"YOU ARE IN THE NIGHT. THE NIGHT IS MY KINGDOM," THE WOMAN SAID.

Jasper's eyes grew wide, and he tilted his head down. There were dozens of water moccasins all about him, some slithering about, others coiled up like rope. An incoherent sound escaped his lips. He raised the rifle. Several shots thudded harmlessly into the ground before one finally ripped one serpent in two.

He swung the barrel toward another, pulling the trigger. There was only a click. And the snakes were slithering forward now.

A wave of panic washed over him. His feet crossed and he tumbled to the ground on top of the snakes. Several of them were quickly upon him.

He thrashed around, crying out, and rolled onto his back. The woman knelt beside him. He felt her lips moving against an open bite on his neck. He realized what was happening.

She was drinking his poisoned blood, just like it was wine. . . .

PINNACLE'S HORROR SHOW

BLOOD BEAST (17-096, $3.95)
by Don D'Ammassa

No one knew anymore where the gargoyle had come from. It was just an ugly stone creature high up on the walls of the old Sheffield Library. Little Jimmy Nicholson liked to go and stare at the gargoyle. It seemed to look straight at him, as if it knew his most secret desires. And he knew that it would give him everything he'd ever wanted. But first he had to do its bidding, no matter how evil.

LIFEBLOOD (17-110, $3.95)
by Lee Duigon

Millboro, New Jersey was just the kind of place Dr. Winslow Emerson had in mind. A small township of Yuppie couples who spent little time at home. Children shuttled between an overburdened school system and every kind of after-school activity. A town ripe for the kind of evil Dr. Emerson specialized in. For Emerson was no ordinary doctor, and no ordinary mortal. He was a creature of ancient legend of mankind's darkest nightmare. And for the citizens of Millboro, he had arrived where they least expected it: in their own backyards.

DARK ADVENT (17-088, $3.95)
by Brian Hodge

A plague of unknown origin swept through modern civilization almost overnight, destroying good and evil alike. Leaving only a handful of survivors to make their way through an empty landscape, and face the unknown horrors that lay hidden in a savage new world. In a deserted midwestern department store, a few people banded together for survival. Beyond their temporary haven, an evil was stirring. Soon all that would stand between the world and a reign of insanity was this unlikely fortress of humanity, armed with what could be found on a department store shelf and what courage they could muster to battle a monstrous, merciless scourge.

NIGHT BROTHERS

SIDNEY WILLIAMS

PINNACLE BOOKS
WINDSOR PUBLISHING CORP.

PINNACLE BOOKS

are published by

Windsor Publishing Corp.
475 Park Avenue South
New York, NY 10016

First printing: December, 1989

Printed in the United States of America

For Rita,
who has been my friend for a long time.

ACKNOWLEDGMENTS

While most of the work of writing is done alone, there are always little helps that come from friends.

Special thanks are due Frances Johnson, for help with research on this project, and Robyn Jones, who helped with the final manuscript.

Greg Langley and Robert Petitt deserve thanks too, for their encouragement along the way.

Part 1

The Awakening

"Death is the evil: so the gods have judged;
For had it been good, they all would die."
—*Sappho*

"And the serpent said unto the woman,
Ye shall not surely die . . ."
—*Genesis 3:4*

Prologue

She had lived ten thousand years, through wars and famine, in lands around the world. She had seen sunrises in the Greek isles, dined in the finest restaurants in the City of Light, but she died on a night of January rain in a place almost forgotten by civilization.

The sky was black, cracked open only by brief bursts of lightning which flared daylight across the landscape of rugged Louisiana clay. She had to make her way carefully as she hurried along.

A misstep could cause her to slip on the slick ground or stumble.

The terrain was uneven and treacherous, riddled with ruts and erosion, and even an occasional protrusion of tree roots.

As she moved, she clutched her cloak tightly around her shoulders against the chill.

Compared to some places she had been, the Louisiana winter was mild; but exposed as she was to the elements, even the mild chill was torture.

The raindrops pelted down onto her pale skin, biting like sharp fragments of stone. It was a feeling she had

9

known before from stones and other attacks.

Perhaps those attacks had been deserved, but she did not want to feel them again. She needed to find a place to hide. It would be dawn soon, and while the fingers of daylight would not turn her to ashes as the legends said, she would be weakened.

Her power was in the darkness. She needed to find a place where she could conceal herself and collect her thoughts while she waited for another nightfall. She did not want to face her pursuers without her full strength.

She would not be able to return to her house. They would be there in the dawn, ready to drive a stake through her heart and perform other rituals of mutilation in order to ensure their safety.

She had seen it happen before, mobs fueled by superstition. Many times her sisters had died in the brutal manner prescribed in the whispered tales told in every language. It was understandable that the mortals wanted to protect themselves, yet she could not stop the hatred that boiled within her.

True, they were her prey; but they hunted as well, often showing little mercy to their victims.

She had watched the traps they used and the weapons that bit into the hearts of the forest creatures. That made her hate the men even more.

Stumbling, she almost lost her balance as she tried to move forward into the forest.

It was a pity she could not transform herself as they thought she could. How easy that would have made things, to simply alter her shape and take wing through this storm.

She almost laughed. How twisted myth could become! In all her years she had heard the stories told and retold, had heard them take new form with each retelling. There was some reality mixed in, but there was also much fantasy.

10

Each tongue added something different to the whispers of the night, embellishing and distorting the truths about her kind. In some ways it was possible for her to live more freely because of the ignorance they thought to be knowledge. On the other hand, new pains were created, because when their fear manifested itself, they could react with great violence.

Pausing, she looked back over her shoulder. Through the darkness her glowing eyes could just make out the faint light of their lanterns, which they managed to keep alight in spite of the storm.

There were at least a dozen of them, led by Sheriff Vince McKinley, a burly, red-haired Irishman. He had made advances toward her when she'd arrived in town to open a small shop as a seamstress.

She was not unaccustomed to attentions from men. She had long ago become aware of her beauty and knew how they were attracted to her hair, which was the color of autumn leaves, and her eyes, which were the color of winter rye grass.

She had learned to turn them away politely. She could do without the complications and the pain love entailed.

McKinley had not given up easily. He had visited her when she first opened her shop at the end of the dirt road that was the main street, offering a polite welcome.

He was from the north. The war had brought him south, and he had stayed to see what he might gather for himself from the ruins. The Union troops had already been moved from town to occupy larger municipalities, but he had remained and gained the respect of the people.

His job as sheriff gave him a feeling of authority. It was rough at times, because the loggers could get rowdy on Saturday nights, but he was more than tough enough to handle it.

As politely as possible, Navarra had declined when he'd offered her dinner. He had grown insistent, finally trying to force himself on her as she was closing up her shop one day. Backing her against a wall, he had ripped her dress and clutched her shoulders tightly as he tried to brush his lips across her neck.

Fortunately, the sun was setting, and with her strength she forced him away, scratching him across the face. She did not kill him because she did not want to draw attention. She was tired of running, and she wanted to stay in the town for a while.

That was why she had taken the trouble of acquiring a shop and making a seven-dollar steamboat ride to New Orleans to purchase stock.

To protect herself, she had concentrated her hunting on the fringes of the community, taking only loggers or hunters and others not so quickly missed because of their customary long forays into the forest.

The unusual strength she displayed in the confrontation with McKinley had tipped him off, however.

When the bodies of a couple of her victims were found, McKinley had talked to people, some of whom still knew the stories their relatives had passed along in the old country. A few foreign-born residents could even recall the stories from the old country, firsthand.

They had told the stories in a town meeting at the Episcopal church. They crowded into the pews together, planters and sharecroppers and storekeepers.

Former soldiers and merchants and craftsmen all agreed to go after her, once they had heard the dark legends of the undead rising from the grave.

Some of the women who had been her customers had come to her to tell her. They didn't realize they were under her influence; they thought they were acting only out of friendship.

Only the young woman named Sarah Wilson had known. Navarra had been planning to change her, to make Sarah like herself with the blessed ritual. That was

12

the way she and her kind had replenished themselves for centuries, ever since the first bond was struck with the forces of the beyond.

That would never be possible now. They would probably try to destroy Sarah as well, just because of their friendship.

McKinley's posse was driven by hatred. The soldiers of the defeated army, the landowners now faced with treating freedmen as equals, and the shopkeepers frustrated by postwar hardship had found a way to vent their anger.

The freedmen, suffering as sharecroppers on dirt farms, had banded with the whites on this rare occasion to battle the common enemy, a demon that threatened their families and their sensibilities.

The prewar days had been prosperous. In the years which had followed there had been military rule. That had at least provided some profit since the soldiers shopped in the stores. Now they were gone.

Reconstruction was not a joyful time here.

The mob had to destroy because they could not understand. They had to destroy to end their fear, to believe they somehow had control over at least some aspect of their fate.

When she was gone, they would turn against each other again. The Knights of the White Magnolia would don their white sheets and hoods again and terrorize their black neighbors.

Tonight they did not need masks. They pursued a different kind of goal.

She moved on across the clay, following its gentle slope. She was not familiar with the landscape, but she believed it would climb to a pine forest. There she would be able to summon the night brothers, the creatures that dwelled in the shadows.

Like her, they had been preyed upon by the men, and they would answer her call. She could command them.

13

She could send the creatures after her pursuers, and perhaps that would allow her enough time to escape.

A gust of wind swept over her, bringing a new chill. She ducked her head and forced herself forward.

They could not have picked a more cruel night.

They had come to her shop, kicking in the door and turning over dressmaker's dummies as they swarmed into the room.

She'd had little time to grab a cloak and escape out the back door. As she fled she heard them behind her, slamming things about and breaking glass.

A new bolt of lightning seared through the clouds, bringing an instant of light to the world.

Ahead of her she could see a stand of trees. Behind her she could hear the mob. They shouted and cursed as they moved together, following McKinley, who was on horseback.

Fear gripped her now. They were closer. Even with her strength and power, they were formidable.

The energy the storm gave her was canceled out by the assault of the elements.

Still another burst of lightning flared, and they saw her. Even without looking back, she knew by their shouts that she'd been spotted.

She ran toward the top of the rise, pain shooting through her legs.

The hoofbeats sounded over the storm. McKinley was not waiting for his band of followers. He spurred his horse on. He was coming after her alone.

She realized she would not reach safety now, so she wheeled around, facing the sheriff at the next flash of lightning.

He reined back his horse. It was fractious from the storm and eager to bolt.

McKinley looked down at her, his army revolver already balanced in his hand.

14

"You're under arrest," he shouted. "For murder."

She did not attempt to hold her cloak as the wind billowed it around her shoulders.

"Arrest, Vince McKinley? You will take me to the jail to await a fair trial?"

"We'll take you in."

"For my death. Those men with you desire my death."

"You're a killer."

"I kill only to survive. Is it the deaths that concern you, or your own pride?"

His thumb drew back the hammer of the revolver.

"Don't make me hurt you."

Navarra laughed.

The explosion of the powder cracked louder than thunder. The bullet struck her shoulder and half twisted her to the side, but she stood her ground.

Clenching her fists at her sides, she drew her head back defiantly and screamed at the top of her voice.

McKinley gripped the reins more tightly, trying to control the horse, which was suddenly moving around, stomping its feet and pitching its head from side to side.

There was another bolt of lightning, and in its glow Navarra's eyes rolled back in her head so that only the whites were visible.

Dropping his gun, McKinley gripped the reins with both hands in an attempt to control the horse.

He lost his grip as his horse reared up onto its hind legs, tossing him from the saddle. He landed on the hard clay ground.

Stunned, he tried to roll to one side to get away from his mount. He had scrambled only a few inches as the horse twisted around and reared again, thumping its hooves down near his body.

"Stop, fella," he called.

But the horse's hooves struck him on the shoulder and near his chest, cracking cartilage and tearing skin. Blood

15

spurted onto his shirt.

He screamed as the horse reared again, coming down this time on his chest, forcing the air out of his lungs. His ribs splintered, sending slivers into his lungs.

Navarra did not wait any longer for the climax of the battle. She continued upward.

The men would not be long in coming; they were running across the distance covered by the horse. Some of them stumbled and slipped on the wet ground, but their determination and anger made them keep moving.

She staggered and gasped for breath. Her head was clouded by the effort required to touch the horse's mind. She needed rest.

At the top of the rise, she stumbled into the trees and tilted her head back again, beseeching the creatures of the night to do her bidding. They would hold off the men behind her.

She ran along through the trees, dodging the branches which struck at her skin.

Her eyes continued to glow, and she plotted a course of minimal resistance.

Behind her the night creatures were swarming in a frenzy, scurrying about in spite of the rain, which normally would have kept them in their dens.

She ran as fast as she could now, hurrying through the darkness.

Ahead she could see an opening in the forest, a break in the trees. She would move across that and then make her way deeper into the woods, further away from inhabited land.

She looked back over her shoulder only briefly to check on the pursuers. She could hear them shouting and screaming as they clashed with the creatures and birds that ambushed them.

Then she stumbled; fear clutched her throat. She was sliding downward. She had miscalculated her position.

Unfamiliar with the geography of the area she had forgotten about another of the legends—a legend which was true.

She could not cross running water. It was something she could not quite understand, something to do with a long-forgotten law of the universe and the nature which governed her and allowed her to exist as she did.

She fought to stop her slide, but the bank of the creek was too steep. She plunged into the water, which was raging because of the heavy rains.

She tried to scream, but her mouth was filled with the water. It poured down her throat and into her lungs. Beneath her it was as if hands had gripped her ankles and were dragging her down.

The pitching water spilled through the narrow channel and tossed her around, dragging her deeper and deeper. More of it filled her nostrils and her ears.

Her body caused the creek to boil, and a spray of white foam rose around her.

She felt nothing as she sank . . . nothing except a soothing sensation. She slowly relaxed as she settled toward the river floor. The boiling slowly stopped.

Drifting backward, she closed her eyes, letting sleep take her as her molecules separated.

It was not an unpleasant feeling. She knew this would not last. Geography changed, tributaries changed their courses. It might be many years, but she would wait. It would not matter. In her mind there was only a single thought which had been drilled into her a thousand years before. *Water does not destroy. It preserves.*

This was the beginning.

Chapter 1

June, 1988

The wind was like the breath of a dragon as it swept across the town, scrapping fragments of paper across the parched sidewalks and whirling dust from the cracked earth of the bordering fields, which had dried to a brown powder.

Shimmers of heat danced over the roadways as temperatures climbed above record highs set in the 1930s.

It was June. There had been no rain to speak of in more than sixty days, and agricultural experts were already speculating about the damage to the crops.

The soybean and cotton farmers were weeping, and the crystal water which had given Bristol Springs its name when it was founded in the 1800s had become no more than a trickle.

Alison Dixon guided her Toyota Celica through the narrow streets. She could feel a tightness in her throat as she cruised past the store windows which had taken on a dingy look in the past weeks.

The town was dying, or at least it seemed to be. People didn't bother to sweep the dust away or clean the windows. There didn't seem to be any reason to. The effort would have been futile.

Her remorse was twofold. She loved the town because she had grown up here. It was a part of her, and she hated to see it waste away. It hurt her to see the darkness in the eyes of people she had known all her life, and she wanted to cry when she heard them talk of losing everything.

She was also worried because she and her husband, Travis, had a stake in the town. A few months before, when the *Bristol Springs Gazette* had become available, they had scraped together the money to purchase it.

Both of them had been working at a paper out of state at that time, Travis as a crime reporter and Alison as a copyeditor. Often they had talked about their dream of owning a small weekly newspaper. There was something romantic about the notion of going back to the world of journalism.

Publishing a weekly paper seemed to offer a fresh creative challenge, and there was something pleasant in thinking about work in a small town where things were simple. It was the kind of place to raise a family.

Leaving the fast pace of big city journalism had appealed to both of them. Travis was ready to do anything to get off the night police beat he'd been working for more than a year. He was tired of looking at bloody bodies and interviewing relatives of murder victims.

In spite of the lagging Louisiana economy, both Alison and Travis had leaped at the opportunity when they received word that Alison's hometown paper was available. Her parents had died only a few months apart, shortly after she had finished college, but Alison had never planned on returning to Bristol Springs.

The thought of it grew on her.

In many ways the paper was what she and Travis had dreamed about, a small operation that focused on human interest items like yam contest winners and local characters.

There was room for improvement as well. In talking it

over, they decided it was something they could turn into a quality publication.

Retaining the paper's folksy quality while developing a more professional edge to its reporting would increase readership, which in turn would help sell advertising.

The paper competed with the *Aimsley Daily Clarion*, thirty miles away, which provided residents with national news and some local stories.

The *Daily* concentrated on coverage of meetings and political issues, rarely devoting a great deal of attention to Bristol Springs. Unless something big arose, it relied on a part-time correspondent who also worked at a local radio station.

By retaining the human interest angle at the *Gazette*, the couple decided, it would be possible to keep people reading both papers—the daily for its wire stories, and the local to see what was going on besides the gossip.

Alison and Travis had closed the deal on a rainy day eight months earlier, purchasing the paper from its longtime owner, who was ready to retire and head back East.

Many were glad to see the paper back in the hands of a local girl.

Accepting the fact that they would be doing most of the work—from selling ads to taking photographs on 4-H achievement day—the Dixons had thrown themselves into their work.

They had found some of the romance they'd been seeking, but they'd also encountered long working hours, battles with printers, and the harsh realities of small newspaper economics.

They had to keep their advertising accounts going in order to keep food on the table.

Beside the romance of a small town, they'd also discovered the sadness and the hardship. It was something Alison had forgotten and something Travis had never considered.

He was from a medium-sized city in central Louisiana. It was not a large place, but it did manage to be impersonal.

In Bristol Springs, people knew all about each other's suffering. They knew how Jessie Mae Eldridge felt when her grandson died of cancer, and they knew how Earl Rodgers was struggling to keep his son in college and pay his bills at the same time.

Lately Alison had found herself wondering if there wasn't a certain "trapped" feeling connected with the town. Turning up the air conditioner against the stifling heat, she turned onto the side street where the newspaper office had been for the past forty years.

As a child growing up in this town, she'd never expected to be an owner of the publication. It still seemed unreal . . . perhaps it was wishful thinking. There would be no waking up to discover it was all a dream. The struggle was very real. The economy in the state had been bad since the oil crisis of 1986, and it had not improved much by the time they'd purchased the paper.

If the drought stretched on and ruined the crops, it might be the death knell for the paper—and the rest of the town as well.

She tried not to think of that as she pulled the Celica into the angled parking slot in front of the building beside Travis's Mustang.

He was back early from the school board meeting. That stood to reason, since school was out. They probably didn't have much to worry about until buying new football uniforms became an issue at the end of summer.

At least Trav's early arrival meant something was working well. They put the paper together on Tuesdays and took it into Aimsley to the printer on Wednesdays so that it was ready for Thursday distribution.

Shouldering her purse, Alison snatched her photo bag from the back seat and hurried through the front door of

22

the office. At 30, a year older than Travis, she still looked to be in her mid-twenties. Her blond hair was long, her features pert and girlish. She was not beautiful, although a sprinkle of faint freckles on her smooth complexion highlighted her deep brown eyes and gave her a look of enthusiasm.

Dressed in her usual jeans and t-shirt, which covered a frame that just escaped being skinny, she looked ready for whatever the town had to offer.

Stepping into the front room, her weight caused the plank floor to creak. She glanced at the bulletin board but saw no messages from Chrisk, the girl hired to work part time to keep the office coordinated. Now, because of her own initiative, Chrisk carried much of the weight of news coverage.

She found Travis in the small newsroom. It consisted of a couple of desks and telephones, some manual typewriters, and a personal computer they used for writing, composing and typesetting.

Travis was standing beside Eula Mae Jeffries, the silver-haired woman who served as their area correspondent. She sat at the IBM computer peering over her bifocals at the green-on-black screen.

"You have to tell it you want to make a new paragraph, Mrs. Jeffries," Travis was saying. "Just like you have to tell it about your margins."

A pencil was stuck behind his ear, and his longish blond hair was in disarray. He'd rolled up the sleeves on his brown shirt just as he always did when he was planning a page layout.

As usual, Mrs. Jeffries was writing her society story at the last minute. She insisted on working on the computer. It gave her a feeling of efficiency.

For Travis, it was a constant source of consternation, but he never let the elderly woman see his exasperation. No one was sure how old she was, but she'd been

23

working at the paper as a volunteer for ten years, since her husband had died of a heart attack.

She was a fixture at the *Gazette*, and since they had taken it over, Travis had helped her polish her writing skills.

In talking it over, Alison and Travis had agreed that they could not do away with the old woman's work. Everyone loved to read her accounts of who visited whom on Sunday afternoons, and how many were baptized at the local revival, and what Esther Everly got for her silver wedding anniversary.

In his role as editor, however, Travis could not in good conscience run the material as a news article. Instead of getting rid of her, Travis had developed a layout which allowed Mrs. Jeffries to have her picture over her column.

"Who knows," Travis had said when the first edition had come out. "Maybe she's writing literature, and we just don't know it yet."

Now he was looking over Mrs. Jeffries' shoulder as she plunked away at the keys.

"You can't say that like that, Mrs. Jeffries. You're writing your story in the past tense. You can't change in the middle of it."

"Ridiculous, Travis. I know what I'm doing."

He looked up at Alison with a knowing smile.

She smiled back and kissed him gently on the cheek.

Hoisting her camera, she dangled it from the shoulder strap. "Pictures of the 4-H winners," she said.

"Page one. We'll let Chrisk develop it when she gets back from lunch."

He motioned Alison over to the drawing table in the composing room. He had spread out a dummy sheet to design the next edition's front page.

Several of his pencil markings were already in place to indicate a long story with a picture at the top.

Taking a ruler from the pocket of his jeans, he blocked off a rectangle at the bottom left corner of the page.

"Is it a standard two-column vertical with the lucky winners staring aimlessly into the camera?" he asked.

"Oh, yeah. They wouldn't have it any other way."

"We'll run a cutline to that effect," he said.

She tapped the top of the page. "You're going with the drought story up here."

He nodded and took an eraser from the pocket of his denim. "It's about 18 inches," he said. "I talked to the county agent and a couple of farmers. It's on the computer. I'll let you edit it when Mrs. Jeffries gets through chronicling the Carter family birthday party for Eric, age 6."

"What's the picture?"

"I got a shot of Duncan Sibley looking concerned over some rows of what are supposed to be soybeans."

She sat down on the stool beside the table. "If it doesn't rain by the end of the week, we probably need to do the story on the namesake of the town drying up."

"I know," he said with a sigh. "I hate to do it. I guess it's almost superstition. I feel as if writing about it will make it so."

"It's been here forever. It's changed form many times over the years, but there's always been some kind of water there."

"It'll be back eventually. It's just scary. What I'd like to do is a story on the fact that the creek bed is almost dry, and then I'd like to talk to some old-timers about memories of it, swimming in it and all that, even some who remember the spring before it changed course."

"They used it for the old saw mill too, even funneled it through a concrete frame to make a swimming pool around 1913. I remember people talking about it."

"We'll do an inside spread," Travis suggested. "We sure won't have any bothersome ads to break up the symmetry of our layout."

"It'll get better.

He leaned back from the table. "I know. But just in case, I didn't say no to the Knight-Ridder deal yet."

She laughed.

He leaned back again and ran his hands through his hair. There was a weariness in his gray eyes. The work they did was taxing, consuming most of their time.

Their only day off was Wednesday, while the paper was being printed. They stayed in Aimsley and did shopping or went to a movie and dinner. That was partly to keep them away from telephones. People would call constantly, wanting this or that photographed, or a story about some important accomplishment by a niece or nephew.

If a major story did break, Chrisk was around. She was young, but Travis trusted her to act if something happened. But nothing ever happened in Bristol Springs, so they were safe.

Alison knew there was more to his weariness than just his long hours on the paper. They had talked about it off and on. While the simple, small-town life had its rewards, Travis was beginning to miss the excitement of reporting. Alison had adjusted to a desk job fairly easily, but Travis had always been on the firing line, and as much as he hated it, there had also been a thrill in it. He had grown up reading Raymond Chandler and other adventure stories. He'd never had a desire to be a policeman, but in covering crime stories there was a certain amount of adventure.

Violence repulsed him, but rushing out to a crime scene with a photographer or talking to the neighbors of murder suspects always started his adrenaline flowing.

He didn't get much of that in Aimsley. There was a chief of police with one cop and a sheriff's deputy who worked part time. They spent most of their days enforcing traffic laws and keeping teenagers from misbehaving in the parking lot of the Dairy Queen on Saturday nights.

Alison looked at her husband as he hunched over the drawing board again to continue his work on page layout.

She wondered if he was dwindling away here. With all the financial problems and a mundane edge to much of the work, she worried that his spirit was slowly breaking.

She wondered about the toll the life was taking on her as well. They didn't have many close friends in town. In a way, that made them closer to each other, but it also carried with it a certain loneliness.

In short order their work had become their life.

"Do you think we ought to look into selling?" she asked.

"Only if the chains make a big enough offer," Travis quipped.

"You don't think the *Clarion* would want it?"

"We're not a big enough threat for that."

"Some other young idealistic couple?"

He laughed. "Suckers? Maybe."

It was not a new conversation. In fact, it never really ended, it just got postponed from time to time.

"There are things I love here," she said.

"Oh, yeah. Talking to the people, hearing their stories. Reading Mrs. Jeffries' copy. Working with Chrisk, and watching her develop her talent. The world could get by without little papers, but it wouldn't be as nice a place."

Alison slid off the stool and headed toward the coffee pot. "Maybe not," she conceded.

As she poured herself a cup, the front door rattled open and Chrisk walked in carrying a sheaf of papers.

"Advertising," she called.

"Okay, we can buy food again!" Travis said.

She carried the ads over to the table to let him plot them onto the layouts.

"Here you go, captain."

"We've got to do better," Travis said, exaggerating the statement with pauses. It was his William Shatner imitation. He and Chrisk shared an affection for *Star Trek* and frequently joked about it together.

27

They had developed a rapport from almost the first day Chrisk had worked there.

Alison and Travis had decided to hire her after she dropped by the shop while they were still unpacking.

She was a slender black girl of nineteen, her wavy hair worn shoulder-length. That first day she'd been wearing faded denim and a torn gray sweatshirt, and she'd been emphatic about her desire to be a journalist.

She'd tried from time to time to get work under the previous ownership, but for whatever reason, she'd been unsuccessful.

Two years out of high school, she hadn't been able to go to college yet because of family finances. She lived with her mother. Her father had been an offshore worker and had died while she was still in high school.

Her sharpness and her wit had quickly impressed Alison, and the writing samples she'd brought along had won over Travis.

She had to work weekends at the Dairy Queen, but she devoted the rest of her time to the newspaper. She did volunteer work for the hours they could not pay her.

Travis was working through a friend to get some scholarship help for her at LSU.

It was one other benefit of running a small paper, according to Travis. They were able to help someone with promise.

In return, Chrisk was a valuable asset. With her volunteer hours, her time came close to matching that put in by Travis and Alison. She helped with layout, sold ads, and wrote everything from features to fillers.

The fresh simplicity of her style contributed to the quality Travis wanted for the paper.

They had Chrisk do special things like pieces on the Bristol Springs recreation scene and atmosphere pieces about the bars where the bands played on Highway 1 and the activities at church fairs and *cochon de laits*.

"How were the 4-H winners?" she asked, joining Alison at the coffeepot.

"A real blast. Is there anything exciting happening around town?"

"Everybody's sweating," she said, adjusting her short black skirt. She always dressed fashionably. Much of what she wore she made herself with her mother's help.

After pouring a cup of coffee, she took Alison's film, put on an apron, and headed into the converted closet which served as the *Gazette* darkroom. "Back in a few minutes," she said. "You think we'll get out of here by dawn?"

"We're shutting it down at 2 A.M. regardless," Travis called. "I want to be home in time to watch the test pattern."

Alison sat down at her desk and scrolled a piece of paper into the manual typewriter.

Absently she also reached over and turned up the police scanner.

"Sounds like the chief's caught some kid racing a motorcycle," she said as she began to tap out a story on the 4-H winners.

Mrs. Jeffries looked up from the computer. "We shouldn't write about that. It would probably embarrass the parents."

Chapter 2

Aaron Briggs felt the same cold sweat on his palms he'd experienced from time to time as a sheriff's deputy when he'd been called on to arrest dangerous men.

He had become chief of police in Bristol Springs to avoid that feeling and the knot in his stomach that always went with it. For the most part, in the past few years he had been successful. He'd never missed his job with the Riverland Parish sheriff's office, where he'd learned the ins and outs of law enforcement.

He considered the chief's job easier and safer. Aside from having to break up an occasional domestic squabble, he didn't run into much hazardous duty. For the most part, people didn't kill other people in Bristol Springs, so he seldom had to hunt down desperate suspects who might be inclined to shoot at him. The drug traffic was also minimal, so he didn't have to worry much about that, either.

As a patrol deputy, he'd had to arrest people armed with shotguns often enough for one lifetime, so he welcomed the occasional burglary investigation or traffic ticket as all he needed to break the monotony.

As he roared along Second Street after the kid on the motorcycle, he felt the old dread return. Dressed all in black, the kid looked like one of the singers Briggs's daughter watched on MTV. There were silver studs visible along the seams of the guy's pants, and he had shoulder-length black hair. Although some of the locals dressed that way, imitating what they saw on television, this guy was not from town. Aaron knew all the local kids who owned bikes. There were only a handful.

Briggs did recognize the blond girl sitting on the back of the bike with her arms wrapped around the guy's waist, however. It was Lou Ellen Johnson. She was a year ahead of his daughter in school. Her father had died two years before, and her mother wasn't able to keep too close an eye on her. She was a waitress at a local cafe and pulled the late shift many nights.

Briggs had a feeling Mrs. Johnson wouldn't want her little girl hanging out with this creep. Since he had a daughter of his own, he felt the need to check things out.

He held off on the siren as he kept pace with the bike along the narrow street, hoping the kid wouldn't make it hard.

Briggs shook his head as he looked at the girl. She was wearing tight black shorts and a yellow pullover that left her midriff bare. It didn't leave much to the imagination, even though she was wearing a black jacket over it.

Apparently the kid wasn't going to give up.

Briggs let the red flashers blaze.

The kid hadn't been going but a couple of miles over the limit when the chase began, but Briggs decided he might as well check him out, let him know the law was around.

A second after Briggs hit the flashers, the motorcycle's engine roared and the bike shot forward through an intersection, gaining even more speed.

The lights had been like a challenge, and the kid wanted to make a game of it. Briggs hit the siren and put his foot on the gas pedal.

Ahead of him the bike roared around a corner by the

drugstore, just missing a Volkswagen that was turning from the opposite direction. The VW driver screeched to a stop, and Briggs guided his car through the same space the bike had taken.

The kid jerked the bike onto the highway, which was also Bristol Springs' main drag.

On the broader road the bike gained even more speed. Briggs pushed his cruiser a little harder.

They shot past the fast food places and the video store at 70 mph.

They passed the store where Mrs. Johnson worked. Briggs wondered if the lady was looking out to see what her daughter was up to.

With the hot weather, the road was covered with a dry film of dust. The kid gunned his motor, stirring up a red cloud as his bike gained more speed. Dust whirled in through the passenger window of Briggs's cruiser. He cursed as it seeped into his nostrils, causing him to cough.

With renewed determination, he pushed the gas pedal again, rolling up his window as he moved.

The motorcycle was roaring along the blacktop now, its speed peaking 75 mph.

Briggs picked up the mike on the Motorola unit and notified the sheriff's substation in the next town that he'd be crossing out of the Bristol Springs city limits in pursuit.

He wasn't sure where Deputy Bill Holyfield was on patrol, but if he was nearby, he might be able to head the kid off. Briggs got a lot of help from Holyfield, more than he really expected, since the sheriff was more concerned about high-profile drug arrests than about minor problems in the corner of the parish. Holyfield provided a lot of assistance because he was a nice guy, not out of obedience to any orders from his boss.

"You'd better see if the state police have a trooper handy in this zone, too," he suggested.

"That's negative. They only have three men working

32

North today. The one on your end is over in Colfax right now."

"Great. Not even in the parish."

He wasn't going to let the kid get away, so he juiced the gas again. The car vibrated slightly, showing signs of its age without quite going under.

He ignored the shudder in the steering wheel, refusing to let up on the gas now.

At the edge of town, the kid hooked it onto a side road which twisted back through the trees, probably expecting to shake the pursuit in the long curves.

It was a mistake. Off the main drag, Briggs felt a little better about maneuvering. Relying on his siren and lights to keep things out of his way, he pulled over into the oncoming lane and put the pedal to the floor.

As they came out of the curve, he picked up speed again, moving back into the oncoming lane and pulling forward.

He passed the kid doing 80 and moved the car a couple of lengths in front of the bike.

Sweat was pouring from under his armpits now, and drops were spilling from beneath his hat brim to run down his forehead.

The sweat stung his eyes, a sensation he ignored as he jerked the wheel hard to one side, spinning the car to a stop across the roadway in a makeshift roadblock.

The kid pulled the bike to the side just in time, breaking hard and sliding it to a stop only a couple of inches from the passenger door of Briggs's unit.

The chief kept his hands on the wheel, ready if the kid tried to hightail it back in the direction he had come.

Instead the biker laughed and threw up his hands as he sat back in the saddle.

Cautiously, Briggs put the car in park and climbed out with his hand resting on the butt of the .38 in his holster.

"Don't make any sudden moves, son," he said, peering over the top of the car past the flashing lights.

Briggs had a pronounced chin, and with his teeth clenched, it looked like stone.

"Step off the bike, son. You too, miss."

The biker killed his engine and dropped the kickstand before casually dismounting. Then he turned and took the girl's hand gently, helping her off as if he were a footman helping a princess.

Briggs moved slowly around the car, keeping his hand ready on the gun.

"Lean against the car, son," he said with a nod toward the cruiser. "From the looks of you, you know the position."

Still smiling, the kid placed his palms on the car and spread his feet apart.

A pat down revealed no concealed weapons or drugs.

Briggs let him straighten up and turned his gaze to the girl. She was wearing too much eye makeup, which made her look slightly older than she was. Her legs were slender, and her breasts, as revealed by the tight fit of the blouse, were full. He would skin his own daughter alive if he ever caught her dressing that way.

"You're Lou Ellen Johnson, aren't you?"

She bowed her head slightly, her hair falling across her face.

"Yes, sir." Her voice had grown meek.

"Does your mama know you're hanging out with the likes of this?"

"No, sir."

"Where'd you meet up with him?"

"The video store."

He looked back at the biker, who he guessed to be around nineteen. "You hanging around there to pick up teenagers?"

"She's got a free will, man."

"What's your name?"

"Dave Pearson. They call me Blade."

"I'll bet they do."

He studied the kid's face, glaring at his own reflection in the kid's shades. He wondered what kind of look the kid had in his eyes. Probably arrogance.

"I'm going to take you in," Briggs said. "You're under arrest, careless and reckless, speeding, resisting an officer by flight." He drew a breath, trying to think of something else to slap the punk with. "Let me see your license."

It checked out. The kid was eighteen, a resident of Penn's Ferry, a little town near Aimsley.

Briggs read the kid his rights in one breath and cuffed him, not taking much care with being gentle as he pushed him into the backseat.

"What about my bike?" the kid demanded.

"I'll send for it."

He put the girl in the front seat. "I'm going to take you by the diner," he said. "Your mama's working there, isn't she?"

"Yes, sir." Her chin was almost touching her chest. She was mad and frightened at the same time.

He shoved the car into gear and wheeled it around to point it back toward the highway.

Estelle Johnson felt dead on her feet. A pain seemed to stretch from the balls of her feet up her legs and into the small of her back, where it nestled for a long stay.

She had almost grown used to the aches and pains her body developed in protest of her long hours of work at the diner. She tried not to think about the ache as she took an order from a truck driver who kept making crude remarks.

He was heavy with black hair and a scruffy blue shadow on his face. People had smelled better to her, also.

She didn't harbor any illusions about her looks, which she considered faded these days, so she wasn't flattered by his suggestions of her beauty. She knew they were false,

35

geared to disarm her.

Her hair was limp and dingy, and she was always hot because the air conditioning in the café was bad. The pale orange uniform she had to wear was shapeless, and her waist was thicker than she would have liked. On top of that, she had developed varicose veins. They bulged beneath her skin and throbbed when she stayed on her feet all day.

Her skin was puffy. With her hours, she didn't have much opportunity to worry about such things, except when she thought about her younger days, when she had been popular because of her milk-and-honey looks. Those days were long gone and not to be regained.

"You should have seen me before I worked here," she told the thick-necked driver.

He ran his tongue over his lower lip and leered at her. "From where I sit, you look right fine," he said.

"What will you have?" she said, letting her tone drip with disinterest.

He tilted his hat back on his head and continued to appraise her.

"It better be on the menu," she said in anticipation of his next line. She was going to have to remember to wear her wedding ring in here. She kept it in her jewelry box. Wearing it didn't seem right, but a bare third finger was too much like having open season declared.

The guy had decided to place his food order just as the bell on the door chimed and Chief Briggs walked in. That was disheartening, since she was tied up. She would have liked to walk over and get him a soup or coffee at the counter.

He wasn't a particularly handsome man, but he was better than many of the sleazeballs who frequented the diner, and he was courteous.

Of the men she considered to be in her league, the chief was the only one she really thought about seriously.

At least as seriously as she could think about a man who didn't seem to notice they were in the same boat since losing their spouses. She had given up on his ever paying attention to her. That part of her life was pushed aside, because most of all she lived for her daughter.

She was surprised that Briggs walked toward her, until she noticed the solemn look on his face. It wasn't romantic . . . it was his business expression.

Oh, God, she thought, something's happened to Lou Ellen.

Briggs reached up and slipped his hat off his sandy blond hair. The band left a ring in his hair.

"I need to speak with you a moment," he said.

Turning her back on the customer, she stared up at Briggs. "What's wrong?"

"It's all right," he said soothingly. "Nothing's the matter. I've got your daughter in the car. She was riding on a motorcycle with a boy I've placed under arrest. I figured you'd want to have a talk with her."

"Is she in trouble?"

He took her arm and guided her toward the door. "Nothing like that. I just thought you'd be concerned about who she's hanging around with."

"I am. It's so hard to keep an eye on her."

"Well, we averted trouble this time," he said.

He pushed open the front door and they walked out to his car, where Lou Ellen remained in the front seat. She sat with her arms folded and her chin tucked against her chest.

When Briggs opened the passenger door, she made no move to get out.

"I told you to stay home today," Mrs. Johnson said. "I don't want you running around all over the place. You know that."

She looked into the backseat and saw Blade leaning against the opposite door with a grin on his face.

37

"I don't even know that boy," Mrs. Johnson said, grasping her daughter's forearm and shaking it. The girl kept her head bowed as she let herself be pulled from the car.

"I was bored," she said meekly. "He just asked me if I wanted to go riding."

"You're old enough to know better than to take off with somebody like that. You know how dangerous it can be?"

"Yes, ma'am."

Estelle turned to Briggs. "Is she under arrest?"

"As far as the law is concerned, she hasn't done anything wrong. It's all up to you."

"I appreciate your help, Chief. I'm going to take her home."

"All right, Mrs. Johnson."

"Are you arresting him?"

"Traffic violations," Briggs said. "Sometimes if you throw a scare into them, it straightens them out before they go too wrong."

Estelle ushered the girl toward the diner. She turned a quick glance back over her shoulder. "Thank you so much, Chief Briggs."

She opened the door and led the girl inside. Quickly they walked over to the counter, and Estelle took off her apron. "Susie," she whispered to the blond girl behind the bar. "Will you cover for me? Just a few minutes. Family trouble.

"I can take it."

Susie was only twenty, and she'd been working at the diner since she'd dropped out of high school. She dated the truckers who stopped along the route and taped soap operas on the VCR she'd saved up to buy.

The friendship between Estelle and Susie stemmed from the fact that they were in the same boat. They frequently covered for each other as a matter of survival. All of

38

Estelle's friends seemed to be young. She worked in the kind of job young women held.

Susie handed Estelle her purse from behind the counter, and Estelle turned her attention back to Lou Ellen.

"I can't imagine what you were thinking," she said once they were in the car.

"It was not any big thing," Lou Ellen said. "I'm seventeen years old. It's not like I'm a child. I was just having a little fun."

"Look at the way you're dressed. That's just asking for trouble. You know what that boy had on his mind. I hope that wasn't what was on your mind, too. I've tried to teach you better than that."

She steered the car across the dry parking lot, the wheels crunching over the gravel.

"You know it's a reflection on me when people see you running around with make-up and clothes that don't leave anything to the imagination. I may have to work hard, but it's honest work. I don't want the people at church thinking my daughter is a tramp. We've got a good name in this town. Your daddy was a respected man."

"These clothes are just the style, that's all."

Estelle shook her head. "I don't care. From now on when you go out I expect you to look decent. You're growing up. You have to take into account how your looks affect other people. Do you understand? And I don't want you to see any more of that boy if he stays around town. There have to be better boys than that for you to go out with."

"You don't even know him," the girl said.

"I could look at him and tell what type he is. You just stay away from him."

Lou Ellen leaned against the door with her arms folded and her forehead pressed against the window, staring down at the passing ground.

If Estelle hadn't been watching the road so closely, she might have noticed her daughter's defiance.

Fifteen minutes later Briggs dragged Blade through the front door of the small police station next to the town hall.

Denise, the part-time dispatcher, was sitting at the radio reading a tattered paperback historical romance.

She put it aside and got out of her chair when she saw the prisoner. It was uncommon for Briggs to show up with people in custody, except maybe on Saturday nights when somebody had too much to drink. He and his officer, Doug Langley, took turns working weekends.

"What's going on, Chief?"

Briggs was pushing the biker toward his office.

"Call Langdon at home. Tell him I need him to get Jasper Leland's truck and go out to Springs Road and pick up a Harley-Davidson that's parked there."

"Tell him not to scratch the paint," Blade suggested with a smile.

"Get in there," Briggs said, grabbing the neck of the kid's jacket and pushing him toward a chair.

Once Blade was seated, Briggs uncuffed him and sat down behind his desk, where he rolled an arrest form into the green IBM typewriter.

He went through it all quickly, getting curt answers from the kid.

"You want to call anybody?"

Blade was leaning back in his chair nonchalantly, fingers laced behind his head.

"Maybe my uncle. Felix Pearson. You've heard of him."

He was the state senator from the district, had been for about twenty years. Briggs chewed on his lower lip.

"Yeah, that Pearson," Blade said. "My daddy's brother. You might have heard of him too. Dr. Richard Pearson."

"I'm sure they'll be happy to hear you broke the law,"

40

Briggs said. "You can tell them, and then you can wait in the cell until they come to bail you out."

"Determined to go all the way with it, are you? *The* cell? You mean you've just got one? First-class operation you run here!"

Briggs didn't smile. He picked up the phone on his desk and turned it around so the dial faced the kid.

While Blade made his call, Briggs leaned back in his chair and took his pack of Salems from his shirt pocket.

He was trying to cut down, but he felt justified in indulging after his ordeal.

He drew the smoke slowly into his lungs and exhaled through his nose, letting the nicotine sooth his nerves.

He'd dealt with kids like this before, the ones who had parents in authority who bailed them out of trouble.

It didn't matter if the senator got mad. Briggs didn't want that kind of conflict, but he would deal with it if it happened.

Once the kid was finished, Briggs took him down the hall and ushered him into the single cell.

The kid promptly dropped onto his bunk and began to make the sounds of a heavy metal band, miming playing a guitar.

Briggs slammed the door and started back down the hall. At least he wouldn't have to put up with the noise for long. The kid would probably be out in under an hour. He went back to his desk to wait for the senator's call.

The sun baked the bed of the creek which had been named Bristol Springs after Edward Bristol, the first man who had settled there and who eventually founded the town.

He had been a shrewd businessman who realized the virtue of ready water. For many years the creek had been the focal point of the town, since it fed down to the sawmill founded in 1872. That had changed in the 1920s, when the mill had closed.

The town had survived the loss of that industry only because a furniture factory remained in operation. It stayed in existence and diversified until the second world war. The location had been on the opposite end of town, so things had gradually moved away from the real Bristol Springs.

The creek, which was not really a creek any longer, was not in the present-day city limits. Through various town acts and ordinances, the actual corporation limit inched away from the Springs area, although most people still considered it a part of the town and expected the local police to take care of any wrongdoing there.

For the past several years, it had been largely neglected. A resort in the area died in the late sixties, and through some geographic shift or some unexplained act of God, the creek disappeared or changed course, leaving only a pocket of water replenished mostly by rain.

Few people drifted out to the site to see what was now not quite a lake but little more than a pond.

Except for the teenagers. They gathered at night on the bank to listen to music, grope in sleeping bags, and occasionally go skinny-dipping. They drank Jack Daniels if someone in the group was old enough to buy it, and some smoked marijuana if there was any on hand. Bristol Springs was not drug free, but most mind-altering substances were in short supply.

With other things to worry about, the Riverland sheriff's office didn't bother the kids much by patrolling the area. Around election time they might raid for drugs to get some news coverage, but that was only once every four years.

From time to time there was talk among the more civic-minded Bristol Springs residents of putting up a museum near the spring as a tourist attraction.

For a while there was even a search to find someone to do a portrait of Edward Bristol.

No one had any idea what Bristol had really looked like, so the first item for the museum had been dismissed. After efforts to locate other early artifacts had failed, talk of the attraction had eventually died down.

Bristol Springs didn't have much to offer in the way of tourism, but anything that might bring in dollars had to be considered. There weren't enough businesses around to provide ample employment. Parents lamented the fact that their children had to go to Aimsley to find work.

The problems created by the drought put any thoughts of tourism temporarily on hold. Edward Bristol's namesake was in no condition to become the focal point of a tourist attraction; it had dried to a cracked bed of red sand.

The afternoon wind swept granules of sand into a rusty cloud which floated over the sloping canal like a pocket of smog. The last pool of moisture had dried up the day before, a victim of the noonday sun.

The emaciated form near the edge of the streambed bore little resemblance to anything human.

The skeleton was covered with a gray, pulpy mass of tissue that looked like tattered rags and stretched streaks of soggy cloth. Only a few black strands of hair clung to the skull, and the eyes which were sunken in their sockets were milky and glazed a yellowish purple. The body was in good condition for something that had been submerged for 120 years, but that wasn't saying much.

She did not feel alive. She was unable to walk. As she dragged herself toward the trees to escape the searing rays of the sun, she could not feel pain or any other sensation.

There was not even hunger, only an awareness that she needed to feed. It was almost as if that was her only awareness. Her vision was clouded, her ears deaf, and her tongue moribund.

How long had it been? How long had she languished on the floor of her watery prison? How long had it taken Fate to free her? She could not guess. She had no way of counting the years as she slept in her suspended state. She had lived in a nonexistence of loneliness and agony.

Finding a shadow from a thick old pine tree, she rolled into its wake. It was not darkness, but it was better than the sun.

Nothing happened immediately, yet gradually an ache spread through the tissue. At least there was some feeling now. Even pain was better than nothingness, that emptiness devoid of any spark of existence which she had known so long.

How would she find food now, when she was almost unable to move? Would someone come by here, ready to offer up a sacrifice?

Her thoughts began to swirl; only fragments floated about in her brain. She could recall vaguely the hour of her death, snatches from the rest of existence, and little else.

She had never been in quite this situation before. She could not seek help, for in her present state she was too hideous. She had no voice, no strength.

She hoped darkness would bring her a little more vigor. Then perhaps she could find prey. If prey came to her . . . that would be the key.

As the sun sank a little further, her thoughts swirled into more order. In the darkness, she would be able to call on the night brothers. They would help her find food.

Chapter 3

Lou Ellen threw a glass against the wall of her bedroom, aiming to miss her poster of the heavy metal group Poison and shatter what had once been a jelly jar on the wall, where the juice it contained would make a noticeable stain. She hit the poster instead and splattered it with a pink splotch of fruit punch. Fingers of liquid stretched down over the lead singer's face, and the wet spot spread outward in a circular pattern.

The poster was ruined. Walking over to it, she ripped it down. She'd been wanting to get one of a group called Guns and Roses anyway.

Her anger at her mother was boiling, and she was furious with Chief Briggs as well. They had treated her like a child. She had a right to go out with a guy if she wanted to.

Wadding the poster into a ball, she hurled it across the room as well. It bounced off the window without doing any damage.

Did her mother expect her to sit around the house all day without going out of her mind? It was summertime. She wanted to enjoy it after the confinement of the school year. Instead, she'd just received a new sentence.

Her mother gave her a couple of dollars for video tapes

and thought that enough to keep her entertained.

She'd grown bored with the tapes down at the video store the first week classes were over. The good movies were always rented out, and she was tired of slasher films and the Australian things that were always on the shelves. It seemed to take forever for new titles to be released.

Bumping into Blade had been like an answer to a prayer—although her mother probably wouldn't consider him heaven-sent.

Lou Ellen had found him sitting on his bike at the curb in front of the store, his feet propped up on the handlebars. He didn't look like he cared about anything.

With his hair and his clothes, he looked like a rock star, and he had spoken to her casually in a deep voice. The confidence in his tone had been exciting. He was different from the hicks she went to school with. She considered them immature and unsophisticated.

She turned up her stereo a little louder and looked around for something else to throw that would vent her anger without damaging her belongings.

She had to settle for turning up the volume on the stereo to an even more unacceptable level. Even though her mother wasn't here to be disturbed by it right now, perhaps the neighbors would complain to her later.

George Michael's voice boomed through the room with renewed energy, and she began to dance about, twisting and turning and bouncing onto the bed, then off, and across the floor in a series of spins and gyrations.

She looked up at the poster of Michael's unshaven face which graced another wall and pretended she was dancing with him. He was so cute.

Why couldn't she live somewhere exciting, where they had live concerts and there were things to do? In Boring Springs there was nothing. Nothing ever happened here. They never even got good concerts in Aimsley or Alexandria, and she never got to go to Monroe or Baton

46

Rouge or anywhere fun, the way some kids did.

She flopped back onto the bed and stared at the ceiling. And if anything fun ever did happen around here, there was Chief Briggs or her mother to put a stop to it before she got a chance to enjoy it.

She expelled a breath from deep within her lungs. Maybe she should have taken a job at Dairy Queen or something. Her mother had frowned on the idea, because she didn't like the notion of her daughter being a waitress too, but at least selling hamburgers would have done something to break up the monotony.

Rolling off the bed, she was about to turn up the stereo again. She almost didn't hear the phone ring.

She expected it to be her mother checking up on her to make sure she was staying home now, or one of the neighbors calling about the noise. It was a pleasant surprise to hear the nonchalant words roll from the receiver.

"Hello there."

It was Blade.

"Are you in jail?" she asked.

"Nah, I'm out already. My dad sent the bail money through the bank, and my uncle made sure they got it over to the jail. He's on some federal board that can give banks a hard time, I think. I've already got my bike back and everything."

She felt a quiver run through her. He'd slipped through their fingers in a few hours.

He was rebellious and good at it. She found that exciting. He'd beat the chief.

"Did your mom give you a bad time?"

"Not too bad. She brought me home. I guess she'll give me a good lecture when she gets off work. She stays too busy with her job to bother me much."

"That's good. Look, what time does your mom get off?"

"Six."

"I could come over for a while. Until it's time for her to show up."

"That would be great. Do you know where I live? Hey, how did you get the phone number?"

"I saw your mom's nametag and looked it up in the phone book. You live on Oak Street."

"Right. You know how to get here?"

"I'll find it. There's not that much of this town."

She laughed. "That's the truth. I'll see you in a few minutes. We'll listen to some records."

"Great."

She hung up and called Julie Briggs to tell her about her good fortune in meeting such a neat guy, and to complain, just a little about what Julie's father had done. She wasn't too rough, though. Julie had it tough, living with the chief. He was strict, and Lou Ellen didn't envy Julie being a policeman's daughter. Sometimes at school, other kids gave her a hard time. She wouldn't blame Julie, she thought as she hung up, if she ran away or did something wild.

Bob made one of his rare appearances from behind the grill with a sour look on his face. Estelle was picking up a sandwich for a guy at one of her tables when the diner manager walked through the swinging door, wiping his hands on his apron.

He was a big man who looked mean, but most of the time he was quiet and easy to tolerate.

He motioned Susie and Estelle together and rubbed his rugged face with an enormous hand.

"I just got a call from Nancy. She's got an abcessed tooth that's swollen her face up to the size of a bowling ball. She can't work tonight."

For one of the first times ever, Estelle noted a certain softness in his eyes.

48

"I'm going to have to ask one of you to stay and work with Roberta tonight. I hate to do it, but I'll pay you the overtime."

Both women felt their shoulders sag. One shift on the front lines was torture. Going through two, especially with one of them encompassing the evening crowd, was agony.

"You guys want to flip for it, or does someone need the extra dough more?"

"Just a second," Susie said. She turned around and took Estelle's shoulder. "I've got to have the evening off," she pleaded. "I've got a date with that insurance salesman. He's so cute, and I'd die if I had to stand him up. He might never ask me again. I'll make it up to you, though . . . really I will. Pick a time, and I'll work it out."

Estelle sighed. She needed to rest, and she wanted to have a talk with Lou Ellen, but she nodded her head. Susie had already helped her out today. At least the extra money would come in handy.

They turned back to their boss.

"I'll do it," Estelle said. "Where's the hash and the sling?"

Bob smiled. "I appreciate it, honey. Really."

Estelle blew a curl off her forehead. "Just let me call my daughter to tell her I'm working late."

Travis walked over to the table where Alison and Chrisk were working on paste-up, sticking long columns of print into place around pictures and advertising blocks.

He placed the design for the front page of the society section beside them and checked the finished pages. The classifieds, which had been done earlier in the week, were in one pile, and the news pages were beginning to stack up.

The entire society section remained, and some of it had

49

not yet been typeset on the IBM. The *Gazette* saved money by producing camera-ready pages to take to the printer, a process which sometimes became grueling. Travis set the type on the computer, and their printer spat out slick repro proofs to be clipped and placed on a page.

The computer made the operation possible, but even with the computer, they still walked the ragged edge of disaster in getting things ready. They couldn't put the pages together until everything was ready, and there was no way to rush the news.

Things like the 4-H contest and Mrs. Jeffries' column could not be rushed.

Alison picked up the layout for the society page and wiped her brow. The air was damp and sticky in spite of the air-conditioning.

"Is it time for a Dairy Queen run?" Chrisk asked.

"Sounds like a good idea," Alison said. "Do you want to take one of the cars?"

"No. It's a while until dark. I'll cruise on my moped. Everybody want the usual?"

"Sounds good," Travis said.

Alison opened the cash box and counted out a couple of bills as Travis ran his hands through his hair and steeled himself for a return to the layouts.

"Back to the old drawing board," he said.

It took most of his strength to force himself onto his stool once again. In his college days he had enjoyed doing layout. He'd gone to a small, private college which put out a weeky eight-pager. With a small staff it had always been a challenge to get it published, but in looking back, designing eight pages a week was nothing.

Back then there had been a certain pleasure in layout, like putting a puzzle together, making all the copy and pictures fit. Now it was a mundane task. He tried for some creativity, but much of the time he wound up slapping down lines and boxes, obeying the modular design rules without getting terribly carried away with innovation.

Lately he felt trapped in a cage of his own making. He didn't find the thrill he'd expected in the small-town newspaper business.

He had hated what he did in the city. The pace of working fourteen-hour days and living on food out of vending machines had begun to wear him down. Getting away from all of that had seemed like a blessing.

There had also been the idea that he and Alison would be able to spend more time together. That had been appealing, and in part it had proved to be what they'd hoped for. Travis loved working with Alison; they were friends on top of everything else. They could trade jokes or fire insults, and they could talk about everything from movies to local issues and find fascination in each other's ideas.

When they'd first begun dating, they'd talked for hours without realizing the time was passing. Now, their schedules left them always tired, even when they had free time together. The tension of running the *Gazette* was creating a new strain. Everything was their responsibility. They had to grind the paper out each week with limited assistance while trying to keep creditors at bay.

They had to cut back on their own take home pay if ads were canceled or revenues weren't high enough.

But even with the difficulties, there had been some triumphs. They'd found some wonderful stories in the town—a profile on an old man who had fought in World War I, a story on a man who trained hunting dogs that could even climb trees, and Alison and Chrisk had worked up a wonderful photo feature on the historic cemeteries around Bristol Springs. Some of the better photos from their efforts were now framed on the office wall.

They were the kind of stories that would win awards in contests for newspapers of their size, solid human interest features.

Travis never would have believed he would say it, but he was beginning to miss the crime beat. He missed rushing across town to check out murder reports and trying to second-guess police officers. It was tough to deal with cops, but he'd won a round or two, and those victories had been uplifting.

Going home exhausted after a rough day had been wonderful. He would cook something simple, usually managing to finish it just as Alison arrived home.

They would eat together, then retire with glasses of white wine to their small living room to watch late movies in black and white—*Anatomy of a Murder* or *The Philadelphia Story*. They both loved Jimmy Stewart.

Lying on the couch in each other's arms with only the silver-gray glow of the television illuminating the room was like being in a magic palace. It was fortunate that they had seen the movies many times, because they frequently missed the endings.

He looked up from the drawing board at Alison as she worked at the keyboard. He still found her beautiful. She didn't do much with her hair these days because of the work schedule, but it was soft and shiny, with waves where it crept down her back. She looked sexy in her jeans and pullover. The shirt fit loosely but hinted at the supple fullness of her breasts.

He forced himself to turn back to the page design. They were going to be at work until midnight as it was. There would be time for romance tomorrow.

He laughed to himself and shook his head. They had reached a point where they needed to schedule lovemaking in order to make sure it did not interfere with production.

He blocked off a space for a photograph and then jabbed the pencil downward to indicate a four inch block of copy beneath it for the accompanying story.

It was tedious. He wanted desperately for something

interesting to happen. He didn't care what, just something to get his adrenaline flowing.

Blade and Lou Ellen watched MTV for a while, until they got tired of it.

"My mom probably won't be home until midnight," Lou Ellen said. "You don't have to be anywhere?"

"I go where I want. My old man doesn't care."

They were sitting on the couch in the living room. She turned toward him slightly, looking into his eyes.

"You want some devil weed?" he asked, letting his eyebrows dance.

"We can't smoke it here. My mother would smell it."

"We'll get out of here, then."

Blade had parked his bike beside the house to keep it out of the neigbors' sight.

"Mom won't be back until late. Could we get out of here without being seen?" Lou Ellen asked.

"Sure. It's almost dark, and that cop has to go home sometime."

"I guess. I can call his daughter again and check. I'll hang up if he answers, but he never does."

"If he answers, we'll know he's still home."

"Right."

She got up and walked to the phone. Blade rested his head on the back of the couch and watched her ass move beneath the denim skirt, pleased with the stirring the view caused in him.

The cop's daughter apparently answered, because Lou Ellen talked for a couple of minutes.

"He's watching television," she said when she had hung up. "If you take the side streets to the edge of town, we'll be all right. More than likely, things will be busy at the diner, and Doug Langley, the other cop, will be hanging

53

around there."

"Sounds good. Where do you want to go?"

"We can go down by the Springs. Kids hang out there a lot. Except it's been so dry, there probably won't be anybody around."

Blade liked the sound of that. He was hoping they'd have some privacy.

Chapter 4

The sun set a little before eight, settling like a huge red globe.

With darkness came quiet. The streets of Bristol Springs emptied, and people either went indoors or sat on their porches. They left the porch lights off because lights attracted bugs.

They sat in silence, sipping iced tea or lemonade or cold beer while watching the occasional glow of fireflies that darted about in the darkness.

Doug Langdon liked working the night shift as a patrolman. Except for an occasional problem with kids who wanted to speed along the main drag, it was easy going. Since he was the only full-time officer under Chief Briggs, he always worked nights and traded off with the chief on handling weekend calls. He had to be flexible in his job, but he didn't mind. It was not bad work.

At night, he usually spent some time at the diner talking with the waitresses and trying to get dates. Usually he wasn't successful. He couldn't quite figure out what was wrong, but something kept him from being attractive to women. Just about all of his advances were rebuffed, making him feel much of the time as if women viewed him as a high school nerd.

He was a big man with broad shoulders, but his face was puffy and rough, with a flattened nose, the remnant of a high school fight.

With his curly black hair and the fact that his people came from the backwoods, the girls in town all seemed to view him as kind of a wild man.

Still he'd seen nice-looking girls hanging out with men who had pot bellies and tobacco stains on their teeth, so he couldn't understand it. They seemed to perceive something creepy about him of which he was unaware.

After a while at the diner, he usually cruised the streets for a couple of hours. He checked shops to make sure no one was breaking into them, and he tried to keep an eye on the houses of people who were out of town. Burglary was not a big problem in Bristol Springs, and the chief wanted to keep it that way. He demanded a careful watch on property.

If Doug happened to spot somebody who looked suspicious, he would check them out. That happened about once every six months, if that often.

Before midnight he'd drop by the diner again and drink coffee. If there was a sheriff's deputy who worked the late patrol on hand in this end of the parish, they got together and talked. He liked it best when Holyfield was around. They talked about fishing and baseball. Sometimes they got into a discussion about politics, but not frequently.

Killing time until dawn was the worst part of the shift. Everything got quiet in town after midnight. By 2 A.M. the boredom could be almost unbearable. Everybody was asleep by then. There wasn't any nightlife in Bristol Springs.

Sometimes he went back to the station and talked to the dispatcher or listened to the calls that other law enforcement agencies were working as they came in on the scanner. Other times he would park and read magazines while he waited for radio calls from the night dispatcher or to catch speeders. He figured that was what he would do tonight, once it got late. He had a new copy of *Cheri* and also a *Field and Stream* to look over. Women and hunting were Langdon's favorite pursuits, although he got to indulge the latter interest far more frequently.

All his life he had loved to hunt and fish, pastimes taught him by his father.

The squirrel tails usually wound up as decoration for the antennas of the family trucks and cars.

On summer mornings they went fishing, taking a boat out onto the lake to catch their quota of perch with an occasional bass mixed in.

Langdon considered himself a sportsman and an angler.

It would be a while until he could do that tonight. He wanted to put in a few hours of actually serving the public before he sat back with his magazines.

Stuffing a pinch of snuff into his lip, he picked up the small paper cup he used to hold the juice and steered with his left hand. He made his way along the main drag at a slow speed.

He saw Chrisk Jackson motor by on her moped and waved.

She waved back. She was a pretty girl, Langdon thought. She was slender and smooth, with a bright smile. She always smiled, was always very polite to him when she saw him.

Too bad she spent all her time at the newspaper. Langdon harbored secret fantasies of dating her. He knew he would never be able to date her publicly with attitudes as they were in Bristol Springs. It would cause all kinds of trouble.

He made a few passes through the neighborhood streets. When he was content that all was well, he headed on over to the diner for a quick sandwich.

The chief had told him to be on the lookout for the kid on the motorcycle, so he watched along the main drag for some sign of the big Harley.

He didn't spot it.

As he was pulling into the diner, Blade's bike was headed up Kelley Street two blocks away.

Three blocks over, the cyclops eye of Chrisk's small motorcycle cut a path for her through the darkness as the wind swept her hair back.

She liked riding the moped at night. It gave her a sense of freedom.

She'd needed some kind of transportation, and it had been all that she and her mother could afford.

Although the purchase was one of necessity, she had quickly come to love the machine. Hopping on it and shooting from place to place on newspaper business matched her self-image. She liked to think of herself as an on-the-go reporter, dashing around to gather information and write stories on deadline. She dreamed of the day when she would fulfill the image in its entirety.

She was putting away as much money as possible for college. She needed to get started soon. Travis seemed to think it would be possible to arrange by the spring semester next year.

In high school she had begun to think of developing a career. Most girls in Bristol Springs, white and black alike, were disposed to local jobs and quick marriages.

She had dismissed that, and she had been fortunate to have an English teacher who encouraged her to pursue her interest in writing.

The English teacher, Phyllis Granger, was young and idealistic, not yet saddled with the cynicism that developed from watching bright pupils wither in jobs in the hardware store or the shopping center. She had loaned Chrisk books to encourage her, things that weren't in the school library—like poetry by Ntozake Shange, and

Gwendolyn Brooks.

Chrisk had begun to look outward, dreaming about things she might do. When the newspaper changed hands, she had been sweating away at a fast-food joint, trying to save money. She had begun to lose hope.

When Alison and Travis arrived, her hope was renewed. She had rushed down to see about a job the very day they showed up. Their enthusiasm had reminded her of Miss Granger, and even though they had warned her about the pay and the hours, she had jumped at the chance to work with them.

Now, as her work appeared in print, she clipped it neatly and pressed it into her portfolio. She knew all of it would come in handy when she was ready to start school, and later, when she started looking for work.

The work brought pride to her mother and her grandfather as well. That pleased her. She often found her mother thumbing through the portfolio.

That nourished her desire to go and continue school.

Eventually she wanted to work for a magazine doing feature articles. Once it had appeared a hopeless dream. Now she was beginning to believe it was attainable, if she worked hard enough.

She picked up a little speed on the bike, eager to get back to the paper and get on with the paste-up. Once it was finished they would sit and talk for a while about the ins and outs of the business.

Usually Travis would start telling stories about crime reporting. Sometimes he rambled, but often it was interesting. It made her long to cover a big story, a trial or an investigation.

She didn't know she was about to get her chance.

The darkness brought new power to Navarra's limbs. She was still unable to lift her weight or carry herself, but she was alive, or at least animated.

Life was a term she had ceased to apply to herself centuries before. She was content with existing, surviving. As the shadows settled over her, she renewed her determination to go on. She would replenish herself and move forward.

Slowly she lifted her hand until it was before her eyes. It was not in her to weep, but the sight of her own flesh disgusted her.

Revulsion churned through her. She could see the tendons and the muscle tissue through the tattered flesh. The decomposure was continuing. The heat seemed to make it worse. Rotting tissue dropped away from her bones.

Touching her face, she felt ragged bulges and cuts. Swollen pockets of gas bubbled in her cheeks and neck. A patch of skin was peeled back from her jaw on the left side, exposing the bone. The nose was a soggy gray mass.

Once she had been beautiful.

She wondered if her beauty would ever return—or would she remain some hideous creature of the night, destined to inspire new legends of nightmare and disdain?

It did not matter.

If her beauty was not to return, she could survive without it.

She shifted her weight and regretted it. As her strength returned, so did other sensations.

She was becoming more aware of pain as well, and there was a burning sensation in her flesh. It would deteriorate completely if she did not find food soon.

There had never been agony like this before. She recalled lives she had once lived and found nothing to compare, not with the pain and not with the loneliness. In all the ages she had known, she had never felt such isolation and emptiness, not even in the beginning, when they had huddled beside the Red Sea and wondered how

60

they would keep from dying.

That was an eternity past, more like the remnant of a half-forgotten dream.

Now she was in a new reality. She did not know the year, and she did not know if any of her sisters remained. She was lost in the jungle of time.

Was she the last, the one who must bear the curse to its ultimate fulfillment, left to suffer the most horrible pain any of her kind had ever endured? Had her kind passed from the face of the earth?

It was time to find help. She had regained as much strength as she could expect from rest. She was strong enough now to call on the night brothers. Gradually she tilted back her head and closed the wrinkled lids of her eyes.

The pain tore at her thoughts as she tried to concentrate. Dragging in rasping breaths, she forced herself to ignore the hurt.

For almost a minute she fought her own consciousness, shutting out the pain so that she could focus her thoughts.

She was reaching out, trying to establish a link with the energy which vibrated through the night, an energy she and her sisters had learned to tap long ago as part of their method of surviving. With her thoughts, she sent a summons through the shadows for any creature that might respond.

Chapter 5

Things were slow at the diner as the evening dragged on. Estelle chatted with Doug Langdon for a while as she polished some glasses.

She felt like a bartender listening to him ramble about things that did not interest her. He was a nice enough man, but he did not excite her.

Too bad Chief Briggs did not work the night shift and spend time hanging around the counter. He dropped by for coffee from time to time during the day, but never at a time that gave her any opportunity to talk with him. She never seemed to be able to let him know she was interested.

She listened to Langdon tell her about fishing trips until she could stand it no more, and then she moved from behind the counter and began to wipe tables. She sensed Langdon's gaze following her, but she was not troubled by it.

It was common knowledge in Bristol Springs that Langdon was looking for a wife. He eventually got around to asking out most of the single women in his age range.

There were not that many, and most of them turned him down. He wasn't different from most of the men in town, and it wasn't because they knew he would spend much of his time away from home on hunting or fishing trips if he was married. There was just some other quality about him, a slight strangeness that turned people off.

The frequent rebuffs he received made him even more desperate and persistent, since he rarely got any companionship from the opposite sex.

Estelle began running a cloth across the shiny simulated wood tabletops, thinking about the pain in her feet.

Eventually Langdon followed her, and she realized as he continued to talk that he was going to ask her out. That had never happened to her before. She'd talked to other waitresses on the night shift who'd had to deal with him, but this was her first experience. She looked around for help, but the other waitress was busy at the cash register.

Then her eyes fell on the pay phone beside the restrooms.

"Doug, I hope you'll excuse me. I need to call and check on my daughter," she said.

It wasn't a lie, really. She wanted to talk to Lou Ellen and make sure she wasn't too upset about the incident that afternoon.

Reaching into her tip pockets, she plunked out a quarter and walked to the phone, where she dialed her home number, turning her back to Langdon as she listened to the phone ring.

She began to grow nervous as she counted it ring twelve times. Usually Lou Ellen answered after only a few rings.

As Estelle hung up, she was telling herself not to worry. Lou Ellen could be in the shower, or she could be listening to her records, using her headphones. That wasn't unusual.

But neither suggestion was comforting. She could not dismiss the trouble of the afternoon. What if Lou Ellen had been so angered by the confrontation that she'd decided to run away?

Estelle tried to hide her concern as she turned back from the phone, but Langdon spotted it quickly. At least in one area he was astute.

"Is anything wrong?" he asked.

"I didn't get any answer."

"Could she have gone out?"

"She wasn't supposed to. She might be showering or something." She smoothed her dress nervously with her hands.

"Well, look," Langdon said. "I was about to go back on patrol. Why don't I head over there and have a look around? I'm sure nothing is wrong. When I've checked it out, it will put your mind at ease."

He put his hat on and adjusted it to give it the tilt he liked. He was trying to be a knight in shining armor for her, and for once she appreciated his presence.

"If it's not too much trouble," she said.

"Naw. I was going to cruise the streets anyway. We'll come up with something. It'll be fine."

From the corner of her eye, she saw a customer wander in. She touched her hair softly, then reached into her pocket for her order pad.

"I'll have the dispatcher call if I find anything," Langley said.

"Thanks, Doug. I appreciate it."

She watched him walk out to his car before she moved over to the customer. She tried to let the work take her mind off her fears.

Blade opened the bike to full throttle once they had turned off the highway onto the road which led back to the Springs. The night wind swept around them like a cool breath.

He liked the way Lou Ellen clung to him as he took the bike through the curves and skidded it around turns.

On the straightaway she rested her chin on his shoulder. He could feel the warmth of her breath against his neck, and occasionally the smooth flesh of her cheek brushed against his skin.

He smiled. He hadn't felt happy in a long while. Most of the time he was bored. Tonight was an exception.

He fired the bike forward, watching the light blaze a trail of white in front of him.

He felt like an explorer on a long journey.

He yanked the bike through another curve and listened to Lou Ellen's squeal of excitement in his ear.

She liked it, so he let it roll through the next one even faster.

He enjoyed being able to impress her. It gave him a thrill.

"Having fun?" he asked.

"It's great," she shouted to make him hear her over the engine.

"How much further?" he asked.

"The next bend," she yelled.

He went through the curve and pulled onto the dirt road. It stretched over a small bluff and led down past an embankment to the dry rut where the spring should have been.

Blade braked the bike hard, spinning it sideways to kick up dirt. Then he dismounted and slipped the bag of marijuana from its hiding place beneath the seat.

Beside it was a small pipe. He put it between his teeth and wrapped one arm around Lou Ellen's shoulders.

"This is good stuff," he said.

"Great."

They walked along the edge of the creek bed looking up at the sky. Away from the lights of the town, the sky was a black canvas with the stars spread across it like sprinkles of silver.

Off to one side, the moonlight burned like a spotlight.

The scene was perfect. Taking his pipe from his teeth, he leaned down and kissed Lou Ellen. It was their first kiss of the evening, but she offered no resistance. He had thought she might be hesitant about physical contact. Instead, she seemed eager for the adventure.

Her lips pressed hard against his for several seconds, then parted to let the moistness of their mouths touch.

Slowly her arms slipped about his shoulders, as she pressed her mouth harder against his, her lips working hungrily.

As they moved into a full embrace he could feel the warm contours of her body pressed against his.

Gently he eased her to the ground. It was dusty and dry, but they ignored that, and she tilted her head back as he began to kiss her neck and throat.

He could hear her breath quickening as he ran his fingers through her hair.

She responded slowly, her breath almost a purr as she slipped off her jacket so that he could kiss her bare shoulders.

He let his face brush against her skin, savoring the touch of her soft flesh. It was flawless and pale in the moonlight.

He closed his eyes, hugging her tightly, rubbing his hands down her sides and across her hips, whispering to her about her beauty. He was careful not to move too fast, careful not to rush anything. She was willing, looking for some fulfillment. There would be time for everything tonight, time for their adventure.

From the shadows, two sets of eyes peered at them.

One set weak and clouded.

One set aglow, blazing with the fire of the hunt.

Langdon saw the porch light on at the Johnson house when he rounded the corner onto the street. That worried him a bit. A porch light on usually meant people were out.

He slowed the car to a stop and looked out through the passenger window. There were a couple of lights on inside, but he saw no sign of movement.

Shoving the gearshift into park, he popped open his door and got out, standing to peer over the roof of the car.

The area was silent except for the chirp of crickets.

He wasn't sure what to make of the scene. People didn't leave interior and exterior lights on. He corrected that. Teenagers probably did, because they didn't pay electricity bills.

Closing his door, he moved up the walk, climbed the steps to the front door, and knocked. When there was no answer, he pressed his ear against the door but detected no sounds inside. Teenagers were always listening to something.

He tried the knob. It didn't budge. A frown furrowed his brow as he chewed his thin lower lip. He didn't want to break in if nothing was wrong, so he walked over to the front window and peered inside.

He could see no sign of life. A lamp burned beside the couch, and a Pepsi can sat on the coffee table beside a half-eaten bag of potato chips. More evidence of a teenager.

He walked from the window to the edge of the porch, his cowboy boots clopping against the dry wood.

He looked around the corner of the house, then hopped off the edge of the porch and walked along the side, heading for the back door.

He happened to notice the tire tracks. The grass was brittle from lack of rain and had remained pressed down in several spots.

Tugging his flashlight from his belt, he aimed the beam down to examine the ground. Judging the narrow indention, it didn't take long to determine that a motorcycle had passed that way.

It had to be the same bike he'd picked up for the chief earlier. Apparently the boy had come back to see Lou Ellen despite the chief's warnings.

He rushed back to his car and slipped behind the wheel to grasp the microphone.

"Yo. It's Doug to base."

"I been trying to raise you," the radio crackled in reply. "There's been a call about a prowler over at Estelle Johnson's house."

"Damn it, that's me. I'm checking the place out for the lady."

"You're supposed to notify me when you do that kind of thing."

"It was a favor, but look . . . you'd better get the chief on the phone. I think the Johnson girl has run off with that biker he picked up this afternoon."

"He told that boy to leave town."

"Well, he probably didn't want him taking Lou Ellen Johnson with him. Call the chief and ask him what he wants me to do."

The chirp of the crickets continued, and somewhere in the distance he heard the deep hoot of an owl. It made him feel uneasy. His grandmother had told him the call of an owl could be an ill omen. He took it as a sign that something wasn't right.

Julie Briggs felt her heart leap into her throat when the call came for her father. Somehow or other, they'd discovered Lou Ellen wasn't at home. When they caught up with her friend, she was going to be in big trouble, probably grounded for a month, maybe even for the rest of the summer.

Lou Ellen had sounded happy earlier on the phone, and a heavy sadness settled over Julie. She knew that her friend hadn't been happy the last few months. She hadn't really recovered from her father's death, and now the first chance she had to have a halfway decent time, Chief Briggs was going off like a platoon leader.

She twisted her fingers through her dark, wavy hair. Part of the regret she felt came from the fact that her father was reacting the way he was because she and Lou Ellen were close to the same age. He felt a responsibility to protect Lou Ellen in much the way he tried to protect Julie.

Since Julie's mother had left, he'd made every effort to be both mother and father to her.

While he was dressing, she entertained the thought of telling him where he might look for Lou Ellen. Then she dismissed it.

Wherever Lou Ellen was, she was probably having a good time. That would come to an end when the police showed up, and it would probably be a while until she had a good time again. It might as well last as long as possible.

Briggs emerged from his bedroom in his uniform. He was pinning his badge to his pocket as he came down the stairs.

"Aren't you overreacting?" Julie asked.

He hugged her and kissed her forehead. "The people in this town look to me for help," he said. "In a big city, they'd have to wait twenty-four hours for help if somebody was missing. It's not that way here.

"I like it here because it's quiet, honey. When it's not, I have a job to do . . . I'm here to help people. Besides, I know if you'd been dragged off by some dirtbag like that boy who's got Lou Ellen, I'd want something done about it quick."

"Maybe he didn't drag her off."

"She might think she's where she wants to be," Briggs said, "but the truth is, she's headed for nothing but trouble, taking up with the likes of that boy. I'm just trying to help her. Do you understand?"

Julie nodded, folding her arms against her t-shirt. There was no point in engaging him in an argument. He was acting more like a father than a cop, but she would never make him see that.

"Be careful."

"We will."

Estelle Johnson was sitting in a booth at the diner sipping coffee when Doug brought Briggs into the building. She'd been telephoned by the dispatcher and apprised of the situation.

"Maybe I was too hard on her," Mrs. Johnson said when the chief slid onto the seat across from her. She was fighting tears. "I never dreamed something like this would happen. She's been moody, but she's never been a bad girl. I've tried to teach her right."

"It's okay," Briggs said. "We found out early. We'll catch up to them fairly quickly, I'm sure. Everything's going to be all right."

"I really appreciate your help," Estelle said.

"It's why I'm here," he said. It was partially true. He also wanted to head off any major problems. If they got a handle on things tonight, hopefully they could avoid going into any lengthy searches to bring the girl back.

It might take a few hours tonight, but it would mean a normal, peaceful day tomorrow, the kind of day Briggs preferred.

Travis sipped his coffee and listened to the chatter on the police scanner as Alison and Chrisk continued to work on the paste-up. While he sat at the drawing board, the radio broadcasts often caught his ear. He'd grown used to monitoring broadcasts in his previous job.

The scanner had come in handy, alerting him of stories to cover, but most of the time the radio was a source of amusement rather than a source of news.

The calls Briggs and Langdon handled usually consisted of double-parked cars, battling spouses, or suspicious characters.

Travis had smiled earlier when he'd heard the broadcast that one of the suspicious characters reported had turned out to be Langdon.

Now he heard the dispatcher broadcast to the sheriff's office substation about the missing Johnson girl. The cops seemed to be in a panic because she'd apparently gone off on a joyride with somebody Chief Briggs didn't like.

Noticing his grin, Chrisk shook her head. "You're not used to Chief Briggs's iron hand yet," she said.

"In Houston or New Orleans or even in Aimsley, they wouldn't start looking for twenty-four hours, probably thirty-six."

"It's a different world here," Chrisk said.

"I'm still learning that," Travis said.

"It's always been that way with the police around here," Alison said. "My grandmother used to tell me stories about the chief of police looking out for the townspeople, doing what was best for them."

"Whether they like it or not?"

"Probably," she laughed. "That's what we've come to expect in Bristol Springs. Absolute protection that we don't have to think about."

Travis sipped some more coffee. "I guess Mrs. Johnson probably appreciates that about now. Maybe it's good."

Chapter 6

The intrusion into the cat's mind was perplexing to the creature, like nothing it had ever experienced. It operated on its urges and its instinct, not on thought.

As it crouched in the shadows of the pine trees watching the two-legged ones, its mind was in a state of confusion.

When the Calling had tripped into its lobes, it had been on one of its solitary hunts, stalking food, following the smell of small animals in the darkness. It hunted at night, always careful not to let its path stray too far from the depths of the forest where it remained hidden, safe from two-legged ones.

Few knew that its kind still dwelled in the region. Living alone, isolated, it had enjoyed the safety for years— the supply of food plentiful in the absence of other large predators.

Stories about big cats were like myths in Louisiana, but few of the myths had any basis in truth. Many claimed to see panthers or hear them cry out like humans, yet no one ever brought one in, not even an accidental kill.

The cat had come from the east, not searching, only wandering. The food supply had stopped it here in the deep woods. It had grown complacent in the land, living well on the small animals it could find.

At a corner of the forest there had been a dwelling of two-legs once, but that had been abandoned long before the cat had come this way.

Most of the time it limited its travels, never moving too far from its lair, seldom even drifting to the river's edge a few miles south.

The panther was rare in many ways. Not only did it live in a place most of its kind had long ago deserted; it also bore the coat of a remote ancestor. Instead of the tan fur that most of its breed possessed, the panther had a sleek black pelt, perhaps the result of atavism. The cat had no knowledge of its genetic traits, however. Its usual concern was only survival.

The urge to obey the Calling had been overwhelming, surpassing the drive for food. It had settled into the night creature's brain like a burning sensation.

At first the cat had resisted, rolling onto the ground and swatting at its head with its huge paws.

When that had failed to rid its mind of the sensation, it had been forced to give in, to follow, feet padding quietly against the dry ground. The cat weighed almost 200 pounds, but it moved with gentle grace.

The Calling led where it did not want to go, toward the place where the two-legged ones still gathered, where there had once been water. The land had been dry for a long time, and the panther had not fed well in days, nor had it found moisture. Its mouth was dry, and its belly ached for nourishment.

In spite of its hunger, it had continued through the trees softly, eyes staring straight ahead, hoping there would be no two-legged ones there. It did not understand the fear of the two-legged ones. It only knew to flee them, for they were an indication of danger.

To reach the source of the unexplained compulsion, the cat had had to travel two miles through the underbrush.

It passed food and ignored it, drawn only by obedience

that was much like the fear of the two-legs. It was something obeyed without question.

When it had reached the site, it had stopped, growling at the huddled gray mass of flesh it found. The tingling sensation of fear shot along the cat's spine, raising the hairs on its back.

The smell that touched its nostrils was like nothing it had ever known. The fear smell of the two-legs was nothing like this smell. It caused the creature's blood to rush through its veins, and its heart quickened as it did on the occasions when feeding was near.

The long black tail swished about, and the creature wanted to turn and run back into the night.

Instead, the compulsion kept it standing as its eyes focused on the thing in front of it.

Slowly the gray mass adjusted and crawled toward it. The cat wanted to spin and run. Instead, it waited as the thing reached for it, touching its head and rubbing its ears to reassure it.

Gradually the fear ebbed, leaving the sensation of confusion. It was a contradiction of everything the animal knew. Taking a few steps from the tree, the cat looked down the slope to the edge of the dry place at the two-legs.

Fear was born anew, the inherent fear of the two-legs. They were not strong creatures, not fast enough to outrun him or strong enough to avert the force of his jaws, yet it wanted no part of them.

It tried to make that known to the presence in its brain. Fear made it struggle against the commands, shaking its head from side to side, twitching its ears and growling deep in its throat. Sound did not emerge from its mouth. The presence had control.

Slowly, crouching, the panther looked down at the two-legs. The smell of them touched its nostrils, and it sensed fire smoldering between them.

Again it tried to rebel and felt pain in its head this time.

74

Its brain seemed to swell against the inside walls of its skull. Its head jerked back, the eyes closed. It almost lost its footing but managed to remain standing.

Resisting was impossible. It would have to obey, or at least allow its limbs and body to follow the invading commands rather than its own.

Again it looked toward the two-legs, waiting for the moment the presence indicated. The moment of the kill.

Briggs and Langdon cruised the streets, swinging through the neighborhoods around the Johnson home in a quick sweep before heading out on the highway.

"You know they might have gone out by the Springs," Langdon suggested.

"It's dried up right now, isn't it?" Briggs asked.

Langdon shrugged. "Kids probably wouldn't care. Not for what they're up to."

"Let's check it out. See if Sarah can raise the sheriff's cruiser and tell them we're crossing the city limits on an investigation."

Langdon picked up the mike and growled the message as he swung the car onto the drag and gave it gas.

"We may not be able to arrest him," he said when he'd hung up the mike. "He's not but two years older than she is."

"He hasn't really violated the law yet," Briggs agreed. "We're just picking the girl up at her mother's request. Maybe he'll try to stop us."

"I guess we can hope," Langdon said.

The evening was ticking on. Travis had joined Chrisk and Alison for the final stages of paste-up. They were all showing signs of weariness, and they had to take great care to avoid mistakes.

When they ran across errors, they used the computer to reprint the paragraphs containing the mistakes.

Corrected paragraphs could be slipped into place where the offending lines were sliced away with small razor-sharp Exacto knives.

They continued to listen to the police department's efforts to track down Lou Ellen Johnson.

"It's kind of sad," Chrisk said. "She doesn't have a daddy." She could sympathize, because she'd lost her own father to cancer.

"I suspect she'll settle down after tonight's incident," Alison said. "Or she'll rebel even more."

Travis poured coffee for each of them. "Well, we won't stop the presses at this point."

Lou Ellen pulled away from Blade and ran her hands through her hair.

"I have to use the little girl's room," she whispered. "I won't be long."

He looked up at her with glazed eyes and grinned. "I'll be waiting." There was a suggestiveness in his tone which was not lost on her.

She walked quickly up the slope, her body tingling from the pot, her skin moist from the touch of his lips.

She moved dreamily, enjoying the sensation of the pot and the warmth of pleasure.

It had been good so far. She hadn't had many dates, and most of her kisses so far had been goodnight farewells. It was exciting to make out with Blade. He was kind of wild and tough.

Her mother would die if she knew what was going on, and that added to it. Besides, it was just casual, nothing big. He wasn't pushing for anything she didn't want to give at the moment. She'd decide when the time came if she wanted him to have it all.

She staggered slightly as she reached the trees, her eyes half closed. The soft night breeze wrapped around her and she let her breath escape slowly through her lips.

He wouldn't have to beg too hard, she decided. Terri Roberts had told her what it, the It, felt like.

Her mother lectured her frequently about the moral aspects and the dangers, but Terri's description of the results hadn't been nearly so horrible.

It had sounded pretty exciting, in fact. She wasn't sure she was ready to give it a try, but who could tell?

Shrugging off the jacket she wore—it was too hot for it, but she liked the way it looked—she placed it neatly on the ground.

She then moved on through the trees a few more steps and started looking for a spot that would provide some privacy. She wasn't used to being away from clean facilities.

Pushing back some branches, she moved into the shadows, still half-staggering.

Looking back over her shoulder, she could still see Blade resting on the ground, the pipe glowing as he puffed on it.

A few more steps were needed just to make sure she was out of sight. She didn't want him seeing her crouched in an unbecoming position.

Finally she selected a tree and reached for the hem of her skirt. Before lifing it, however, she happened to glance down at the ground.

There was some kind of mucus near the base of the tree, something gray and sticky. It shone a little in the moonlight that streamed through the branches.

As she bent down to study it, the smell touched her nostrils and caused her stomach to churn. It was the smell of something decaying.

Placing her hand on her nose, she turned away. It must have been the remains of some dead animal. Perhaps it had

77

died here from lack of water.

She took a step further into the darkness, looking for a tree that was unsoiled.

Stopping at the next big oak, she again prepared to relieve the growing pressure in her bladder.

She hadn't reached to her underwear before that release occurred in a sudden flush, triggered by the swipe of the cat's huge paw.

It caught the calf and part of the ankle of her right leg, knocking her off balance as the sharp nails ripped through skin and muscle.

She screamed as she hit the ground, rolled onto her stomach, and began to scramble toward the edge of the trees.

From here she could not see Blade, and she wasn't sure if he had heard her cry out.

She had moved only inches across the forest floor before the cat was on top of her, its claws digging into her back and its mouth pressing against her neck, trying to sink sharp teeth into her throat.

She kicked and fought to drag herself from under the creature's weight, but she found it impossible to break free. The claws raked along her bare shoulders, ripping through the cloth of her tank top. Thin lines were drawn through her skin by the beast's nails.

The pain stunned her numbed brain, shocking her into an awareness that made the agony more acute.

"Blade!" she screamed, the first vowel building to a crescendo before her lips completed the name. The monster pressed a paw against her shoulder to steady her as it bit through the trapezius muscle.

Something else tore, and a stream of blood spurted up across her face. She stopped moving. Her eyes were clouding, a dimness beyond the night's darkness blotting out her vision.

She looked through the trees to see Blade standing a few

feet away, his face filled with shock.

She tried to lift her arm to reach out to him and found it would not respond.

Then she watched him turn away and begin to run.

She lay still as the cat pawed at her, rolling her onto her back.

The next rake of its paw tore open her throat. She felt the blood but not the pain now. The fluid washed over her neck—what was left of her neck—and she felt what she thought was the panther's tongue.

She realized moments later the cat had stepped back. It stood watching, her blood dripping from its jaws.

As the dimness continued to overtake her, she tilted her gaze downward.

The horror began anew, but mercifully it lasted only a few seconds as she stared at the huddled gray form which crawled toward her.

The hideous mouth pressed against her, and the coated gray tongue licked hungrily at her ruined throat.

She did not know what it was, but as it drank her blood, it seemed to take new form. Its puttylike skin bubbled and contorted, slowly taking on an appearance that was some-what . . . she could not believe it . . .

. . . human.

Blade jumped onto his bike in a frenzy to get it started. His hands grabbed at the handlebars. He almost lost his balance trying to kick the starter.

He was terrified. Cold sweat poured down his back, and he felt the muscles in his bladder and bowels trying to give.

His breath came in dry gasps, and he could hear his own heartbeat thundering in his ears like a kettledrum.

As the engine roared to life, he turned the bike hard to aim it toward the roadway. It almost moved from under him as it shot forward.

He guided it up the rise, using his feet to balance it until he could get it on flat ground.

Before he could angle it toward the highway, he was compelled to look back over his shoulder.

What he saw he dismissed as a combination of fear and the buzz of the marijuana. He could not believe there was a beautiful naked woman with flowing dark hair standing at the edge of the trees, her skin glistening as white as ivory in the moonlight as blood dripped from her face and down across her breasts.

Later he would realize his eyes had not been mistaken. Later he would wish it had all been a nightmare.

Chapter 7

A few minutes after the pages were finished and the *Gazette* staff had settled down to a final round of coffee, the scanner broadcast brought word of an animal attack. An ambulance was requested from Riverland Hospital in Aimsley. They called for the Med-Evac helicopter, if it was available.

As Travis sat up to take notice, the sheriff's department was asked to notify the coroner's office, and the air ambulance was turned back. It seemed there was no rush for medical attention.

For a second they were all silent. Travis looked at Alison. Alison looked back at him. Chrisk looked at both of them, wondering about a course of action.

Alison could tell by the look in Trav's eyes that he wanted to roll on it, and a glance at Chrisk conveyed the same information. People who didn't work in the news business would have misunderstood it as morbid sensationalism.

Alison understood the desire to get the story. She knew how badly Travis had languished without the spark of spot news.

For Chrisk it was a new experience. Working at the *Gazette* had not provided her much opportunity for this sort of thing. At the scene she would probably be shocked, but she would function. She had proved herself in too many ways not to. She would not go to pieces in the presence of death. She knew she would have to get used to such things if she was going to succeed in journalism.

"If we don't get it tonight, it won't be news by next week's edition," Travis said. He was like a little boy asking for permission to go to a movie.

"We'll be up all night," Alison said.

"I'll come back and do the film and the paste-up," Chrisk volunteered.

A second ticked by, then Alison heaved a sigh. "I'll start figuring out how to remake page one," she said. "You two hit it."

Without hesitation Travis was up, grabbing a note pad and some pens. Chrisk followed him, picking up the camera bag and snatching some film from a drawer.

Their sneakers squeaked on the tile floor as they rushed about. It took them a total of fifteen seconds to make it out the front door.

Alison had to smile as she sat down at the drawing table with the paste-up of page one. Theirs was the killer instinct. For a second she felt like the mother of two children running off to a baseball game. Unfortunately, this was not a sunny afternoon event played on green grass.

She stripped the main photo off the page and prepared to move the drought story down. The major news story had ceased to be the lack of rain.

Travis's Mustang peeled a strip of rubber onto the pavement as he backed it out of his parking slot and shoved the stick shift forward.

Chrisk steadied herself by pressing her hands against the dashboard when he slammed the gas pedal.

The look in her eyes was intense. He glanced over at her for only a second. He had to concentrate on the navigation of the narrow streets. It had been a while since he'd had to get anywhere in such a hurry, but his driving skills in such situations had become a reflex.

He didn't look forward to whatever scene awaited them. He didn't like seeing death. At times he had questioned the need for the public to be informed about such things in detail, but it was news. Getting to it quickly was everything, and it was that challenge that pumped his adrenaline.

It was the difference between truth and the version the cops put into their reports. Sometimes they had a way of simplifying things, or adjusting facts. If someone had indeed been killed by a wild animal, the cops might play it down in an effort to stave off panic. If there was a danger, the newspaper had to let people know about it.

Chrisk was trembling. Images of the potentially grisly scene they were approaching filled her head. She envisioned blood and torn limbs, and she knew that it would inevitably be someone she knew.

"You okay?" Travis asked as they sped through the dark.

"Fine," she said. "Just nervous."

"If it turns out to be rough out there, let me know if it gets to you. These things can be nasty."

"Have you ever seen someone killed by an animal?"

"No. I just know the human body holds a lot of blood."

"I'm ready."

"I'm not interested in close-up photos of the body," Travis said. "We'll try to get a good shot of the accident scene. Keep your eyes open. I want you to help me write the story. We'll do a dual by-line."

He spotted a sheriff's cruiser with its lights flashing. It

turned off onto the Bristol Springs road, and Travis followed, not worrying about speed limits. He put the pedal to the floor, keeping close to the patrol car as its red lights blazed a trail through the darkness.

The Mustang had seen better days, but its engine roared to life. The battered frame rattled, shuddering both occupants until they reached the end of the road.

There were several law enforcement vehicles parked near the creek bed. The lights flashed blue and red.

Travis and Chrisk climbed from the car and walked together toward the cluster of sheriff's deputies.

Beyond them other cops were visible, shining lights through the trees toward some men standing just inside the perimeter of the forest.

The coroner had not yet arrived. He would have to drive from Aimsley after someone phoned him.

With Chrisk in tow, Travis strolled up to the deputies, who were talking casually while they waited around.

"Whose investigation is it going to be?" Travis asked.

One of the men looked over at him, then turned his gaze toward Chrisk. A toothpick rolled around in his broad mouth.

"Who are you?" he asked.

"Travis Dixon. I'm from the *Gazette*."

A thin, blond-haired deputy, whose nametag read Roberts, turned around to look at Travis.

"It's in our jurisdiction," Roberts said, "and we pulled a couple of cars over here, but Chief Briggs was already involved in it."

"What kind of animal was it?" Travis asked, motioning casually for Chrisk to move behind him and get pictures of the men working with the lights.

"Hard to say right now. Something big, is my guess," the deputy said. "They'll probably have to check the teeth marks and everything."

84

"Have they got the next of kin notified?"

"They're going to tell her mother now."

Travis nodded. Turning, he looked back at Chrisk. She had been shooting pictures for a couple of seconds now. A few people had turned to look at the flash, but they were largely ignoring her.

He saw Briggs emerge from the trees and speak with someone, then walk toward his car.

Travis detached himself from the deputies and approached Briggs. He and the chief had not become friends in the time Travis had been in town, but they had exchanged conversation while having coffee at the diner from time to time.

"The Johnson girl?" Travis asked.

Briggs stopped and looked at him, his expression an unhappy one.

"Not for publication yet."

"I know."

Briggs took a handkerchief from his pocket and used it to wipe sweat from the back of his neck. "I've got Langdon notifying her mother. I don't know how I'm going to keep her from looking at the body. I don't need that for identification, but I'm afraid she'll want to see it." He winced.

"Pretty bad?" Travis asked.

"It's the worst I've ever seen."

"What did it?"

Briggs took off his hat and smoothed his hair down. "I can't be sure at this point. Something big, to do as much damage as it did. It scared her boyfriend off, so we're going to try to find him and see what he saw. We passed him coming out here. He was going like a bat outa hell. I thought we were going to be tracking him for a murder."

"You came on here first?"

"We could have chased him, I guess. Thought the girl

85

might need help first. I radioed the sheriff's department to look out for him. He slipped through their fingers."

Briggs looked past Travis to where Chrisk was shooting pictures of the patrol cars.

"You're not going to try to get pictures of the body, are you?"

Travis shook his head. "I couldn't use it. It would upset people too much."

"It'd do that," Briggs agreed. "They're gonna be plenty upset anyway. Let me make a radio call and I'll take you up there to the scene if you behave yourself."

"Thanks, Chief."

Trav walked over to Chrisk. "I'm going to walk up there with the chief. You don't have to go if you don't want to."

"I'll have to do it someday," she said. "I guess I'd better learn."

Briggs joined them a few seconds later and ushered them up the slope. He knew Chrisk as he knew everybody in Bristol Springs and trusted Travis's word that no pictures would be taken.

The deputies who were scurrying about the area with flashlights ignored them as Briggs led them through the trees. A yellow strip of police tape had already been stretched around the area. Briggs lifted it up, and they passed under it.

The body was not yet covered. Travis shook his head sadly when he saw it. The throat was ripped out. The abdomen was shredded, and one arm was almost torn from the socket.

Seeing it, Chrisk gasped and turned away, pressing her face against Travis's shoulder. He placed his arm around her shoulders to comfort her.

"It's bad," she said.

"You okay?"

"I'll make it."

86

Travis looked down at the ground around the body, then at the base of the tree which it rested against.

A frown furrowed his brow.

"What is it?" Chrisk asked.

For a moment Travis was silent. Then he spoke hesitantly. "There should be . . . more blood," he said.

"What?" Chrisk asked.

There were several patches of drying blood on the ground, in the dirt, and in the dried grass. Some of it was smeared where the girl had obviously dragged herself, and there was blood on the body itself. Yet there was far less than Travis had seen in police photos taken under similar circumstances.

"Chief?" he said.

"Yeah, son?"

"This is where the body was found?"

"Langdon and I came up here together."

"There's not much blood."

"Not gory enough for you, Dixon? A girl's been ripped apart here." He sounded angry.

"No. It just doesn't seem right. I've been in apartments where people were murdered where whole walls were covered with blood."

"Dead is dead. I guess you can say what you want to in the paper about it. All I can tell you is I don't know. The coroner will check it out."

Taking Chrisk by the arm, Trav led her away from the scene.

"What do you think?" she asked.

Travis shrugged. "I don't know. It could be nothing. Or maybe she was killed somewhere else, and the body was dumped here to make it look like an animal attack."

"You mean a person could have done this?"

"People do bad things," Travis said. "The mutilation could have been done to cover it up. They should find that if they do an autopsy. We'll have to be careful how we write it up."

Estelle knew by the look on Langdon's face when he walked through the front door of the diner that something was wrong. She ran around the counter to meet him.

"What is it?" she demanded.

He touched her shoulders, attempting to offer support. "You'd better sit down, Estelle."

Her voice rose. "What is it, damn you? Is she hurt?"

He swallowed and tried to let his words come softly. "It was . . . it was some kind of an animal. It musta happened because there's no water."

"What animal? What do you mean?"

He swallowed again. "She was killed, Estelle. She was out at the Springs with the boy, and some kind of animal got to her. It must have come along out of the bottoms looking for a drink."

"Are you sure it wasn't that boy that did it?"

"We're going to check that out. It don't look like he did it. I don't think he coulda done it."

"He's to blame. She wouldn't have been out there otherwise." She burst into tears now, sobbing uncontrollably. "No, please God in heaven no, not my little girl."

The other waitress came over and they helped her to a table. She sipped some water that was brought to her, and she used a napkin to dab her eyes.

"Where is the body?" she asked.

"It's probably going to have to be sent to Bossier City for an autopsy," Langdon said softly.

"I want her buried next to her father. They'll give her body back, won't they? For the funeral."

"Yes, ma'am," Langdon said. "They'll do that. We just have to figure out what did it. We're going to have to get it so it can't hurt anybody else."

"I know." She got to her feet slowly. She almost looked as if she was not going to be able to continue standing. "I need to go to the rest room," she said.

She walked over to the door and pushed it open.

Inside she moved to the sink and splashed water on her face. Already her eyes were ringed in red.

She put her face in her hands as the pain burned in her stomach. It hurt as if someone had struck her with a fist. She drew breaths in quickly, moaning as the feelings cut through her soul.

Tears filled her eyes, and she felt a darkness settle over her. Her world was shattered. The emptiness she had felt since her husband's death was multiplied tenfold.

The last vestige of her reason for being had been taken away. She only sweated in this job to support Lou Ellen. There was nothing else. There was no meaning to anything.

She remembered holding her child as a baby, and all of the things she had hoped for her flooded her mind.

How often had she thought about the girl's future, college possibly, something bright. How many times had she dreamed of helping her plan her wedding, picking out the gown and the arrangement of the flowers.

Lou Ellen could not be dead. She wasn't finished with high school. She hadn't learned to drive yet. She hadn't taken typing or finished home economics. She hadn't even been to a prom.

Estelle had a Polaroid camera in a drawer at home she had planned to use when Lou Ellen got her first formal.

That would not happen now. There would be no silk dresses, no corsages pressed flat in the backs of old books.

The spirit ribbons from high school football games pasted to her mirror had no meaning any longer.

Estelle was bombarded by images.

Her daughter wouldn't be around for arguments anymore. She wouldn't refuse her vegetables, and she wouldn't be waiting at home after work for their casual conversations.

Estelle's stomach tightened, and she moved into the toilet stall to throw up. Her world was ruined. In a matter of seconds it had been destroyed.

She sank down to her knees, her back against the wall of the stall as she wept uncontrollably, a numbness settling over her.

Dr. Phillip Warren, the parish coroner, showed up in a pickup truck with a camper covering the bed. It was the vehicle always used to collect bodies. It was driven now by one of his assistants.

Travis watched them climb from the vehicle and walk toward the area the deputies had cordoned off with yellow tape—the assistant a young man in faded jeans and a work shirt, the coroner a tall, thin man, his head bald on top, his chin covered with gray whiskers. He carried a black bag. It made him look like a country doctor on a house call.

"Here they are to determine she's dead," Travis said.

Chrisk snapped some pictures as the men followed Chief Briggs, stepping across the tape.

"Will he be able to tell anything here?" Chrisk asked.

Trav shook his head. "Not much. I've never dealt with animal deaths. If he can recognize the type of bite, he might make a determination. He might measure them. Otherwise, it's going to be a couple of days."

"What about the blood loss?"

"Or lack of it? Anybody's guess."

They waited. Minutes ticked by before Warren climbed back over the tape with the sheriff not far behind him. The assistant had been left to do the basic prep of the body before moving it.

Travis watched them walk together toward the sheriff's car, talking as they moved.

He couldn't hear what they were saying. He let them stand together beside the car for several seconds before he began an approach.

As the chief slipped into the front seat to pick up the radio, Travis moved in on Warren.

"Any comment?" Travis asked. "I'm with the *Gazette*."

Warren was used to dealing with the press. He gave a friendly smile and touched Travis on the shoulder.

"It's going to take us some time."

"You can't tell what kind of animal it was?"

Warren hesitated. "Not at this point. It may have been several animals. It's not clear until we check it out."

"Any evidence that the body was moved?"

"Not that we can tell. It's being investigated."

"Do you have an opinion on the lack of blood present?"

A frown crossed the coroner's features, and he wet his lips with his tongue. "I can't say. The body is badly mauled. Off the record, there isn't a lot of blood, considering the condition of the body. I can't explain that. I've never seen anything quite like it. How did you spot that?"

"I was a crime reporter in a city where people got hurt a lot," Travis said.

"They get hurt in the country too," Warren said. "You never know what kind of animal you're dealing with."

He turned back to the chief. Travis caught just a portion of the chief's words into the microphone.

He was trying to reach Langdon to step up the search for a kid called Blade.

"Anything?" Chrisk asked when he returned to her.

"There's more here than we're hearing," he said. "They're looking for her boyfriend. Maybe as a suspect."

"Weird."

"Weird it is."

91

He turned back to find the chief approaching him.

"I want you to be careful what you print in that paper of yours," Briggs said. "It better not cause a panic."

"I'm not the one you have to worry about," Travis said. "You've got a big paper and a couple of television stations to worry about."

"Don't remind me," Briggs said.

"Can you confirm the name?"

"Yeah, they got her mother notified. It is Lou Ellen Johnson. She was just sixteen." He rubbed his eyes. "She was my daughter's friend."

Anticipating a search by the police, Blade had pulled his motorcycle into a rest area on the highway about two miles from the Springs.

Parking his bike out of sight beside the small restroom unit, he walked into the narrow men's room. It stank of stale urine and had no ceiling. The tile floor was tracked with mud, and cigarette butts littered the drains of the urinals.

He relieved himself of what he hadn't lost into his shorts at the moment of the death, when fear had struck him.

Reaching into his jacket, he took out a Marlboro, lighting it as he planted himself on the dry lavatory. It was the only place to sit in the room, except for the stained commodes concealed in stalls covered with peeling green paint. He tried to ignore the smell.

He was going to have to get to a phone somewhere and call his father, probably his uncle too. He wanted them to know where to find him before he got picked up. He frequently went for long stretches without talking to them, so if he dropped out of sight they might not find it unusual.

He didn't want the bastard police chief exacting justice on him for the accident. He had visions of winding up in some shallow grave somewhere, joined by the ghosts of other unfortunates deemed undesirable by small-town cops.

His father was going to love hearing he was in trouble twice in the same town in less than twenty-four hours. He had not been terribly popular with his father since his decision to drop out of LSU, where he'd been taking pre-law courses.

The thought of being a lawyer had held no great thrill for him. He had entered the program because it seemed a good way to keep his parents off his back. Law in their eyes was an acceptable pursuit for their son. For him it just meant that he didn't have to bother with the messy specimens in biology classes required for pre-med.

Putting up with college after surviving high school had been more than he could handle, however. The parties were okay, the girls available, and with his family's reputation, good fraternities wanted him, but the tedium of lectures and the demands of tests and term papers had been too much.

He didn't know what he wanted out of life, but he knew the life-style his family had mastered did not appeal to him. He didn't want to devote endless hours to some job that would strangle him with stress only to have the rest of his time dominated by obligatory social engagements and community causes.

Since leaving school, he'd tried a couple of jobs, devoting more of his time to biking around the state, looking for adventure he was fond of saying, humming the tune of *Born To Be Wild*.

He wanted excitement.

He let his hair grow long and began wearing black, fancying himself some kind of rebel, although he stopped short of James Dean impressions.

Bumming around, he ran across people who tried to push him. Years under his father's thumb had worn down

93

his tolerance of that sort of thing, prompting more than a few fights.

He had been bailed out of his various altercations in recent months because his uncle could not afford the adverse publicity. Politics were unstable in Louisiana because there were a lot of dissatisfied people, and anything stood a chance of sounding a death knell for incumbents.

And here he was. Another misunderstood rich kid for whom no one would have any sympathy.

He spat out smoke and stared into the darkness. He was involved in a death now. It wasn't his fault, but it might be more than his uncle wanted to touch. Disowning him might be easier than trying to cover this one up.

He churned his tongue to generate saliva because his mouth was growing dry. He might as well get used to the smell of the room, he decided. He was in deep.

Thumping his cigarette away, he slid off the sink and paced the room, kicking the door on the toilet stall and then slamming his fist against the wall. He cracked a piece of tile and managed to bruise his hand at the same time.

"You seem upset, David Pearson."

He twisted around with a start. His heart rattled into his throat as he gasped and let out a slight cry.

The woman laughed at him. He clenched his teeth, about to hurl an insult when his eyes focused on her.

She stood near the doorway, the bare light of the lamp which jutted from the wall washing down over her.

Her beauty was incredible. The dark auburn hair which fell to her shoulders was glossy and full. Her face was formed like the perfect art of a sculpture, the bones giving fine structure to her rounded face, and her gray-green eyes seemed to glow with golden flecks.

Her flesh was as pale as ivory, flawless and sleek. He recognized the jacket she wore as Lou Ellen's, but his eyes were drawn to survey the slender legs and the curves of her body, hinted at beneath the jacket.

Barefoot she stood with one leg bent slightly, her delicate hands holding the jacket closed with a plunging V that accented her breasts.

She looked at once soft and elegant, yet wild and uninhibited.

Her tongue moved across her lips slowly, and she tilted her head slighty as he studied her.

"I need your help, David," she said.

He took a step backward. "What do you mean? I'm in trouble too."

She raised her eyebrows. "Then we stand to benefit one another." Her words were crisp with some undefinable accent. He was stunned by every aspect of her.

Yet a cold knot of terror entwined itself around his intestines and slowly tightened.

"I saw you," he said. "Out there. I must be crazy. You killed the girl."

She pushed a lock of hair from her face and continued to gaze across the room at him, her eyes making him uncomfortable.

"I have to survive," she said. "If I do not kill, I do not live."

He pressed his back against the cool tile. He had no escape. She was between him and the doorway. His mind was racing. This seemed unreal. What was she? Some wild creature of the forest?

She laughed again. "No, David. I did not turn into a panther," she said. "I only called on a brother of the night to help me." He could not make out the accent. It was deep and rich, exotic.

He heard the flutter of wings in the open air above the room, and suddenly a large brown owl swept down into the chamber. It sailed past him and settled on her shoulder with its huge eyes locked on him.

"I have many that I could call on," she said. "They can

95

do much for me, be my eyes, my hands. There are things that they cannot provide, however. Things only a human can offer."

"What?"

"Protection. Assistance . . . warmth."

"What are you? What's going on here? You train animals? To kill people?"

Without warning, the owl flew from her shoulder and landed on his own. He jerked to one side as it settled.

"Do not harm it."

The owl perched gently, curling its claws into the leather of his jacket.

Blade felt dazed. His head was spinning.

"I got some bad shit," he said, half laughing. No pot had ever produced anything like this before. "I'm hallucinating."

"It is not that."

"What, then? What the hell are you?"

"That does not matter."

"What good can I be to you? They're going to throw my ass in jail when they catch up with me."

She took a step toward him, then another, reaching out with one hand to touch his face.

"You have done no wrong."

"That doesn't matter. I still don't see what I can do to help you."

"I need your knowledge. I have been gone for many years. Much has changed. I am lost, confused, and without friends. If I am to survive, I must have your assistance."

Her eyes locked on his now. He stared into their glowing fire. The heat enveloped him. He should be running, but he felt drawn to her. He could not flee.

There was a promise of something in her, a promise of purpose and thrill. She was a different world, a far cry from the drudgery he wanted to escape.

With her there was a chance for something totally

different and new.

"You will help me?" she asked.

He nodded.

She kissed him softly on the lips. "I will see you soon," she said. "Soon." She disappeared through the doorway, and a moment later the owl took wing, rising silently into the night.

Part 2

The Blood

"But flesh with the life thereof, which is the blood thereof, shall ye not eat."

—*Genesis 9:4*

Chapter 8

When sunlight became visible through the crack in the curtains over Chrisk's bed, she rolled over and looked at the narrow sliver of sky.

She'd made it home at 3:30 A.M., only dozing in the interim. The sight of the body and the blood had produced a more traumatic effect than she'd expected. She was thankful the scene had not been as bloody as Travis seemed to think it should be. If it had been any worse, she wouldn't have been able to stand it.

Slipping from bed, she adjusted the seams of the long black t-shirt she wore and walked into the kitchen to the refrigerator. There she pulled out a carton of milk and poured herself a glass.

She felt her weariness in her muscles, but her reeling thoughts prevented her from trying to sleep any more. When she put her head down, an instant replay of the death scene flashed across her mind.

She sat down at the table and drank, thinking back on the story she and Travis had composed back at the office. It had been quick and precise, with the facts up front.

Travis had worked at the computer first, to hammer out what he knew, turning it over to her to chronicle her description of the scene.

She had been pleased with the finished story, which Alison had gone over for errors, smoothing a few transitions without changing the story's essence.

By 3 A.M. the revised page one with the new photograph of cops clustered together near the forest had been completed.

Normally Wednesdays were a day of rest for her. Sometimes she worked at the Dairy Queen in the evenings, if they needed an extra hand, but most of the day she rested, taking the opportunity to do some reading or clean house.

Fortunately, since she'd been working, her mother had become lenient about household chores. She understood Chrisk needed time to herself.

Today would not be a time of relaxation, however. She had talked it over with Alison the night before. While the Dixons were in Aimsley getting the printing done, she would be pounding the streets of Bristol Springs.

Word of Lou Ellen's death would be spreading, and they had agreed a reaction story would be needed. She was going to talk to a few people on the street or in the shops to try and capture their feelings for a story for next week's *Gazette*.

Also she would drop by and talk with Chief Briggs and get an idea of what course of action would be taken about the animal. Travis suspected there would be precautions to make sure no one else was harmed.

Chrisk shared his concern about what might develop along those lines. Once the fear surrounding the matter had time to manifest itself, people were apt to do all sorts of things. There was a possibility they would start killing everything from house pets to neighborhood children if they moved at the wrong time in the dark.

If it was possible to lynch a bear, Travis suspected some of the locals would find a way.

She had to agree that there was potential for danger among those in the town whose collective IQ dipped precariously into the red zone.

Travis referred to them as the dangerously inbred.

Finishing her milk, she headed toward the bathroom. Her mother passed her in the hallway, already dressed in a simple print dress. She worked at the town hall as a custodian.

"You need some rest," she said.

"I'm all right, Momma," Chrisk said. "I've got work to do."

"At least let me fix you some breakfast."

"Don't worry. I'm fine. This is important news. It'll be good for my portfolio."

"You won't be doing yourself any good if you build up that thing and wear yourself out in the process. Besides, I don't like you talking that way. A girl is dead."

Chrisk walked back to where her mother ws standing. "It's not that I don't feel bad," she said. "I just have to go on with what I'm doing."

"I know, I know," her mother said. "I just wish you'd slow down a little bit. This is Bristol Springs. You ain't in the big city yet, child."

Chrisk hugged her mother's shoulders and kissed her forehead softly. "It's okay. I'll survive."

She turned and walked on into the bathroom, closing the door to end the discussion.

Chrisk knew her mother worried about the dangers involved in newspaper work. She had almost screamed when she'd learned Chrisk had been at a death scene. She'd lectured for ten minutes about the possibility of the animal still being around.

Chrisk also knew there were other things her mother worried about. From time to time Chrisk got warnings about being seen too frequently with Travis. No matter how many times she reminded her mother that they worked together, the warnings persisted, and sometimes when she visited her grandfather, he issued warnings as well.

He came from a different era and had a different sense of propriety.

"You know how people think in this town," he said. "Black and white. They look at you-all together and snicker behind your backs. That's not good for you, and on top of that he's a married man." Chrisk's insistence that Trav's wife frequently accompanied them didn't quell the concern.

There was racism in Bristol Springs, but there had not been real tension in years. It was more subtle than that.

From time to time someone would make a remark, but for the most part it was live-and-let-live. The town council had both blacks and whites serving on it, although it was at times an uneasy alliance.

Chrisk pulled her hair over her head and let it fall back to her shoulders. Some people she knew accused her of trying to look like a white girl. She resented that, but kept quiet. She was proud of her heritage, as proud as anyone, but she saw it as no indignity to her ancestors to try and make something of herself. She wanted more than a quiet little life in Bristol Springs, and she wanted more than just a degree that said she had completed coursework and written term papers. She wanted to do something important; she wanted to write stories about all the injustice in the world. She wanted to capture the frustrations of people and inspire change.

Trying to forget about her turmoil, she moved over to the shower stall.

The soothing water helped melt away some of the weariness. She lingered for a while under the spray, moving from beneath it only reluctantly.

After drying her hair, she dressed in jeans, a black pullover shirt, and turquoise high-top sneakers. She put her notebook and camera into a shoulder bag, downed another glass of milk, and then went out and climbed on her moped. It was early, but life started early in

Bristol Springs.

Briggs sat in his office eating a doughnut and reading a folded copy of the *Clarion* sports page.

He was wearing a neatly pressed blue uniform, his tie knotted tightly against his throat and his sleeves buttoned at the wrists in spite of the heat that was building outside. He'd had no sleep, but he was cleanshaven. He was expecting reporters today, the ones from Aimsley and possibly other towns, and he had to be ready to deal with them. PR on this was going to be almost as important as catching the animal if the media descended.

It was Briggs's hope that they tired of it quickly, and he was counting on Bristol Springs' home-court advantage—the town was isolated at its end of the parish. Traveling to it took awhile, and the trip wasn't on good roads.

Even with the advantage, things were going to be hectic over the next few days, until they could find whatever killed the Johnson girl or until the whole matter blew over. The third possibility was that it might rain and put an end to the drought and all of it.

He'd never dealt with an animal attack before, so he wasn't sure what the public response would be. He wasn't sure if people would be as quick to blame him as they would if they thought he had failed to prevent a murder on the city streets.

There was some information he didn't want to get to the public until Blade Pearson was found. He hoped to have the kid in custody before the autopsy report came back with a determination on the possibly human bites the coroner had spotted.

Briggs's own supposition was that they had occurred during a moment of passion while she was rolling around with the punk.

He'd found evidence of that in the dust by the springs,

105

along with an extra set of woman's footprints. They didn't match the shoes the girl had been wearing, but he dismissed that, figuring the girl might have had her shoes off at some point.

Before word of any of that got out, he wanted to question Blade about it. He also wanted to know if the kid had any ideas about the sticky gray substance they had found on the ground near the body. The coroner hadn't been able to make a guess about what it was. He hoped the doctors would come up with an explanation about that also. He was uneasy about all of this.

For the time being, he was taking other steps to deal with the situation.

In a cooperative effort, Langdon was out with Holyfield and law enforcement's stalwart supporter, Jasper, wandering around in the woods, looking for whatever animal was out there that looked dangerous. A few other volunteers were spread out in hunting parties as well. Though the majority of the region's residents had a propensity for hunting, only a few dogs had been available this morning. Everybody had given him excuses when he'd called. Many of the dogs were sick from the heat and the dry weather. The men had wound up using a couple of sickly bloodhounds.

At least that was something. It looked good to have people out beating the bushes.

He hoped they didn't shoot each other while they were out protecting Bristol Springs' widows and orphans.

As he checked over the baseball scores in an effort to keep his mind occupied, he rested one hand absently on the handle of the pistol at his side. Normally he would have taken the belt off when he'd come into the office, putting it on only to go out on patrol. He wanted to have it on today if any of the reporters wanted to take pictures.

*   *   *

Sweat poured down Langdon's forehead and dripped from his nose and chin. The curls of his black hair were plastered to his head beneath his hat, and his hands were slick on the stock of the .30.30 rifle he carried.

Beside him Holyfield was slogging along as well, his green and tan uniform soaked with sweat, just like Langdon's blue one was.

Stopping in the shade of an oak, they shared a drink from Holyfield's canteen, then leaned against the tree and wiped sweat from their brow as they listened to the voices of other hunters which carried through the woods.

A few yards away they could hear men moving through the brush, sweeping along in search of some sign of the animal.

"We're never going to get him," Langdon said. "Not in daylight." He hunted enough to know there was little hope of success in searching for a nocturnal animal while the sun was out. That was why you went out at night to hunt raccoon.

"What do you think it was?" Holyfield asked.

"Beats me. Not a wolf. They travel in packs."

"A bear."

"I figure a bear would have torn her up a lot more, left some tracks, too."

Holyfield rubbed sweat from his face. "I didn't think there were wild animals around here anymore. Leastwise, not dangerous ones."

Langdon pursed his lips. He knew better. His people had come from these woods, and he'd heard them talk about the things that were out there.

"These woods are thick," he said. "Lots of things run around out here that we just don't see. I'll tell you what, they're coming up out of the bottoms, looking for water in this drought. We may see more stuff before it's all over with."

"What all you think is out here?" Holyfield asked.

107

"Shoot, you name it. There's probably some panthers, bobcats. I wouldn't be surprised if we saw a bear." He spat a glob of saliva into the dirt. "Anything that ever was here has probably left some of its kind behind." He pointed to the right, out in the direction of the springs. "A lot of places have been bulldozed and everything, and you had some building back toward the old highway once." He pointed in the other direction. "Not these woods. They go way back and stretch behind where that old steambath place was. They're the same as they were when old Andrew Jackson sailed down the river to fight the British."

Jasper wrinkled his nose as the hot breeze rustled through the brush around him. It was an effort to pick up some unusual scent.

Jasper had no record of being able to track animals by scent. He wasn't that good a hunter, even when it came to squirrel, but he liked it when Chief Briggs called on him for help, so he was doing his part.

Jasper's father had been killed in the Korean conflict, and his brother had served in the U.S. Navy. Jasper hadn't been able to get in.

He didn't do too well at many things. He supported himself doing odd jobs around Bristol Springs. He helped out the soybean and cotton farmers, mostly, but lately there hadn't been much work on the farms because things were so dry. They kept saying if it didn't rain soon, there wasn't going to be any crop.

That worried Jasper, because he didn't have a great deal of money put away. His wife Sudie made a little money doing sewing for people, but that wasn't enough for them to pay all the bills. He had basics like utilities to take care of. He kept that down by not allowing Sudie to use the air-conditioner during the day. Sometimes he shaved the food bill down by fishing, which he was fairly good at.

108

Right now there wasn't much fishing around, however. The area lakes were getting low.

The satellite-dish payment came in every month like clockwork, too, and that was on Jasper's mind. He had to keep that up because he didn't want them coming out and repossessing the dish. He needed it for football season so he could watch the sports channel and the games on the superstations that hadn't been scrambled yet.

He hoped if he came through on this hunt, the chief would slip him a couple of extra dollars that would help him get by. The chief knew times were hard, and he'd always been pretty good about paying Jasper something when he helped out.

Jasper tilted his red baseball cap back over his stringy blond hair, which fell almost to his shoulders. His mouth opened while he scanned the area around him. He didn't see any animals at the moment. There were plenty of trees, but just as when he'd tried squirrel hunting, he had a feeling that he wasn't going to be terribly successful.

That made him feel discontent. Things just didn't work out for Jasper. He hadn't been much good in school, which was why the Navy and the Army had turned him down. He'd only finished eighth grade. He couldn't read very well.

With his hands clasped tightly around his rifle, he moved on through the brush, his shoulders slightly stooped as he peered at the ground.

Even with the leaves above him breaking some of the sunlight, he still felt like he was going to melt in the humidity, but he forced himself to devote his attention to the hunt. He could hear the others talking, which meant they had stopped to rest.

If he didn't stop, that might give him an advantage, and he might collect money on it. It also occurred to him the town might look to him as a hero, not just that old dumb Jasper who was good for odd carpentry work.

They all had a tendency to look down on him, but if he got the animal that killed the little Johnson girl, then people might give him a little more respect.

He curled his finger around the trigger and envisioned aiming it at some charging bear. Although it would be a frightening situation, he was confident of the weapon's power. He'd never killed anything with it, but it kicked hard when he fired it at targets in his backyard.

He spotted the track almost by accident. His thoughts were drawn back to reality as he moved over to study it. It was in a patch of loose, powdery dust near a myrtle bush that had shielded it from the wind.

He squatted beside it, tracing its form gently with his fingertips. It was large and deep, almost a perfect cast of the paw that had made it.

So it wasn't a bear, he thought. He'd never seen panthers. Everybody had heard of them being in these woods, some even claimed to have heard them scream—the scream was supposedly like a woman's—but nobody Jasper knew of had ever seen one.

He rubbed his face with his fingers and bit his lower lip. The track was headed deeper into the woods. Apparently, after the kill it had moved back toward its lair. He wasn't such a bad hunter after all. He could figure this out.

Cautiously he looked back over his shoulder. There was no sign of Holyfield or Langdon or the others.

He turned back to the track. If he took the men with him, one of them might make the kill, or one of the fellows with dogs might lead them to it, and that would mean he wouldn't get the money.

He hesitated a moment. The cat was probably back in its hiding place now, concealed as it had been before.

It would not come back out until darkness, he suspected.

He could come back then and hunt alone. That would give him an advantage. He'd be able to get all the credit for sure.

"Jasper," he heard Langdon call, the sound almost causing him to lose balance.

"Yeah," he shouted back through the trees.

"You finding anything?"

"Naw."

He reached down and wiped the track away. He wouldn't be finding anything until tonight.

By noon Chrisk had talked to a handful of people. Most of them had heard of the death and were troubled by it.

She talked to older people and younger ones. She came to realize it was all unreal to them, something they did not quite believe. They hadn't actually seen the body, and word of the death left many people numb.

But not all. One of the teenagers wept in speaking about Lou Ellen, who everyone remembered as a sweet girl. Someone said they had talked to Julie Briggs, who was really upset.

Chrisk took it all down in her notebook, the words making her feel more and more somber. She kept remembering seeing Lou Ellen in the Dairy Queen with her friends, laughing and playing the jukebox.

Even though she had seen the body, she decided it did not seem real to her either.

On the moped she rode through the streets looking for people who might have comment.

She was headed toward the police station when she spotted the television van from Aimsley. Another car parked beside it was unfamiliar. She decided to go inside.

She found Briggs preparing for a press conference. A black guy was setting up a television camera on a tripod at the corner of the room while the chief talked with a woman in her twenties dressed immaculately in a skirt and white blouse.

Beside her a reporter from the *Clarion* was making notes

in a narrow reporter's notebook.

She walked over to join them. "Hello, Chrisk," the chief said brightly.

She nodded a greeting, remaining silent as the other reporters glanced at her. She could tell they didn't think she was important.

She ignored the scrutiny of their gazes, not worried whether they approved of her or not. The *Gazette* was a newspaper just as real as their organizations, and she was a real reporter.

She started formulating questions in her mind, readying herself to compete with the others. Travis had warned her that in press conferences it was often important to hit quick if you wanted your questions answered.

Once the cameraman had completed setting up the camera, he held a sheet of paper in front of the lens to balance the color reading. Then he gave a nod to the girl.

She raised her microphone, and Briggs gave a brief statement about what had occurred, providing Lou Ellen's name and age.

"Did anyone witness the event?"

"That's a possibility," Briggs said. "We're looking for her boyfriend to check. He was frightened away."

Chrisk tried to ask a question, but before she could speak, the *Clarion* reporter had raised his pen toward the sheriff.

"Any ideas about the type of animal?" he asked.

"Not at this point," the chief said, half smiling. Chrisk could tell he was enjoying the limelight in spite of the severity of the situation. He was at the same time trying to downplay the trouble.

Chrisk spoke up. "What steps are being taken to find the animal?" she asked.

"We've got men out in the woods hunting it right now."

"Have you thought about calling in any experts on

112

this?" she followed up.

His mouth dropped a little bit on that question. It was clear by the look in his eyes that the thought had not occurred to him.

"At this point we're confident we can handle the situation ourselves with the assistance of the sheriff's office," he said. "If it gets complicated, we'll get someone from Wildlife and Fisheries."

"Is anyone else in danger?" Chrisk asked. She was shooting her questions out quickly to keep a footing with the city reporters. She was determined that they not be able to dismiss her.

"We're going to make every effort to protect the citizens," Briggs said.

"Is there some suspicion that this is more than an animal attack?" Chrisk asked. "Could there be foul play?"

Briggs glared at her.

"We don't have indications of that at this point," he said.

"So there's no evidence the body was moved?"

The other reporters were shooting glances toward her now. She seemed to have thrown Briggs a little off balance.

She was acting on the remarks Travis had made. It seemed to be chiseling away at something.

"We are not sure if it was moved or not at this point. We're awaiting autopsy results from Bossier City."

"What about this boyfriend you aren't naming?" the *Clarion* man asked, picking up on the questioning. "Is he a suspect?"

Briggs cleared his throat, glancing toward the white lights from the television camera. When the still photographer's flash unit went off, the chief's eyes darted toward that.

"We're only trying to clear up a few things," he said. "We have a few questions for the boy. We want to learn what type of animal he saw. That's to help us track it better."

113

Chrisk could see his enjoyment of the conference had faded. He was rebounding, but there wouldn't be as much pleasure in watching the six o'clock news as he had anticipated.

A few more questions were asked, and things calmed down. Finally they shut down the cameras, and after a few more casual comments, they began to pack things up. The city reporters didn't seem to be too excited about the incident, even though their material had a chance of being picked up by the networks and the wires. It was just another death in a small town to them, a little unusual, but the kind of thing in which interest would quickly die.

Briggs followed the crews to the door, trying to keep a polite smile on his face. As they disappeared, he tapped Chrisk on the shoulder, indicating that he wanted her to stay.

As the others got into their cars and pulled away, she followed him back into his office.

"What the hell were you trying to do out there?" he demanded before she could sit down.

"My job."

"What is your job? To stir up trouble? Do you want to start a panic?"

"I'm just trying to get information."

"You came close to getting those other reporters stirred up too. This is a nice quiet town. We've had a tragedy, and we're dealing with it. That's all there is to it. I'm not going to let you mess this town up. It's my job to keep things quiet around here. You tell your bosses to look out."

Navarra slept in a shadowy spot amid a cluster of trees deep in the forest. There was a small indentation in the ground blanketed with leaves and pine needles. It did not provide the total darkness she would have liked, nor was it

114

comfortable. She nestled under the jacket and coaxed her mind into relaxation in spite of the circumstances.

It was nothing like the pillows she had known in the Roman halls, and it did not rival the bedrooms of the French palaces she had occupied, but it was far better than the nonexistence she had suffered in the watery tomb.

There she had had no feeling, no discomfort, and no dreams. It had been a terrible nothingness. It had been worse than the pains and tortures her sisters had described.

This was bettter. When she spoke with David Pearson again, she would get him to provide her a better shelter.

She would need a fortress, and she would need to establish an oracle, for she did not intend to go back to what she had been, and she did not intend to die.

This time she would protect herself.

This time she would accomplish her goal.

Chapter 9

After killing some time shopping, Travis and Alison went back down to the *Clarion*'s printing shop, where huge machines whirred reels of newsprint along, spraying pages out in a rapid-fire staccato.

Sitting at a rugged worktable, they inhaled the dizzying smell of ink and newsprint until they were able to pick up a couple of test-run copies of the paper.

Travis thumbed through it slowly, studying it with intensity. He glanced over the front page story. He spotted a couple of misspellings, but those did not disturb him. Considering the rush with which it had been completed, it was in good order. It might even be able to garner some awards in competitions among papers of similar size.

After a few seconds, he turned inside to the less sensational matter. He looked at his school board story, then turned to the editorial page.

Alison had written a column this week discussing the dry weather. Wrapped around it were some lesser-known syndicated columns which their budget allowed, and a political cartoon was centered on the page. It had been provided by Harry Iberville, who was also the high school industrial arts teacher.

The religion page closed out the first twelve-page

section of the paper. It featured a smattering of briefs on gospel sings and revivals, some press releases from some religious institutions, and a column by the Reverend Lory Burns of the Episcopal church.

This week Burns speculated over controversy regarding the upcoming film based on *The Last Temptation of Christ*.

"It looks good," Alison said, peering over his shoulder.

She had been looking over the second section with its wedding announcements, assorted public notices, classified ads, and their two-page spread for the Handy Dandy Supermarket, which offered low prices on bleach, canned corn, shortening, produce, and beef.

"Makes me hungry," Alison said, standing behind him and rubbing the tired muscles of his neck. They had both slept about three hours before getting up to drive in for the printing.

"Let's get lunch. It'll be another couple of hours before everything is ready."

They walked out of the printing building and wandered through the downtown streets.

"Let's have lunch at the Clairmont."

"Agreeable."

They walked on down the street to the hotel, which was relatively new but built as a replica of a grand hotel which had been a focal point of the downtown area in the twenties. A renewal had led to the destruction of the original, but nostalgia and the hope of revitalized tourism had led to its regeneration.

In the dining room they ordered, their eyes meeting once the waitress had disappeared.

For a moment they were like schoolchildren experiencing a crush, staring at each other. Finally Alison broke into a smile.

"You're no tough guy," she concluded.

"I don't really pretend to be," Travis said. "I don't want

117

to be anymore. My tough reporter days are over."

"You jumped on that story last night."

"Not the same. In the city I was a tough guy. I thought I was missing that until last night. I was just going through the motions out there. I knew the animal would be gone by the time we arrived. Wild animals don't scare me as much as people used to."

"Do you think they'll find whatever it was?"

"Eventually. The girl probably stumbled over it. Does that sort of thing happen much?"

"You're a Louisiana native."

"It never happened in Alexandria," he said. "There's more forest in Bristol Springs."

"It's never happened that I can remember," Alison said.

"I've read of attacks in other places," Travis said. "They're fairly rare. A lot of the time there's no real explanation for them. Except predatory instinct reacting to a person who's in the wrong place at the wrong time."

"Maybe we could go through the old issues of the *Gazette* and find out when the last animal attack on a human did occur in this area," Alison suggested.

"It'll take forever to do that."

"We could take turns." She reached over and touched his hand gently. "There's time enough between now and next week. We'll dig it out if it's there."

"Fine. It'll give you a chance to do some more of your family research in the process."

"That's the only way I'll get it done, by incorporating it into the work for the paper. There are all kinds of trunks in my cousin's attic that I haven't even had time to look at."

"Your cousin is strange."

"She's just a little slow. I need to go by and have a look around her place if I'm ever going to get anywhere with tracing my heritage here. I found a little information when I went out to the graveyard with Chrisk, but not enough. It seems family names wander in and out of my

118

amily. I may be dangerously inbred myself, Trav.

"We need to know about that before we reproduce, don't we? You wouldn't want some arbitrary recessive trait making a surprise appearance in our offspring."

"That's why your cousin worries me a little bit."

She hit him with the cloth napkin from beside her plate.

"I guess I do need to help you with that. I'd probably like finding out about what Bristol Springs was like back in the old days."

"I suppose it was fairly traditional small-town America. In the fifties we had freshly cut lawns on summer afternoons, football games that the whole town turned out for on autumn evenings, long walks to school on cold winter mornings."

"Regular Norman Rockwell stuff. One of these days we will pay a visit to your old home place," Travis agreed. "No two old-style white frame houses are alike. I promise I'll take a look at your family tree soon, really." He'd been playfully teasing her about things ever since they had moved into town. The house belonged to her cousin now, who lived on her father's insurance money and watched soap operas all day long.

It was nestled back in Bristol Springs' residential section, far enough out of the way to make it inconvenient to drop by, considering the newspaper schedule. Also, hanging around the cousin made Travis nervous.

"Maybe tonight after we get back," Alison suggested. "Terri would be glad to see us."

"I was hoping we might just spend a quiet evening at home," Travis suggested. He let his voice become deep and soft. "Candlelight and wine. Soft music."

"We never seem to get the candles lit or the wine poured," she said, smiling.

"Maybe one candle."

*   *   *

119

Estelle Johnson lay in bed watching a soap opera on the small black and white set she had wheeled into her bedroom. She could not follow the plot because she could not stop weeping.

She sipped the bourbon she had been nursing all morning. Again the liquid traced a path through her abdomen that burned like a streak of fire. It seemed to sizzle in her stomach. It wasn't serving its purpose. It did nothing to ease the pain.

She had developed a taste for it slowly, but it had intensified. She'd struggled with her craving, usually coming out successful because of Lou Ellen. Being responsible for her daughter had been an anchor.

Now Lou Ellen was gone, so there was no responsibility. She mourned the loss and clung to what she saw as her only source of stability.

Yesterday she'd been hoping for a date with the chief of police. Today all she wanted was relief from the agony. She didn't know what she was going to do.

There was no point in staying at the diner. That had been for Lou Ellen too, so she had no reason to continue the work.

Lou Ellen wouldn't be needing new school clothes this year, and there was no need to save for her college any longer.

Estelle sank deeper into the bed, her head dipping back into the pillow, her eyes aimed toward the ceiling.

She'd struggled to keep the roof up there for Lou Ellen as well. Now she felt indifferent to everything.

Some women from the church had come earlier, bringing food. It was on the kitchen table now. She'd seen no need to refrigerate it. She didn't expect to eat the noodle casseroles or the rice dishes which had been prepared. She wasn't hungry.

Not hungry at all, she thought. Just thirsty. She tilted her head up just enough to keep from strangling as she sipped again.

It burned, causing her to cough. She had not had a drink in more than a year. The bottle had been pushed back in the pantry behind the canned pork-and-beans and cream-of-mushroom soup.

It was a forgotten old friend, just waiting to be there when she needed it.

Blade was dragged into the police station around 2:45 P.M. by a state trooper. He didn't struggle as he was guided into Briggs's office.

The kid looked more rugged than he had the day before, with a day's growth of beard on his face. The dark circles under his eyes indicated he had not slept well.

There seemed to be a nervousness in his eyes as well. They darted from side to side, yet his face remained arrogant when he looked at Briggs.

"Welcome back," the chief said while the trooper poured himself some coffee.

His name was Dugan, and he was a tall guy with sandy hair that he wore in a flattop cut. His complexion was ruddy, although he had not been burned by the sun. The look in his dark eyes conveyed little compassion as he looked at Blade over the paper cup he lifted to his lips.

"Found him hanging out around the old resort," Dugan said. "Musta been there most of the night."

"He give you any trouble?"

"Not a bit."

Blade's expression was sullen. He sank deep into his chair and folded his arms across his chest.

Briggs walked around his desk and stared at the boy. "You didn't do what I told you, did you?"

"I guess I forgot."

"You got a girl killed. That's a hell of an attitude to take."

121

"It was an accident."

"She's dead," Briggs said. "You caused it. How does that make you feel?"

"Bad, but I couldn't help it."

"You could have helped it if you'd left her alone and kept your hot little hands off her."

"Come on, man. How was I supposed to know you had wild fucking animals out there?"

"It wouldn't have mattered if you had left her alone."

"Yeah, well it happened. I liked her and she liked me, so we went out together. People do that. It's a free country. You trying to charge me for what some mountain lion did?"

Briggs opened his eyes a little wider. "Is that what it was? Did you see it?"

"It was dark, but it looked like a big cat."

"Did you try to help her?"

"Yes. There wasn't anything I could do, so I ran before it turned on me."

"Why didn't you come to us?"

"I saw your car coming. I was scared. I've heard stories about small-town cops."

Briggs leaned back on his desk. "You've got Trooper Dugan here to keep an eye on you. Make sure I don't rubberhose you or anything."

Dugan raised his coffee cup in a mock salute.

"Now tell me," Briggs said. "What were you doing out there?"

"Fooling around. Kissing. Stuff like that."

"Smoking a little weed?"

Blade looked over at the trooper then back at Briggs. "Fuck it. I'm not answering that."

"How rough did you get with the girl?"

"I didn't even try to feel her up. I figured she was a country girl and she'd get bent outa shape by that. All I did was, you know, make out with her a little."

"You bite her?"

"What do you mean?"

"Did you bite her? While you were slobbering down her dress, did you bite her shoulders or anything?"

"No." Blade said emphatically, his brow now furrowed.

"Did you see any bite marks on her while you were fooling around?"

"No. I don't know what you're talking about. She was attacked by a damned mountain lion. What do you expect to find but bite marks?"

"We also found some gray stuff under a tree. Some kind of pulpy stuff. Any idea what that was?"

"I didn't see anything. I wasn't around the trees. Look, are you going to charge me or what?"

Briggs raised his hand and patted the air. "Calm down. I need your help. How big was the cat?"

"I don't know. Big. I've never seen one of those things before. I guess it weighed a couple hundred pounds."

Briggs thought a moment before posing his final question. "Did you see anyone else out there? Any other people?"

"No. Not a soul."

"Think the kid's lying?"

Dugan stuck out his lower lip. "Could be."

"Why would I lie?" Blade demanded.

"I don't know," Briggs said. "We don't have the reports back. Could have been human hands that tore that little girl up."

"Bullshit," Blade said.

"Cut the language," Briggs said. "As long as you're being questioned here, you can be civil."

Blade clamped his mouth shut once more.

"You pouting?" Briggs asked.

"If you're going to keep hassling me, I want a lawyer, and I want to call my uncle."

Briggs walked back behind his desk and propped his feet

up with a heavy sigh.

"I can't lock you up," he said slowly. "If I tried, your uncle would be in here in no time to pry you out. As far as I can tell, you're more guilty of negligent stupidity than anything else. I hope you realize what you've done, boy."

Blade remained silent.

"I hope you use better judgment from now on."

There was still no response.

"Get out of here."

Blade rose slowly and walked to the door, turning up the collar on his jacket as he moved.

He didn't bother to ask for help in getting back to his bike at the resort. It wasn't that far from town.

He wasn't in a hurry anyway. Although he wasn't showing it, he was disturbed. He knew it didn't matter where he went now. At nightfall, he could expect to be visited again.

"A cat," Briggs said once the kid was out of the office. "At least that lets me know what I'm up against."

"You got men out there?"

Briggs nodded. "No luck so far. It must have headed back into the deep woods once it killed."

"Probably scared. They don't like people."

"Normally they don't kill them," Briggs said.

"This one may not have ever seen people. I've lived in these parts all my life, hunted at night since I was kid. I never saw one."

"Any ideas about how to hunt one?"

Dugan shrugged. "Beats me. I'm a coon-and-squirrel man. Deer, in season . . . I don't know about anything like a panther."

Briggs poured himself some coffee. "I'm going to have to get some Wildlife and Fisheries people in here," he sighed. "I'm going to need some help to kill the bastard."

"You going out tonight?"

"While the thing's hunting? I don't think so. I don't have the men for it. I can't risk volunteers. If somebody got hurt, I'd be in deep. We'll try to go out tomorrow, with dogs and all. I wanted to do that today, but I couldn't get it organized in time. The drought's got everything screwed up around here. Everybody's involved in digging irrigation ditches."

"The sheriff's office didn't have anybody? It's their jurisdiction."

"The sheriff let me use his deputy. That's as far as he went. He's probably planning a marijuana raid to get himself on television."

"Well," Dugan said, "I'd better get back out and make the highways safe."

Briggs watched him go without getting out of his chair. Today was not a happy day. All his efforts to handle things quickly last night had failed.

He looked at the picture of his daughter which sat in a golden frame on the left side of his desk.

Her brown eyes peered back at him. That inspired his feeling of responsibility. He wanted nothing bad to happen to her. That was as much an inspiration to him as anything.

That and keeping the citizens and the town council away from the door.

He just hoped that Blade's necking with the girl was the source of the human teeth marks. He couldn't imagine how he would deal with it if some kind of mad cannibal was running around out in the woods.

125

Chapter 10

Night settled slowly, beginning with a slight fading to the sky from blue to a dull gray. The sun hung at the edge of the horizon, a huge orange ball. Finally the sky faded to black.

The air cooled slightly, and the crickets began to chirp. Moths darted into the air, making love to porch lights and street lamps.

Another sensation made the night different in the forest.

The animals felt the Calling almost immediately. It rang into their minds, superseding the instinct to nestle somewhere within the synapses which carried messages through their bodies.

There were no definite demands, just a compulsion to be ready if called upon for service. It was like a voice of darkness commanding obedience.

They continued to flutter about or wind in and out of the trees or slither along in their foraging for food, which occupied most of their time. Yet they responded, knowing they could not disobey.

If needed, they would respond—any of them, or all of them.

*   *   *

Blade sat in the center of the deserted bathing area of the old resort. It consisted of a maze of individual stalls surrounding a central tiled steamroom with numerous slabs designed for sitting or reclining.

It seemed cold and impersonal now, with everything shut down. Mildew had formed in some corners of what had once been a stark white room, and the floor was dry and dingy, covered with a layer of grime.

It was like a tomb except for the skylight above, which had several cracked panes. Through it starlight filtered, silver and soft.

He sat on one of the slabs, his cigarette smoldering in one hand. He waited for an hour after nightfall, until he heard the soft touch of her bare feet moving across the tile.

She had found him, even though he had given her no indication of where he would be.

She emerged slowly from the shadows near the massage tables, still clad only in the jacket. The zipper in front was tugged about halfway down, plunging between her breasts.

In the faint light her skin remained pale, reminding Blade of fine porcelain. As the muscles of her legs tensed and untensed with each step, he realized their sleek, smooth perfection.

He swallowed as she moved closer. He had heard of people feeling the hairs on the backs of their necks rise. This was the first time he'd ever experienced it.

He stared at her beauty, all the while trembling inside. He did not know why he had not fled to his home when the chief had released him. This was odd and unknown. He knew that by opening himself to her, he would be setting off on some bizarre journey.

He could not quite believe it, and throughout the previous night, he had been unable to think because of the anticipation that tingled through his body.

He was terrified by the possibilities, yet here was the

127

opportunity for something fresh, something so different from his life that it could never have been imagined before now.

He could tell that she was aware of his desires, and that she intended to fulfill them.

She walked toward him slowly, her movements sensual, as if she had absorbed some quality from the panther she controlled. Perhaps she had, and that had contributed to the legend.

When she reached him, she walked around him in a slow circle.

"You were not harmed, David?"

He stood straight, looking forward as she walked behind him.

"No," he said.

She walked in front of him once more, lifting one hand to her lips, kissing the tip of her index finger.

Her eyes were studying him—probing, in a way. He could feel something inside him quiver.

"You knew I would be here," he said.

"I sensed it. I am not omniscient." She looked around at the building. "What is this place, David?"

"It's a resort. This was like the steamroom."

"Oh?"

"Health and shit. They piped water up from the ground here. It's supposed to be like Lourdes, or something."

"The water has dried up."

"There's a drought. This place bought the farm way before that. That water's still down there, they just shut the pipes off. Nobody's ever bothered to reopen it."

"I have been gone a long time."

"How long?"

"The War between the States, you've heard of it?"

"The Civil War. Who hasn't?"

"Shortly after that."

"That's hard to believe."

128

Her eyes glowed. "Yet you know it is true."

"I can tell, somehow. I didn't believe things like you existed 24 hours ago. Now I know you're real. You killed a girl, had her killed. So here I am ready to help you. Weird."

"Weird."

She walked toward him now, lacing her hands behind his neck and kissing him on the lips.

Her warm touch stirred him. He felt his desire for her building. It was an unusual desire, stronger than any he had ever known.

She leaned against him, one of her bare thighs rising to rub the side of his leg.

"You will help me, David, won't you? There is much that I can do for you, much that you could never know from any other woman. The pleasure of your body can be enhanced by the pleasure of your mind, which I can touch."

He let his hands slide around her waist, resting them against the fullness of her hips. Her lips parted as he kissed her again, this time a lingering kiss that triggered new sensations throughout his body.

She took a step back from him, smiling. "In time we will explore those possibilities," she said.

He nodded, his control maintained precariously by a force of will.

"What do you want?" he asked. "You're not going to ask me to kill people."

She gave a coy smile. "Not for my feeding. Only if it is necessary to protect me. I need a protector. I have no strength in the daytime."

"That part is true too?"

"I can walk in daylight, but I have no power."

"Why? Where do you come from? What . . . makes you a vampire?"

"In time, we'll discuss that also. First I need to get some

129

help from you. I need some clothes. You'll get those for me. I'll trust your estimation of size. I would prefer something more traditional than the clothing your girlfriend wore. Is this place safe?"

"I don't think anybody comes here anymore . . . unless they just want to break windows."

"This will serve as a haven. I will need something to make a comfortable bed."

"You don't need a coffin?"

"More of the myth, the mortals' myth. Pillows, blankets will be fine. Just so I can sleep in comfort."

"Okay. There's a shower room in there we can convert. There are some rooms, but someone took the beds out of most of them. I think we'll be safer if we keep our quarters centralized."

"I agree. As for my clothes, you will get them tomorrow?"

"Yeah. I'll go over to Aimsley. It'll take longer, but I won't draw suspicion there."

She turned, pausing before moving away from him. She looked back over one shoulder.

"I will be back . . . later. You can wait for me."

Jasper wore a headlamp strapped around his baseball cap when he parked his truck at the edge of the creek bed.

Climbing from the cab of the battered red truck, he leaned over into the bed and picked up his rifle. He'd attached a strap so he was able to sling it over his shoulder, if need be. Then he fished out a vest with numerous pockets which he had filled with shells.

Shrugging on the vest, he gripped the rifle in his hands, stuffing a flashlight into his hip pocket.

He had a bone-handled hunting knife in a scabbard at his hip, and he'd stuffed a fish bellet into his boot. He didn't know what use he would have for it, but he'd never tracked a panther before, so he figured he might need it to finish the monster off once he'd shot it.

He wanted to take care with the hide, because he might be able to sell it and make a little money on top of what the chief would pay him.

He took a sip of water from the half-gallon jug he'd brought along, recapped the jug, and hung it over his shoulder by the string attached to its handle.

Then he headed into the forest, moving briskly but as cautiously as his heavy work boots would allow.

He didn't expect to run into the panther right away and wanted to get back to the point where he'd seen the track as soon as possible.

Moving from there back into the creature's lair, he expected to make the kill quickly. Then he would drive back into town and give the chief the good news.

Visions of becoming a hero ran through his mind like a newsreel. They'd interview him for the paper and for television shows, and they'd take pictures of him standing beside the big cat's carcass.

He knew that would make Sudie proud; that as much as the money he was going to get would make this extra effort worthwhile. He liked to do nice things for Sudie.

They had grown up together, had known each other all their lives. As little children they had played together in the junk-strewn yards that surrounded the homes of their parents.

Neither of them had gone very far in school. They had married in the old nondenominational church when he was seventeen and she was sixteen.

Their house had been one left vacant when Jasper's Aunt Madelyn had died. It was an old shack down the road from the homes where they had grown up. Madelyn's husband, Harvey, had built the place in the late forties.

He hadn't done it very well either. Electricity had been added haphazardly, and the indoor bathroom wasn't attached to the building very well. There were cracks along the seams where it was joined to the house.

By the time Jasper and Sudie had inherited it, the whole structure had begun to sag. It was a dry, gray building with a rusted tin roof. They had remained there, with Jasper constantly making repairs, for all the years of their marriage.

Jasper was forty now. In truth, he had never hoped for much more than having a wife and a roof over his head, but he was unhappy about the fact that they'd never had children. There was something wrong with Sudie that prevented her from having kids.

All the same, they got by fairly well. He had a garden in the back of the place that gave them tomatoes, and the fish he caught helped. He and Sudie froze those and shared them with other family members, who sometimes provided squirrel and deer meat in return.

Jasper wasn't sure why he'd never grown good at hunting. Just about every other male in the family, and most of the women, took it as second nature.

He'd been along on many a trip without killing anything.

As he slowly stalked back through the trees, he wondered if he should have taken along one of his cousins or nephews.

Then again, why should he share the limelight? Old Jasper had never done anything but exist. Now he had a chance to be something; for just a few minutes he would be worth something. He could do it alone.

He rubbed a hand across the stubby red beard on his face. The humidity in the air made him perspire while the weight of everything he was carrying made his muscles sag.

As he moved, the bobbing light of the headlamp richocheted off trees and branches in front of him.

When he reached the point where he'd seen the tracks,

he paused and looked around, his fingers tense on the rifle.

No monsters yet, but he was getting into the territory.

A step to the left would carry him back through the deep woods where nobody ever went.

To the right the forest extended back toward the network of back roads that led to people's houses and around to the old resort.

Jasper had worked there for a time when it had been open, doing minor repairs when they were needed. He'd liked that job. It had paid fairly well, up until the place closed.

The panther wouldn't be drawn that way, so he turned and headed deeper into the forest.

Chapter 11

Travis pulled the car into the old garage while Alison went to unlock the front door. He planned to leave the papers in the back until morning, when Dean Vickery came around to get them to distribute to the various paper boxes around town.

He would also throw them to the subscribers on his route, having most of them distributed by one P.M.

Their house was a white frame two-story with a broad porch and large windows. It had a quaintness they both liked. They regretted that they did not have more time to keep it properly.

Alison went inside and put the packages from their shopping trip on a table beside the door.

She'd bought a summer dress to wear while she was out covering stories in the heat, and Travis had picked up a couple of paperbacks which weren't in the budget. They would be added to the stacks of books in the back room which served as a second office for them. They had nicknamed it the hellhole because it was impossible to keep neat. Trav's paperbacks, old newspapers, bills, and other items cluttered it up.

Alison turned the lights on in the living room, pleased at least with the look of this room. Travis had helped straighten it, and for a change it looked neat.

People at the paper where she and Travis had worked before had warned her about marrying someone in journalism, citing the fact that it was difficult to spend a workday with a person and then go home for even more hours together.

She'd also been warned about the difficulty of marriage, the commitment it required and the things one had to give up, like partying with friends.

She'd been ready to put some things behind her, however. In spite of seeing many marriages among friends and acquaintances get flushed, she'd decided to take the risk.

Many had taken bets on how long she and Travis would last, since he was regarded among people who knew him as irresponsible in everything but his work.

In spite of that, they'd come to terms with each other quickly, developing a relationship that allowed them to deal with their respective idiosyncrasies and differences of opinion.

The bottom line was that at this point she did not want out. She wasn't restless or disgruntled. The day-to-day bothers didn't override the pleasures and the comfort of having someone to turn to. She'd seen people leave marriages because their partners were no more than roommates. That hadn't happened with Travis.

She got some wineglasses from the kitchen and poured from a bottle of Blue Nun, returning to the living room just as Travis entered.

She put the glasses down on the mantel over the mock fireplace, and he moved to her, taking her in his arms.

Their lips met, mouths moving together with a hunger. Their tongues dueled for a moment before he brushed his lips across her cheek and then to her neck.

She tilted her head back, eyes closed, sighing softly as his mouth moved across her skin.

Her arms were folded around his neck. His hands crept slowly down her sides, tracing the outline of her hips, then curving backward to cup her buttocks.

She felt her breaths quickening, and she began to steer him toward the couch.

They tumbled onto the couch together, tugging at each other's clothes. She unbuttoned his shirt, pushing him back on the cushions as she kissed his chest.

He reached up and pulled the tail of her t-shirt from her jeans.

Sitting astride him, she lifted her arms to let him pull her shirt over her head. Then she unhooked the clasp of her bra between her breasts, letting it slide off as she bent down, letting her breasts rub against his chest as their mouths met again.

His hands were sliding beneath her jeans when a knock sounded at the front door.

"*Shit*," Travis muttered. They disentangled as quickly as possible, and she scrambled for her shirt while he moved for the door.

A moment later he entered the room with Chrisk at his side.

She saw Alison and smiled. "I guess this was one of those moments."

Alison smiled back. "Briefly."

"I'm sorry."

"From you we'll tolerate it," said Travis, dropping into an armchair.

"I just wanted to go over what I've got," Chrisk said. "I talked to several people today. Some are pretty upset."

Alison got up. "You want a glass of wine?"

"That'd be fine," Chrisk said. Alison went out.

"We'll have to try to get a picture of her," Travis said.

"We could probably lift one from her school yearbook," Chrisk suggested. "Then we wouldn't have to bother her mother. I talked to some women who went by there to take some food. She's going to pieces."

Travis shook his head. "That's too bad." He got up and got his wineglass, passing the other to Chrisk.

"That's not really why I dropped by," Chrisk said.

Alison returned with a third glass and settled onto the couch beside Chrisk.

"What is going on then?" Travis asked.

"Chief Briggs chewed me out for asking questions in front of the television people. It was strange. He wanted everybody there so he could bask in the attention, but he blew up when I pressed him on the killing."

"Could he be hiding something?" Alison asked.

"Cops are always hiding something," Travis said.

"A state trooper brought a guy in today," Chrisk continued. "The guy Lou Ellen was with when she got killed. The guy was there awhile, then they let him go."

"Could be routine questioning," Travis said.

"That's the way it looked. The way Briggs acted, I was watching for anything that didn't add up."

"We'll try to keep an eye on him this week," Travis said. "If there's something wrong, we'll find out."

"Something doesn't seem right," Chrisk said.

"Cops blow up about things," Alison said. "You never know what's going to trigger their temper."

"That's just part of it. It's what Trav noticed about the blood, too."

"What's that?" Alison asked.

"There wasn't enough of it," he said. "At least, it looked that way last night. I asked them about it at the scene."

"So she was possibly killed somewhere else?"

"Could be," Travis said. "The boy they questioned . . . is he local?"

"No. I couldn't find anybody that knew his name."

"Did you see him?"

"No, but they said he was a biker. I think Briggs tried to run him out of town yesterday."

"Could he have mutilated her to make it look like an animal did it?" Alison asked.

"It's possible, although they seemed pretty sure last night that she'd been mauled," Travis said. "Maybe he's one of those self-styled satanists and he cooked up some kind of ritual involving an animal."

"I've heard of those groups using dogs."

"I doubt he's part of a group," Travis said. "I think a lot of that stuff gets exaggerated."

"You're skeptical about everything," Alison said.

He sipped his wine. "Somebody has to be."

"So what's our plan of action?" Chrisk asked.

Travis smiled. "I think you need to get some rest," he said. "You look tired."

"We're working on a story," Chrisk protested.

"Judging by the hollow look in your eyes, you haven't rested in a long time," he said. "Go home and sleep. We have a week on this, we'll try to find out what the autopsy results reveal. Do they know what kind of animal yet?"

"A panther, they're saying."

"I didn't know we had those around here," Alison said.

"We've got one, I guess," Chrisk said.

Trav nodded. "One's enough."

Jasper swatted mosquitoes as they zeroed in on his face and neck. Trying to ignore the torment of their stings, he refrained from scratching.

He was wet with sweat now and growing discouraged. It was getting late, and he was further back in the woods than he'd ever been, yet there was not a sign of the cat.

His hopes for the money were fading along with the potential for fame. Before long he was going to have to turn back and hope that he'd be called tomorrow to continue the search with the police.

He was beginning to wonder if he should have revealed

his findings earlier. At least he would have gained a feather in his cap for putting them on the right trail.

He could not tell them about it now, not without revealing that he'd kept it a secret. Briggs wouldn't be happy about that.

He had to keep moving if he was going to accomplish anything. That monster was out here somewhere.

He stalked on through the trees, moving down a slope where a trickle of water had cut a gully through the ground. Like the creek bed, it had basically dried, so he stepped across it with ease and moved on into a tangle of brush.

He was fighting his way through the branches of the growth when he heard a twig snap. It cracked loudly, reaching his ears over the sounds of his own movement. That made him stop dead still. He quit fighting the brush in order to still the rattling leaves.

For several seconds he heard no other sound. The forest was still. Running his tongue across his lips, he looked from side to side, wondering if he had stumbled upon the cat.

It must be close. Maybe it had a den out here somewhere in these gullies.

Lifting one foot, he moved it slowly forward, placing it carefully to avoid making any sound. Then he followed with his other foot, twisting his body to avoid the reach of the branches.

He emerged from the tangle to find himself standing at the edge of a thick stand of trees. Vines and other vegetation twirled around their branches and grew together, reaching from tree to tree to create a thick, almost unified structure.

He couldn't go in there. He reached up to his hat and touched the rim of the headlamp, directing the light into the thicket.

It could not penetrate very far. He found himself

looking at more vines and brush.

He knew he wasn't going in there; that was settled—cat or no cat. He was willing to go back and just hook up with the chief's people tomorrow.

"Giving up so easy?"

The voice made him try to climb the air. He jerked around, almost stepping out of his boots.

When he saw her standing there in the beam of the headlamp, he almost dropped the gun.

His eyes widened, and he stared. She was beautiful.

"You're frightened," she said.

He nodded, unable to bring his voice out of his throat.

"It is unusual to find someone out this far."

He saw something move beside her, and his gaze moved downward. A rush of air escaped his lips as the headlamp fell upon the green eyes of the panther.

It was black, as black as the night.

"You seek him to kill him," the woman said. "You fear him."

"He—he killed a girl."

"You think?"

"That's what they said. I'm working for the police."

"Yes. Just as your ancestor did."

"My who?"

"You are the descendent of one called McKinley. I smell his blood in you."

"I don't know 'bout that," Jasper said. "My folks have always lived in these parts, but we ain't named McKinley."

"Names change. You are of his line."

"What of it?"

"It matters little. You will not harm this brother of the forest."

"Miss, you better look out. That thing's dangerous."

She stepped in front of the cat. "Do not harm him."

Jasper leveled the gun. "I've got to take him in."

The woman laughed.

140

"I'm warnin' you, lady."

"You are the one who deserves to be warned. You are in the night. The night is my kingdom."

He flexed his finger and tightened it around the trigger.

"That will do you no good."

She smiled once more. "Think of where you are. You just crossed a drying stream. You know what lives in water?"

Again his eyes grew wide, and he tilted his head down, the lamp bobbing against his forehead, causing the beam to bounce across the ground.

He had not heard them approach. They had arrived on their silent bellies, but there were dozens of them, probably from a nearby nest.

He'd heard the stories of a man in Pineville who had waterskied into a nest of water moccasins, but he'd never seen so many on land.

They lay all about him, some slithering about and others coiled up like rope. There must have been dozens of them, all black, shiny in the light of the headlamp.

They surrounded him, spread out for several feet in any direction.

His mouth dropped open as he looked from side to side. An incoherent sound escaped his lips.

He wanted to run, but couldn't. Even with the fear that gripped him, his simple mind warned him that running would only get him bitten. The things were ready to strike, and they would tear into his legs as he stepped among them. This far in the woods, he wouldn't be able to make it out before the poison got to him.

He'd seen what could happen when a cottonmouth struck.

He raised the rifle and started to shoot. Several shots thudded harmlessly into the ground before one finally hit a snake.

It ripped the serpent in two, spattering blood onto

141

the ground.

He swung the barrel toward another and pulled the trigger again. There was only a click.

All the snakes were slithering forward now.

Desperately he turned the gun around and began to use the butt like a club, hammering it down on the snakes. The blows caused them to jerk back or twist around, but they were not stopped.

Several of them began to rear back their triangular heads, opening their mouths. He saw the exposed fangs and twisted about in his tracks.

They were all around him. He reached to his boot and tugged out the knife, slashing it about in a futile effort.

In his calf, just above the top of his boot, he felt a pain like he'd been pricked by a tiny pair of needles.

He turned and swung the blade downward. Its razor-sharp edge sliced off the snake's head.

Another pain caught him on his forearm. The snake's teeth hung in his skin.

He began to shake it frantically to dispel the creature, but it remained, its thick body flapping against him as he moved.

A wave of panic splashed over him, and he began to claw at the snake with the knife.

His feet crossed and he tumbled to the ground, falling headlong. He lay on top of several snakes, and several others were quickly upon him.

One struck his face, another his arm, and he felt another slither up his pant leg.

He thrashed about, crying out. The burning sensation of the poison corrupting his tissues began to bring agony.

He kicked and clawed at the snakes that covered him, trying to get to his feet.

He began to feel himself choking. One or more of them had struck arteries, carrying the venom quickly toward vital organs.

He rolled onto his back, paralyzed. He looked up through the darkened trees, seeing only a thin shaft of light reaching up through the blackness.

He thought it was a light from heaven for an instant. Until he heard the footsteps.

His eyes rolled to one side, and he saw the woman's bare feet stepping through the piles of twisted black snakes.

They made no move to harm her, and in moments she was standing over him, looking down.

He tried to speak but failed as she knelt beside him, bending toward his neck.

One of the snakes had left an open wound there. He realized blood was dripping out.

He felt her lips against his flesh, felt her teeth open the wound a little further. Her lips continued to move about on his neck, until he realized what was happening.

She did not seem to mind that his blood was filled with poison. She was drinking it anyway, just like it was wine.

Chapter 12

Travis was in the office early the next morning, going through the mail, halfheartedly planning the copy for the next edition when the telephone rang. There wasn't enough deadline pressure yet to give him any real inspiration.

He had his feet propped on the desk, so he had to stretch to reach the handset.

"They're going out with the dogs," Chrisk said. "I'm at the diner. You want to pick me up?"

"Yeah, I'll be right there, just give me time to call Ali." He hung up and dialed home quickly.

The phone rang several times before he got an answer.

"That took forever," he said. "What were you doing, boffing the milkman?"

"Worse than you think. He brought his dog," Ali answered.

"There better not be fleas in the bed. Funny you should mention dogs. Briggs is going into the woods with some hounds."

"A cat hunt?"

"Evidently. I'm going to pick up Chrisk and head out there."

"I'll go do the interview on the magnolia party, then get

144

to the office. I think Donna Shows is supposed to bring in her wedding announcement today."

Donna, the recently graduated homecoming queen of Bristol Springs High, was marrying Lonnis Smith, who planned to get work on the offshore oil rigs.

"She'll be expecting a half page."

"Probably a full page. She's having the pictures done in a studio in Aimsley."

"Well, we'll block it off for her," Travis said. Hanging up, he gathered up the camera bag and trotted out to the Mustang.

He found Chrisk at the counter in the diner finishing a plate of eggs.

"Momma insisted I sleep late this morning, and she left me money for a good breakfast," she explained.

"You slept late?"

"For Momma six A.M. is late."

"I see."

"Morning, Travis," Bob said from behind the counter.

"Morning." Travis looked around but caught no sign of Estelle Johnson.

"The autopsy is delaying the funeral," Bob explained. "I couldn't expect Estelle to work under those conditions."

"He's trying to talk me into filling in," Chrisk said.

"I'm afraid I need her more than you do," Travis said.

"And I wouldn't pass up this story," Chrisk added.

She placed money on the counter and walked with Travis across the room. As they neared the door, Travis heard mumbles from some men in baseball caps and plaid shirts who were sitting in a booth.

Travis held the door for her and ignored the rumblings. Let them speculate.

"Bob saw them go by in a couple of different trucks," Chrisk said as they climbed into the car.

Travis put his sunglasses on and wheeled the Mustang

around, churning up dust in the dry parking lot.

"We should catch up to them without any problems," Travis said.

"They'll probably still be getting organized," she said. "Everybody around here does some hunting, but I'm not sure any of them knows how to track a panther."

At the creek bank they found a cluster of parked trucks with a crowd of men standing nearby.

A couple of them were unloading dogs from cages on the backs of the trucks, while Briggs stood nearby talking with a man in a Wildlife and Fisheries uniform.

All the stops had been pulled out this time. People who had good dogs had been prevailed upon to show up.

Langdon was sitting on the hood of the police cruiser dangling his legs as he watched.

"This would be the ideal time to hit the bank," Travis said. "Maybe I should call Alison. Our money troubles could be over."

They climbed out of the car and walked over to Briggs, who gave them a nod of greeting.

"We're going back into the thick of it," Briggs said. "We aim to get that thing today."

"We'll stick behind you for a while, if it's all right," Travis said.

"Yeah. I want you to be careful. We think it's a panther, and we don't know what it's liable to do. It had to be a little crazy to come up here and kill that girl." He nodded toward the old red pickup parked a few feet away. "Looks like Jasper got an early start on us."

Travis looked back at the truck and then nodded at the chief.

"We'll watch our step," Travis said.

They sat on the hood of his car while the men began to prepare for the hunt, loading shotguns and rifles and trotting the dogs around.

A few of the men were stuffing snuff into their cheeks or pouring coffee from thermoses.

"It's going to be hot," Chrisk said, rolling up the sleeves of her shirt.

"It's already hot," Travis said.

When the troops began to move into the forest, they slid from the hood of the car and followed.

A silence fell over the group as they began to move back through the trees. They were taking the task seriously. They walked in a line with their guns held in front of them. Some of them who served in the National Guard had army surplus equipment, and others were wearing camouflage so that they looked like soldiers marching into battle.

Chrisk snapped a few pictures as they moved deeper into the forest, fighting outstretched branches and dodging briars.

A half hour into the endeavor everyone was soaking with sweat. They stopped and sat at the bases of trees, sharing water from various jugs and canteens.

The dogs sat around with tongues and tails wagging.

After a few minutes everyone picked up their things and started moving again, the dogs trotting far ahead, sniffing the ground and barking occasionally.

"Do they know what they're looking for?" Travis asked.

"I guess they'll know if they smell it," Chrisk said.

"How far back do these woods go?"

"We're traveling north?"

"I think so."

"Probably to Canada," Chrisk speculated.

"We're going to run into Canuks or Cajuns. Either way, we won't be able to understand what they're saying."

"They'll be saying, 'You sure picked hot weather for hunting.'"

For another half hour they trudged along behind the

hunters, watching sweat spill off the men's necks.

Suddenly the dogs started howling.

One moment they were trotting along with their noses to the ground, the next they were stopped in their tracks, and their moans rose through the air in a mournful wave.

They quit sniffing and cowered. They turned back toward the men, obviously frightened, their tails tucked between their legs.

The howls turned to whines, and the dogs crept toward their masters, hanging their heads as if they expected to be harmed.

"What's going on?" Briggs demanded angrily.

"I don't know," one of the dog handlers said as the dogs continued to scramble about. They were panicked, and it showed in their eyes and their movements. One of them tried to climb into its master's arms, almost toppling the man over. The man grabbed its collar, swearing as he tried to control it.

"They've smelled something they're afraid of," another handler said.

"That's obvious," Briggs said. "Would a cat do that?"

The dogs almost drowned out his voice with their cries. They rolled onto the ground, meekly raising their legs as if to beg for mercy.

"I ain't never seen nothin' like that," said an old man with a thick gray beard. "Those hounds are scared to death. It don't make sense. It must be a bad scent to them."

The sound of the dogs' cries continued to build into a deafening concert.

One dog rolled over onto his back and kicked his paws into the air, and Nat Stuckey's bloodhound Lucky began to rub his face in the dirt, as if he were trying to clear his nostrils of the terrifying scent.

A mongrel that belonged to Jack Ellroy tried to take a piece out of D.B. Hargrove's prize hound Bessie. The men began to swear at each other.

"We're going to have to get them out of here before they drive us all nuts," Briggs shouted. "Round 'em up if they belong to you. The rest of you, stay put. And keep your guns ready . . . we may be getting close."

It took several minutes to get the dogs gathered. Finally they were leashed, and they offered no resistance in being led back in the direction of the trucks.

"Why wouldn't they have caught the smell of the cat back where the girl was killed?" Travis asked.

"Colder trail," Chrisk suggested. "Maybe they didn't get this far back with the dogs yesterday. Or could be the cat was through here last night."

They walked along behind the now-diminished party, taking careful steps because the ground was more rugged here.

"We're really going where no man has gone before," Chrisk commented.

"If a tree falls out here and we don't hear it, is there sound?" Travis asked.

They followed the men on down a slope as the breeze started to rustle through the brush below them.

The smell was not frightening but replusive. Chrisk put her hand on Trav's arm, and they both gasped for fresh air.

It was the smell of something dead, or something rapidly decomposing in the heat.

In front of them the men began to cough and curse as well.

Raising their arms in front of their faces to cover their nostrils, they pushed on across a drying streambed to keep moving through the thick brush.

They were expecting to find the remains of a deer or some other animal the panther had killed.

Instead they stumbled on Jasper.

He lay on his back, his mouth open and his eyes staring into nothingness. They were glazed over with a milky coating that masked pupils that looked purple.

149

A headlamp strapped to his forehead still burned, though faintly.

It was his skin that looked hideous. One cheek was swollen into a huge lump, and his flesh was covered all over with purple and greenish discolorations which surrounded fang marks. In other areas, the flesh was extremely pale.

It had decomposed quickly in the morning heat. In a day the smell would probably have been unbearable.

Chrisk turned her back on the scene. Although repulsed, Travis kept looking as Briggs knelt beside the bloated body, examining the wounds.

"What is it?" Elmo Dearmon asked.

"Snakebites," Briggs said.

"Musta been hunting out here last night," somebody said.

"Trying to find that damned thing on his own," Briggs noted, getting back to his feet. "That explains why his truck was parked out there. I should have figured something was wrong."

He accepted a light jacket from one of the men and placed it over the body. He took his handkerchief from his pocket and held it over his lower face as he turned toward the men.

"Langdon, go back and call for the coroner. Everybody watch your step. There must be a nest of those damned things around here."

"Looks like he fought 'em hard," Leon Williams said, nodding toward the spots where Jasper's gun had torn up the ground. Elmo kicked at the coiled bodies of the dead snakes Jasper had taken with him into death.

"They must have been in a frenzy because that stream over there is dried up," Briggs said. "Same thing that got the panther stirred up. Lack of water." He took his hat off and smoothed his hair down.

Travis and Chrisk walked back through the trees, get-ing out of range of the smell.

"You all right?" he asked.

She sat down at the base of a tree. "How do you get used to it?"

"You just learn that bad things happen and that you can go on after you see them. Although I think one of the reasons I wanted to get away from the city was because I didn't want to become totally immune to it all. You have to hang onto your humanity."

"It's not easy."

"No, it isn't."

She got to her feet and dusted off her jeans. "I'll survive."

"No need for pictures down there," Travis said. "The body's in too bad a shape."

Chrisk tilted her head back. "Something's not right here, Trav."

"I know. It's strange. I can feel it."

"What are we going to do?"

"The only thing we can do is wait and see what happens."

Chapter 13

The Reverend Lory Burns was a tall man with light brown hair that fell onto his collar and a beard which, even though he kept it neatly trimmed, still generated discussion among some of his older parishioners.

He took a little satisfaction in that. At least it meant he was getting some response from them.

He sat in his small, dark study at the old church where rays of blue sunlight fell across his desk from the stained-glass window above it. He was going over his sermon for Sunday morning, trying to give it a pleasant, uplifting message. That task grew more difficult with each passing week.

Burns was not happy at St. John's Church. He was from New England and had trained in Boston, served in New Hampshire, and then been lured to Bristol Springs by the desire for a change of scenery and an escape from the conflicts within the church hierarchy over doctrine and tradition. He hadn't become a priest to debate whether or not women should be in the clergy or squabble over tradition versus current morality.

He wanted to be a pastor, to help people and watch them go through their day-to-day lives.

He'd expected to find in Bristol Springs a haven where

he could serve a basic pastorate without dealing with politics and other disagreements.

It was not unheard of to find an Episcopal church in a small southern town, but this congregation was unique. It had existed for a long time, and that had an appeal for him. He expected it to be unaffected by things going on in other places. He dreamed it would be simple and special.

In his naiveté, he'd failed to consider the other difficulties. The Southerners did not appreciate his personality. He considered himself reserved, perhaps even a little shy. Some townspeople tended to view him as cold and intellectually aloof. He was alienated from many of the people, except for a circle of affluent church members, basically yuppies who worked in Aimsley.

Those other church members, who were Episcopalians because their parents had been Episcopalians, bore a Bible-Belt streak that caused them to view Lory as a liberal. On religious television they always heard about how bad liberals were, so a few of them viewed Lory with real disdain.

Coupled with hard economic times, he found himself struggling to keep the more radical wing of his congregation from migrating to the Pentecostal church on the other end of town in search of spiritual renewal. The emotional services appealed to many.

Lory had attended some of the revival meetings at the Pentecostal church out of interest, and he was thinking about doing some writing on the subject, but he still found the process alien and different from the worship to which he was accustomed.

His own concept of God was more quiet, and he preferred to think of Christ as a quiet man, a peaceful man.

It amazed him how divergent worship of the same figure had become, and how much conflict had been generated in recent years.

People were still talking about the Jimmy Swaggart

153

scandal which had broken a year ago in New Orleans and Alexandria. Lory felt as far removed from that as he did from the controversy brewing over the film he had written about for the paper.

He did derive some satisfaction from writing the column for the *Gazette*. It let him play with theological ideas which he might be able to develop into papers at some point in the future.

He liked Travis and Alison also. They were pleasant. Frequently he took the time to drink coffee with them. He was always pleased on the infrequent Sunday mornings they attended church. He often spotted them sitting in the third row. It gave him a feeling of solidarity to have people present who might enjoy and find meaning in what he was talking about.

Still he desired to do more, to offer more help to his people. That had been part of his motivation for entering the priesthood. He wasn't doing as much of that as he would like. He sometimes could not think of what to say to a man out of a job or to a farmer sifting through the dust of his dying land.

He had prayed for guidance, and now he waited, trying to be patient.

He knew God had a purpose for him. He didn't know what it was yet, but he had devoted his life to his studies and his work. He tried to be confident that an answer would come.

With a feeling of some weariness, he got up from his desk, straightened his Roman collar, and shrugged on his jacket. His shirt was black, but he preferred his suits in light gray. They were better for the southern heat, and they prevented him from being mistaken for a Catholic priest.

Although he had been informed by the funeral home it was not yet time to make arrangements for services, he needed to speak with Estelle Johnson about her daughter's death. The ladies who had visited reported that she was

154

terribly despondent.

Throughout the morning they had been dropping by to urge him to pay Mrs. Johnson a visit.

He kept putting it off, but he knew he would have to go.

He walked from the church to his car, cursing the heat as he climbed into the ovenlike oppression of the front seat of the Buick Century.

He flipped the air conditioner to maximum as he backed from his parking slot and adjusted the vent so that the lukewarm air was blowing in his face. The oil light flashed on and off, and he made a mental note to himself to get it checked.

What a terrible summer it was going to be. No wonder the animal had gone mad and killed. The heat must certainly have fried the creature's brain, and the poor girl had inadvertently stepped in its way.

He angled the car down one of the narrow residential streets, which was lined with towering oak branches that entwined to form a vaulted ceiling. He enjoyed the shadows that danced across the car. The shade helped the heat a bit.

He was just beginning to get comfortable when he reached Estelle's house. He pulled in behind a small red sports car and got out, spying a woman rounding a corner of the house.

Without seeing him, she walked to a front window and tried to peer inside through a small crack left at the base of the shade.

She was wearing a summer print dress with a scarf tied around her hips, and her hair fell onto her shoulders in carefully arranged curls. She didn't look like a burglar, but he felt awkward moving up the walk.

He had reached the edge of the steps before she turned and saw him, gasping slightly, then resting her hand against her heart as she laughed.

"You frightened me," she said. He recognized her now

155

as a clerk from the local video store.

"I can't get no answer," she explained. "I'm a friend of Estelle's. We used to work together at the diner."

Her jaws were grinding on a piece of gum as she spoke.

"I'm afraid she's so upset she's gone and done something drastic. She don't have any other kinfolk around here, so there's not anybody to look out for her."

He looked into her dull eyes for meaning. He supposed her concern was sincere.

"Let me see if I can get her to come to the door . . ."

"Danya," she said, supplying her name.

"All right, Danya." He walked up to it and banged on the door facing with his fist.

"Mrs. Johnson, it's Lory Burns. Are you all right?"

There was no answer. He turned and looked back at Danya, who could only offer a shrug.

"I already tried the door. It's locked."

"In back?"

"That one's locked too. I thought I heard a television playing."

"In which room?"

"I guess it's the bedroom."

He followed her around the side of the house to a window. A faint sound of voices was audible.

Lory peered through the curtains and saw Estelle sitting propped up on some pillows, an empty shot glass clenched in one hand. Her eyes gazed ahead with a blank stare. They looked glazed.

"We'd better try to get in," he said.

"You mean break in?"

"I don't think she's aware of what's happening," he said. "We've got to get to her." He carefully removed the screen.

The catch on the window itself required the assistance of Danya's metal nail file from her purse. He was not skilled in the technique, but he managed to flip the catch.

156

He had to struggle to pull himself through the opening once he had lifted the window as far as he could manage.

"Hello, preacher," Estelle said, tilting her head in his direction.

"Hi, Estelle." He gave her an awkward smile.

Once he was inside and on his feet, he leaned back out the window to speak to Danya. "Meet me at the front door. I'm going to need your help with her."

"What's wrong?"

"She's inebriated," he said. He turned and hurried through the house to meet Danya at the front door.

The gum was starting to get on his nerves.

"Why don't you start some coffee?" he suggested.

He walked back through the house and sat on the edge of the bed, gently taking Estelle's hand.

"My little girl is gone, Reverend."

"I know," he said softly. "It's been a terrible blow. I'm here to help."

She muttered something and let her head drop back on the pillow. Her words were slurred and unintelligible.

He spoke to her softly until Danya returned with cups and a pot of coffee. Lory poured a cup and lifted Estelle's head, forcing her lips to accept it.

She tried to turn her head away, but he urged her to drink. Finally she did. While he'd heard it said that coffee would only produce a wide-awake drunk, he wanted to jolt her a bit before forcing her into the shower.

After she'd finished a couple of cups of coffee and begun to come around, he took her arm and gently tugged her from the bed.

She was awkward in standing, unable to support her weight. He had Danya get her other arm and they moved her into the bathroom.

They had her sit on the closed lid of the toilet, and while Danya turned on the water, he removed his jacket and rolled up his sleeves.

157

Together they guided Estelle, helping her step into the tub. She was still wearing her nightgown.

She screamed when the needles of the shower water hit her, splashing over her face and soaking her hair.

Danya stepped back to avoid getting drenched, leaving Lory to support Estelle's weight until she began to revive.

Reaching forward, she pressed her palms against the wall, supporting herself as the water continued to splash down on the back of her head.

She moaned, staggered about, and then stepped from beneath the spray.

Lory was waiting with a towel. She accepted it and wiped the water from her face.

Danya helped her once again to a seat on the toilet lid, throwing another towel over her shoulders.

"I've never had a preacher do so much for me," Estelle said. She was sitting in her kitchen now with another cup of coffee on the table in front of her. She was wearing a white bathrobe, and her hair was brushed back from her face, hanging down her back in wet strands.

He'd had Danya search the house and pour out all the liquor she could find.

"It's not often I get a chance to do something so useful," Lory said. "I just saw something that had to be done."

Estelle closed her eyes, holding her lips together tightly. "I was trying to forget everything."

"I'm afraid that would only bury the emotion," said Lory. "You loved your daughter very much. It is not easy to accept the loss, but grief is natural."

"I kept thinking I had nothing to live for . . . that I couldn't go on."

"That's not so," Danya said.

"I know. I just felt so hopeless."

"Well, I'm going to stay here with you," Danya said.

"No . . . I'm okay now. I don't want to be a burden to anyone."

"I'm sure there's someone at the church," Lory suggested.

"No—it really won't be necessary. I feel terrible. I'm upset, I admit that. But I'll manage. I made a mistake. I'm thankful you two came along."

"I don't feel right about leaving you," Lory said.

"No, you have other things to do. You've already helped me so much. I couldn't impose."

Lory sensed Estelle still wanted to be alone. She was embarrassed by the state she'd been found in, and she didn't want to rely on additional support.

She was vulnerable, deeply in pain, but he had learned long ago he could do only what people allowed him to do to help.

"I'll come back to see you tomorrow," he said.

"Okay. I appreciate it."

He said a brief prayer with her and urged her to contact him if she needed anything.

He left her with Danya. In a way, he felt as if he had done nothing.

Travis and Chrisk wound up back at the diner for lunch. The heat had sapped the energy out of both of them.

Travis felt half dehydrated, and the sight and smell of the decomposing body lingered in his mind. He was concerned about the impact it had had on Chrisk, but so far she seemed to be holding up.

As he bit into his hamburger, he found himself wondering what had ever inspired him to become a journalist.

In twelfth grade, between studying *Macbeth* and English literature, he'd picked up some writing skills in composition work.

He'd quickly gained the attention of his English teachers in college when they noticed his flair for writing, in spite of his difficulty with placing commas in the right place.

Advisers had directed him toward work on the school paper, and doors had opened from there.

There had been no desire in those early days to pursue crime reporting. The closest he came was writing English papers on Raymond Chandler and James M. Cain.

He'd loved detective fiction since he'd accidentally come into possession of an old paperback copy of *Farewell, My Lovely* in high school.

When he landed his job on the paper in the city, he'd first been assigned to working on a consumer affairs column. He worked with better business bureaus and chambers of commerce across Texas and the southwest.

His enthusiasm for that had gained him consideration on a major murder case. It had involved the murder of two elderly ladies in a quiet residential neighborhood. They had been brutally beaten in their home while they slept.

Finding little new in the police investigation, he had gone over to the neighborhood and trudged the sidewalks, talking to people. He'd been able to write an impressive profile of the women, as well as a characterization of a neighborhood coping with the shock of two horrible deaths.

That had led to more and more crime assignments until he'd been elevated at twenty-six to the night crime beat, where he had stayed for three years.

He had sometimes brooded over the fact that he was more an observer, questioning the validity of his work.

His editor had consoled him by reminding him he didn't need to make the arrests. His job was only to report them when they occurred.

Deep down, he still had a feeling of emptiness because he'd never quite been what he had dreamed of being, but

160

he was working at happiness.

Alison helped a great deal in that area. He had found something fresh and warm about her. As they began to date, he felt his sagging spirits lifted, and the loneliness that had plagued him melted away.

Her humor was well concealed because she was quiet most of the time—shy, as Travis learned after a while.

It almost matched his own shyness, making working through their insecurities about relationships a difficult task.

They had managed because for the first time in both their lives they had found a relationship that seemed to be charmed.

They had come to realize that they complemented each other.

They were each a part of the other, and love seemed natural. Although there were different interests and compromises to be made, things worked. Their love was deep and consuming. It was real, and he prayed that it would last. Above all, he wanted to love Alison.

Everything else that he did had ups and downs, but it all revolved around their love.

He let himself think about that very little, because in a way it was frightening. It made him think of losing her, and he could not abide that.

"You're awfully quiet," Chrisk said from across the table.

"Awash in a sea of thought," he said. "Thinking about Alison."

"Yeah, when I get ready to tie the knot, where do I go to apply for a marriage like you two have?"

He laughed. "You have to find a sorcerer and promise him your firstborn," he said. "I used to think I'd never meet anybody right for me. Love can be discouraging."

"I can drink to that. There are no guys my age around here. Not black guys, anyway, and white boys don't date black girls, not publicly. I've had a few offers to go out behind some barns."

"When you get to college, you'll find somebody. You'll run into somebody who's concerned about the world like you are, somebody you can share things with."

"You think?"

"People lied to me like that for years, so yeah, I guess it's possible."

"I'm putting my money away. Spring semester, I'm out of here. If the scholarship comes through."

"It'll be there. You're good, and you'll prove yourself. I've got confidence in you."

"If I can just keep the stomach for it."

"That was pretty gruesome. You could work a long time without seeing anything else that bad."

"I'm getting this *really* weird feeling. What if all the animals go crazy? Did you see that movie *In the Shadow of Kilimanjaro* on the late show?"

"What about the baboons reacting to the drought in Africa?"

"Yeah, they tore up the place. That really happened."

"Hopefully it'll rain before that happens around here."

"Well, I talked to the man from Wildlife and Fisheries, and he said he'd never seen anything like we've got going on."

"Was that on the record?"

"Yeah."

"We'll include his comments. We don't want to start a panic, but if it hasn't rained by next week, maybe people should know it's okay to worry."

Chapter 14

When he returned to the resort, Blade expected to find Navarra in the same trance she'd been in when he'd departed that morning for Aimsley.

It had been an awkward shopping spree, consuming more time than he had expected, but he still made it back before dark.

He'd endeavored to explain to sales clerks how he needed a gift for his sister but he didn't quite know her size.

Using his father's credit cards, he worked through several shops, amassing a wardrobe. He had no idea what Navarra might like.

All of the packages had been strapped to the back of his motorcycle for the trip to Bristol Springs.

Walking into the resort's main building, he found Navarra awake and at work in spite of the sunlight which filtered in.

She had moved into the dusty chamber at the end of a long corridor where the pit of an indoor swimming pool languished under a skylight overgrown on the outside with vines and brush and cloaked inside with cobwebs and grime.

Navarra was at the shallow end of the pool toying with a table she must have lugged there.

"What are you doing?" he asked.

One eyebrow tilted up as she looked at the things in his arms. "That will become apparent in time. You brought the clothes?"

"I did."

She walked up the steps of the pool with a slow, graceful stride and took the packages from him to spread on the tiled floor.

Tossing open boxes, she began to lift out the various garments to look them over. Her fingertips caressed the fabric, and she examined each article, considering its style and texture.

Finally she selected a long white dress decorated with lace. He had chosen it in an effort to find something that would please her, and by the way she held it up and spun about with it he knew he had succeeded.

"It is lovely," she said. "I once made dresses, so I have a particular affection for pretty things."

She held it in front of her, pressing it against her body. "It will be perfect," she decided, placing it aside while she began to look at the other items.

"I was trying to give you a variety," Blade said.

"These will all be ideal, and they should fit well enough. You did well." She turned to him and put one arm around his neck, kissing him gently.

"I didn't know about perfume and stuff," he said. "I picked a few things, and some soap and junk like that."

"All is well."

Blade stood beside her, feeling a bit uncomfortable.

"Are you going to keep killing people?" he asked.

Her head turned slowly, eyes focusing on his with a stare that throbbed into the marrow of his bones.

"I will survive."

He swallowed, unable to look away from her gaze. Sweat beaded on the back of his neck. He did not quite understand his feeling of being controlled. It had seized

164

him as they stood in the old bathroom, and it remained. It was rooted somewhere deep within his brain, with fingers that gripped him deep inside his heart.

His desire for her was only a part of it. Her favors were as erotic as anything he had ever experienced, but he felt bound to her in a deeper way.

He belonged to her, and there was no way to rebel. He had submitted to her, and it allowed her to ensnare him.

The stare she offered now was not establishing new control. She had no power to do that in daylight. It only reminded him that he was not a free man any longer.

He had somehow sworn a fealty. His heartbeat slowed a little, almost becoming normal again.

He liked that image of himself. It fit in with his black leather motif. He was her knight, a black knight for a dark angel of death.

"I have to survive," she said. "You can understand that, can you not?"

He took her into his arms, looking down into her eyes. "I understand," he said, and she brought her mouth up to his.

Her lips were hot. Her body was warm where her skin touched his. As the kiss ended, she began to kiss his neck and throat, her hands moving swiftly over his body, finding the buttons on his shirt and pulling them open so that she could move her hot kisses to his chest.

He put up no resistance. If this was a part of his duty as her knight, he would not complain. He was to be her protector. It was perhaps the most purpose he had ever known in life.

Yes, Blade liked being a knight.

Early Jackson sat in the wicker chair on the front porch of his home, rereading his granddaughter's story about the killing. The thought of it touched his heart, but he got a warm feeling from the knowledge that Chrisk had done her job so well.

She had a talent. She was not just doing a job, she was fulfilling potential. He ran a hand through the thick gray whiskers which covered his face.

He could remember the days when he had helped his father work the dirt, trying to produce crops on land that had not been fertile for many years.

Although his father had hoped he would stay on the farm, his mother had urged him to look for a better life.

He had worked for a time in the old sawmill, then moved on. Traveling by rail, he had seen the country, heading north to Chicago, where he found work in the stockyards, then west to California to work in the orange groves.

His youth had been exciting. He'd had to endure the usual bouts of racism, the hatred that was hurled at him just because his skin was black, but he had for the most part avoided dangerous encounters.

He still had on his forearm a scar he'd received from a sailor in San Diego who'd thought Early was looking at his girlfriend.

He had another scar he'd received in a tavern in another sawmill town in South Louisiana. He'd been trying to break up a fight between two younger black men when one of them pulled an ice pick.

The point had ripped a bad gash in his side before he'd been able to take it away from the younger man.

He had grown good at surviving over the years. He'd taken a stand, when possible, and he'd walked away from fights he'd known he could not win.

Early's belief in God had carried him through much of his struggle.

Whenever his anger boiled too high or he felt his heart about to give way to hatred, he called on the good Lord to give him strength, and it always came, just as his momma had promised it would.

Sometimes Chrisk could not understand how he stayed so happy as age crept over him.

"I'm going to enjoy what I got," he told her. "And not worry about what I'm not."

He didn't try to say more, didn't try to explain how immense was his sense of accomplishment when he saw the stories she wrote.

All that he had done, all that he had suffered and worked toward, was for her now. To see the daughter of his daughter strive for great things made him aware that he had not labored in vain.

He listened to Chrisk express her concerns about politics in America and the injustices in South Africa, and he knew she would go out and work to change the wrongs. She had a chance to succeed, and probably to encourage others.

He liked to think the stories he had read to her while she was a little girl had helped inspire her.

She'd sat on his knee on this very porch listening intently as he read fairy tales or folk stories or told her stories of his own, handed down through the generations.

He saw a lot of himself in Chrisk, a lot of the man who had wandered before finally settling again in his hometown to start a family late in life. He counted himself lucky to be able to see his grandchildren grown up.

Chrisk was his favorite.

He worried about her, pursuing this job as a journalist. He did not want her getting involved in something that would get her killed.

And he wanted her reputation to be sterling as well. She scoffed when he warned her about being seen too frequently with Travis, dismissing his concerns as old-fashioned, but he'd heard the whispers in the barber shop and at the grocery store. People in Aimsley loved a good scandal.

Closing the paper, he put the bad thoughts out of his mind as he climbed from his chair and walked back into the narrow front room of his house.

The rumors would pass. He'd fought too many battles in his life to be concerned about words.

His youth was behind him now. Chrisk's life was unfolding. He'd put a little money away. He intended to give it to her when she went away to school.

She would need it as she pursued her studies.

He wondered if he would live to see her graduate. He was 84, so it wasn't likely. He didn't have much time left.

He was just thankful to the good Lord for the time he'd had. Picking up the tattered King James Bible from the table beside his chair, he ran his hands over the cracked leather cover, enjoying the texture before he flipped it open.

He liked to read the Psalms in the afternoons.

They had Jasper's body spread out on the embalming table in the back room of the Rosewood Funeral Home, a white sheet partially concealing the body.

The upper portion, including the badly swollen face and neck and the discolored chest and arms, was exposed. It was not a sight Briggs enjoyed as he stood beside Barney Simmons while the old man completed his examination.

"I think it's a safe assumption he died from the snake-bites," Simmons said, standing back from the body.

They were both wearing masks to filter out some of the stench of decomposure, which found its way into the air in spite of the antiseptic scent of the room. The decomposure smell was worse than it should be, Doc had said.

"No signs of any other injuries?" Briggs asked.

"What were you looking for?" Doc asked. "If you had a specific suspicion and you were to fill me in on it, I might be able to come up with something."

"No sign of human teeth marks?"

The doctor looked at him over the rims of his half-glasses.

"You serious?" he asked.

"We think the other body may have had that."

"You think there are cannibals in those woods?"

"I don't know what to think. Maybe some kind of cult," the chief said. "I'm waiting for autopsy results."

"Well, you might want to go through that with this body too," the doctor said. "I've never seen anything like this."

"The coroner said that wouldn't be necessary because the cause is more obvious this time. He must have stumbled into a nest of snakes."

"I've never seen a nest of them. What are you going to do? Get a posse and go hunt down all the snakes? You might find one panther, if that boy was telling the truth, but I don't see how you're going to get the town appeased about this mess."

The old doctor adjusted his white lab coat and continued his examination of the body. "He's been struck 52 times, if my count is accurate, and it probably is. That's a lot of snakebites made by a lot of snakes, even if some of them struck him two or three times."

"It's got to have something to do with the drought," Briggs said.

"Did you talk to the Wildlife and Fisheries man?"

"Yes. He didn't have a definite answer either. He's . . ."

"Never seen anything like it?" Doc finished.

The chief nodded.

The doctor ran a hand through his hair. He had a weariness about him that was etched deeply into his bones. He had been the general practitioner for Bristol Springs for an eon, watching the births and the deaths.

He had to admit he didn't feel right about this. Snakebites occurred from time to time, and he had ways of treating them if the venom didn't get into a vein.

With Jasper it was a question of which vein the venom didn't get into. Even his clothes had not blocked the fangs as they bit into him.

There was no way the funeral home was going to make this body presentable for an open-casket funeral, even if there was not an autopsy.

"Well, I've got a few things I need to do if I'm going to make an appropriate report to the coroner's office for the death certificate," he said.

Walking over to a steel table near one wall, Simmons peeled on a pair of rubber gloves and then picked up a large syringe.

He watched the look on Briggs's face as he moved back to the table. As many times as Briggs had watched such things, it still made him uncomfortable.

Almost casually Doc slipped the needle into the body, planning to get a blood sample.

He was unsuccessful on the first try.

He tried again, plunging the needle into the waxy flesh with determination. As he eased the plunger back, it drew nothing into the syringe.

He looked up at Briggs, who was staring down quizzically.

"It's stranger than we thought," Doc said. "Your snakes must have sucked out all the blood."

Chapter 15

The shadows on the resort floor began to creep lazily toward the wall, indicating the impending darkness.

"Do you have to kill every night?" Blade asked.

Navarra lay beside him in the tangle of their clothing, her cheek pressed against his shoulder and one leg draped across him. Her breath softly tickled his neck.

"I take only what I must. It is best for the mortals to remain unaware of my presence if possible, so some nights I do not feed."

She kissed his cheek and then his lips, moving her hand across his chest in a gentle caress.

He closed his eyes and grunted slightly at her touch.

"I was thinking," he said in a moment. "This is a small town. They'll figure you out sooner or later, won't they? I think you'd be better off in a city, a big city. I could take you to New Orleans. They wouldn't notice if people disappeared there."

She laughed. "There is no rush," she said. "Perhaps in time we will travel there. There are other things which must be done first. They will not be a danger, these townspeople. They are fools."

"What do we have to do?"

She picked up a strand of her hair and used it to tickle

his face playfully. "You ask so many questions, David Pearson. These things will come in time. I do not want to overwhelm you with too much at once."

She ran her fingers through his hair, kissing him again, then smiling. "You will have much opportunity to serve me, and there will be much time for us to enjoy the cities. I want to find out how this world has changed. I would love to see New Orleans again, then Paris and Rome once more. Unfortunately I cannot rush away from here. I have business, if you will. And there is work to be done."

He twisted to the side so that they were facing each other. Her body was warm and soft against him. He hugged her and rubbed his face against hers.

"Will you have to hunt tonight?" he asked.

"No. I will not hunt. I will not stay here, either. I have something I must do."

"What's that?"

"Something necessary."

"How do you decide what you have to do?"

"I follow my instinct, and there are things I can see which are beyond the scope of mortal knowledge. With the help of my adopted brothers, I will see even more."

"This is all confusing."

"A world you never dreamed of is opening before you."

"Yeah. It makes me feel good. Like I belong somewhere."

She placed her palm against his face. "You serve me well."

She pulled away from him, getting to her feet. Barefoot, she padded across the slick floor, selecting the white dress. He watched it slide slowly over her slender form as the final rays of the sunlight filtered through the skylight.

He did not rise as she paced across the room, disappearing through the doorway just as the day gave way to darkness.

*　　*　　*

Estelle sat in her kitchen, sipping the last of the coffee Danya had prepared before leaving.

The grief still throbbed in her throat, and now a new cloud hung over her, one of embarrassment.

She had never intended to sink so low that her priest had to come to her physical rescue.

She had needed the help, no question about it, but now she was troubled by that.

Danya, as much as she was a friend, would talk about what she had seen. The girl couldn't help herself. She was young, and she would blab about Estelle to everyone who came through the video store. That would include just about everybody in Bristol Springs.

There wasn't much to do in town, so everybody who didn't have a satellite dish rented movies for his VCR.

She realized she was dropping even deeper into depression, and there was so much left to do. She hadn't even begun to plan the funeral. She hadn't made contact with the funeral director; she hadn't even thought about covering the cost of the casket.

Lou Ellen would be buried next to her father, that at least was planned. The burial plots had been purchased years before, one of the few things her husband had left in perfect order.

The thought of Lou Ellen being lowered into the ground was nasty, a terrible thought.

She finished the coffee in her cup and got up from the table. A walk through the house was disheartening.

It was too empty, too quiet without MTV blaring. She swallowed back her anguish, thankful and devastated at once, because she wanted a drink again.

She'd never relied on alcohol before, but now she felt a need burning deep inside her.

She moved through the living room like a zombie, dropping onto the couch without uttering a sound.

She stared straight ahead, seeing nothing. The pain was

173

worse than ever, so immense that she could not even weep. She could do nothing but sit there as it consumed her.

She was about to lie back when she heard the sound. In her dazed state it almost failed to register, but somehow a signal reached her brain.

It came from the backyard, the sound of something being knocked over.

She did not feel fear. Thoughts of her own safety had no meaning. She did not care if someone sought to harm her. Death might bring relief.

Mechanically she got up from the couch, tightening the tie on her robe as she moved down the hallway toward the back door.

She listened as she walked, hearing nothing new.

Still staring straight ahead, she pulled the curtain back from the window.

There was only darkness in the backyard. There was no sign of what might have caused the sound. She saw no overturned trash cans or flowerpots. There was no movement at all, except for the gentle swaying of a few branches touched by the wind.

Absently she placed her hand on the doorknob and gave it a twist. The lock sprang free with the movement, and she pulled open the door.

The humid night air was carried through the opening, touching her nostrils with the smell of the night. It was as damp and empty as the house seemed to be.

She stepped out onto the patio, feeling for the first time a sensation of anxiety.

What had caused the sound?

She scanned the small area, the lawn Lou Ellen had reluctantly kept mowed with the old Lawn Boy push mower.

She could picture her in cutoff jeans and t-shirt as she shoved the machine along, churning up a spray of green under the afternoon sun.

Estelle's hands closed tightly around the edge of the door as she thought about the process. How many times had Lou Ellen actually done it?

Only a handful, really. A handful of days which reminded her how finite life could be. When you thought of it in those terms, there just wasn't much there.

She leaned against the door frame, her lips tightly pursed as she fought the tears.

When she lost the battle, she raised one clenched fist to her mouth, as if she were catching her sobs in it.

She almost didn't hear the hoot of the owl which rose through the darkness like an eerie knell foretelling something dark and final.

It was that and more.

Travis sat in a lawn chair on the patio behind the house. He was sipping an RC Cola from a can and listening to the quiet. Sometimes he preferred that over watching television or reading during the evenings he was at home.

He and Alison had decided to let the work on the paper slide until tomorrow rather than spend endless hours in the office tonight.

After a day in the woods, Chrisk and Travis were both exhausted, and running the office all alone had taken its toll on Alison.

Behind him, the glass door slid open and Ali walked out. She was wearing a loose-fitting Bloom County t-shirt over a pair of faded cut-offs. Barefoot, she walked over to the edge of the patio and sat down on the red tile so that she was looking up at Travis.

Her slender legs, which she crossed in front of her, Indian-style, appeared even more pale in the moonlight.

They had left the porch light off to avoid attracting insects.

"The body must have been pretty gruesome," she said.

He nodded. "It was already starting to decompose. You could smell it, and there were several dead snakes around him. They smell really terrible when they're killed. I'm surprised no one tossed his breakfast."

"How did Chrisk take it? She didn't say much about it to me."

"She was tough about it."

"She's really put in the hours this week. We need to pay her something extra. A bonus."

"Yeah. We'll find something that we can cut back this week and put that into her check."

"Good."

He swallowed some of the sweet cola and tilted his head back to let it run down his throat.

"Are you getting a rush from all this?" she asked.

He chuckled. "Not a rush. It's a break in the monotony. I feel like a journalist again, more than a gentleman publisher."

"Anything not to be a yuppie."

"I guess."

"What are we going to do with all this material? It's almost enough for a special edition."

"I don't want to try to fund that," he said, arching his eyebrows.

"Neither do I, but it's the biggest thing that's happened around here in eons."

"I guess you were right about digging out the old editions to see if there's a precedent for these kinds of deaths."

"Do you feel strange about it all?" Ali asked. "I got goosebumps when you told me what had happened."

"Oh, it's weird. I'm surprised CBS and NBC haven't piled in here. I'm sure the *Clarion* put the story on the wire."

"They're all in the Midwest, where the drought is really going to hit hard, or they're on the campaign trails."

Trav nodded.

"I'd rather be here," Alison said. "The people with all the glitz and glamor reporting don't know what they're missing."

"At least we go to our own home each night," he said, reaching for her hand. She accepted it and moved from the patio to sit in his lap.

He encircled her with his arms, resting his chin on her shoulder while she tilted her cheek downward to rest it against the top of his head.

The smell of her skin touched Trav's nostrils. It was sweet, only faintly scented with perfume. He loved the smell of her and the touch of her skin.

She was not beautiful, but he rarely thought of that. Her presence always stirred him.

He knew he was lucky. Few people found such a relationship. They bonded together to avoid loneliness and the darkness of endless nights, but they didn't find the magic.

He'd thought for a long time he would be one of those people, one who slogged through bad relationships with a few good ones which terminated for reasons beyond anyone's control.

For a time he had thought that would be his curse, to watch love slip away, to live with the memory of might-have-beens.

When he'd met Alison, he had been paranoid, fearing she would be taken away. He expected some unseen act of God to separate them, some job offer in Hong Kong that was so good she could not turn it down, or the interest of some oil man who'd wine and dine her away.

It had taken a long time for him to feel secure with Alison, to let his fear recede. He had worried that something he would do would offend her, that she might think him childish because he read detective fiction or immature because he laughed at Garfield cartoons.

177

He looked around every corner for the oil man. Commitments were no longer based on "I do." The phrase in the eighties had become, "Until I can do better."

Holding her in his arms now, he began to kiss her neck, brushing his lips across the pale blue lines the veins displayed under her ivory skin, tributaries to the heart, where he could feel the gentle throb of her pulse.

As his lips moved to hers, she took his hand and slid carefully off his lap, both of them stretching to maintain the kiss until they were standing against each other in an embrace.

"Let's continue this inside," she whispered. "We wouldn't want the neighbors watching."

He followed her to the door.

They ignored the sounds of the night, the crickets and the insects, the birds, and the owl which sat on a pine branch behind the house, watching.

Part 3

The Deception

"... they delight in lies: they bless with their mouth, but they curse inwardly."

—*Psalms 62:4*

Chapter 16

The phone call on the autopsy came earlier than Briggs had expected. The backlog at the crime lab usually prevented response for at least a week.

The phone rang while Briggs was sitting in his office drinking his morning coffee and reading the Aimsley paper. It carried only a brief notice about Jasper's death, mentioning that it roughly paralleled an urban legend. Otherwise there was nothing in the paper to indicate that there was anything strange about it.

When he got on the line, Briggs listened as the technician from Bossier City introduced himself as Mark Robinson. He proceeded to describe things like massive trauma and contusions.

"I don't need all that right now. I know she was killed by a mountain lion," Briggs said, cutting him off. "I can get those particulars when you send the written report to the sheriff's office."

"I thought it was urgent," Robinson said.

"It is. What I need to know is whether or not the body had human teeth marks on it as well as claw marks. I don't care about the scientific language."

Briggs felt his face reddening. He had not intended to get angry, but he was really beginning to feel the tension of the situation. It was unknown and it was strange.

"We couldn't be conclusive about human teeth marks," Robinson said.

"What? With all the technology you guys have?"

"There were some cuts that initially looked like human teeth marks, but they were near other scars, so it was impossible to determine. The body was torn up too badly. I will say this—there was no human saliva in any of the cuts."

"She'd been necking with some guy. You didn't even find that?"

"Not in the cuts."

Briggs gripped the handset tightly, dreading the answer to his next question, which he did not really want to ask.

"It was mentioned to me," he said, "that at the scene there was not a lot of blood. Did you find that in the autopsy?"

He had thought he might have to explain his question, but the technician seemed to know what he meant.

"Extreme blood loss is not unusual in something this bad," said Robinson. "Our findings indicate there was a larger than normal blood loss, however. Almost as if all the blood had been drained from the body. Almost like a dialysis machine."

Briggs drew in a quick breath. His chest felt tight, and his head was beginning to hurt. Travis Dixon had been right, and that angered the chief as much as it worried him. He had something on his hands he didn't know how to explain.

He licked his lips before asking his next question. "What would cause that?" he wondered.

"We didn't come up with anything conclusive. It has to be attributed to the attack. Weird things happen, Chief. We also have indication that the cat did a lot of its damage after she was dead. It must have just kept pawing at her. A bite to her throat killed her, then whatever it was just kept pping at her."

"Did you do a test on that corrosive we found out there?"

The technician had to make a check of another file, so Briggs was left waiting on the line.

Finally the voice returned. "That was tissue. No indication it was part of the girl's body. It was as if it was very old."

"It was human?"

"Possibly. The properties of it were not unlike human tissue. Nobody could really be sure what it was. The cat may have dragged it up from somewhere."

"Thank you," Briggs said. He hung up the phone without waiting for further reply.

He didn't feel like talking anymore.

Alison flipped through the brown pages of old issues of the *Gazette* in the storeroom. She had been through them several times in the past few weeks, doing research on her family through the birth announcements and the obituaries.

Travis was out on an interview, and she had insisted that Chrisk take the afternoon off since she'd be working the night shift at the Dairy Queen.

That left Ali some quiet time alone to try and find records of previous animal attacks.

It was a lurid subject, but along the way she was finding pleasant memories of her childhood.

News reports of *Greet Your Neighbor* festivals in the town's park reminded her of the spring days when she was a child, watching her cousins chase small pigs which had been smeared with grease to make the contest of catching them more interesting.

The picnic tables all around the park were set with fried chicken, potato salad, and pork and beans. Watermelon usually followed, and as afternoon crept along, accordions

183

and violins (fiddles, they were called) were brought out as dancing got underway for all but the strictest Baptists.

Old Man Carter (someone said his name was Wilbert, but no one was sure) always stepped into the center of the dance floor. He stepped high, executing the dance steps of his youth despite his ninety years.

The old man was dead now, the festival no more than a memory, but in the yellowed pages and faded pictures it was alive to Alison again, just as were the memories of fishing or hunting for pirate treasure with her cousin Putnam.

He'd read that Jean Lafitte had pursued the pirate trade in Louisiana, and it didn't matter that the notorious Buccaneer's journeys had never taken him within a hundred miles of Bristol Springs.

In between the searches for pirate treasure they'd found time to go swimming in the springs, ignoring their grandmother's warnings about drowning or the woman who lived beneath the waves.

The woman who slept on the water's floor was a local legend used by everybody's grandmother to keep children from being careless while swimming.

She smiled in recalling it. No one was sure where the legend had begun, but it had been around as long as anyone could remember, passed along by word of mouth among all the Bristol Springs family.

If the town survived the drought and its other problems, and the spring or at least the creek was reborn, she would probably tell it to her own children.

It would be a while, both the town recovery and the Dixon procreation. She and Travis were not in a hurry to have children, although they agreed that eventually they did want some.

In a way, deep down, that had been a contributing factor to her agreement to move back to Bristol Springs. It was a better environment for children. It was not perfect, but it

184

was an improvement on the dingy world of the city. There were green things here when nature was not being cruel. There were flowers and blue skies.

She smiled inwardly, realizing she was guilty of the same romanticism Travis harbored. She was supposed to be searching for stories of animal attacks, a needle-in-a-haystack endeavor which didn't really afford the leisure of childhood recollections or family planning.

She shifted the stack of papers off her lap and moved over to another stack, blowing dust off it before beginning to peruse the columns.

She was back to 1962 with still no sign of a killing by a panther. Checking her watch, she realized the morning had crept away. It was past noon. There was other work to be done.

She was restacking some of the back issues when she heard the front door open and close.

Thinking it might be Travis, she hurried into the front room. Instead she found a woman waiting near the receptionist's desk.

She was young and attractive, dressed in a smart-looking suit. She wore her brown hair pulled back and tied in a ponytail, and it accented the cat-like look of her face.

Her green eyes pierced Alison's heart when she looked at her.

"Can I help you?" Alison asked.

The woman smiled. "I am not sure. I hope so."

"What were you looking for?"

She was not carrying a purse. She put her hands together in front of her, motioning with them in unison.

"I was hoping you might have some information that might go back a few years."

Alison shrugged. "We haven't owned the paper that long, but we have issues that go back into infinity. Unfortunately, they're not indexed."

"I was hoping to find information about my relatives,"

she said. "I'm in town a few days because of Lou Ellen Johnson's death, and I thought I might find some information."

"You're related to her?"

"I am Estelle's cousin. She called me yesterday. She is very upset," the woman said.

She seemed a bit mysterious, yet Alison found her interesting, appealing in some way.

"Did you have to travel far?" Ali asked.

"Out of state. I thought while Estelle was sleeping this afternoon I might do a little family research, see if I might locate something on my roots. My immediate family hasn't lived here in ages, but they started out here. We know around the Civil War time there was a woman named Sarah Wilson. There was some artifact in an old box in an attic with her name on it. Otherwise, not much else. I could have relatives all over this place without knowing it."

"More than you think," Alison said. "I grew up here. You might even be related to me. I've done a little research along those lines myself."

"One never knows. The secrets of the past can be quite fascinating."

"Well, our old issues are in the back," Alison said. "I might as well help you, since I've been plodding through them all day. I've been trying to locate stories on previous animal attacks. I hope that doesn't sound too morbid. People look down on the press these days, I know, but we have to do these things."

"Certainly," the woman said, following Alison into the storeroom.

"What did you say your name was?" Alison asked as she pulled a chair around for the woman, positioning it between some shelves that stood against one wall.

"Neva. Neva Wilson."

186

"I'm Alison Dixon. You've been to Bristol Springs before?"

"From time to time. Our family is not that close to Estelle."

"I understand," Alison said. She sat down on a stool and picked up the stack of papers she had been working on.

The smell of the old newsprint filled the room, but it did not mask the scent of the visitor. It was a stirring smell, not quite like perfume.

Alison found herself glancing at the guest from time to time, observing her beauty. It was a pure, untouched beauty, not enhanced by makeup.

As they conversed casually while going through the papers, she discovered she liked the woman even more in spite of the fact that she spoke only in crisp, brief phrases.

She had not realized how long it had been since she'd had a friend besides Travis and Chrisk. She had so little in common with her own cousin and the people she'd known before leaving Bristol Springs that without realizing it, she had let a side of herself languish.

Talking with Neva provided the kind of release that made her aware of her need for companionship.

Somehow the conversation turned to literature, which Neva seemed to be schooled in. She knew all of the poets Alison mentioned, unlike so many people, who remembered the names only long enough to get through college survey tests.

They found a common interest in history as well. They wound up putting the papers aside and sharing coffee in the outer office.

Alison had not given much thought to her appearance lately. She'd kept her makeup minimal, and her hair was allowed to do as it chose. Sitting across the worktable from Neva, dressed in her jeans and t-shirt, she felt like a dishrag next to a satin napkin. Yet she was not threatened by the guest. There was no sign of haughtiness or superiority in her, which Alison had expected when she'd first set eyes on her.

She had anticipated arrogance, but there was none.

"Are you happy here?" Neva asked.

Alison smiled. "Good question. Not as happy as I thought, not as miserable as I could be. Actually, it's not bad. We have money problems, but we've been lucky. It hasn't caused too much friction between me and my husband."

"I imagine being married would be difficult," said Neva. "I find it hard to imagine giving up so much freedom."

"Trav isn't the typical man. He has his moments, but he's sweet. He doesn't always understand what I'm talking about when we get into feelings and emotions, but he tries." She raised her eyebrows and looked upward, searching for a word. "He's devoted, I guess you'd say. Sometimes he really seems dependent on me. It's not an unhealthy thing, just a real bonding. I guess it's what you're supposed to have in marriage. When I first met him, I thought he was this tough police reporter. He can be gruff on the surface.

After I got to know him, I started realizing how much of that was a protective shell. He's tender—gentle, really. He's not like Mickey Spillane anymore."

"Who?"

"Oh, a detective-story writer. Tough fiction," Alison said, slowing down a bit. It was easy to talk to Neva, and she realized she was pouring out her soul.

"I have never read detective fiction," Neva said.

"Travis loves it. I think he used to fancy himself a detective hero. That goes back to the toughness I was talking about."

"So often men set ideals which they cannot live up to."

"Well, Travis is realistic at the bottom line. He's tried

really hard to make this newspaper work, and I think he tolerates a lot here on my behalf. He's not from a big city. Alexandria is small compared to most cities, but he's not at home in a place like Bristol Springs."

"That's what has always made me cautious about marriage," Neva said. "You wind up having one partner stifled for the sake of the other."

"Oh, I don't think Travis is stifled," Alison said, defensively. "He's enjoyed being away from the city. Covering crime news was wearing him down. I can see in a lot of ways he's happier now."

"I do not mean to draw conclusions," Neva said. "Forgive me. You know your husband better than I. Your Travis sounds like a good man." Neva glanced toward the window. "I must be going," she said. "I have to help Estelle with the funeral arrangements. Perhaps later in the week we could get together."

"That would be nice," Alison said. "Lunch?"

"All right. I will come by one day."

"You didn't get much of your research done."

"Well, there will be time."

Alison watched her walk through the front door. She felt oddly uncomfortable.

She had loved talking with Neva, but she found herself contemplating some of the things they had discussed. The talk had revealed to Alison that she was not completely content. Was Travis stifled without realizing it?

As she returned to the storeroom, she wondered how long they could expect their bliss to continue.

Navarra returned to Estelle's house to find the woman sitting in the living room.

Looking more washed out than ever, her hair limp and oily, Estelle seemed to be in a daze. She looked up with glazed eyes as Navarra walked through the front door smoothing her skirt.

"They called from Shreveport," Estelle said. "They'll be sending the body tomorrow. But they didn't say body. They said remains." She began to cry, her eyes closing and her chin quivering.

Navarra moved to her, kneeling in front of her and hugging her gently. She embraced Estelle's shoulders and let the weeping woman's face press against her shoulder.

She comforted her until the tears had stopped, then helped her to the couch, where she whispered to her, offering a calming voice which helped her drift off to sleep.

Things were going well. She removed her clothes as she walked toward the bedroom. The box containing the white dress was there.

Peeling back the tissue paper, she lifted it out and smoothed it on the bed before moving into the bathroom.

It was clean and shiny, an improvement over anything she had seen even in the palaces of old.

She turned on the shower and let the spray warm. She had not desired to be near water for some time, but she knew she would have to clean herself eventually.

The prospect of the shower was an improvement over the notion of a bath and submerging even a part of her body in water once again.

When she stepped beneath the spray, she found the warm sensation pleasant. She let her muscles relax as she smoothed soap over her skin.

Her thoughts wandered back to the papers she had scanned at the office. Although Alison had not been aware of it, she had easily traced the information she had needed.

The papers did not go back to the 1860s, but she was able to pick up the line fairly easily and follow the descendants of her friend Sarah Wilson.

The notices of births and deaths carried the handed-down names which had been in Sarah's family in the old days. The names confirmed the sensation Navarra had felt when she first walked through the doorway into the newspaper office.

Family names had changed back and forth over the years with marriages, but there was no doubt. Alison was the granddaughter of Sarah Wilson. The count of generations was not exact enough to determine how many greats should be placed before the word, but that was not important.

All that mattered was that she had found the one who would certainly carry in her blood some trace of the process she had begun with Sarah Wilson so many years before.

That would make things easier.

Stepping from the shower, she reached for a towel and looked at the crack in the curtain. Darkness was near, and tonight she would feed, for survival and for celebration.

Chapter 17

Bats twisted through the night sky, hurling their small bodies about in aimless circular patterns, their thin, leathery wings flapping almost silently in the darkness as the skin of their tails adjusted to guide their courses.

They chased insects which served as their nourishment while night breezes buoyed their furry bodies.

They traveled unseen. Although most people knew of their existence, few actually ever set eyes on a flittermouse, as the old-timers called them.

As Duncan Sibley walked along the narrow strip of land which stretched through the rows of planted soybeans, kicking up dust with each step, he heard the creatures overhead without paying much attention to them. They might have been birds.

Although they sometimes carried rabies, they seldom got near people, and he had other things on his mind.

He was worried about the land. It could not get much drier before the damage became irreversible. He had driven his old Ford pickup out to this section of land after finishing supper, the windows of the vehicle rolled down to let in the cool night wind.

Normally he would have settled down in the den with his wife to watch television, whatever showed up on the

Aimsley station, be it special or game show.

Tonight he had been unable to relax. The problems with the drought were weighing heavily on his mind.

It would be devastating, not just to the town, but to his pocketbook as well. He feared he was going to have to take one of the Chapter Elevens bankruptcies designed especially for failing farms.

Squatting beside one of the rows, he picked up a handful of dirt and let it sift through his fingers. It was a dry, gray powder almost as fragile as smoke. The *Farmer's Almanac* hadn't warned him about this.

Straightening, he wiped his hands on his jeans and pushed back the brim of his cowboy hat.

His forehead was covered with perspiration. It was another humid night. There was no rain, but there was plenty of moisture in the air.

It was moisture that could not be transferred into the ground, just as the money tied up in his crop could not be transferred into the bank.

He looked out along the seemingly endless rows of dirt illuminated in the faint moonlight. They represented everything to him, to his wife, and to their two children, one fifteen and one ten.

He had worked a farm for as long as he could remember, helping his father with the land since he was a boy, and droughts had come and gone. They had survived them, but this time around it seemed worse, and Duncan had an uneasy feeling that there was no end in sight.

On the news they weren't offering any hope of an end to this thing, and he'd read in the paper that the other farmers had the same fears he did.

It was as if the sixth sense developed by those who worked the ground and relied on the weather was kicking in with the same message for all of them: this was the end, the one that would make the Louisiana farmers weep the way the men in the Midwest had wept.

Louisiana had not been untouched by previous hardships, and Duncan knew of many men who'd received money from Willie Nelson's farm aid through Louisiana churches to keep their farms going, but now it seemed like the final blow was being dealt.

He was forty. It was too late to find another line of work, too late for school or apprenticeship, too late for a career in the military. He'd served in West Germany during the Vietnam War, probably because his mother had spent so much time praying for his safety. The prayers had paid off. Boys he'd gone to school with had died in the jungles along the Mekong delta.

He had worked in communications, learning languages, but he had not pursued skills he could apply much to civilian life. He had always planned to come back to the farm.

He had returned to marry his high school sweetheart. He'd never regretted it.

Nowadays he found himself wondering about what opportunities he had passed up, how much of life had passed him by. He'd never believed that crap about midlife crisis. He'd always figured it was an excuse for men to walk out on their families, but now he was beginning to understand there was more than just discontent.

It was like a lust for going to find the things he had never known, for somehow creating for himself a life like they talked about on *Lifestyles of the Rich and Famous* or to meet women like the ones who tried out in the spokesmodel category on *Star Search*. All of Duncan's television viewing was confined to local stations. He didn't waste money on cable.

He remembered days when he'd thought about just kicking off and traveling across the country. He'd never had a chance to do that, and he knew he never would, because as much as he thought about it, he knew he couldn't go away and leave his family.

194

He wasn't that kind of man. He could never be unfaithful to Betty, formerly Betty Brown, who'd worn his letterman's sweater back in 1965 and dangled his Bristol Springs class ring from a chain in 1966.

She wasn't pretty anymore. She'd put on weight after the children, and she wore her hair short, kind of whacked off. He loved her anyway. He'd never expected her to remain a beauty queen.

With his hands in his pockets, he walked back along the easement between the rows, headed for his truck.

He was halfway there when he sensed someone watching him.

He turned abruptly and saw her standing there, silhouetted at the edge of the field. The moonlight filtered through the fabric of her dress, revealing the shape of her body beneath. The sight stirred him even as he felt a rush of fear.

He shifted the matchstick from one side of his mouth to the other, frowning as he looked over at her. There was no sign of where she'd come from, and it seemed a little strange that a beautiful young woman would be out here all alone in the dark.

As he walked toward her, he saw her eyes glowing. She was standing still, waiting for him.

He reached her in several quick strides, his mouth almost dropping open when he saw her face. It was perfect. Her appearance was soft and delicate, as beautiful as any he had ever seen.

"Are you lost?" he asked.

"Not lost. Just out for a walk."

"In my field?"

"I was enjoying the darkness."

He felt his eyes drawn to the neckline of the gown which revealed the curve of her breasts.

He started slightly when her hand reached up to caress his cheek. That made her smile.

195

"Are you so frightened of touch?"

He chewed on the match and tried to smile back. "It's not that. It's just that I'm . . ."

"Married? Are you happy?"

"Yeah. Very happy."

There was something that was not natural. She seemed to know more about him than was possible. He felt vulnerable and naked in front of her.

She reached up and took his face in both her hands, using her fingertips to trace the firm line of his jaw.

His face was rugged, browned from long hours of work in the sun, but that gave him a form of attractiveness which he knew some women liked.

"You are handsome," she said, again seeming to read his thoughts. "A fine and strong man. You do feel a need for something, don't you?"

She let her hands slide across his shoulders and down his sides, and the stirring in him was now undeniable. He felt his heartbeat quicken.

She whispered something else and stepped toward him, letting her body press against his. He offered no resistance. His mind reeled back to Betty and the kids, but he found his hands moving around her, touching her back, moving down her hips and across the smooth curve of her ass as she began to place small, delicate kisses on his neck.

She kissed him quickly, again and again, gripping his shoulders, touching his flesh with her tongue.

He closed his eyes, allowing himself to enjoy the sensation and the feel the fullness of her body offered. It was so different from what Betty had become. It was firm and perfect, and he wrapped his arms around her, pressing the heat of her flesh against him as he offered kisses of his own.

He ran his fingers through her soft hair and inhaled the scent of her skin, felt her hands moving over him again as well.

He had tilted his head back again when his head began

196

to swim, and he realized something was wrong. He pulled slightly away from her and raised one hand to the side of his neck.

He felt moisture, more than there should have been from her kisses. He pulled his hand in front of his eyes and saw the liquid gleaming black in the moonlight.

Blood.

How much had he lost? What had she done? He touched his neck again, and his fingertips found punctures near his jugular vein.

Placing his palm flat against the wound to stop the flow, he stumbled back from her. His eyes were filled with fear now, and he felt a new sensation sweeping over him.

This was not a woman. It was a witch or some other creature of darkness. He knew that was impossible, yet the evidence contradicted the unreality.

He managed not to scream, but he continued to twist backward, almost stumbling over his own boots. His feet had to scramble to maintain a foothold.

His hat tumbled off his head, and he spun around, beginning to make preparations to run.

He was like a character in a slapstick comedy, except that he would not escape pain and injury, the way they always did.

He knew he would have to get to his truck; then he would be able to get away.

He seemed to be moving in slow motion; it was like being in a bad dream in which he couldn't quite seem to get going.

The slick soles of the boots skidded on the dry dust, and he stumbled again, just managing to keep from falling.

He was finally beginning to pick up speed when the first tiny pinpricks of pain shot into his ear.

He didn't realize what was happening at first, not until he felt the fur against his face and heard the flutter of the wings.

A bat had attached itself to the soft tissue of his earlobe. Its razor-sharp teeth were clamped down hard.

He swatted at it as he ran, the effort to dislodge it fruitless. For an instant his mind let him believe the bat was the woman transformed, but even in the sudden state of fear he could not accept that.

He charged on for the truck, fighting the bat as he moved. The struggle caused him to veer from the pathway, and he tripped over one of the planted rows.

He went plunging forward, headlong across other rows. His face landed in the dirt, and he began to cough and spit at the taste of the dry ground.

He could feel blood coursing through the fingers of the hand still pressed against his neck, and he realized he was also bleeding from the ear as the bat's wings beat against his face, slapping his cheek.

He pushed with his knees and his feet, rising with difficulty to continue his rush toward the truck.

The second bat hit the back of his neck and stayed, transmitting a new sensation of pain into his head.

He staggered about, clawing at the two creatures, trying to rip them away. Their stubborn mouths held fast, and they were quickly joined by another, this one selecting his left wrist. He felt the teeth rip through the softer skin on the under side, partially damaging a tendon.

He twisted about, stomping the ground as if he were attempting to execute some practiced dance step.

Still another of the creatures found his scalp, tangling its feet in his hair while its teeth tore into the skin near his forehead.

Blood began to stream across his face, washing down into his eyes, stinging, at first.

He wiped some of it away and continued to stagger toward the truck. He also continued to twist, flailing his arms against his attackers.

He happened to look back at the woman, and he saw her

standing there, still silhouetted by the moon.

The breeze fluttered at her dress and toyed with her hair, but all around her, from out the endless darkness, more and more of the winged creatures appeared.

They flew past her, sailing on their thin, umbrella-like wings toward him, the screeches from their throats sounding a shrill attack cry.

One tangled in his shirt, biting through the fabric. Another found his cheek.

He pushed his legs harder. He had covered more distance than he had realized, and his truck was only a few feet away.

Even with all of these monsters on him, if he could get there he could escape. He could fight them off and drive to Doc Simmons' place. He might have to take a lot of shots in his gut to prevent rabies, but he would beat these bastards, just like he'd beat the drought that was threatening his farm.

Swallowing, he ignored the pain and the blood that was now covering his face. He stumbled against the side of the truck, and his hands slid down to the handle.

Fumbling with the latch, he got it open and pulled the door toward him, almost ripping it loose with his summoned strength.

With a cry, he grabbed the body of the bat on his cheek and ripped it free, tearing a strip of his skin with it.

Next he yanked one off his ear. It took most of the lobe and uncorked a new flow of blood.

He dived into the front seat, kicking at the creatures fluttering about his legs.

Then, still fighting against the ones clinging to his body, he yanked the door closed and fumbled to get the truck started.

He had forgotten the windows were open.

A wave of bats flowed in, first on the driver's side, but soon they were swarming in through the passenger window as well, hundreds of them, more than there should have been in the whole state.

Their small, dry bodies, covered with fleas and pits of dirt and shit, bounced off the inside of the cab, hitting the ceiling and ricocheting off the windshield as they all scrambled for his flesh.

His shirt was torn to ribbons in a matter of seconds, and it was covered with his blood as they bit his stomach and his chest.

He fumbled a wrench from the glove compartment, using it to hammer at them.

He struck one or two before teeth closed on his lips and his eyelids. Other bats managed to pierce his jeans, and one tiny mouth closed on his testicles.

He tried to scream but his mouth was filled with fur, and they circled his lips, biting at the corners of his mouth. One of them hung from his lower lip.

He began to choke and cough, tasting the fur and dirt on their bodies. He vomited, and the bodies blocked its escape, causing the acid bile to flow back down his throat, gagging him again and choking him.

His vision was obliterated by the blood, and the pain was unreal. It numbed his brain.

His head rolled back on the seat, and more of them crowded onto him, battling each other for exposed flesh, teeth piercing into his chin and throat.

He continued to cough, but he stopped thrashing. He had no strength left in his arms.

He'd never thought anything completely hopeless until now.

He gave up, realizing at least the worries of his farm were now gone.

He didn't even struggle as he heard the truck's door open. He ignored the loud sound of an approaching motorcycle engine. If it was help coming, it was too late.

Some of the bats were pushed away, and then he felt new

teeth. They sank easily into the puncture wounds the woman had placed on him earlier.

Then he felt nothing at all.

Blade pushed some of the dead bats off the seat. Several of them had been crushed by the weight of Sibley's body or the thrashing of the wrench.

They smelled lousy, so the biker tried to breathe through his mouth as he worked around them, edging Sibley's body aside to give him access to the steering wheel. The springs in the seat creaked under his weight.

Fortunately the key was in the ignition. He was glad he didn't have to dig into the guy's pockets for it. The corpse was covered with globs of blood and saliva from the bats. It was a sickening sight.

Trying to ignore it, he pressed the gas pedal and fired the engine to life. It sputtered a bit as he wheeled it out of the field and back onto the highway. He followed the highway a couple of miles, pressing the gas a little harder as he distanced himself from town.

His stomach was quivering. The more he thought about it, the more difficult his task seemed.

He jammed his boot even harder against the gas pedal, fighting the wheel on the vehicle as he took it into the next curve.

He didn't complete the turn. He let the vehicle leave the roadway, spinning it through the loose gravel on the shoulder of the road.

He shoved the passenger door open and dived as the truck plunged into the ditch.

He was pitched into the gravel, where he skidded along for several feet, scraping skin off in a couple of places and ripping his jacket.

The truck's momentum carried it across the narrow canal, slamming it hard into an oak tree which stood a few feet away from the edge of the forest. For some reason, it had escaped the trimming of the highway right-of-way.

The crash of the crumpling metal rose into the night, and the ruined engine of the truck seemed to heave a heavy sigh.

Sitting in the gravel on the shoulder, Blade waited for the blaze, but it didn't happen the way things did in movies.

He'd told himself most wrecks weren't as spectacular in real life while still hoping this one would be, just to simplify things. He would have to see that Navarra's wishes were fulfilled.

With a groan he got up and dusted off his clothes, discovering his left leg had been twisted slightly.

He had to limp over to the vehicle. It looked like an avant-garde sculpture now, with the front fenders stretched around the tree and the windshield shattered inward. The safety glass had been crushed so badly that the network of cracks made it look like uncut crystal.

Sibley's body was pressed back against the rear of the cab and held in place by the dashboard. His chest had been crushed, and the head rolled to one side, dangling like the head of a discarded marionette.

The mouth hung open, revealing the tattered lips and tongue.

Averting his eyes from the hideous scene, Blade ran his hand along the bed of the truck, using it for support until he reached the area of the gas tank.

It had ruptured after all. He could smell the fumes.

Given time, it might catch fire on its own with the gasoline dripping onto the hot muffler.

He decided it was better to urge it along. He took his cigarette lighter from his pocket, searched around, and found some dry leaves.

Wadding them under the edge of the vehicle, he set the outer leaves ablaze before making tracks.

He moved as fast as his injured leg would allow back to the roadway. The fumes didn't catch for a few seconds after that.

When they did, the gas burst into a orange ball of flame that belched up into the sky, scorching the bark of the tree and setting the lower limbs ablaze.

Blade didn't stay to watch. He hurried into the woods on the other side of the roadway, praying the flame wouldn't spread to the forest.

The owl had been waiting on a branch there. It raised its wings slowly and lifted its weight in the air, leading him back toward the resort, where he knew Navarra would be waiting.

She would make everything right again. He trusted her for that.

Chapter 18

"You think he was drunk?" Langdon asked as he looked in the passenger window at the charred body.

Dawn had found the wreck, but a few wisps of smoke still crept up from cracks in the blackened metal.

"I don't think Sibley was much of a drinker," Lucky Winnsboro, the wrecker driver, said as he wiped sweat from his brow with his engineer's cap.

He was a fat man with curly brown hair, and across his sagging belly he wore a grimy white t-shirt which was already wet with perspiration.

The day was warming up early. It was going to be a hot weekend.

"Lucky he didn't burn up creation," Langdon said, stepping back from the mass.

"Don't see how it didn't," Lucky said.

"The oak is just far enough away from everything else. The leaves could have floated over to the other trees, but the wind must have been blowing toward the highway."

The deputy coroners pulled a stretcher from the back of their truck and wheeled it over toward the wreck.

Chrisk snapped pictures of them while Alison stood beside her scribbling notes about the scene. They'd been there about a half hour after hearing about it on the scanner. Saturday was just another day for reporters and crime fighters.

Chrisk seemed a little tired, even though she hadn't worked a full shift the night before at the Dairy Queen. She kept rubbing her eyes when she wasn't shooting.

"You're going to have a full paper next week," Langdon said, walking over to her. His grin was broad, bordering on lewd, but she suspected he was just being friendly for a change.

Behind him the coroner's men put on gloves while Lucky attacked the passenger door with a crowbar.

The metal squeaked and groaned, and the door resisted, prompting Lucky to begin swearing.

After a few seconds, he stepped back from the door and raised the crowbar to strike it several times.

"There seems to be a lot of tragedy lately," Alison observed.

Langdon shook his head. "More than we can handle around here, on top of everything else. Poor old Sibley there had a wife and children. I don't know who's gonna handle what's left of his farm. Terrible time to have an accident."

"I guess these things run in cycles," Alison said, folding her arms in front of her because of Langdon's gaze.

She didn't mention her thought that it was often difficult to determine if automobile accidents were caused by suicide.

"Jasper's wife ain't right in the head, so I don't know who's gonna take care of her. They say Estelle Johnson's a mess too."

"I think a relative of hers has shown up."

"She needed somebody," Langdon said just as the truck door sprang open behind him.

The coroner's men moved in, motioning Lucky along. He had to use his crowbar to allow them to retrieve the body.

205

"Where's your husband this morning?" Langdon asked.

"Trying to figure out where we're going to put all the bad news," Alison said.

Travis was chained to the computer, trying to write the mounting number of stories concisely enough to avoid additional pages and subsequent costs for the next edition.

The struggle was one more reminder of their situation. The printer in Aimsley didn't allow for insertion of only two additional pages, which would have been a single sheet. It had to be four front and back, and that meant more money than they had to spend.

She found herself wondering once again about their happiness. Was it real, or were they kidding themselves?

A steady feeling of unease had been growing in her stomach since her discussion with Neva.

What if she and Travis were being stifled or destroyed by this world they had created for themselves? Had it brought happiness? They were not kids any longer. Would they grow settled, complacent in the quagmire of marital indifference and occupational stagnation?

When Travis had the writing finished, she would need to talk to him about it.

She forced herself to watch as they tugged the body from the front seat, trying to keep it from coming apart.

She had to turn away when the melted face came into view. The streaked, pulpy flesh which had become seared to the skull was too much.

The workers wasted no time in sliding the remains into a green body bag and zipping it shut.

Lucky, however, looked back into the truck. There was a puzzled look on his face.

"What is it?" Langdon asked.

"The sumbitch musta been huntin' squirrel out of season," Lucky said, raking a lump of matter from the seat.

It thudded into the dirt at his feet.

Langdon knelt beside it, taking a pen from his pocket to poke at it. Reluctantly Alison walked over to stand beside him. Chrisk followed.

"That's no squirrel," Langdon said. "It's a bat."

"Cab's full of them," said Lucky.

"I'll be damned," Langdon said, looking in at the charred bodies. "Looks like there might be more to this wreck than we thought."

The feeling of dread gained new ground when Briggs got word about the wreck.

He could not fight a growing feeling that he was losing control of what was going on, and hearing that Sibley had apparently run off the road because the cab of his truck was filled with bats only added to that feeling. The world was going wild.

He'd read somewhere that bats were so afraid of people they would do almost anything to avoid humans. He'd read about a movie company that had tried to film a scene in which a horde of bats flew out the mouth of a cave, bombarding the film's leading actor.

Although the actor was prepared to stand in the path of the bats brought in for the picture, the bats had other ideas. They wouldn't fly where a man was. They couldn't be made to take such a course.

Even if they were thirsty, and Briggs wasn't sure about how much water these bats required, he couldn't understand them flying into a truck.

He doubted rabies could explain the odd behavior of the animals in Bristol Springs, and so far, no one had turned up any evidence of rabies.

The only thing he had was a couple of reports that people had been drained of blood and a possible indication that one victim had human teeth marks on her body. He didn't know if he should believe those or not. It kept making him think of the black and white Universal movies he and his brother had watched on the late show as a kid, or the show about the reporter that his daughter liked so well. Kolchack, they called that guy, and he was always discovering the old legends were true.

It sounded silly, insane, but it was inevitable. He knew it was not possible, and that there had to be some medical explanation for what was going on, yet the notion of vampires kept popping into his head.

What if there were people who craved human blood? Would they be able to function like the vampires of stories, sucking blood from a victim's neck?

He didn't expect them to turn others into vampires, because he knew there couldn't be any supernatural involvement. That was impossible. He was no scientist, but he knew that.

Except that he kept remembering a part of the novel *Dracula*, which he had also read as a kid. The Bram Stoker novel explained that vampires could control the creatures of the night.

He felt he was wasting time thinking about such foolishness, yet the thoughts kept returning. Although it was impossible, it would sure answer some of the questions about what was going on.

He looked down at the pile of pink message slips on his desk. The mayor wanted him to call. He was not a full-time mayor, but he did have political power, and Briggs served at the mayor's pleasure.

Other calls were from worried townspeople, All of them wanted something done. No panther had been killed yet, and in less than a week's time, animals had caused the deaths of three people.

Messages had also been taken from the paper and television stations in Aimsley and the *Town Talk*, the newspaper over in Alexandria. The thing had the potential to become a phenomenon, a thought he did not relish.

A press conference over one death was one thing. A swarm of media attention, even if it was just by telephone, didn't appeal to him. Briggs knew he had better figure out what to do about the problem.

The idea of the vampire kept coming back, and he kept forcing it away. He didn't even have anybody he could ask about it . . . not without being taken over to the mental hospital in Penn's Ferry, or the one at Pineville. He wondered if anyone over at Pine College in Penn's Ferry might have knowledge of pertinent folklore.

Finally he picked up the phone and dialed the mayor's number to tell him some lies about how fine everything was going.

The mayor's wife answered at his house, which also doubled as his real estate office.

A few moments later the firm, dry voice of Mayor Henry Adamson came on the line.

"How are you doing, Chief?"

"Plugging along," Briggs said, trying to keep his voice light.

"I know things have been keeping you busy," Adamson said.

"It's gotten a little crazy around here," Briggs admitted.

"I've been getting plenty of phone calls," the mayor said. "People are scared to go out their front doors."

"This thing's got to be connected with the drought," Briggs said. "If we could just get some rain, everything would settle down."

"We've had droughts before," Adamson said. "Nothing like this has happened. The council has decided we need to have a special meeting tonight. Even if it is a Saturday, the people will turn out." Town meetings were never held on Saturdays.

"We'll have you there to tell everybody everything is

209

going to be all right," Adamson said. "We'll take some volunteers. I'm sure several of the men will be ready to help. That will be good for appearances. Then we'll have another hunt, and maybe we'll find that panther. If you could string that bastard up, it would put an end to our problems."

"It's probably gone back into the deep woods again."

"Doesn't matter. We'll find it. That will calm people down. I don't want people out hunting on their own. That'll be worse than you can imagine."

"I know," Briggs said. He could imagine the accidental gunshot victims they'd be carrying over to Riverland General.

"I hope we can get this over before it turns into a political situation," said Adamson. He liked being mayor, and the tone in his voice conveyed to Briggs that he didn't want his office to be jeopardized.

"Is there something stirring?" Briggs asked. If the mayor left office, so did he.

"We can expect a little trouble at the meeting," the mayor said. "We'll settle it quickly, before anybody gets out of control. I'll see you tonight."

Briggs hung up.

He hoped the mayor was right. Somehow, he knew he wasn't. Nothing was going to be over quickly, and nothing was going to be over easily. They were headed for a nightmare.

The ruined face of the farmer stared through the spiderweb windshield cracks. Through the leering grin a thick, purple tongue was swelling.

The lips were torn into ribbons, revealing the wide white row of teeth, and the eyes stared through the glass with a glazed, yellow stare.

Bats fluttered around his head until one of them

swooped over and plucked out one of the eyes, ripping it free of its socket and pulling out blood vessels like strings of spaghetti.

Blade sat up with a rush of fright. He was shuddering with the clammy sweat that covered him.

He rolled off the pallet where he had been sleeping in the old steamroom and stumbled on his aching leg to a basin where he threw up, coughing and retching until the contents of his stomach were gone.

Then he opened a bottle of water he had brought from town and splashed some of it onto his face.

He had managed to open a tap on one pipe in the steamroom, but he wasn't fond of drinking from it. The taste was metallic.

Being a black knight hadn't been as easy or as clean as he had expected. The noble cause of defending the dark lady had given way to the gritty reality of death.

The smells from the truck and the images of the body would not purge themselves from his thoughts.

He wondered what he had allowed himself to become. His motives had been vague at best, cajoled in part by the promised pleasures which Navarra had indeed delivered.

Upon his return from the truck, she had massaged away the pain from his limbs. Afterwards they had made love furiously, relentlessly, and the experience had carried him through waves of ecstasy he had never imagined possible.

There were things she knew, things she could do that no human had dreamed. They involved pain and the threat of pain, yet they were wonderful. They carried him temporarily away from the emptiness he had known all his life, and last night they had walled out the shock of what he had done.

Now the walls had crumbled with the cool breeze of dawn, and he felt more empty than ever.

He leaned against the basin, lifting a hand to his face to wipe away the perspiration.

He had nowhere to go. He couldn't go home. Things would be no better there. Nothing had changed.

He could not run elsewhere. He belonged here. He was the knight in spite of his weaknesses.

He felt Navarra's touch at his neck and turned to find her gaze. She was beautiful, as always, dressed now in one of the dark suits he had bought. That meant she would be going out somewhere.

"Things like this are always difficult at first," she said. "When I had to kill the first time, I was devastated." She ran her hands across his chest, soothing him with the soft purr of her voice. "You must realize that you have entered a different realm. The rules are different now, for we are in a game of survival. They will kill me if they find me and realize what I am. They would say it was because I am a threat, but the truth would be that I am different and that would be the reason."

"It's just tough to accept," Blade said.

"Change always is. This world seems so abrupt to me. Imagine how different it was when my rest began. I have been forced to adapt, not an easy task. Yet it is one I cannot deny, David."

He hung his head, almost pouting. "It was just hard on me last night. I'll manage."

She ran a hand through his hair until she cradled the back of his head in her palm. "It will get better. We have much to do. You must find a piece of wood."

"Wood?"

"Suitable for carving. We are going to make a statue, an oracle."

"Why?"

"It is necessary. It will bring power." She said no more.

As she turned and walked away from him, he felt his anxiety give way to a quiver of anticipation.

Something was going to happen, and he was going to be

212

a part of it. That was what mattered.

He realized a few lives did not mean that much to him, not when other things were considered.

Soldiers died in battle, guinea pigs died in laboratories. If people passed away as a part of some greater experience, he could accept that. With Navarra's help he could understand it all and that would be enough.

He found his shirt and shrugged it on. If Navarra wanted a statue, he would carve her one.

Estelle Johnson could not seem to keep her attention on the funeral director as he explained the details of Lou Ellen's funeral, which was to be held the following day.

Her thoughts kept wandering, but she couldn't quite figure out where they were going. Something was worrying her, something worse than the grief about her daughter, something she was unsure about.

Thank goodness Neva was on hand to discuss matters with the thin man who sat behind the desk. He looked like a funeral director was supposed to, with a gaunt face, pale skin, and a balding skull.

Characteristically, he kept wringing his hands, promising a lovely and economical service.

He'd tried to sell Estelle an incredibly expensive casket which Neva had convinced her to forget.

Neva had handled things well, keeping expenses within a manageable range. She was being very kind and helpful. There was no reason for Estelle's fear, no reason she could lay a finger on.

She sat in her chair across from the mortician, Mr. Dunfellow, watching him wringing his hands and listening to Neva determine particulars.

She had also called the priest and taken care of getting the obituary on the radio and in the Aimsley paper.

Neva was being so good to her. She was lucky her cousin had been willing to come and offer her help at such a difficult time.

Neva didn't seem to mind giving up time from her own life. It must be putting a strain on her job. Estelle couldn't remember what Neva did for a living, but it had to be tough for her to take so much time off.

Chapter 19

The Reverend Burns sat in the newsroom with the Bristol Springs press corps, discussing the recent events in Aimsley.

"It does seem to be reminiscent of a biblical plague," Travis said.

"Biblical plagues were dispensed by God upon the wicked. While our little town has a few skeletons in its closet, it doesn't strike me as qualifying for that type of retribution," Burns said, rubbing a hand across his beard.

"Maybe you should put that in your column," Alison suggested. "There's a town meeting coming up tomorrow. When it's over they'll probably go on a slaughter hunt."

"Alison wants to call in Greenpeace and PETA," Travis said.

"Hopefully it won't get that bad," Lory said. "One can never tell. The people are getting quite upset. Grief is a difficult problem to handle."

"Two of them were your parishioners, right?"

"One. Mr. Sibley was a Baptist and Jasper was a Pentecostal. We do have other churches in town."

"I guess that rules out a heavenly vendetta against any religious group that might have stepped off the straight-and-narrow," Trav said.

"Without the supernatural to blame, it still leaves the logical explanation vague. We're seeing different species of animals go wild and attack men. It's highly unusual for predators to be given to that kind of behavior."

"You could exclude the snakes," Alison suggested. "It's a natural reaction for them to strike when their nest is disturbed."

"It's still an unusual phenomenon," Chrisk said. "It really looked like those cottonmouths had surrounded Jasper."

The reverend shook his head. "It is unusual. For the most part, animals do their best to coexist with man. They know they're better off staying out of his way, and most of the creatures we're so frightened of are intelligent beasts. When they start killing people wantonly, it's out of the ordinary."

"You've studied animals?" Travis asked.

"I've worked with some environmental groups. I've come to realize there are myths about the ferocity and the gentleness of animals. When you get to the root of the matter, most humans know very little about animals."

"So what's your judgment of the current situation?" Travis asked.

"In a word? Perplexing. I don't know what could cause this sort of thing. The lack of water could be a factor."

"Does all this stop when it rains again?" Alison asked.

"Who knows? It could stop right now. People are frightened. That could make them stay out of wooded areas. With reduced contact with wildlife, it probably could end. Maybe it's already over. I don't think we have a group of animals out there plotting to kill people."

"Unless there is something supernatural going on," Travis quipped. "Or something like *The Birds*."

"Yes, unless there is something supernatural going on." A few moments after he had spoken, the priest smiled.

"Have you had any luck finding records of other

216

killings in the old papers?" Travis asked, turning to Alison.

"Not so far. I got interrupted yesterday when a visitor stopped by."

"You know who might know about that sort of thing? My grandfather," Chrisk suggested.

"How old is he?" Travis asked.

"I don't really know, exactly."

"Well," Alison suggested, "it might be a good idea if you go and talk to him. I have to write up my story, and that might get y'all out of my hair. That doesn't refer to you," she told the priest.

"Oh, I have other things to attend to," he said, setting down his coffee cup. "I've got to get a funeral sermon ready, and I need to check on Estelle Johnson again. She's taking this terribly hard."

"Is her cousin helping?"

"More than anyone else, I guess. It's hard to tell," Burns said. "The ladies from the church couldn't get through to her, and she didn't seem to want my help."

"Her cousin is very nice," Alison said. "We're probably going to get together for lunch."

They traveled out to Early Jackson's house with the top down on Trav's Mustang. The wind ruffled Chrisk's hair, billowing it back over the seat. The breeze was cool in spite of the stifling heat.

She knew her grandfather wouldn't approve when he saw them drive up. There she was, sitting in an open car with a married man. He would tell her it didn't matter if nothing was going on, the Bible said to steer away from even the appearance of evil.

Fortunately, he would wait until later for that. He would be polite to Travis.

When they reached his house, they found him sitting on

the front porch, reading the Aimsley paper. He got up when the car pulled into the driveway.

"We want to pick your brain," Chrisk said.

"You gonna find slim pickin's," the old man joked.

"You've been here a long time," Travis said. "We want to chat with you awhile about the past."

Early chuckled. "Well we'll do that, but it's too hot to be sittin' out here without a drink of iced tea. Y'all both want a glass, I know."

"It would be good," Chrisk said. She and Trav sat down in some rockers and waited while Early moved slowly into the house. His knees popped audibly as he moved.

He returned a few minutes later with a tray which held a pitcher of tea, three glasses of ice, and a sugar bowl. Rings of lemon had been slipped over the glass rims.

He poured and sweetened the tea and passed it around before settling into his own chair.

Travis sipped the drink gratefully, savoring the taste and enjoying the coolness of the moisture beaded on the glass.

"Now, then," Early said, sitting back into his creaking chair. "What can I tell you about?"

"It's kind of gruesome," Chrisk said.

Travis agreed with a nod. "Mr. Jackson, we were wondering if you knew anything about any animal killings in the past. Anything from way back?"

"Any wolves making off with babies? I don't think that ever happened," Early said with a chuckle. "Lot of stories get told. My grandmama used to warn me about alligators and bears. I never saw either one. I've been in and out of Bristol Springs all my life. I traveled all over, up in the northwest and everything. I didn't hear much of animal attacks anywhere."

"You don't recall there ever being an animal attack here?" Travis asked.

The old man rubbed his face, which was damp with

218

perspiration. "Let me think."

He closed his eyes and seemed to be straining to reach back into his memory.

"Some dogs attacked a man one time," he said. "Funny, but it seems the animals that are around men get meaner than those that ain't."

"They lose their fear of men," Travis said.

"Must be it. These were some German shepherds. They were guard dogs. That must have been back in the thirties. The only other thing like that I can remember is a case that my grandmama told me about. Seems a horse bucked a man off and trampled him to death."

"When was that?" Travis asked.

"Way back. Just after the Civil War. I don't know that that story's true."

"Why is that?"

"It's part of a wives' tale. I told you I got warned about alligators. Well, more than that, I was warned about the lady under the water, the woman who lives beneath the waves. Everybody that ever went swimming around here has heard that one."

"I can attest to that," Chrisk confirmed.

"What's the story?" Travis asked.

"It's one of those things they tell kids to scare them so they'll be careful. The story goes that there was a witch woman that lived in the town. She came here after the war and collected little boys and girls.

"The townspeople finally got wise to her, and they chased her out of town. Tried to, anyway. The sheriff was riding a big black horse, leading the others after her.

"So she turned around and gave his horse the evil eye, and it pitched him off, and its hooves trampled him to death before anybody could do anything."

"Then she fell into the springs and sank to the bottom, where she went into a deep sleep," Chrisk picked up the narrative. "She stayed there, waiting for some little boy or girl who wasn't careful swimming. She would reach up and grab them and pull them down with her to eat them. She's supposedly still there on the bottom of the springs."

"It's dried up now," Travis reminded.

"Well, she'll be back if it ever rains again and produces a pond for her to live under. You know how legends are—the truth doesn't make a lot of difference."

"Is there some basis for it?" Travis asked.

"I suppose there was some woman they ran out of town way back," the old man said. He frowned again, delving back through the years for another fragment of information. "I think there really was a man trampled by a horse, too. Right after the war. Some say the witch woman put a curse on his horse. I don't know that they even happened at the same time. You know how history gets distorted."

"It would probably be on microfilm at the public library in Aimsley," Chrisk suggested. "I could take a trip over there and look it up. We could get the real story."

"You can do it Monday. Consider it a day off," Travis said. "She works too hard, Mr. Jackson. I can't make her get any rest."

"I taught her not to be lazy when she was growing up."

"I'm afraid she's going to burn herself out before she gets to college," Travis joked.

"I'll make it," Chrisk said. "I just don't see how you're going to run a newspaper without me."

She glanced at her grandfather and was glad to see that his smile was genuine. In spite of his concerns about society, he understood the importance of what she was doing. She was glad she could see that in him.

It confirmed what she'd always believed: what a great man he was.

She reached over and squeezed his hand as he began another story about the old days in Bristol Springs.

*   *   *

"Have you traveled much?" Alison asked. It was early afternoon, and she and Neva were sitting on the floor in the living room, where they had eaten sandwiches for lunch.

"A bit," Neva said. "Paris . . . Rome. It was long ago, however. I do not know if they have changed or not."

"I've traveled around in the South more than anything," Alison said, chewing on her lip as she thought about it. "Texas and Mississippi. I was in New York once for a while. Then Atlanta, for a newspaper seminar. I've always wanted to go to Europe, but Travis and I don't have the money for that right now. Maybe when we retire we'll be able to do those things."

"It's sad when one has to wait for age to allow the enjoyment of life," Neva said.

"Sometimes you get tied down without realizing it," Alison said. "I've always been basically satisfied with life. I grew up here, living with my family. I got good grades in school and worked the summers because it was what was expected of me. I always knew I'd go to college, knew I'd go to work after that. When my parents died, I suppose the patterns of my life were already set."

"Patterns are easy to follow," Neva said. "They can become traps."

"I've never really thought of myself as trapped," Alison said.

"I sense you are experiencing some discontent."

"It's a minor thing. I guess you just reach an age like this, I'm thirty, and you realize you're not going to be quite as great as you expected. You start to see you have limitations, and there's not some magic about you that's going to make you more than a common person."

"Did you dream of greatness?"

Alison flicked a crust of bread around on the plate in front of her on the coffee table. "Well, like I said, I always did what was expected of me, even when it came to my job.

221

Copyediting isn't particularly fulfilling, but I viewed it as a necessity and plunged ahead. I think deep down, maybe I always expected something more. I just never reached for it. I don't know if I thought it would be handed to me, or what."

"So you went into journalism?"

"It was my other option because I was good in English. And I like what I do here. You can't expect everything to be perfect and exciting. I have a good marriage, I have food on my table. I could be much worse off."

"You mention your marriage and your husband often . . . almost as if you define yourself by your bond to him."

"I guess I do, in a way. That's sort of what marriage boils down to, isn't it? You're one member of a team, a part of the other person."

"Yet you remain an individual."

"I try to," Alison said with a laugh.

The visitor smiled. "I guess I am just curious. Our lives are quite different. I have always tried to plot my own course, set my own patterns."

Alison bowed her head, still flicking with her index finger at the crust of bread.

She smiled weakly. "I don't guess I ever knew how to do that."

"It should not be impossible to learn," the woman suggested. "No matter when you start."

Langdon stopped in at the video store to catch a look at Danya. He liked to do that if things were quiet enough to allow it. She was prettier than any of the girls in the other stores along the main stretch where he could stop by while still appearing to be on the job.

She was sitting behind the counter, reading a video newspaper called *Take One*. She looked up when he entered, a huge pink gum bubble puffing from her lips.

"Afternoon," she said. "How come you're not out huntin'?"

"The chief's doing some planning. There's gonna be a town meeting."

She leaned forward in her chair, resting her arms on the counter, unconsciously giving Langdon a glimpse of cleavage as the neckline of her floral print dress dipped slightly.

He ran his tongue across his lower lip as he gazed at the pale white swell of her small breasts.

His imagination took care of what he could not see.

"When's it ever gonna be safe around here again?" she asked. "Estelle Johnson's half crazy over what happened to her daughter. I'm scared to walk home at night."

"Easy, now," Langdon said, trying to sound reassuring. He looked into the dullish gaze in her eyes.

They were brown, offset by the dark curls of hair which framed her face. Although it was shoulder length, she sprayed it heavily.

"We're doing all we can," he said. "So far, these things have taken place only in the woods."

"Those bats got that man while he was just driving down the road. Think about all the critters that are around here."

"What, house cats and stray dogs? So far we haven't had any trouble with domestic animals."

"I hope it don't start," Danya said.

"It'll be over as soon as this drought breaks," said Langdon. He rested his hand on the handle of his gun for emphasis. "But if you like, I could come by and walk you home after you get off. I work a split shift on Saturdays anyway."

She chomped on her gum for a few seconds, thinking it over. She didn't much care for Langdon, but she wasn't put off by him in quite the same way the other girls were.

223

Besides, he did wear a gun, and having him along was preferable to walking the three blocks to her house alone. Her sister got the car on Saturdays.

"I guess that'd be all right," she said. "You can just come by after that meeting."

He tipped his hat. "Just doing my duty, ma'am."

Actually, he was answering above and beyond the call of duty, because on weekends he wasn't really working, he was just on call.

He didn't know what he was letting himself in for.

The dry bed of the old swimming pool was beginning to look more like a temple. The makeshift altar was taking on more definition with Blade's efforts, becoming a rough-hewn holy place.

The block of wood on which he had spent most of the day working still left much to be desired. He was no carver or sculptor, and he had no idea of what Navarra wanted in terms of the appearance of her deity.

There was much he did not understand about her existence. He had not believed in such things only days earlier, and he had never given much credence to talk of God or Satan or any of the stuff Shirley MacLaine talked about, either.

As he worked on the wood with his knife as a carving tool, he questioned again why he was staying. She was involved in death and dark things, things he did not understand.

He'd never sought such things. Even in his rebellion against his family, he hadn't really had dreams of power. The family had power, so he was indifferent to it, as indifferent to it as he was to money. It was the kind of indifference born of having grown up with both things in his life.

He could grasp the desire for money and power no more

224

han a man who has walked all his life might understand an invalid's desire to get up and run.

More than anything, he supposed it was the continuing sense of purpose he had with Navarra. In spite of the terror he had felt earlier about the farmer's death, the tasks she kept giving him had meaning.

He was performing his fealty, displaying that allegiance which made him worthy of his knighthood. A knight was suitable for the noble task and not unwilling to perform the menial.

He worked without a shirt, occasionally wiping sweat from his lean muscles. The enclosed pool was a stuffy workplace, but he was impressed by the seeming vastness there.

He imagined himself creating a temple of the magnitude and elegance of those he had seen in films.

He had never seen a temple quite like the one Navarra described, but his imagination would suffice until she returned from town.

She seemed to approve of his efforts. She offered him some help carving the statue, her hands guiding his with precision and skill. It was something she had done before, perhaps many times.

"Time is short," she whispered.

Chapter 20

Normally only a handful of people showed up at the Bristol Springs Town Hall—a sturdy gray building constructed in 1962—for council meetings, so the old wooden-floored meeting room with four rows of chairs usually sufficed.

Concern about the killings brought the citizens in better than a high-priced evangelist at a tent revival, however. They filled up the chairs and stood along the walls with their arms folded, fanning themselves against the heat and bumping into the framed black and white photographs of former mayors which lined the walls.

The sound of their collective voices rumbled through the room while they waited for the appearance of the people they had chosen to represent them.

The voices stopped when the council members came in. Most of them didn't look happy about being in the limelight, aware they were going to be called on to do something about a situation which they believed could be alleviated only by an act of God.

Lester Worthy kept fumbling with his mustache, while Betty Neely, who had a weight problem, puffed on a cigarette. Usually she didn't smoke in public, for she considered it unladylike.

As the council was getting seated, people started to whisper again.

Alison, Chrisk, and Travis worked their way in the back door of the room and elbowed through the crowd to the middle aisle so they could hear.

Chrisk had the camera around her neck.

"Keep it ready," Travis whispered. "If they lynch one of the councilmen, we'll be able to sell it to the wires."

A few minutes later, Lory Burns strolled into the room with his hands in his pockets and made his way over to the journalists.

"Amazing what a common enemy will do," he said.

"And somebody will find a way to work this to their advantage," Alison added.

Eventually, Mayor Adamson walked in along with Chief Briggs, and the buzz that had risen over the room again dwindled quickly to silence.

The men ignored the gazes that fell upon them and moved along in front of the dais where the council sat, taking their stance near the center of the floor.

Almost casually the mayor raised his hands.

"I want to thank y'all for coming," he said, a broad smile crossing his face. He was wearing a plaid shirt and tan slacks. With the sleeves of his shirt rolled up, he had assumed his common-man appearance, the focal point of his campaigns.

"I know everybody is concerned about what's going on in town," the mayor continued. "It's been frightening for all of us."

There was a rumble of confirmation from the crowd.

"What we're going to ask you to do is remain calm," Adamson said.

That produced another rumble, but he continued to keep his hands raised, gesturing for everyone to keep the noise down.

"We have a problem here. It's very bad, what has

happened so far. It's been a tragedy. We can't undo what's been done. All we can do is try and prevent more problems and more deaths."

There was a mumur of agreement.

"We're going to be asking y'all to stay inside as much as possible," the mayor said. "I know y'all can't do that all the time, but it'll help if you do it as much as you can."

"We've got to work," Herman Atwood shouted, jumping to his feet. He took off his dirty blue baseball cap and shook it at the mayor. "We can't stay inside. With this drought, we got more work than ever. Besides, Mr. Sibley was in his truck, and look what happened to him."

"We can't expect to stop living our lives," the mayor agreed calmly. "What we want to do first of all for y'all's benefit is reduce the risk."

"What are you going to do about solving the problem?" Alden McClain piped up. He was the owner of the video store and leader of the citizen's faction that opposed anything done by the mayor or the city council. His gray-blue eyes indicated he was ready to rally his troops against the mayor's suggestions if he didn't like what he heard.

"We may be witnessing a power play," Travis whispered.

"What's been done?" Alden demanded.

"We've had teams out hunting for the cat. We've got our police on this, we've got Deputy Holyfield from the sheriff's office, and we've had some consultation with the Wildlife and Fisheries people," the mayor answered, showing only a bit of fluster at having to tip his hand. His dissertation on what was being done was probably designed to come later in his discussion.

"Is that enough?" Alden persisted. "Maybe you need more people. What are we going to do? This is all crazy. How can people be safe anywhere?"

"That's why we're going to try to keep people inside," the mayor shot back, letting a sharpness creep into his

228

voice as a warning.

"We need to do something else," Alden said. "We need more people involved. We need to get organized. We need people with guns, and we need torches. Animals are afraid of fire."

"Hold on a minute," the mayor shouted. "Let's think this through. This thing has started because of the drought. Everything is dry around here. If you start running around with a bunch of torches, you're going to start a forest fire and wind up burning down the whole town, not to mention everybody's crops."

"Well, what can we do?" someone else demanded.

Briggs stepped forward. "Like we told you, remain calm. If everybody gets hysterical, we're going to have more than just the animals out there to worry about. I want you to remember this drought can't last forever. When it rains, our problem will take care of itself."

"With that cat still out there?" Alden asked. "He's tasted blood once."

"I don't think we need to be concerned about that sort of thing," Briggs said. "We don't need to borrow trouble."

Travis caught sight of something in his expression that troubled him. He'd seen cops get that expression before. It came when they knew something they couldn't tell. He found himself staring hard at Briggs, searching for some clue about what he might know.

Something was definitely bothering him. What did he know that nobody else did?

"Have you heard anything about the medical reports?" Travis asked, leaning down to whisper in Chrisk's ear.

"No." She cast a gaze over at him. "What's wrong?"

"Gut instinct."

As the squabble continued, a new voice rose above the crowd. It was hoarse, yet firm. "It's the Lord's will," the speaker called.

Heads turned until everyone realized it was William

Fendler Clark.

W.F., as he was known, stood up with a fistful of biblical tracts in his hand. He seldom ventured from the old shack where he lived, and most people were glad of it. His yard was piled with junk and trash which would have repulsed neighbors, if he'd had any. Everyone was thankful that he lived near some overgrown fields. He apparently saw no need of keeping his place up, since he expected the end of the world soon.

"It's a pestilence just like was brought on Sodom and Gomorrah," he shouted. "It's written that as it was in Noah's day, men will stray from the Lord, and they'll pay the price. The end is near."

He tried to get the people around him to accept little red and white pamphlets which predicted the end of the world by Rosh Hashanah in the fall.

Travis turned his attention back to Briggs, who had faded back a few steps to let the mayor handle a little more of the heat. The council sat quietly, grateful they had people out front to run interference.

"How long will it be before the animals overrun the town?" another resident called out.

W.F. attempted to answer with a reference to biblical prophecy, but he was drowned out by a call from another man across the room. This fellow was heavy-set and pissed off.

"We need the National Guard," he said. "That's our only hope. We've got to clear those woods of any vicious animals. If we don't, they might overrun the town."

At his side, his small son bowed his head with embarrassment at having his father become the center of attention.

Shouts continued to rise for another forty-five minutes as the mayor tried to get things under control.

He didn't have much success until every fear had been stated and reiterated and everyone had a chance to say his piece.

Finally, with little actually accomplished, the meeting began to break up. The mayor stood before the people, telling them the chief had the situation well in hand, while more and more walked out, shaking their heads.

When Travis saw the chief move from in front of the council dais and head back to his office, he followed him out the back way. He found him standing, shoulders slightly slumped, in the mayor's doorway.

The man looked up to see Travis approaching, and his expression was not cordial.

"I already took one beating in there," he said, trying to sound jovial. "If I'm going to be battered by the press, you might at least let your wife do it. She's better looking."

Travis gave a nod. "She's tied up with the crowd. I was wondering if you have any theories about this situation."

"Theories?"

Travis studied his expression and reaction and was ninety-eight-percent certain Briggs was hiding something.

"Is everything as it seems?" Travis asked. For the first time since the deaths had begun, he was beginning to feel his old intuition kick in. For the moment he was alive again, not just going through the motions.

Briggs turned away, looking toward the floor, bringing a hand up to rub the back of his neck.

Travis decided it was time to push.

"There was something in the medical reports, wasn't there?" he asked, playing his earlier hunch.

Briggs's face immediately turned toward Travis, his eyes wide in a "Who told you that?" query.

"What was it?" Travis asked. "Is there a person involved?"

"I don't know. It's inconclusive," Briggs said. "I can't answer any more questions. You better not come up with a bunch of crap in that newspaper of yours."

"Then come clean."

Briggs grabbed Trav's t-shirt and slammed him back against the wall. Trav hit the tile with a heavy force that jolted him like a charge of electricity.

"Don't push me. I've got a lot on my hands, and I don't need problems from you. If you stir things up, you'll have the Aimsley paper down on me and then the television stations."

"If there's something wrong, maybe that's what's needed," Travis said. "You're being left high and dry on this by other authorities."

"That's my problem, and you're just speculating." His eyes were wide and hard, and his face was only an inch away from Trav's.

"Am I? I've been in town long enough to see how things work. The sheriff has elections to think about, and the state police have problems of their own, between the state economy and what's going on in Baton Rouge with the new governor." He was summoning every piece of information that floated in his head, hoping the things he was right about might jar the chief's composure even further.

"Just be careful," Briggs said. "That's all I can tell you. Pass that on to your readers. I don't know what is going on here. I don't know how bad it is. All I can tell you is, it's strange."

Coming to his senses, the chief let go of Trav and backed away. But he looked at him for a long time. "I'm sorry," he said finally. "I got carried away. There's a lot of pressure right now."

"What is it you suspect?" Travis pressed.

The chief only shook his head and walked back into the mayor's office. "I've said more than I should already. I can't tell you anything because I don't know anything. Get out of here, Travis."

He closed the door, and before Travis could pursue it

rther, the council members began to swarm out of the
meeting room, where they'd been trapped by constituents
making demands of them.

Travis wandered back into the outer hallway, where the
others were waiting.

"That was a productive evening," Alison said. "What
did you learn back there?"

"I wish I knew," Travis said. "I wish I knew."

It was Langdon's hope that Danya might invite him in
for coffee at the small house she shared with her sister.
He'd had his mind on other things for the last few days,
but his thoughts never wandered far from his loneliness. If
he invited him in, it might mean she was interested in
him. And that might lead to other things.

He had known Danya a long time, and he didn't think
he looked down on him as much as some of the other
town girls did.

He was trying desperately to break his backwoods legacy
and find a nice girl to settle down with, or at least to release
a little passion with.

Being in law enforcement alienated him from his past.
In spite of his pent-up desire and lust, he didn't much care
for going back to the limp-haired girls in faded print
dresses that he had known in his adolescence. He was
interested in different things now.

He was banking on the fact that Danya didn't have a
date on a Saturday night, it might mean she was available,
or at least not serious about anybody.

He knew she saw a lot of people coming through the
video store, but he hoped she didn't find any of them
interesting. After all, what did they have to offer,
compared to him? He was a man of action. He'd been
involved in the hunt for the killer panther, and he was the
protector of Bristol Springs. He'd come up from the dirt to

take his place in the town, and that earned him som
respect, to his way of thinking. He deserved a nice girl i
his life.

He made a few jokes as they moved along, but Dany
didn't smile. She just kept chewing her gum. This mad
him nervous, because it seemed to indicate he was no
impressing her.

That made him try harder, and it only increased hi
nervousness.

No matter what he tried, she didn't say much except ye
and no.

It was not that far to her house. He saw hope slippin
away. She walked along with her arms folded around som
tapes she was carrying, her expression stoic.

He watched her unchanging countenance as the
walked along, in and out of street lights and shadows. Hi
sense of futility continued to grow. By the time the
reached her door, he realized he was in a hopeless state

He told her good night with a brief smile. She echoed hi
comment, sans smile. She really had just wanted him fo
protection.

Dejected, he walked back down the steps of her porcl
and put his hands in his pockets as he moved back alon
the walk.

At the front gate, he turned back toward Main Street.

He was looking down, so he didn't see the dog emerg
from the shadows. He was almost on top of it before it
growl made him stop in his tracks.

It was a large black animal, a mixture of several breed
that didn't go well together. Its huge white teeth wer
bared as if in warning, and its growl came from dee
within its body.

He started to take a step backward and heard anothe
growl from behind. In turning he found another dog, a
German shepherd he recognized as belonging to Rutl
Beauboeuf. It was normally kept indoors, but now it wa

nleashed and appeared as dangerous as the first beast,
vhich he supposed to be wild.

Flight in any direction was impossible, and to one side
he white picket fence which bordered Danya's yard
locked his path. His only option was to move into the
treet.

As he prepared to turn, another dog showed up, a
nongrel with grayish fur. Like the first, it hunched low,
ts jaws clenched tightly.

It was ready to kill him if he moved.

Danya stepped through the front door into the darkened
ront room, turning the latch back instinctively. The
ouse was quiet; her sister was not back yet.

Without turning on the light, she moved on into the
iving room and shrugged off her shoulder bag.

She'd brought some tapes home from the store, but she
lidn't feel like watching anything right away. She was too
ired to concentrate. Placing the small plastic boxes on top
of the television, she walked back to the hallway.

The mail rested on a table where her sister must have left
it. She thumbed through it quickly, finding little of
interest.

She kicked off her shoes, intending to go into her
bedroom and change into pajamas in order to relax.
Staying on her feet behind the counter at the store all day
had a way of taking its toll.

Unhooking her belt, she pulled her dress over her head
and draped it over her arm as she went into the hallway.

She was moving in darkness. She'd lived all her life in
the house, so she didn't feel any need to turn on the lights.
Her sense of danger had stopped at the front door.

There were no animals inside.

As she walked along the hallway, she heard a plank in
the hardwood floor creak.

A woman stood at the end of the hallway, almost invisible in the darkness except for her white dress.

Seeing her, Danya stopped with a start, almost swallowing her gum. She quickly pulled her dress in front of her, holding it against her body.

"Who are you?" she whispered, unable to make any louder sound.

"A friend. Just call me a friend."

The woman reached out and took her hand. For some reason, Danya did not feel the need to resist. The woman seemed to need something, something only Danya could offer.

Langdon tried to remain completely still, with his hands out at his sides. The dogs' eyes were locked on him, and he feared any move might make them pounce.

He began moving his right hand a fraction of an inch at a time, easing it toward his body.

The dogs slobbered, strings of saliva dropping from the corners of their mouths. Their feet were flat on the pavement, their traction firm.

Langdon lifted his hand until it rested on the handle of his revolver.

The dogs continued to growl. Their teeth gleamed through the darkness.

He yanked the weapon from the holster, trying to level it at the dog in the street.

Before he could squeeze off a shot, the German shepherd had launched itself. Its teeth sank into the flesh of his upper arm, causing him to cry out in anguish.

He let go of the gun, and the force of the dog's body dragged him to one side.

He landed on his left shoulder and began to shake his arm in an effort to disengage the dog.

Its teeth were holding fast. It was determined. He began

to swat at it with his hand as a few drops of blood spilled off his arm.

Then, without apparent reason, it stopped and backed off, turning suddenly to scurry away into the darkness.

He rolled back on the pavement and looked up to see Danya staring down at him. The night breeze swept around her, playing with strands of her hair and pulling at the hem of her short robe, which she held closed in front of her.

"You'd better come inside and let me have a look at that," she said.

Alison stood at the mirror in her bathroom, brushing her hair, unable to find an arrangement that satisfied her. She had been distracted during the excitement of the meeting and Trav's burst of investigation. He was finding the spark again.

Now, at home, her sense of frustration returned. Her hair was such a problem. It frizzed in the wrong places or framed her face in a way that seemed to accent the length of her nose.

She threw her brush down and stepped away from the mirror, unsure of what she was trying to achieve.

Her summer robe hung limp about her frame, shapeless and faded. She eased the cloth off her shoulders, letting it flutter to the floor. In the stark white rays of the fluorescent light over the mirror, her skin appeared so pale that it was almost transparent. Veins were visible beneath her flesh, and here and there tiny moles or freckles seemed to stand out.

Her breasts were small, almost nonexistent, her hips not so developed as she might have hoped. Her frame was almost straight. Travis had never found her unattractive, yet she couldn't help wondering.

Lifting her hair back with her hands, she studied her

face, turning it from side to side.

Would other men find her pretty? Or did men really matter, anyway? There was more to life than men.

She flipped off the light and walked through the doorway into the bedroom, where Travis was propped up on the pillows reading a paperback.

He looked up, a bit surprised to see her. She hadn't come to bed naked in quite some time, but she approached him brazenly, tugging his reading glasses from his face and running her hands over his cheeks and then down across his shoulders and chest.

He did not resist, although he was a bit confused by the abruptness. She smothered him with kisses, pushing him back on the pillows and climbing on top of him.

They quickly entwined, and in moments, she impaled herself on him, pursuing the act roughly and with an aggression rare to her. It was not like the tender couplings in which they usually engaged, and there seemed to be something artificial about it as well. They were like strangers completing some act of mutual need with mechanical efficiency.

She did not think of Travis at all. There was almost no feeling from either of them. It was perhaps the most impersonal moment of their lives together. She tilted her head back, letting her thoughts wander to other things, far away from Bristol Springs.

The climax was uneventful, an ending that took both of them unawares.

Finally she rolled off him, slipping beneath the covers and rolling onto one shoulder so that her back was toward Travis.

He started to speak, then flopped onto his own side of the bed to deal with his confusion in silence.

Chapter 21

The sun was bright on Sunday, too bright for a funeral. The blue skies and golden light seemed better suited for some jovial activity, not for mourning the passing of a young girl.

Everyone had stayed after church for the services, then followed the procession of cars out to the cemetery.

Chrisk stood among the ranks of the mourners, trying to deal with the emptiness she felt. A lump had formed in her throat, but she was not crying.

Across from her, Chief Briggs's daughter, Julie, was not so controlled. Tears streamed down her face as she continued to sniffle without making any effort to wipe them away.

Danya was crying also and clinging to Doug Langdon's arm for support. Chrisk raised her eyesbrows at that. She knew Langdon had been lusting after every woman in Bristol Springs for ages, but she'd heard no indication that he was having any success with Danya.

The last she'd heard, Danya had been dating a pipe fitter from Penn's Ferry. You learned new things at funerals.

Estelle Johnson sat in a chair across from the coffin. Her eyes were moist, but she was not crying. Her face was like a death mask. She showed almost no emotion.

Chrisk observed the woman who sat beside her, Neva, the one who was becoming a friend to Alison. The woman held Mrs. Johnson's hand, gripping it gently to offer support.

As Burns spoke the final words of his graveside service, Chrisk studied the two women, uncertain of the bond between them.

She sensed something more than just a family relationship. The dependence Mrs. Johnson was showing to her cousin seemed to be greater than that.

Chrisk had not met or talked with Neva, but there was something about the woman she disliked. She could not say exactly what it was. It was not jealousy of her beauty, nor was it anything Neva did. Chrisk just didn't care for her or trust her. She was not usually given to instant dislikes of people, so she couldn't really understand it.

Suddenly, the woman turned her head toward Chrisk. Their eyes locked. The stare with which the woman gazed upon Chrisk was cold and piercing, malevolent.

An icy feeling touched Chrisk, and she averted her eyes. The discomfort was immediate. She felt as if the woman were looking straight through her, or deeply into her, perhaps, seeing her soul.

Raising her hands, she rubbed her shoulders. In spite of the June heat and the stiff material of her black dress, she felt like she was standing in a January wind.

She tried to ignore the situation and concentrate on the words the priest was speaking. It was difficult.

She turned back to Neva, but the woman was no longer watching her. Her attention seemed to be back on Estelle.

Burns's voice lifted slightly as he reached the conclusion of his sermon, and Chrisk turned her attention back to him. "We watch the passing of our loved one with comfort in the knowledge that God has promised us eternal life through his son Jesus Christ," he said, closing

240

his small Bible as he finished speaking.

People began to disperse. Some of them walked by to pat Estelle on the shoulder, while others passed by the casket. It had not been open for any of the proceedings. Chrisk realized many of the people were imagining what must be concealed within.

Chrisk moved along the row of flower sprays, surreptitiously studying Mrs. Johnson and her guest through the leaves.

Neva stood stoically behind Estelle, watching the people who muttered words of comfort. Some of them offered to drop by the house, but Neva politely declined.

"Estelle needs to rest right now," she said.

As soon as possible, she hoisted Mrs. Johnson from her chair and began to usher her across the stretch of gravesites toward the roadway where the cars were parked.

Chrisk eased from behind the flowers and followed, watching Neva place her arm around Mrs. Johnson's shoulders, walking her along.

"Are you practicing your surveillance skills?" Burns asked.

She turned abruptly.

"Just watching," she said, forcing a smile. "I guess it's not anything suspicious. Travis has me trained to be on my toes."

"I find it a little peculiar too," Burns said, stopping beside her to watch the pair get into Estelle's car. Mrs. Johnson climbed behind the wheel.

"You'd think her cousin would drive her," Burns said.

"We're all jumpy in light of what's going on," Chrisk said.

"And we've lived safely in our little community here so long, we have a fear of outsiders," Burns said.

*   *   *

241

The argument between Travis and Alison started after lunch. Finances served as the catalyst, but it quickly deteriorated into a discussion about other problems.

"I don't know what it is," Alison said as they moved into the living room. "I just feel so much pressure suddenly. It's like I'm trapped."

Travis was silent for a while, unsure of what to say. "Is it the paper?" he asked. "If it is, we can stop joking around and get out from under it."

"I don't know if it's the paper or you or what. I'm just wondering if I've made some wrong choices."

"What do you mean?" He held out his hands, trying to understand. She pulled away from him, clenching her fists in frustration. "I don't know," she said. "I can't explain it. I've never been anywhere. I've never done anything but work. I've always accepted that as the way it had to be. The way I was brought up, you had to go out and get a job and work, and you didn't think about things like fulfillment.

"Maybe there's something out there, something better. I've never looked for it. In the last few days it's become more apparent. I feel trapped, like I don't know what I want anymore. I thought I knew, I thought I understood my life. Now I'm not so certain." Tears were beginning to form in her eyes. It surprised Travis.

"This has just developed?" he asked. "It hasn't been building or anything?"

"Maybe. I'm just beginning to feel it. There are things I want to do with my life. I want to be alive. I want to feel alive."

"Look, I can start making calls. I've felt a little trapped by the paper myself. I thought covering the deaths would wake me up, but it hasn't. We can find a buyer and probably turn a little profit. Then we can travel, if you want."

She plopped onto the couch, crying as she pulled her

242

legs under her. "I don't know if that's what I want either."

Trav's mouth dropped open slightly. "Is it me? Have I done something?" He closed his eyes, as if that allowed him to look inside himself. "I've thrown myself into the paper too much, I guess."

"It's not that. I've always worried about you being happy here. The paper has been a joint effort all along. Travis, don't blame yourself. You and I have always been equals. I just don't know if I belong in this life. Maybe I shouldn't be married."

Travis ran his hands through his hair, letting it fall down around his face. He was halfway between hurt and anger and not sure of how to deal with the feelings.

The one thing he had always counted on was his relationship with Alison. Amidst everything—the turmoil on the crime beat and the difficulties at the *Gazette*—that had been the stabilizing force.

Now it was wavering, and he did not like the feeling. It was a threat of a return to the loneliness he had known before Alison. He was reminded of the emptiness he had felt when she was not a part of his life, back when he had believed there would never be someone to share things with.

Back when he had believed there would be no one for him to love.

Julie Briggs could not contain her guilt when she returned home from the funeral. She had spoken to no one about her knowledge of Lou Ellen's date with the biker the night of the attack, but she could not rid herself of the feeling that she was somehow responsible.

She kept thinking that she should have told her father when he set out to look for the girl. She lay on her bed staring up at the ceiling, remembering Lou Ellen.

243

It had always been fun to be around her. Julie remembered times they had cut classes to sneak behind the gym and try cigarettes, and the times they'd sat in the bleachers after school talking about boys.

She could not believe the remains of her friend's body were now in the big metal box they had carried to the cemetery.

The tears which had begun at the graveside continued. She listened to the wind and wondered if heaven was real.

When she rose and walked into the kitchen for lack of anywhere better to go, she could hear her father snoring in his bedroom.

His Sunday afternoon naps were always deep and noisy. He took them after church because he liked to make a few passes around the town after Sunday supper just to make sure everything was quiet.

She walked on through the kitchen and out the front door without disturbing him. He wouldn't wake for several hours, and she planned to be back by then. It wouldn't take long for her to go over and speak with Mrs. Johnson.

She hoped it would ease her conscience a little bit.

Chrisk went back by the office after the funeral and sat at the computer, where she began working on a column. Travis had encouraged her to try anything she wanted, so she worked at the keyboard for a while, striving to come up with something that captured the feelings of loss the funeral had conjured.

After a half hour she found she wasn't quite creating what she'd wanted. The feeling of sadness did not translate into words in the way she had hoped.

She spaced down a few lines and absently tapped out a stream-of-consciousness passage.

WHAT HAS CAUSED THE FRENZY FROM THE ANIMALS?

WHY DO THINGS SUDDENLY SEEM SO STRANGE? NOTHING EVER HAPPENS HERE IN HOOTERVILLE.

WHO IS OUR MYSTERIOUS VISITOR?

She paused a moment and looked at that last line. It seemed to sum up much of what she had been wondering all afternoon.

WHO IS NEVA? JUST A WOMAN. ALI LIKES HER, SO WHAT'S THE BIG DEAL? SO SHE HAS A BITCH OF A STARE.

She pushed herself away from the terminal, and walked over to the coffeepot, and set it to brew.

It was ridiculous to be suspicious of someone for no reason. Reporters were supposed to deal in facts, not suppositions. What did Neva stand to gain from coming here if it wasn't just to comfort a relative in a time of need?

Estelle Johnson didn't have anything worth snatching away in a confidence game.

Was there any other gain she might be missing? She drummed her fingers on the counter while she watched the coffee drip.

What other treasures did Bristol Springs have to offer?

When the coffee was ready she returned to the computer and entered those questions beneath her others.

She had nothing, she decided when she scrolled over the material.

WHAT DOES BRISTOL SPRINGS HAVE

TO OFFER? IT'S DYING. THERE'S NOTHING HERE. IT'S THE MIDDLE OF NOWHERE. YOU CAN SEE NOWHERE ON BOTH SIDES.

She scrolled up a few more lines, deciding to play with something else for a while before going home. She would make the trip to Aimsley tomorrow to check out the microfilm.

WHO DIED BEFORE?

Her imagination played a little.

WERE THEY VICTIMS OF THE WOMAN BE-NEATH THE WAVES?

The statue was continuing to take shape, and Blade seemed to have developed an affinity for the work. He stood beside the pile of shavings wiping his brow with a handkerchief as Navarra approached through the evening shadows. She was dressed in her white gown.

"It is becoming beautiful," she said, running her delicate fingertips over the gentle curves of the figure's face.

"Am I doing it right?"

"Perfect. As good as any of the craftsmen or artisans from my past could have done." She turned to him and placed a hand on his face. "You have never done this before?"

"I played with clay when I was a kid . . . not much more. I guess I just had a talent I didn't know about. I've been trying to follow the picture you put in my mind."

"You are amazing, David Pearson. You achieve as I might have hoped and more."

She kissed him gently on the lips, then walked back to the doorway.

The darkness was complete now, and she exulted in the feeling of the night. Raising her hands, she let the night's energy flow into her, breathing deeply and closing her eyes.

She could feel the forces of nature pulsing through the atmosphere, and she sensed the life essence of everything around her—the plants, the animals, and the people. The oracle was working its magic. "I grow stronger," she whispered, and then she stepped forward through the doorway, disappearing into the night.

W.F. Clark's shack was on the edge of town. It sat back on a lot overgrown with weeds and littered with tin cans and hubcaps.

The trash had been allowed to pile up, and bags of garbage lay along one corner of the yard. Some of them had been torn open, and there was a stench of decaying food.

A worn out and forgotten Ford shell rusted on the front lawn. Thick clumps of grass sprouted through the section where the windshield had been, and weeds poked out through the headlight wells.

Beyond the car, the house sagged like a gray cloud of smoke. The faded timber seemed ready to splinter and collapse, with the tin roof, now covered with oxide dust that made it a reddish color, balanced precariously on top of it all.

The council had discussed condemnation of the place from time to time, but whenever anyone approached W.F. with such a notion, he screamed at them and shouted them away with rebukes from the Old Testament.

Sitting in his living room, he read by the oil lamp which cast a faint orange glow over the room. He was going through some pamphlets about various topics of concern to fundamentalists.

W.F. donated money to a variety of causes, from television ministries to Bible translators.

Some were legitimate and some were con games, but W.F. had little ability to discern between them. He worried about the trilateral commission and read supermarket tabloids.

He'd seen a couple of UFOs over Miller's field, which stretched out at the end of his street, and he'd considered sending a letter to the theaters in Aimsley, asking them not to show *The Last Temptation of Christ*, which he'd heard about on the religious radio station.

An old southern gospel album played on his phonograph in the corner of the room, and the sounds of old, familiar hymns filled his ears.

He hadn't felt strong enough to go to evening services, so he sought solace in memories of old sermons that the tunes recalled.

He'd grown up going to church services and camp meetings. Now, as he grew older and his health declined, he sought refuge in his religion. It was all he had since his wife had died. It was enough.

He was oblivious to the condition of his home and his yard. He didn't worry about intrusions from the elements or other forces of nature, and the cracks in his walls which let daylight through didn't concern him.

People seldom saw him except on occasions like the council meeting. He spent most of his time reading or watching the small gray images on his portable television set. And praying. He prayed a lot and talked to his dead relatives. He knew that God let them hear him, and he thought of the day when he would be called to join them in their heavenly home.

Putting aside his tracts, he picked up the dusty and cracked family album, which contained pictures of himself as a younger man. He looked at shots from the fifties, when he'd been younger. He smiled for the camera, flanked by his hunting dogs.

There were pictures of the wedding also, and of him and his wife Sally as they prepared to leave for their honeymoon. Flipping through the pages he found reminders of his children, too.

A tear streamed down his cheek as he remembered Sally. So much time had passed since he had seen her, since the Lord had called her home.

Poor Sally. The cancer had ravaged her. Asbestosis, they had called it. She'd gotten it from the wallpaper in the farmhouse.

There were so many bad things. Perhaps it was running away from them that had driven W.F. so deeply into his faith.

He turned to another page and found a young Sally standing on the front porch of that old home. She wore her blue dress and waved at the camera.

He swallowed. That had been taken with his old Kodak in 1959. She was so pretty there.

He hovered over the picture, studying the faded colors, contemplating the memories it conjured. After they had taken the picture, they had gone inside and had their dinner in the kitchen with the children.

How long ago that had been. It seemed like another lifetime.

W.F. was so engrossed with the past that he did not notice the sounds around him. There were always sounds in his creaking old house. He had learned to shut them out because they had no meaning for him.

He turned another page, and a loose photo slipped from beneath its photo corners to the floor. He heard the floor creak. His eyes spied the feet standing near the doorway, and he looked up to face the woman.

Her beauty was striking, enough to take his breath away, and the first thing that crossed his mind was that she was an angel. As he looked into her eyes, he realized that was not the case.

He licked his lips and clutched his photo album against his chest, as if it might protect him.

"What do you want?" he asked.

"I came to see you." She took a step forward, reaching out with one hand as if to touch his face.

"Stay back," he warned.

"Don't you want my touch?" she asked.

"No. You ain't something pure."

"What am I?" she asked, smiling.

"I don't rightly know, but you ain't good. I can tell that."

"You sense that?"

"The Lord tells me what is good."

"Who do you worship?"

"I'm a child of the King. I am a child of God. I am washed in the blood of the Lamb."

She raised her eyebrows.

"I am saved by the name of Jesus."

"Ah," she nodded slightly. "You are touched by the Nazarene."

"He came to judge the quick and the dead."

"I remember. I was alive when he was born. You could feel the force of the universe change. I cursed that day."

Dropping his album, W.F. ran across the room, grabbing at the bookshelves which sagged on one wall.

He was off balance, so he stumbled and grabbed at the shelves. That dragged them down with him.

The shelves dumped their contents onto his head. Books and old letters and other clutter rained down into a pile around him.

He began pushing with his feet to try to right himself. His back pressed back against the wall.

Navarra stood without moving.

He scraped around in the rubble until he found what he

vanted, the old cross that Sally had worn around her neck.

Raising it in Navarra's direction, he squinted, hoping it vould drive her away.

Instead, she stepped forward. "Your symbol is not nough. It represents, but it does not act alone. Your priests and holy men have always thought the symbols to be enough. They threw holy water on us and thought it vould protect them."

"I ain't no papist. I'm a believer."

When he spoke, she wavered slightly and readjusted her balance. Something seemed to have caused a disturbance n her calm demeanor.

He kept the cross in front of him and began trying to struggle to his feet. She turned away, lifting an arm in ront of her face.

He took a step toward her, then another.

"Leave this place," he demanded, drawing even closer o her now hunched form. She seemed to be cowering from him.

He stepped even closer, intending to touch her with the cross.

She wheeled around smiling, laughing as she hit his and to send the cross flying. It sailed across the room and clattered against the wall.

Then, with a wild scream, Navarra grabbed his shoulders and shoved him backward. He stumbled over his feet and crashed to the floor.

The rats were waiting. They scurried from the shadows as he thrashed about, trying to get his hands under him to lift himself.

A large black rat with oily fur which stood up across its back charged out from a hiding place and sank its teeth into his right hand. Like little needles, they cut into the webbed spot at the base of his thumb, giving it a grip as he began to shake.

The next rat was smaller but more vicious. It had not eaten recently, and it rushed in and found a spot on his other arm. He began to shake that one as well.

He was making no progress when the next team moved in, wood rats almost big enough to be mistaken for opossum.

They scurried onto his legs and ran up toward his stomach, their tiny paws clawing at the cloth of his shirt until the flesh was exposed.

It was soft and wrinkled skin, and they wasted no time in beginning to rip at it with their teeth.

The skin peeled back quickly, spurting blood over their gray fur as they began to devour muscle and fat.

A small rat ran up his pants leg and began to chew at the back of his knee, tearing flesh and biting into a vein which uncorked a fresh stream of blood. It sprayed out like a hose, soaking into the cloth of his pants.

The next string of attackers joined the rats at his stomach area, which was now ripped open. They were burrowing into the gaping hole, gnawing at the exposed tissue and almost swimming in blood and other juices.

More of his shirt ripped open as other rats rushed in, their teeth cutting along the sides of his ribs.

His head rolled to one side, and his tortured eyes spotted the cats, his cats, standing near the corner. There were grays and tabbies, one that was half Persian. They were watching.

Lifting his hand, he beckoned them with outstretched fingers.

Slowly they began to move. They padded out of the corner toward him. He began to weep. They would end the torture for him, certainly. They had preyed on the rats daily. They were natural enemies.

He watched their small feet prance across the floor until they were upon him, and then their teeth began to sink into him as well. Next came their claws, shredding skin.

252

They ignored the rats, working instead on their master's body.

They steered clear of his throat, leaving Navarra room at his neck. He screamed when her teeth touched his flesh.

She pulled back, bright red fluid running across her chin. A smile crossed her lips.

"Bless you," she said, and then returned to her feeding.

Chapter 22

Travis went in to work alone early on Monday morning. He had slept—or at least spent the night—on the couch, and he and Alison had not spoken when daylight found them.

He had decided he needed to do the work anyway. Unshaven and bleary-eyed, he had headed for the office. The future of the *Gazette* was not bright, but he had to think of its readers. In spite of his personal problems, the subscribers were entitled to what they paid for.

The argument, or the discussion, as he preferred to think of it, had lingered only a brief while before it dropped into silence. Neither he nor Alison was sure of what they would do next, whether they would arrive at some way to remain together.

He hated the idea of her leaving. It ached in his chest, as if a cold piece of stone was lodged in his heart. Coming as it had, without warning, made the hurt even more acute.

Chrisk showed up around nine, wearing jeans and a t-shirt. Her hair was tied in a ponytail on the side, which made her look more hip than ever.

"How's it going?" she asked.

Travis tried to offer a smile. The effort wasn't quite successful. Finally he shrugged.

"What's wrong?"

He ran a hand through his hair. "Ali and I had a fight."

"Oh? Finances again?"

He hadn't intended to discuss it with Chrisk, but he threw up his hands. "I don't think so. She's going through a crisis."

"It'll work out. You guys are too perfect to split up."

"I hope that's true. I wish I knew what to do." His face was pale, and his eyes seemed sunken in their sockets.

For the first time she realized he must be talking about something more than a spat. "Give it time. Maybe Reverend Burns can talk to you guys."

"I don't know. I'll worry about it later. Right now we've got to get a paper together."

"I was going to go over to Aimsley and look up those articles my grandfather mentioned. I could stick around to help here."

"No. The idea sounds good. Let's get it. People will be interested in it . . . maybe."

"You're sure? Trav, if you want me to, I can stick around. We could talk."

He smiled at her. Her face was always so bright and vibrant. "Thanks," he said, "but I'm okay. Really."

She got a notebook from a desk and tucked it into her handbag. "If you insist on wearing your Charles Bronson face, I'll be back this afternoon."

"See you then."

He turned back to the layout he'd been playing with. The pain in his chest was almost debilitating, but he managed to suppress it enough to continue. He'd survived pain before.

He was still huddled over his work when the phone rang. It was his friend from LSU, telling him the arrangements had worked out for **Chrisk's** scholarship.

255

It was good news, but he couldn't find any enthusiasm.

He thanked his friend and hung up. At least he'd have some good news for Chrisk when she returned.

Not everybody's life had to fall apart.

When Langdon called in sick, Briggs almost hit the ceiling. He was up to his ears in trouble and filled with anger over the confrontation with Alden, not to mention the fact that Julie had been acting strangely since the funeral.

Without Langdon, he'd have to patrol the town himself and keep in touch with Holyfield in case there was trouble. That meant postponing any cat hunts.

Was there no end to this trouble? He sat in his office looking over the medical reports on the first two deaths. The paperwork had finally arrived. It provided little in the way of answers, and comparing Doc's report with the findings from Bossier City didn't help a great deal.

Briggs was still troubled by the unexplained blood loss. There was no reason for it. He'd quizzed the doctor about it repeatedly without obtaining a satisfactory answer.

He didn't know where to turn, and if he didn't come up with something soon, he knew he was going to have a vigilante group to deal with.

If he wasn't able to keep control, the sheriff's office would have to be called in.

Not to mention the fact that Travis Dixon seemed to have some idea that something was out of the ordinary. If Trav printed something wild in the paper on Thursday, that would really put things out of control.

He was about to get his second cup of coffee when Alden showed up. He was wearing his standard plaid shirt and blue jeans, and the outfit made him look like a cowboy ready for a gunfight.

"Morning, Alden," Briggs said, trying to seem as

256

rdial as possible. "Coffee?"

"Don't play games with me," Alden said, leveling a
nger at him. "You know what I'm here about."

"What do you want me to do, Alden? Langdon is sick.
olyfield is on patrol, and the cat is long gone. I can't
oot every other animal in the world that might get
irsty."

"You ever thought of calling in some kind of animal
pert? Not from Wildlife and Fisheries, but from one of
nem big zoos or something? You know as well as I do,
nimals hardly ever attack people, and it's happening
erywhere you look around here. People are going to start
noving away, and the town's about to go belly-up as it is."

"A good rain would solve a lot of problems. You want to
o a dance, Alden?"

"You takin' me lightly?"

"It's a very grave situation. What can I tell you? Just the
ther day in Florida an alligator got a little girl. He'd come
p out of the canals looking for a mate. There's a lot we
ust don't understand about animals."

"I'll tell you what's to understand—you don't get
omething done, I'm gonna organize a vigilance commit-
ee."

"Alden, will you calm down? You're just going to create
nore problems if you go off half-cocked."

"You listen to me, Briggs. This is a serious matter. You
et one more person die, and we're going to do something
about it."

"What do you want me to do? Round up all the animals
n town? I've just got the one jail cell."

"Screw your sarcasm. You ain't gonna be laughing
ong. You get that straight."

Alden turned and clomped out of the store, his heavy
cowboy boots rattling against the hardwood floor.

"Just remember those X-rated video tapes you keep in
your back room are illegal in this parish, even if you rent

257

them only to preferred customers," Briggs said under his breath.

Alison sat alone in her bedroom, wondering about what she would do next. The explosion the night before had surprised her as much as it had Travis. Although the feelings had been boiling in her heart for the past couple of days, she hadn't really expected them to come to a head so suddenly.

She didn't want to hurt Travis in the process of trying to work out her own problems. He had never done anything intentionally wrong, had never given her reason to mistrust him, and had never had a wandering eye, like some of the husbands of her friends.

In so many ways he had lived up to all her dreams. The sudden discovery that things were not right still made her feel dizzy and confused.

She got up from her chair and slipped on her jeans. She would have to talk to Travis more. There were things they had to work out in addition to the newspaper.

She would go in to the paper in the afternoon and help him put out the edition for this week. There might be friction, but the paper had to be published.

She paused, remembering that a week ago she had felt content. She must have been dense to have been so easily deluded.

She walked through the house, enjoying the effects of the sunlight streaming in. She and Travis would also have to leave the house. The things she did not want to give up she could stow at her cousin's until she was ready to send for them, once she was established somewhere.

She'd have to get her résumé ready. With a sigh, she admitted to herself she would probably have to stay here longer than a week. She couldn't just strike off to parts unknown without at least some kind of hint at a job

oortunity. There were no savings around the Dixon
usehold.

Wiping a tear from her eye, she realized how badly she
eded to talk to Neva. Neva's advice had brought her this
. She would know what was appropriate.

Navarra slept.

It was a trancelike state, and the others sat around her in
e darkened chamber which had once been a shower
om at the old resort. She had gathered her protectors.

Between work on the statue and the construction of the
mple, Blade had sealed the skylight and constructed a
adle-like bed for her, using discarded benches and other
ms from the resort's rooms. The beds had been cleared
it along with most other items, but enough things
mained to make salvage practical.

Candles set up on a pair of stands provided the only
ow in the room. It was golden and warm as it touched
e dark shadows.

Some sheets and pillows from Estelle's house had been
ded to make the new bedchamber almost elegant.

The tiled walls and exposed pipes were still stark and
nappealing, but Estelle had done her best during the
ght. She had come there with Navarra under cover of
rkness. Working had done much to take her mind off the
neral. She felt little remorse now. She felt little of
ything except a desire to befriend Navarra.

Estelle did not blame the visitor for her daughter's
ath. She now understood the necessity, and she saw that
r daughter had fulfilled a purpose. She did not
nderstand it all yet, but she knew something was to
appen, something important and lasting. Just knowing
at Lou Ellen had been a part of it was comforting.

Blade's adoration was continuing. He was stunned by
avarra's beauty as she slept. Her face was peaceful and

perfect in the glow of the candles.

He wanted to touch her again and trace the lines of her face, but he refrained. It would not be appropriate in presence of the others.

For now he was a guardian and nothing more. would protect her as long as she was vulnerable. He kn she feared the daylight, when others might come to do harm, and he accepted this duty as part of his knighthoo During the course of preparing the statue, he had al fashioned a club for himself. It was from a sturdy piece oak, and he practiced twirling and fencing with it. would wield it well when the skill was needed. He h made certain of that.

The club rested now in the crook of his arm, ready if should need it.

Julie was still a bit confused by it all. Little had be said to her about what was going on. She was drawn by t sense of awe that she felt for Navarra. The image rebellion against all things hung over the dark wom like an aura. It appealed to Julie, and it soothed her.

The touch of Navarra's thoughts had warmed her a excited her. Nebulous concepts of the darkness filled h thoughts, and an eternity seemed to expand before her

She closed her eyes, wondering what would transpire the next few days. She was told things would happen soo as soon as the oracle was complete and ready to chann power and energy into Navarra's grasp.

None of them turned when Langdon walked throug the darkness. His footsteps were soft, and he did not spea

Dressed now in his civilian clothes, jeans, and a loos fitting cotton shirt, he did not intimidate anyone as lawman. They could sense he too was an ally.

The circle of protectors was growing. Navarra woul not be destroyed as easily as she had been before. She ha taken care to assemble a powerful group, a group that wa strong in its essence and capable of striking at th weaknesses of her enemies.

Langdon provided another important link in the chain which surrounded the small group's leader: he carried a gun beneath the folds of the loose-fitting shirt.

Anyone wishing to penetrate the circle would be facing a formidable task.

Chapter 23

Chrisk's ride to Aimsley was a hot one as the summer sun climbed toward its meridian. Only the wind whipping around the small bike kept her from being drenched in perspiration on the trip along the black ribbon of highway which led out of Bristol Springs.

When she reached downtown Aimsley, she was already tired and thirsty. She stopped for a Coca-Cola at a little drugstore before heading to the library.

As she sipped it down, she reasoned that at least she was having a different kind of Monday.

She found herself thinking of Travis as she sat on the bike in front of the store. She didn't want bad things to happen between Trav and Alison. They were her friends.

She hoped things would be patched up by the time she got back to the office.

There were several smaller library branches around the outskirts of the small city, but she knew only the main branch would be likely to have what she needed. She didn't rule out the possibility that she would return home empty-handed, because she had learned there were always gaps in research materials.

She walked through the glass doors and managed to attract the attention of a librarian.

The woman looked like the classic archetype, with a severe white blouse and a dark skirt.

Her gray-streaked hair was pulled back into a bun, and she wore wire-rimmed glasses which had a tendency to slip down her nose. She introduced herself as Miss Gilchrist.

"What can I do for you?" she asked.

"I needed to see if you would have back issues of the old *Bristol Springs Gazette*," Chrisk said.

The woman's eyes brightened as if she were glad to hear a request she could fulfill. "Oh yes. We have microfilm of all the area newspapers." She started to take a step, pointing toward the circulation desk. "Let me get the key to the cabinet."

Chrisk held up her hand to stop her. "I think I should tell you that I need to look way, way back."

The woman hesitated. "To what date?"

Chrisk bit her lower lip and raised her eyebrows, almost hesitant to speak for fear of finding a negative answer.

"How about the 1860s?" she said.

"The *Gazette* hasn't been published continuously since then," the librarian said.

"I know that. I'm looking for something specific. I work for the *Gazette* today and this goes back further than our file copies."

The librarian ran a finger thoughtfully across her chin. "That does stretch back. I'm not sure if any of those editions have been available for copying. Our best bet would be to check the basement."

She disappeared through a doorway and returned a few moments later with a key attached to a huge metal loop.

"I'll help you look," she told Chrisk.

She led the way down the darkened stairway into the musty old underground chamber. It reminded Chrisk of a cave: the floor was bare concrete and the walls were bland, except for a few ten-year-old posters which encouraged reading.

A forgotten coffee urn sat in one corner, and along another wall stood a row of old green dented file cabinets.

They strolled past several which were marked *Aimsley Daily Clarion*, then past a few more which held other papers. Finally they reached a couple of cabinets which were labeled *Gazette*.

A brief check revealed they didn't contain anything before 1890, the era when the paper had become permanently established.

Chrisk's disappointment showed on her face. She started to turn, but the librarian touched her shoulder.

"That doesn't mean we should give up hope," she said.

"Do you know of somewhere else I might find some?" Chrisk asked.

"I might," Miss Gilchrist said. "Let's go make a phone call."

Chrisk rode her moped through the afternoon traffic with calm skill, threading in and out of congestion and making fairly good time as she traveled across town.

The house she was looking for was on the far side of Aimsley. She followed Mason Street until it gave way to the residential streets in Fenton Park, the elegant section of large houses with wrought-iron fences and cobblestone driveways. Majestic oaks loomed over the roadway like guardian giants.

She found the house she was looking for on a slight hill and steered through the open gate. She pulled up the circular drive and parked beside a huge old oak tree that stretched its branches over the roofline of the structure providing deep shade.

She used the heavy brass knocker at the front door, and after a few moments she was greeted by a teenaged girl in hite shorts and a pink polo shirt.

"Are you the reporter?" she asked.

Chrisk nodded, feeling awkward. The girl was only a
ouple of years younger than she was and probably had
nore advantages than Chrisk would ever dream of. She
vasn't having to wonder how she was going to go to
ollege, yet she seemed a bit in awe of Chrisk's presence
ecause she was a writer.

"My grandmother is back this way," she said. She
notioned Chrisk inside and led her through the entry
oyer, down through a sunken living room, and into a
mall solarium where a woman with bright red hair sat in
. motorized wheelchair.

A tray was spread across the arms of the chair, and on it
ested a notebook and a stack of paper and materials.

"Hello, Mrs. Galloway," Chrisk said, introducing
nerself and extending her hand.

The old woman offered up a badly twisted claw, spotted
vith age and bent with the arthritis that confined her to
ner chair.

"So nice to meet you," she said. "I was excited when
Bess called. You're interested in the post–Civil War era?"

"Yes, I am."

"I've been working on a book for a while about this area
during Reconstruction. We were a bit isolated in this
parish, so things were somewhat different."

Chrisk smiled politely, not wanting to offend the
woman by rushing to her exact topic. She'd been warned
that Mrs. Galloway was eccentric.

"I've collected all sorts of materials over the years," the
old woman said. "Diaries and old papers and everything I
can find. You're interested in the papers from Bristol
Springs?"

Chrisk gave a nod.

"This way," Mrs. Galloway said.

Chrisk followed the whirring motor of the wheelchair

265

as it rolled along a narrow hallway into a neatly kept workroom.

A desk sat along one wall, but the room was dominated by a complex set of bookshelves. In order to save space, the shelves were compressed together. A lever at the end allowed them to be parted to allow access to the desired section.

Mrs. Galloway stopped her chair at the lever and tugged it into place.

Two sections of it opened, and she scooted between them to a spot where she tugged out some pages sealed in plastic.

Before being laminated, they had turned brown, and in the plastic their edges were visibly tattered.

With the pages resting on her lap, she directed the chair over to the desk, where she began to spread them out.

In those days, all the news had been crammed onto the front page of the paper, the columns separated by thin black lines.

Chrisk stood beside Mrs. Galloway, and together they poured over the pages. The print was small, so the old woman kept adjusting her glasses while Chrisk squinted to read the lines.

"What specifically are you looking for? These pages come from right after the war."

"I'm trying to find information about a sheriff who was killed by his horse—trampled to death. We want to tie it in with what's going on in Bristol Springs now."

"Oh yes, I've heard. Terrible what's happening over there. Animals gone wild. I would have thought they would have called out the National Guard."

"They may yet," Chrisk said.

They began to go over the papers.

"I guess the world has improved just a little bit," Mrs. Galloway said as they looked at a story which told of how "Thornton Washington, a Negro, died in a drowning cident." The distinction had been made in print in Louisiana well into the modern era.

"You know, there was a time when papers around here couldn't run photographs of black people," Mrs. Galloway said. "Hard to believe how bad it once was."

Chrisk nodded. "My grandfather has told me about the old days. He was lucky. He had friends who weren't. Now looks like things are moving that way again."

"A shame," Mrs. Galloway said. She picked up another of the laminated pages. Her eyebrows shot up suddenly. "I think we may have something."

Chrisk looked down at the headline: "Sheriff Dies under Hooves of His Own Horse."

"That has to be it," Chrisk said.

"Well, we'll just make you a photocopy," Mrs. Galloway said, beckoning to her granddaughter.

Alden stepped from the afternoon sunlight into the thick air of the café. Although an air-conditioner puttered, the place was warm, and the smell of the grill filled the room.

He walked over to a table where he found Dexter Hemphill sitting. Dexter was a thin man with weasel-like features. He wore overalls and a baseball cap. A hammer hung from the loop at his side, and a tape measure stuck from one pocket.

Dexter was a jack-of-all-trades who did odd jobs all over town and drove a school bus when school was in session. He had dropped by the café at Alden's request.

"What's goin' on?" he asked in his thick southern accent.

"We need to do something about these animals," Alden said. "The town ain't gonna do anything. That means it's up to us."

"I heard that you give 'em a talkin'-to at the meeting the

267

other night."

"Had to. They won't do anything. Briggs is scared. So' the mayor. It's typical. It's up to us. This here's my home and I'm bound and determined to make sure that Bristo Springs is a decent place to live."

Dex nodded. He'd heard Alden say that many times Alden liked to say it. It was his mission, Dex had learned

"We've got to get some people together," Alden said "We need some men that know what they're doing in the woods."

"Fellers good with guns," Dex said, picking up or Alden's line of thought. "That'd be you and me. Paul Winslow would help us."

"Steve Murphy."

They rattled off the names of a few more cronies.

"We need to have a meeting, Alden said. "I say we get the word around and get everybody together tonight at my store. We'll make a plan, get organized, then do like I said we ought to do."

"Hunt?"

"Exactly. We'll get out of there and we'll find that ol' panther and plug him. Then we'll get whatever other monsters out there are likely to attack people. We might not be able to get the bats that got Sibley, but we can damn sure take care of any other four-legged bastards. Two-legged ones too, if they get in our way."

Dex picked up his cup and tossed back the final swallow. "I'll put the word around to meet at your place tonight, then."

"Better bring some beer. The men'll be thirsty."

"Yeah, I imagine so. See you later."

Alden nodded and gave a smile. He looked like he was pretty pleased with himself.

Alison couldn't get an answer at Estelle Johnson's door,

so she decided Neva must have taken her somewhere to help her cope with the grief.

Turning from the door, she walked back down the front steps and along the walk at a slow pace. She wasn't quite ready to go to the office yet. If she got in by late afternoon, Travis might be ready to take a break, leaving her to work alone into the evening.

She could pick up where he was leaving off, and that would let her escape spending time in close quarters with him. The way things were at the moment, she was afraid another discussion might be sparked, and she wasn't ready to try and describe her feelings again. Things were just too complex, and she didn't know how to make Travis understand.

She would have liked to talk to someone about her conflicting feelings—Neva, ideally—but even Chrisk's ear would have been welcome.

Instead, she climbed back into her car alone and plugged in an old Joan Baez tape. The soft music touched her sometimes, offering a little soothing to her pain or at least some background for her suffering.

As she cranked the engine, she decided she'd just ride around for a while, until she was ready to drop in at the office.

She was in no rush.

There was no air conditioning in W.F.'s home. In summer, he kept the windows open. As the sweltering June heat baked the house, a faint scent of decomposure began to drift out on the breeze.

It was not unusually rank at first, so by the time it reached the street, it didn't seem to be much more than the usual smells which drifted out from W.F.'s.

Besides, people didn't move down his street too much. His piece was almost as isolated as Bristol Springs was.

A few kids played in the area that afternoon, but otherwise, people didn't pay much mind.

Like most fixtures, W.F.'s place was something people never thought about much.

Beside the smell, there was not much indication anything was out of the ordinary. It was not uncommon for him to go several days without being seen. People suspected he spent long hours in religious meditation.

There was also no indication that there was anything going on inside. People couldn't hear the teeth from the street. The ongoing feasting was uninterrupted.

Lory Burns had left the paper he was working on spread across his desk and struck out across town toward nowhere in particular.

Since he'd come to Bristol Springs, he'd been trying to complete an article on apathy toward world hunger in the American religious community, but life in the sleepy little town had kept him from making much progress. He wanted to be a pastor, and that work kept him busy.

He found satisfaction in writing for the newspaper, and he enjoyed his sermons, and while world hunger was important, he knew his article would not bring it to an end.

Driving through town, the more immediate problems held his attention. He watched people walk past with empty expressions, going through the motions of their lives without any enthusiasm.

The heat was bad enough. With the drought and its accompanying spirit of hopelessness, the last vestiges of life seemed drained from the people.

Stopping at the café, he got an RC Cola to go and was pulling back out onto the street when he noticed Alison's car parked at the edge of the café's lot.

She had her hands on the wheel, but her head was bowed

and her eyes were closed.

With a twist of his steering wheel, he moved his car in a loop around the lot. He pulled to a stop beside Ali and rolled his window down.

By then she was looking up. She rolled her window down as well. She tried for a smile.

"What's wrong?" he asked. "I'm not being nosy . . . it's my job."

"Fighting a little confusion," Alison said.

Burns studied her for a moment. There was something wrong in her eyes. For some reason, it reminded him of the look he'd noticed the day before in Estelle Johnson's eyes, even before Chrisk had expressed her feelings to him.

The look was not quite like grief, although it seemed to be connected to feelings of remorse.

"Would you like to talk?" he asked.

"I need to head over to the office soon," Alison said. "I'm just trying to . . . pull things together."

"Are you and Travis all right?"

"I guess I'm just having my midlife crisis early, to avoid the rush."

Shifting about in his seat, he leaned out the door. "If there's anything I can do, let me know."

"Sure, Lory. We'll do that. I guess everything will be all right. Really."

She turned and started her engine, putting on a smile as she turned back to him. "I'll see you."

In a quick motion, she shoved her car into gear and pulled away.

Chapter 24

By mid-afternoon Travis discovered he was not accomplishing much in the office. Everything he tried to get started seemed to fizzle out. He walked from the drafting table to the computer, answered the phone, and forgot whom he had talked to as soon as he hung up.

He considered calling Briggs and pumping him for more information, then thought better of it.

He'd let Chrisk check the rumors on the street before he confronted Briggs again. He didn't seem to have his usual go-for-the-jugular drive to find out what the chief was concealing.

Normally the thought of some kind of cover-up would have sparked him to life.

Now he felt his indifference creeping deeper and deeper into his heart, as if it were nestled there, pumping through his bloodstream.

He didn't want to admit to anything so futile, but it was as if he didn't want to go on if Ali wasn't around.

If they were not together, work on the paper meant nothing to him. It was their newspaper, their brainchild, their joint effort. Without her, his sense of purpose was lost.

The sick feeling in his stomach, the feeling he kept

trying to push away, the feeling he was pretending did not exist, kept overwhelming him.

He was sitting at the desk drumming his fingers on the blotter when he heard Chrisk's motorcycle putter up outside. It made him realize how much of the day had gone, but it also lifted his spirits slightly.

At least he would be able to give her the good news about the scholarship. She'd be excited. He knew that, and the thought of her enthusiasm was appealing. He hoped it might rub off on him.

Getting up from his chair, he walked back into the news area, where he picked up the note he had taken earlier. He decided to slip it into his pocket. He'd build up to it slowly.

He walked back toward the front of the shop. Chrisk opened the door and walked in wiping her brow. She looked dusty from the trip, and her shirt was damp, but she was smiling.

She had a large rolled photocopy tucked under her arm. "I found it," she said, raising the roll triumphantly. "It wasn't easy, but it wasn't hard either. There was this lady working on a book on the period."

"The article?"

"About the sheriff being trampled. It's wild, Trav. He was chasing a woman out of town, just like Grandpa said. I didn't read it all, but it's here."

"That's good," Travis said. "We'll get to that later. It'll be good for the story. Right now I have other news."

"What?" She looked puzzled.

He raised a finger and twitched it slightly in warning. "If you rush into good news, you ruin it." His grin was broad.

"Is it about me?" she asked, her eyes brightening.

"You might say that. Think about what you've been waiting to hear about."

Cautiously her expression began to melt into excite-

273

ment. "School, Trav? Is it about school? Stop playing games and tell me." Her voice was rising to a squeal, and she bent forward, feeling the growing thrill.

Casually, Travis reached into his shirt pocket and pulled out the note.

"My buddy called, and he's been able to put together a scholarship package for you—a good one that should go a long way toward handling your tuition and books."

"Oh, Travis, that's fabulous."

She clenched her fists, almost ready to burst.

"And he's been able to get you lined up for a job at the bookstore."

Her mouth opened. "I'll be able to eat, too. Oh, God."

"And, to cap it all, after the first semester, based on your experience, they'll probably have a position for you at the *Reveille*. Once you're in the saddle, it'll all be up to you, but you should be able to parlay that into an internship at the *Morning Advocate*."

Chrisk threw up her hands and twirled around for a moment, then spun toward Travis, unable to contain herself.

She wrapped her arms around his neck and lifted her feet off the floor so that he had to place his hands around her waist to keep them both from falling.

Still squealing, she kissed his cheek and clenched his neck tightly.

"Oh, Travis, it's so wonderful I don't know what to do. I never dreamed it could be possible. I must be dreaming."

"It's reality," he said. "Pinch yourself."

They were so engrossed in the discussion that they failed to notice that Alison had walked into the room.

The realization came a split second later, when Trav happened to notice her standing in the doorway.

There was a stunned expression on her face, a good sign she was taking things the wrong way.

He pushed Chrisk gently away just as Alison began to

urn from the doorway. She was across the threshold and he door was slamming violently into its frame before Travis could take a step.

Chrisk's expression melted. "Oh, God, Trav—she hinks . . ."

Travis was already moving across the room. He grabbed he doorknob and yanked it back, slamming the door against the wall as he moved. With the abuse it was taking, t was a miracle the windowpane stayed in place.

Alison was in tears and had made it halfway to her parking place when Travis got to the sidewalk. He ran after her, grabbing her arm to halt her escape.

When she felt his touch, she jerked away from him, anger burning on her face.

"I guess you were glad when I told you how I felt. You were hoping I would leave, I guess. Now you can be together. What were you doing? Celebrating?"

"Ali, you're overreacting."

"Travis, I never dreamed anything like this would come from you. You bastard. I knew people whispered about us, and about you and her, but I never thought it could be true. I must look like an idiot to everybody around here."

"Alison, she got her scholarship. She was excited about it."

"Bullshit. Bullshit."

She started toward her car.

"Alison, for God's sake, listen to me."

"How long has it been going on? You two always did seem happy after you came back from long assignments together."

"Alison, will you listen to yourself?"

"It's better than listening to you." The hurt in her voice was thick and deep.

She fumbled with her purse until she had her keys free and stomped to the driver's door.

She scratched the paint when she missed the lock, swore

about it, and then managed to get the door open, slamming it into Travis's car in the process.

He was at the door, holding it, before she could close it. "Let's talk this over."

"There's nothing to talk about. Get back to your girlfriend."

"Damn it, this is ridiculous."

"No it isn't." She grabbed her door and yanked it, pulling it from his hands. When the engine roared, he stepped back, just avoiding her fender as she backed up.

Her tires screeched on the pavement as she pulled away. Travis stood in the street watching her disappear.

He was stunned, and only when Chrisk shook his arm did her presence creep into his awareness.

"She'll cool off," Chrisk said. "She'll realize how silly it is."

He walked with her back toward the office. "I hope so. I feel sick."

It was like someone had just cut off his arm.

The tears filled Alison's eyes, blurring her vision. Her car screeched around a corner and just managed to avoid a collision with a pickup truck.

Fighting the wheel, she managed to right her vehicle and aim it out onto the main drag.

She pressed the gas hard, whisking past the stores, heading out of town. She didn't know where she was headed, but she wanted to get away.

On top of the feelings she had been experiencing before was a new anguish and confusion. She was angry at Travis, betrayed by her husband and her friend.

She couldn't bring herself to hate Chrisk, however. She was young and didn't really know better. She had probably given in to her feelings.

The hurt there came because Chrisk was so pretty. Her

slender, rounded body always looked so firm beneath her jeans and t-shirts.

The thoughts collided with her own insecurity about her appearance. She was not as pretty as she might have hoped. How could she compete with a young woman whose appearance was so distinctive that it made her unique in this small town?

She envisioned Travis with her, touching her dark skin, enjoying her flesh, tasting her kisses.

She swore as she drove, damning him to a thousand hells. How could this happen, and how long had it been going on?

The car swept past the city limits sign, and she decided to go down by the springs.

Perhaps it would be comforting to stop there where she had once played pirate with her cousin. She could sit in the car and collect her thoughts.

It would give her a chance to stop crying and figure out where she was going to go, She wouldn't stay with Travis. She didn't even want to see him.

The thought of going back into Bristol Springs was horrible as well. How could she go back there where they would whisper about her, about how her husband had been seeing a girl ten years younger than she was.

It would be too embarrassing. Her hometown was ruined for her now. It would always be a tainted place, a place of whispers and silent, knowing smirks. Damn Travis for that too.

She continued to hate him as she pulled along by the dry spring bed. Shoving the car into park, she reached into her purse and found a tissue.

She had thought her sobs were about to be under control, but instead tears began to flow again and her nose began to run.

She wept into the tissue, almost unable to bear the pain. Above her, the night began to take slow control of the

277

sky. Beyond the pine trees across the way she could see the sun making its slow descent. It took longer in summer, it seemed. Too long. She wanted the solace of darkness, the comfort of shadows which would make her feel protected from reality. Reality was not nice at all.

She hoped Neva would turn up soon. She needed to talk to her now more than ever.

Pete Taylor and his buddy, Chester Hutchison, headed back along the route from Aimsley, where they had traveled that morning with a load of tin cans and pie plates.

Pete's father had loaned them the truck to let them make the run, which had been for the purpose of earning some spare money. Summer jobs weren't plentiful, so boys like Pete and Chester did what they could to bring in cash.

They had walked the roadsides for almost a month, filling up plastic garbage bags with beer and soft drink cans discarded by passing motorists.

They'd also done their share of searching through garbage bins and other undesirable places in order to add precious ounces to their collection.

After making their stop at the recycling center in Aimsley, they had pulled over at a 7-Eleven on the way out of town and picked up a box of Bud Lite in cans and a six-pack of Corona. Both of them preferred the Mexican beer, but it was more expensive. They hadn't wanted to blow all of their new $75 fortune on the celebration.

They planned to head down by the spring bed and pop back a few cool ones. If things hadn't been so dry lately, they might have planned some night fishing as well, or some skinny-dipping, if any of the local girls were around.

They had accepted the need of a private party tonight. There was no water, and the girls wouldn't be out because of the fear over the killings. Pouring down large quantities of beer was a good enough pastime if nothing else was available.

Pete and Chester were juniors at Bristol Springs High School, good old B.S. High, as they were fond of calling it, and they knew the parties they would be enjoying during their final year of school would make up for a slow summer.

Neither of them made very good grades, but both played football. The Bristol Springs team wasn't too hot, but there were some great parties to dull the pain after the losses.

"It's getting dark," observed Chester, who sat on the lumpy passenger side of the truck. He was an incredibly large boy, with a huge head which stretched down to his shoulders without much sign of a neck.

"Maybe there'll be some other people out there," Pete said. He was not a small kid either, but beside his friend he seemed small of stature.

"I doubt it," said Chester. "They're all scared to peek out their doors."

"'Fraid a panther's going to get them," Pete said. "We'll be all right." He nodded toward the glove compartment.

Chester opened it, pulling out the .38 revolver which was nestled there amid crumpled road maps and Skoal cans.

He liked the way it felt in his hand. He and Pete had used it to shoot rabbits on late-night excursions on numerous occasions. It belonged to Pete's father, but it always remained in the glove compartment.

The bumper sticker on the old Ford read, "When guns are outlawed, this outlaw will have one."

Pete's old man was a firm believer in the right to keep and bear arms. In his mind, their primary purpose was for hunting, but he liked the idea of having one in the truck just in case he got attacked by two-legged animals. He was never specific about who he feared, but in Louisiana the

279

vehicle was considered an extension of the home, and it was thus legal to have a pistol stashed in the glove compartment.

Spinning the reluctant crank on his window, Chester swapped the gun to his right hand and leaned out the window to practice another use he and Pete frequently found for the weapon.

No road sign was safe.

Turning his baseball cap around on his head so that the brim stuck down his neck, Chester braced his arm against the door and squinched one eye closed as they approached a highway marker.

It was a small square with a green map of the state at its center and the highway number painted on it in white.

Some people used shotguns to blast the signs, but Chester and Pete liked the challenge of using a pistol. Chester squeezed off a shot which struck the sign slightly northeast of center just as they sped past.

"Got it," he said. "That sucker has a locator dot for our hometown, the armpit of the state."

He spun the chamber of the weapon and leaned out again, watching for more signs.

"Too bad there's no pedestrians," Pete joked.

"Yeah. I'd like to blast me some slobs," Chester said.

"We can line those bottles up once we get 'em emptied," Pete said.

"Yep. What we'll do is check our aim after each beer. See if we get worse or better."

They both laughed, and Pete reached down and turned on the lights. It was getting late enough to turn dark.

Travis sat quietly at the computer, hammering away at the keys with a new determination to finish the story on the deaths. He had gone home to try to find Alison, and he'd driven the streets for a while trying to locate her.

Without success he had even checked her old place, but her car had not been in the driveway, so he had not stopped.

Finally he had returned to work, seeking refuge.

Chrisk watched him for a while in silence. She sat on a stool, knowing she should be doing some kind of work, but she was unable to turn her attention to anything. She didn't know what she should do to remedy the problem that had been created.

When Travis finally looked up and caught her staring at him, she said, "I could try and talk to her."

He shook his head. "She'll realize eventually. I hope she'll let me talk to her." His voice was soft and lacked confidence.

"Where do you think she went?"

"Somewhere to think, I guess. She knows this area better than I do. If she wanted to hide, I don't have a chance of locating her."

"I grew up here too, Trav. I could help you look."

"Let's let her rest. If I can stand it. Maybe time will help."

"I feel so terrible. It's my fault."

"No it's not. Something was already wrong." He sighed heavily and bowed his head, lacing his fingers behind neck.

"Trav, is there anything I can do? I know you must be eaten up inside."

When he looked up, she could see the pain in his eyes. It reverberated from deep inside him. His features looked drawn and haunted, like some ghost had reached inside him and pulled out something vital.

"People are going to talk a lot," he said finally. "You need to get prepared."

"I can deal with it."

281

"I'm sorry."

"Don't worry about it."

"They'll be snickering."

"I know. It'll bother my grandfather more than anything. There've been rumors about us, you know."

"Yeah, now people will think they're confirmed."

"We'll get through it. The important thing is Alison."

"I don't know what to do." He looked off into nothingness.

"I could call Lory Burns."

Travis shook his head. "Not right now. He'll feel obligated to counsel me. That's not what I want at the moment."

"My grandfather says prayer does a lot to heal the emotions, you know, just the calling on a higher authority for help."

"I'm sure I'll get to that too, begging God to make her come back. Unfortunately I don't think God manipulates other people upon request."

He turned and punched some keys, saving what he had written in the computer's memory.

"We'll be lucky if we get this ready for the printer."

"We'll just have a long day tomorrow. We'll make it."

"I suppose we ought to knock it off for the night. We're not going to get anything done."

Chrisk nodded. "I guess I'll head home and let my grandfather lecture me. I'm going to hear my share of 'I told you so's.'"

Travis nodded, but he did not speak. He followed Chrisk from the office and turned off the light.

Part 4

The Inferno

Whoso sheddeth man's blood, by man shall his blood be shed: for in the image of God made he man.

—Genesis 9:6

Chapter 25

When darkness came, Navarra awoke slowly, emerging from the trance state like someone surfacing from the depths of a dark pool. Her eyes fluttered open, and she looked up at the faces of her guardians, who sat watching her as if mesmerized.

Their features glowed in the eerie light of the candles, and when she was ready to rise, Blade offered his hand.

She accepted it, stepping from her resting place with a graceful movement, like a duchess stepping from an elegant carriage.

This rest was the most complete she had known since returning to existence. With the comfort of protectors—a coven of sorts—around her, she had been able to sleep without fear.

The release had brought rejuvenation.

Her body felt fresh and powerful, and the energy of the darkness coursed through her. She could feel the growing power from the oracle.

She stretched gently, then surveyed the faces of those around her, touching Blade's cheek softly.

He smiled and led her from the chamber into the temple where the statue was taking its final shape. His work had gone swiftly.

She nodded only slightly, closing her eyes and letting the power it channeled course over her.

He smiled, glad of her approval.

After a moment, she opened her eyes again and walked on past him toward the doorway. The others had followed her. She dismissed them now with a nod, indicating that they would not be needed for a time.

Danya took Langdon's hand and led him silently into another room. The others dispersed to find resting places.

Blade followed Navarra until she reached the main entrance. He opened the locks he had set up there, then pushed the door open for her.

She walked past him silently, the wind catching her hair and billowing her gown as she strolled out into the darkness.

Blade pulled the door closed and sat down on the floor beside it. He could hear the others in other rooms. Some of them were eating the food Navarra had picked up as Neva. Danya and Langdon were producing loud sounds and grunts.

Blade found he preferred being alone, waiting for the lady to return.

She glided through the darkness, her footsteps soft. She left no tracks where she stepped. She seemed to move almost effortlessly.

The breeze continued to waft over her, and her eyes glowed. All around her the night creatures stirred, stopping their endeavors and peering at her as she walked past them. They were ready to respond if the summoning came again.

From out of the shadows, the owl fluttered. It sailed past her, moving on through the trees ahead of her as if to lead her in a predetermined course.

She followed its flight with ease, keeping track of it even

in the darkness.

Occasionally, as it flew forward, it called out in its deep voice, making sure she had not been forgotten in the underbrush.

The owl had learned its purpose well in the last few days. It followed its directives without hesitation, seeking prey for her with the same determination with which it sought prey for itself as it soared through the night skies. It was her eyes, her guide through the dark world.

Alison was asleep in the car with her head against the backrest when the high beams hit her mirror and seared her eyes.

She sat up with a jolt, her heartbeat quickening. She was afraid it was Travis coming for her. She wasn't ready to see him right now. She wasn't prepared for a confrontation, and she didn't want to hear him try to convince her how wrong she was.

A glance through the back glass assured her it was not Trav at all. She could see the outline of a pickup truck rumbling along the roadway.

It was an old model and it rattled as it moved, following the roadway down and along the spring bed's edge.

The vehicle pulled to a stop a few feet away from her car. She could make out two heads in the cab, one of them huge.

She had rolled her window partway down earlier to let in the night breeze, so she heard their laughter as they began to climb out.

Leaning into the back of the truck, they opened a cooler and pulled out some beer bottles, then carried them around to sit on the hood of the car. They weren't looking in her direction, although she speculated that they had seen her car as they had approached.

Climbing onto the hood of the truck, they tilted their

heads back and poured down some of their drinks.

Then they spat out across the dry bed where there should have been water. She heard them swearing.

She moved around a bit in her seat. The brief nap had left her stiff and feeling slightly gritty with perspiration and dust.

She thought about just starting her engine and pulling away. She didn't want to stay around where the boys were. She didn't think about them being dangerous. She just felt it was their hangout more than it was hers.

She sat still for a while as they drank more beers. She was wondering where she ought to go. Then one of them noticed her.

"Hey, there's somebody over there."

"I thought it was empty."

"Nah. It's a lady."

"Is she okay?"

They would come over now. She would have to put on a smile and try to explain she'd just needed a place to think. Would she be able to do that without looking totally strange to them? They didn't seem to be the type to understand the need for solitude.

As they slid off the hood of the trunk and started stomping across the ground, she put her hands on the steering wheel.

She didn't recognize them even as they drew close, but they looked like town boys, maybe a little rough . . . hopefully not threatening.

The key was in the ignition, in case she needed to get away in a hurry. She wanted to go ahead and crank the window closed, but that would seem impolite if they were just checking.

"You okay, lady?" the smaller boy asked.

She smiled and nodded as he bent over to look through the window at her. She could smell the beer on his breath, but he wasn't drunk yet.

"What's happening, Pete?" the big boy asked.

The smell of beer grew stronger.

"Nothing, Chester. This is Chester," Pete said.

"Hi," Alison said.

"You sure you're okay?" Chester asked. His speech was a little slurred.

"I was just sitting," she said, trying to keep a pleasant expression. With her hands on the wheel, she turned her face away in a hope that they might leave her.

"You're not broken down?"

"No."

She clenched her fists around the wheel, beginning to grow nervous. She had no way of knowing if the boys were dangerous or not. She didn't know them. She couldn't remember if she'd seen them around town.

She decided to start her engine and back away. She moved slowly. Her hand slid down the arc of the steering wheel a few inches at a time until she could drop it easily to the ignition.

At the same time she eased her foot forward to the gas pedal, preparing to press it down and twist the ignition in the same instant.

A split second later the sound was not her motor.

She jumped at the noise, pulling her hands back as she turned to look at the boys.

Pete was yanked from her line of vision in the blink of an eye, and Chester began to move backward with a look of horror on his face.

He did not cry out, but his mouth dropped open and his eyes seemed ready to pop from their sockets.

The next sound was Pete's cry. It was loud and long, a deep agony.

Terrified, Alison could not bring herself to look out the window. She sat frozen in her seat, unable to move to close the window or start the engine.

There was another cry, then another deep roar. *The sound she had heard before.*

Then something slammed against the lower portion of

her door. The vibration shook the car. She realized it must have been Pete's body.

A scream started to rise only to be muffled into a gurgle.

She had come to the place where the first death had occurred. How stupid she had been, sitting here with the window open, inviting trouble.

A splatter of blood sloshed up onto the edge of her window, and she did begin to move, rolling the window up and positioning herself behind the wheel. She had been drawing back toward the center of the car, away from the sound.

She managed to get the engine going when she saw Chester coming back from the pickup. He was carrying a gun. Stopping several feet from her car, he pointed downward and fired.

His target was beneath her window. He missed, and the bullet thudded into her car.

She shoved it into reverse and backed up wildly, swerving as the car moved. She had little control over it because her hands were trembling so badly.

After traveling a few feet, the scene she had been imagining unfolded in her headlights.

The boy was beneath the panther. It had come back, and it had already succeeded in ripping open his throat. It was standing on him now, its front paws pressed against his chest, now tearing at his chest, peeling back shirt and flesh alike in blood-streaked strips.

Chester was motionless, the gun frozen in his extended hands.

The black beast was looking up at Chester. Its tail twitched slightly as it peered up the barrel of the gun.

Chester squeezed off another shot that missed the cat and tore into his friend's leg.

Alison slammed on her brakes and hesitated. She needed to do something, had to help the boy, but she didn't know how.

Keeping her foot pressed on the brake, she tugged the

ift back into the drive position.

Perhaps she could run over the thing. It would tear up
e car, but it might kill the animal before it got Chester.
She was about to act when the cat pounced, leaping off
te and plowing into Chester. The gun did the boy no
od as the cat sank its teeth into his neck.

The blood sprayed like a fountain, and the gun dropped
om Chester's hand. He fell back under the cat's weight,
d his struggle was only momentary.

He lay still, and the cat prepared to continue its assault.

"No," Alison screamed. She shoved the horn down,
awing the cat's attention.

"Oh God," she screamed. It was turning toward her.
Forgetting the notion of running it over, she shoved the
r into reverse and began to back up again.

Her hands kept slipping on the steering wheel. She had
clench it tightly to hold on. Her foot put the pedal to the
or, producing a roar from the engine which propelled
e car backward.

With speed she traveled about two seconds before
amming into the embankment where the road sloped
wn to the springs. The bumper and trunk crumpled,
d the shattered glass from the taillights tinkled out.

Ignoring the damage, she tried to gather her thoughts.
Tires whirred in the loose gravel, and she lost traction.
e shoved the car into drive again and tried to move
rward without success.

As the wheels spat rocks and sand, the cat bounded
ward her. It moved swiftly, its eyes wide and bright in the
ams of her headlights.

She frantically struggled to make some progress in
eeing the car by twisting the wheel from side to side.
The movement provided no success. She was stuck.

She began to fumble around, trying to figure out some
ay of escape, but she couldn't afford to get out of the car.
was her only protection. The cat would certainly get her
she tried to run. She could only stay put and pray for the

best. If that was enough.

An instant later the vehicle rocked as the cat jumped onto the hood.

Its green eyes peered through the glass at her as it began to lift its paw and scrape at the glass. Its mouth and whiskers were covered with blood and spit. Drops of it trickled off and dotted the windshield with pink spots of foam.

Then it hurled itself against the glass, its weight smashing a network of cracks in front of Alison's eyes.

Its mouth pulled open, exposing the rows of sharp yellowed teeth, and with its paw it continued to rake at the glass. The fractured window began to give. It began to peel from the edges of its frame, crumpling inward.

Tears blurred her vision. The snarling countenance peering through the cracks became even more hideous and threatening.

She fumbled open the glove compartment, looking for something that would serve as a weapon. She found only badly folded road maps and crumpled credit card receipts.

A loud roar burst from the panther's lungs, the wisps of its breath fogging the battered glass as it continued to paw the cracks inward.

Alison tried to scream and found she could not utter a sound.

She felt her lungs tighten; her brain felt like it was constricting. She could not move her muscles.

She looked up at the cat one final time. It looked now like some hideous dragon. Her eyes rolled back in her head, and she blacked out, dropping down into a sea of nothingness which provided the only refuge she could find.

Navarra emerged from the shadows at a dead run, summoning strength she had not utilized in an eternity kitting across the area between the trees and the spring ed, she was no more than a blur of movement. She ecognized Alison's car and knew something was wrong.

The cat had been attempting to fulfill its commands vithout consideration of individuals. It would have ttacked any humans in the area.

She reached the edge of the car just as the windshield ollapsed completely inward.

She spoke to the cat softly, stopping it before it moved hrough the jagged opening toward Alison.

Coaxing it toward her, Navarra reached up and rubbed ts head.

"You serve me well, my brother, but for now there is to e no more."

The panther hopped to the ground and stood at her side, ooking up into her eyes.

She stroked its head gently until it was calm again.)ismissing it, she watched it move back toward the forest. Vhen it was out of sight, she hurried to open the car door.

Alison lay back on her seat, arms curled in front of her in a helpless, almost fetal pose. Her head rolled over limply vhen Navarra attempted to move her.

Gently, Navarra laid her down across the seat, then urned off the ignition. Alison was unharmed, and she vould remain unconscious for a while.

Relief washed over Navarra. Gently she brushed curls away from Alison's forehead.

She closed the door softly, content that Alison would be all right. She was where she should be now. She wouldn't be going back to Travis no matter what he tried. Navarra could read all of that in her sleeping thoughts.

Satisfied, at least on that level, she walked over toward the warm bodies which awaited her attention.

Chapter 26

Briggs and Doc Simmons tied handkerchiefs around their faces as they prepared to enter W.F.'s house. Briggs was using a red bandanna and Doc a white monogrammed handkerchief. Neither cloth was really effective at filtering out the smell which had drawn them to the home this morning.

Some kids playing in the street nearby had noticed it first shortly after 8 A.M., when their mothers had ushered them out of their homes for some peace and quiet.

Only when Stephen Dove had ridden by on his rickety old red bicycle and figured out something was wrong had anyone begun to take notice, however. Dove's academic progress to grade six—his final year of schooling—had been spurred by social promotions. A spurt of growth had made the tall, lanky Dove too big for the furniture in the lower grades.

He was thirty now, and the lankiness was still with him. Wearing an old yellow baseball cap, he rode around town offering to do odd jobs.

Rumor had it Dove had been dropped on his head as a baby, and the community felt a certain spirit of responsibility to care for him.

Now he stood on the sidewalk watching Briggs and Doc

eeping toward the splintering front door of W.F.'s place. They had to wade through piles of garbage and Kentucky ied Chicken wrappers.

"Don't you come in here now, Dove," Doc said as they ached the step. "It's probably going to be pretty bad."

With his hands in the pockets of his overalls, Dove odded. Briggs had placed him in charge of crowd control, hich at the moment consisted of keeping back several ds who had taken time out from their skateboarding to atch the proceedings.

A few adults were also beginning to approach. When ch new person arrived, Dove single-mindedly issued his arning. "Don't get too close, folks. We've got to keep the ea clear 'cause the chief is checking out a situation here."

"Looks like you've found a replacement for Jasper," oc said as they shoved the front door inward.

"Hell, he may be in line for Langdon's job if he don't get ack to work soon," Briggs said, half gagging as the full rce of the smell burst through the opening. It was thick nd sickening, having been contained in the house nderneath the June sun.

"How long could he have been here?" Don asked Doc.

"Couple of days at most. That would be enough."

Turning together, they grabbed the last breath of fresh ir and then walked into the front room.

The state of disarray was worse than Briggs had xpected. There was evidence of more than just W.F.'s sual squalor.

He surveyed the overturned items and the other mess efore his gaze fell on the body. He almost vomited.

W.F.'s body rested on the floor against the wall. His face vas a mask of decaying yellow, with the flesh beneath his yes already sagging into wrinkled bags. His eyes were pen and covered over with a milky glaze.

All of that Briggs could have dealt with. The rats were what jolted him to his bones.

They were huddled together in the chest cavity, their coats covered with coagulated blood and bits of yellow tissue and muscle.

A hoard of them were piled up at the stomach area where they had apparently entered. Others were scurrying about underneath the rib cage, which had been stripped of flesh.

A few more emerged at the throat where a second opening had been gnawed. Other rats were around the neck, their teeth ripping away strips of flesh and chewing on veins and fatty deposits.

Some of the creatures were dead. They had drowned as they gorged themselves on the juices of W.F.'s body. Their brothers had not been merciful of the carcasses, but they had shown less enthusiasm for cannibalism than they had for eviscerating W.F.

"I didn't know rats were carnivores," Briggs muttered through his kerchief.

"Live and learn," Doc replied. "It'd be my guess that they were after the liquids in his body."

"Is that an educated guess?"

"Just wild speculation, considering our previous circumstances. I'd guess W.F. keeled over of a heart attack and the rats were thirsty."

"Any way to confirm that?"

"It'll be hard. I doubt his heart's still intact."

Briggs had to wipe perspiration from his brow. The heat and the smell were making him sick. The sight of the body didn't help much. He happened to glance into a corner where a couple of rats were working on fragments of what he guessed to be a pancreas.

Some cats, also filthy with W.F.'s bodily fluids, were also on hand.

"I don't guess I have an explanation for that," Doc said.

He tromped through wads of rats to peer down at the body, his handkerchief tight against his face.

"Will you be able to tell about the other thing?" Briggs asked.

"The blood loss?"

"Right."

"I can tell you that right now. There's not enough. You've got a little on the floor, a little on the rats, and a little more here and there. Not enough, unless these bastards drank it."

"How can that be explained?"

"I don't know that it can."

"There's been a struggle in here," Briggs added, moving around the room. He picked up one of W.F.'s photo albums and spotted a cross on the floor.

"And these aren't the kinds of things W.F. would throw around. Not a cross and pictures of his family."

"You thinking there's a human culprit involved?" Doc asked.

"I've been wondering that from the beginning. I hope it's a human. I can catch a human."

"You turning superstitious there, Chief?"

"I don't know what I'm turning. What am I supposed to think? You tell me all these people are drained of blood. There's no answer. It's like one of those old horror movies."

"Maybe you've got a nut who likes old horror movies and has found a way to reenact them."

"By doing what? You think he's got a dialysis machine he hooks up to people, then whistles and lets the animals come chew them up when he's through?"

They both walked to the doorway and stood in the opening for fresh air. Despite the thick humidity, the taste of it was clear and sweet compared with the inside of the house.

"What have you got?" Dove called. He was now holding back a crowd of a dozen people.

"Heart attack," Briggs called back. He saw no sign of

Alden in the crowd, but he didn't see any need to star panic by mentioning the rats.

"You want me to call an ambulance?" Dove called.

"You just hold the crowd," Briggs said. "We'll get th coroner in a few minutes."

They turned and walked back into the house. The rat were still hard at work. Disgusted, Briggs kicked at couple of them. They dodged him defiantly and continue to gorge their already bloated bodies.

"What are we going to do with all these bastards? Briggs asked.

"I vote we let the coroner's boys worry about it."

"It'll take an hour to get them here. We can't just le them keep eating."

"They've already been at it a couple of days. They can do much more damage in an hour," Doc said.

Briggs rested his hand on the butt of his gun. Shootin would do as much damage to the body as the rats had. H wanted to find a place to throw up. This was worse tha any death scene.

He was about to take a step toward the body when h heard Dove's voice behind him.

"Holy sweet Jesus."

He twisted around angrily to see Dove sticking his hea through the doorway. The man's mouth hung open i shock.

"I thought I told you to stay outside."

"They ate him up," Dove said, oblivious to the smell

"Dove, you're not supposed to be in here. You better no go out there and scare people by telling them what you've seen here."

"I had to come in," he protested. "They need yo outside."

"What for?"

"They just found two boys out by the springs. The panther came back last night. They're ripped up, jus

298

ke before.''

A dog that belonged to Rick Boudreau, who lived in the cinity of the springs, had actually found the bodies.

Rick had managed to get a leash on the beagle before it ad done much additional damage to the remains.

Out of decency, he had put some old green tarpaulins ver the corpses before calling for help.

Briggs pulled the cruiser to the edge of the roadway and limbed out with Doc not far behind.

A cluster of spectators had already gathered. It didn't ke them long, even though nobody actually lived at the rings.

The sun beat down without mercy, and the smell of ecay was in the air, though not as badly as it had been in V.F.'s house.

Flies were buzzing around, lighting on spots where lood had soaked into the dirt in thick black patches.

Briggs ordered the people back a few hundred feet and walked with Doc to the tarps. Doc lifted the first one and odded.

The chief looked down reluctantly. Half the face had een clawed away. A sick half-grin was on the features vhere the teeth were exposed. The round orb of one eye tared up in stark abandon. The edge of the socket had een ripped off in a jagged line.

By what was left, he recognized Pete immediately. The oy had once dated Julie.

He let the tarp fall and went with Doc to the next.

It was worse than the other, the flesh almost totally hredded. The face was no more than a mass of raw meat, and the throat had been ripped out.

"Well, Doc?"

"There's blood around. I can't tell if there's enough or not."

Using the same kerchief which had covered his nose earlier, Briggs wiped new sweat from his face.

He'd called his office on the radio, asking for the coroner's office and some help from Holyfield.

As he turned back toward the crowd, he saw a vehicle approaching. He wished it was the deputy's cruiser. Instead, it was a pickup he recognized as belonging to Alden McClain.

It was followed by another truck with a camper. It belonged to Alden's friend Dexter, and there seemed to be several people in the front seat.

By the time Briggs had walked back to the mouth of the roadway, men were piling from the vehicles with guns in their hands.

"Just stop right there," Briggs said, raising his hand.

Alden, carrying a high-powered rifle, walked forward with his troops piling along behind him.

He stopped only when he was standing face-to-face with Briggs.

"We're gonna do something about all this," he said. "You've had your chance. We're going into those woods and get that fucker."

"I don't want a disorganized party going crazy in there," Briggs said. "Somebody'll get hurt."

"We ain't disorganized. We had a meeting last night."

Briggs stood his ground. "Put the brakes on, Alden. You're going to cause a massacre."

"There's already been one. We're here to stop it from happening anymore. Those boys' folks are gonna be grieving. It's time something was done 'fore somebody else's kids wind up dead."

Doc walked up beside Briggs and glared at Alden. "If you take your bunch out in those woods, I'm going to have more work than I can handle picking lead out, and you'll probably wind up leaving some kids without fathers."

"What do you suggest, then?" Alden asked. "We've got to do something."

"You've got manpower. Let us organize them into

300

groups of two or three and make a sweep of the woods," Briggs said. "Deputy Holyfield will be here in a minute. We'll plan zones so they don't crisscross. That's better than sending one mob in there."

"When do we start?" Alden asked.

"As soon as I can take care of this scene. We've got to get these bodies out of here and let these kids' folks know what's happened."

Alden looked a bit dejected. "We'll wait here. You just better understand we expect some results, Briggs."

Briggs cast a hard look at the faces of the men who stood behind Alden. "So do I."

Travis had arrived at the office early. He had not been able to sleep. At work he had managed to get quite a bit done, bringing regular publication into the realm of possibility if he worked through most of the day with Chrisk.

He had given up hope on hearing from Alison unless he hunted her down.

The death story was in the system. He had worked from his own notes, from Chrisk's, and from Ali's to put it together.

He was working on layout when he heard the call on the scanner. He decided not to roll on it. The scene would be no different from the others, and he could get the names from Briggs later.

It was not the best way to do business, but he did not have the motivation to look at another set of bodies.

It meant the problem was growing even worse, and it meant he should probably call the Associated Press in Baton Rouge, but he had to take care of his own business first.

Besides, surprisingly little interest had been shown in the trouble. A reporter from the Associated Press had

301

called a couple of times for updates, but otherwise they didn't put much attention on it.

They were busy gearing up for the Republican Convention, which would be held at the end of the summer in New Orleans, or doing stories on the drought in other parts of the state. Some freak deaths somehow were just not worth the trouble. A child killed by an alligator in Florida had drawn national attention, but that had been in a residential area and not a jerkwater town in the middle of nowhere.

Noticing a slight tremble in his hands, Travis jotted a quick line to mark off the headline for the page. Alison normally composed the headlines, so he would have to remind himself to come back and take care of that.

He was going to have to get used to doing a lot of things himself.

Early Jackson was in his usual place on his front porch, sipping coffee and reading the *Clarion*. He was dressed in a clean white shirt and dark trousers, and he looked no different than he had on a thousand other mornings, but Chrisk had never felt more apprehensive about approaching him.

She pulled her bike to a stop in front of his house and dismounted slowly to move up his front walk, her head slightly bowed. Her face was solemn, and she did not want to look into his face.

He would remind her of his warnings, and she would have to look at the pain in his eyes. She prayed he would understand.

Standing in front of his chair, she found it impossible to look into his face. She kept her head bowed, a few locks of hair falling across her face.

She should have been here with joy to tell him about her scholarship. She had dreamed about the pride he would feel when she brought that news. Now there was only grimness.

"What happened?" he asked.

"A misunderstanding," she said.

"People have been talking about it for months."

"It's not true. We weren't doing anything. Ali walked in and thought she was seeing something she wasn't."

"You haven't made love with him?" His words were low and blunt.

"No. I was hugging him because he'd just told me my scholarship had come through. I'm going to go to college, Grandpa."

He shook his own head. "People will say you paid for it. You know how."

"I can't help that. I can't change what they think. They're wrong. You know they are. This is just that kind of town. I know I haven't done anything wrong, and I came here to let you know that. I can hold my head up in front of anybody in this place. They can whisper, but we'll know they're wrong."

"The good book says flee from even the appearance of evil."

"The good book says to forgive, too," she said. "That's always the way you've lived. When white people mistreated you, you didn't turn around and return hate for hate. This is different, but it's the same. It will pass, and they'll find something else to gossip about at the video store. We're not ruined. You can still go to church on Sunday and shake hands. Tell them there that the rumors are wrong. Tell them that Travis is a good man, and that I work for him and that's all. It's the truth."

He sighed a heavy sigh. He looked as if a great weight had been laid on him, but he nodded.

His hands still gripped the pages of his newspaper; his lips were tight. He almost seemed frozen, but then another sigh came. It seemed to indicate he would be able to accept things.

It would take a while for him to feel good again, it would take a while for him to brag about Chrisk's accomplishments, but that would come in time.

Right now there was nothing for Chrisk to do but walk back down the steps and climb onto her bike, but she knew eventually her grandfather would get over it all.

She puttered out of his neighborhood without pushing the bike. She wanted her stomach to unclench before she reached work, and she wanted to be ready to see Travis. She wasn't sure what she would say to him.

She passed in front of Estelle Johnson's house and saw Alison's car parked there. It looked dusty and battered. Ali must have done some driving around of her own.

She didn't notice the windshield because it was facing away from her.

Finally Chrisk headed over to the office. Parking out front, she walked to the front door, braced herself, and went inside.

Travis looked up and gave her a nod. "You ready for a long day?" He was making an unsuccessful effort to be chipper.

"You think we'll be able to get it all done?" she asked.

"Sure. Romulus and Remus worked fast, didn't they?"

She told him where she had seen Alison's car, blurting it out even though she had intended to mention it casually.

"I guess she's spending time with Neva," he said. "Looking for comfort." His expression showed he was not as calm about it as he tried to appear. He placed his hands flat on the drawing table and looked down at them.

"You're not going to try to talk to her?" Chrisk asked.

He shook his head without looking up. His eyes were closed. "Not right now. I can't go over and kick in the door and expect to get anywhere. I'd like to do that, but I don't think it will help matters. I'm trying to occupy myself to keep calm."

"How can you stand it?"

"It's not easy. I just don't know any other way. I'll need you to call Briggs in a while. There's been another death. We'll need to get it into the edition."

"Who was it?"

"I think they said on the scanner it was a local kid."

"Where?"

"Same as the first. Out by the place where the water is supposed to be."

Chapter 27

Lory Burns had heard all the news by mid-morning. Ladies dropping by the church office brought word of the split-up of the Dixons because of the black girl that worked for them.

Although the word of more deaths disturbed them, and their hands trembled nervously with the growing terror in town, they were more inclined to discuss rumors about what Alison had caught Travis and Chrisk doing. Speculation on scandal was more fun than discussion of carnage.

"Any time you saw one, you saw the other," Barbara Hebert said of Chrisk and Travis. "I've been figuring something was going on. That's just the kind of times we live in."

"There's no proof," Burns told her, reclining in his desk chair.

"You're too trusting, Reverend. I know how people are. There's no telling what all's been going on. They're not the only ones, either. Lots of people in this town are slipping around. I wouldn't be surprised if these animal killings weren't some kind of punishment sent from the good Lord. You know, a plague, just like in days of old.

hy, like Sodom and Gomorrah."

"That was a very long time ago," Burns said. "I don't ink God exacts his justice in quite that way. If he wanted punish, I'm afraid all of us would face some problems. 'hile he frowns on sin, he has shown us grace through ır Lord Jesus Christ."

Mrs. Hebert didn't argue, but she didn't appear to be vayed from her opinion. She thanked Burns and left him lone in his study without mentioning her real reason for opping by. He suspected she had none, other than to hare her gossip. He had discovered some people enjoyed eaking to him about the sins of others as if they expected to earn them brownie points in the hereafter. Perhaps it st made them feel more righteous since their sins didn't heasure up.

"Let him who is without sin . . ." the priest muttered nder his breath.

He was personally unsettled by all the news. Things vere not right anywhere. The town was not as disturbed as t should be about the nightmare that was taking place.

He could not dismiss the strange way Alison had been cting the day before, nor the odd relationship between Neva Wilson and Estelle Johnson.

The break-up between Alison and Travis did not make ense either. They had been happy in spite of their inancial circumstances. One relationship in a thousand licked like theirs.

What was going on?

Lory sat at his desk running a hand over his beard as he nulled it over. Was there anything in his experience to uggest an answer?

Nothing.

He thought about praying for inspiration as he pushed aside materials about the Episcopal convention which had come in the mail. He would think about those later.

307

What would he think about now? He wasn't going t
come up with anything on this subject by constar
consideration.

Yet perhaps he could find a relationship to somethin,
from the past. There had been things he had studied–
legends, Greek and Hebrew myths.

Had any of the ancient stories paralleled what wa
happening in Bristol Springs?

He got up from his desk and pulled a book from hi
shelf. Something had struck him, something about deadl
animals.

There was a Greek word which described them, but h
couldn't remember it. It had been too long since he ha
dealt with the language. He hoped that digging throug
the books from his seminary days would jog his memory

Alison awoke with a start, jerking up in the strange be
and looking about for some clue as to where she was
Nothing was familiar. She was in a room where she had
never been before.

Sunlight washed in through the windows and across the
hardwood floor. She had slept soundly for a long time.

As she tried to calm herself, she placed her hand against
her forehead as if the touch would help her remember. She
could find little recollection of the night before. Not after
witnessing the deaths of the two boys.

What had happened after that, after the panther had
tried to attack her? Had she fainted? Had someone found
her and brought her here? This did not look like a
hospital. It was someone's bedroom.

When the door started to open, she grabbed the sheet
and pulled it to her body, because she was wearing only
her t-shirt.

She felt relief when Neva entered the room carrying a
breakfast tray. She was wearing a white gown and a robe.

They were at the Johnson house, Alison decided.

"I hope you're feeling better," Neva said, moving to her with the tray. She set it on the bedside table. It held a poached egg, grapefruit, coffee, and toast. It was simple yet appealing. Alison realized it had been a long time since she had eaten.

She propped up her pillows, then lifted the tray across her lap as Neva took a seat in a chair across the room.

"How did you find me?" Alison asked.

"I was out for a walk." She said no more.

"That thing, that panther tried to get me," Alison said, the memory of it renewing her fear. She trembled as she tried to eat.

Neva only nodded, her eyes remaining locked on Alison. The gaze was almost as disquieting as recalling the night's events.

Alison smeared some jam on a piece of toast and bit into it, following it with a swallow of the strong coffee.

"I feel strange," Alison said as she leaned back against the pillows with the cup still in her hands. "I'm confused. I guess you've heard the rumors about what happened."

Neva gave a slight nod.

"I can't believe it," Alison went on, the hurt opening her up. "I just can't believe Travis." Her shoulders sagged and her chin dipped. "Or maybe I can."

She closed her eyes, battling hurt and anger. "She's so pretty, her body's so perfect. I'm a skinny schoolmarm, and she looks like she stepped out of a French perfume ad, or something. Trav's a nice-looking guy, too. And in her eyes, he's a former hotshot crime reporter. I guess she found him glamorous. Hell, they had to work together all the time. I guess they just couldn't help but get horny for each other."

She glanced at Neva, who remained silent.

After a few more sips of coffee, she put the tray back on the night table, climbed out of bed, and walked to the window.

The warmth of the sunlight felt good against her skin. She ran her hands through her hair, letting it fall in tangles about her face.

"I'm completely lost," she said. "I don't have a clue about what I want to do now. I don't want to stay here, that's been decided for me. I guess it's time to go somewhere really far away."

Neva did not disagree.

"I guess I need a way to start over," Alison continued.

Neva said, "Perhaps I can be of help."

By mid-afternoon, the coroner's office had removed the bodies. Doc had done only a cursory examination of them, but he sat in Briggs's office sipping Jack Daniels from a bottle the chief kept in the file cabinet.

"It's a mess," he said. "There's no explanation."

"None we want to accept," Briggs replied. He had convinced Alden to wait on an assault of the forest, but it had not been easy.

"Guess that leaves the unacceptable," Doc said.

Briggs took a swallow from the paper cup he was using. "What the hell am I supposed to do?"

"Beats me," Doc said, raising his own cup in a salute, then tilting it to his lips.

"Holyfield is supposed to go out with me tonight. We're going to have to bring that panther in. That's all there is to it. If we don't get him, there's no way I'm going to keep Alden at bay."

"Well, lend me a rifle, and I'll go along," Doc said. "I haven't been hunting in a long time. Besides, you might need me on hand in case you shoot one another."

"You sure about that?" Briggs asked.

"It's always a possibility when you take men and give them guns," Doc said.

"I mean, are you sure you want to go?"

"A few more of these, and I'll be ready to go anywhere," he said, lifting his glass.

Briggs took his pistol from his holster and spun the chamber. "I just hope guns are enough."

Doc laughed. "Maybe you want some holy water."

"Isn't that what we're both thinking?" Briggs asked. "I know it's crazy, but what else am I supposed to think? People keep turning up almost completely drained of blood. I look at that, and I think the old legends had to come from somewhere. I don't believe the dead are rising from their graves or anything, but something strange is going on. Maybe this drought has brought out some kind of animal we don't know about. You know, there's people that have hunted the woods around here all their lives without ever seeing a panther. What else could there be?"

"The woman who lives beneath the waves," Doc suggested. "The waves ain't there no more, and there's no sign of any skeleton. Like you say, all legends have to come from somewhere."

Travis picked up the layout sheets he was working on and threw them across the room. They fluttered through the air and scattered across the floor.

Chrisk, working at the computer, whirled around in a start to see him pick up the coffeepot and hurl it against the far wall.

The bowl shattered, splashing coffee along the paneling as the remnants of the container rained down onto the floor.

He started to pick up a chair but stopped himself, his anger almost under control.

He stood in the center of the room, shivering. Chrisk got out of her chair and walked over to him, touching his arm gently.

For a moment he didn't move, didn't acknowledge her presence. Finally, he turned, crying. He hadn't expected it to happen, but he could not control the sobs.

Taking his hand, she guided him over to a chair. He settled into it, trying to wipe his eyes. He couldn't stop the tears.

He realized the pain had been bubbling inside him all morning. His strength hadn't been what he had hoped. He had wanted to remain calm and collected, but his stamina had failed him.

His desire to leave Alison alone and give her nerves time to calm was not going to be fulfilled.

He wanted to let her think he was being mature and nonchalant about it all, but he couldn't. The rules didn't seem to matter anymore.

He couldn't let her go. He had to find her and explain what had happened. For some reason he viewed it as a sign of weakness, but he no longer cared about appearances.

The only thing that mattered was getting her back. He knew if he could just talk to her, he could make her see the truth.

He felt like a schoolboy with an obsession, but he couldn't help himself. His shoulders quivered as he tried to control his crying.

He looked at Chrisk through his blurred vision. She was staring back at him, trying to keep her features pleasant.

"Let it out," she said. "You shouldn't have tried to keep it bottled up so much."

"I couldn't help it. My God, I feel like such a wimp."

They both laughed at the remark. He sputtered through the tears. It lifted his pain, but only by a miniscule amount.

He had to make the hurt deep inside him end. It was an ache that gnawed at his insides. The only way to stop it was by going to Alison. He would have to go over to the Johnson house and see her, admit he had been childish in not coming before, and try to explain everything.

He was ready to grant her any concessions in order to restore their union. Selling the paper or burning it down for the insurance would be viable options.

"I'd get you some coffee," Chrisk said, "except you took your anger out on the pot."

"It was handy." He got out of his chair and pulled his handkerchief from his pocket, using it to wipe his eyes and face.

"I've got to go see her," he said. "I've got to talk to her."

"Don't you think you need to compose yourself a little more?" Chrisk asked. "You're not in the best frame of mind here."

"I'm fine. I've waited too long as it is."

He pushed past her and yanked the front door open, almost running to his car, peeling rubber as he backed out.

He felt like Dustin Hoffman rushing to the church to stop Katharine Ross from marrying the wrong man.

He fought back a new round of tears as he sped through the narrow streets. Images flowed through his head, recalling moments of his life with Alison, their meeting, their courtship, their honeymoon.

They had gone to Florida, borrowing a beach house that belonged to a friend of his who'd landed a job as the Key West bureau chief for the *Miami Herald*.

He remembered their walks along the beach. One moonlit night they had made love in the sand as the waves lapped in.

It hadn't been as neat as they had expected, but they had wrapped their sand-encrusted bodies together and laughed, enjoying the warmth they felt between them.

He remembered their first apartment, too, how they had had to adjust to sharing it. It had been an awkward period of discovery. She had been shy around him, modest about uncovering her body. They had joked about how old-fashioned their romance was, but it had worked well,

313

so well.

He couldn't let her go, couldn't let her believe a mistake and slip away.

He careened around corners, jumped a curve, and skidded across a sidewalk before finally wheeling the Mustang onto the street which led up to the Johnson house.

His heart leaped when he saw Ali's car. From its condition, he feared she might have been hurt. That as much as his desperation forced him to jog up the walk and bound up the front steps.

He prayed Alison would appear, but instead it was Neva. She pulled the door inward and stood looking at him through the screen with her arms folded.

Her face was expressionless, but the gaze in her eyes seemed to be filled with hatred for him.

"I need to see my wife," he said.

"I do not think she wants to see you," she said.

He looked away from her with exasperation. "I just need to talk to her. Would you tell her I'm here?"

"She's been very upset and she's resting."

She kept her arms folded, and she showed no signs of relenting.

"I have to see her," Travis said. "She's wrong about what she thinks happened."

"Is she?"

"Yes, damn it! She's wrong. I don't care what you think, there's nothing with Chrisk. She was excited because her scholarship came through, and that's the only reason she was hugging me."

"I see." Her lips were tight. She still made no movement.

"I have to talk to her."

"Mr. Dixon, I perceive that you're very upset. You need to go somewhere and get calm. I am not going to let you near Alison in your present state of mind."

Travis slammed his fist against the door facing. "Don't make me out to be some obsessed psycho. I just want to talk to my wife."

"I am sorry. It is not the right time."

He tried to look past her into the house. "Ali," he called through the screen. "It's Travis. We have to talk."

"Mr. Dixon, please try to get ahold of yourself."

"Just let me talk to her."

She started to push the door shut. He slammed his fist against the wall again. "Damn it, if you close that door I'll kick it in. I'll kick it off its frigging hinges."

She paused, looking at him with perfect composure. Suddenly her gaze froze him. He felt chills along his spine, and he stopped shouting.

Taking a step back, she pulled the door open a bit wider, letting Alison emerge from the shadows of the room.

She wore a white robe. Her hair was uncombed, and she had no expression on her face.

"I don't want to see you," she said. Her voice was cold, devoid of emotion. "There's nothing for us to talk about."

Travis swallowed. He had expected things to be different when he saw her. Seeing her was supposed to make everything all right. Instead it was only fueling the agony inside him.

"Ali, you've got to believe me. What you saw with Chrisk was innocent. Completely. You know she's been waiting to hear about her scholarship. I got the call from LSU yesterday morning."

Her expression didn't change. "It doesn't matter about Chrisk. What was wrong was wrong before I saw the two of you. I have other things I have to do with my life, Travis. Things that don't involve you anymore."

"You don't mean any of that." He looked at Neva. "You're listening to her. Alison, we belong together. You're a part of me. You've got to listen to me. Neither one of us is going to be happy without the other, no matter

315

where we go. It's not where you are or what you're doing that matters. You know that as well as I do. As much as we hated what we were doing in Texas, we were happy with each other. You know we were. You know how we both felt when we first got together, how happy we were."

"Emotional things lead to mistakes," Alison said. "I can't continue to gauge my life as if it were part of yours. I have to move on."

"To what?"

"You should go, Mr. Dixon," Neva said, pushing the door forward once again, narrowing the opening.

She positioned her body between Travis and Alison. He tried to look around her.

"Ali, please. Ali."

"Enough has been said," Neva said. "You have heard her wishes."

"Something's wrong here," Travis said. "I don't know what the hell's going on, but it's not right."

She eased the door forward even further, leaving only a narrow crack through which her face was visible.

"Pull yourself together," she said. "I know it's painful, but you must let her go. If you love her, you will respect her wishes."

And then the door was closed, and he was staring at the white paint which covered it.

The chill remained, seeping into him. It was a feeling of strangeness that he had never known before.

He breathed heavily as he turned and walked back toward his car. He had to do something, but he was confused.

Not just confused, frightened. He was lost, and he didn't know what it would take to help Alison.

He climbed behind the wheel of his car and wondered what was happening. Other people had been left by their wives. He could just be overreacting, imagining some mysterious influence to help his mind accept the matter. It

316

could be a way of laying blame on something beside his own failure.

Except he knew better. In spite of the hurt, he knew something was wrong.

It was as if he had been lost in an alien land, far from home and with no map to guide him to safety.

Chapter 28

Travis returned to the office to find Burns sitting in the news area talking to Chrisk. They were looking over a printout.

Trav guessed the minister had come to drop off his column, but Burns's expression made it clear he had deeper concerns.

The priest rose when he saw Travis standing in the doorway and moved across the room.

"I'm sorry," he said softly.

Trav wiped one hand across his face. He felt like someone had struck him very hard in the stomach. He knew his face must show it.

He walked over and sat down. It was Alison's chair, technically, an old swivel job they'd picked up in a secondhand store in Aimsley. It creaked—the sound he was used to hearing it make when she sat in it. Because it was old, he could feel the shape of her molded into it.

He wanted to be polite to Burns, show the usual hospitality and amenities, but at the moment that wasn't in him. He found it almost impossible to speak.

The priest sat down beside him. "I know it's rough," he said.

"She wouldn't talk to me," Travis said. His words were

ery low and coarse. "It was strange. She was cold, motionless. Neva did most of the talking."

"Emotionless," Chrisk noted. "Like Mrs. Johnson at he funeral."

"Chrisk and I have been talking," Burns said. "She wrote down some suspicions about Neva. They match ome of mine. Something very out of the ordinary is going n around here."

Travis nodded. The words were not fully registering. His thoughts were on Alison. The scene at the house kept eplaying in his head.

"We think there's something strange going on," Burns epeated, trying to make Travis hear him.

"Alison acted strange," Travis said. "She wasn't herself. She's upset."

"Travis, I saw her yesterday, before she would have come in the office and found you. She was at the diner. She acted strangely there. Dazed or something."

"What could it be?" Travis asked.

"I don't know yet," Burns said. "We have to try to find ome answers."

"I'm torn between loving her and hating her," Travis said.

Burns leaned in front of him in order to look into his face. "Trav, there's more to it, I believe. I don't know what it is. I don't think it's just a marital spat. I tried to look up some things, but I don't have the right books. I have to find something."

"What are you saying?"

"The woman, Neva, no one had ever seen her around here before. She's supposed to be related to Mrs. Johnson. The ladies of the church don't know her. You know what it's like around here. Everybody knows everybody's cousins and aunts and brothers."

"Everybody *is* everybody's cousin," Travis said.

"Then where did Neva come from?"

The three of them looked at each other. No one had an answer. No one wanted to voice his fears.

"I wrestle constantly with my understanding of the world," Burns said. "I struggle with notions of spiritual and physical reality.

"My entire life was shaped by my belief that there is more than just the physical world. That belief is removed and distant, however. Heaven is somewhere else. The possibility that some forces beyond our typical understanding exist in the earthly realm is difficult to accept."

"What are you saying?" Travis asked.

"I'm not saying anything definite. I'm only speculating."

"About what?"

"What have we said? People are acting strangely. Animals are out of control. There are legends about that sort of thing."

"About what?"

"Evil forces."

Travis felt his mouth drop open. Unwillingly he stared at the priest.

"Don't look at me like I'm some kind of fanatic. I didn't just pick it out of the air. A few years ago we thought zombies were just legends. Now we know there was some truth to the stories they told about them in Haiti."

"There's a logical explanation for the animals," Travis said, almost forgetting about Alison.

"What? Water? We're not that far from the river. It's not dry. The animals would find that water, wouldn't they? Why hasn't anyone thought of that?"

Trav shook his head. "I don't know, Lory."

"You yourself said something was strange."

"Are you suggesting that Neva is some kind of evil force who has the ability to control the animals?"

"In ancient times they spoke of that kind of thing. Legends associated with the Bible, Greeks, medieval

320

urope. All of them have the same stories. The legends had to come from somewhere. Something had to give people the ideas for their myths."

"This is crazy," Travis said.

"Everything around here is crazy," said Burns. "You said yourself the chief was acting strangely."

"What could he know that would indicate what you're talking about?" Travis felt his journalistic skepticism creeping back. It was his job to poke holes in theories if he could, even if they were his own.

"He could know there was something about the deaths that didn't add up."

"Maybe the animals are being used to cover up some kind of blood sacrifice," Chrisk suggested. "Maybe they're trained by some cult to cover up their rituals."

"Then these people have it backwards. Usually it's the cults that mutilate the animals," Travis said.

"Travis, if what he's saying is true, Alison is in more trouble than you think," Chrisk said.

That turned him around. He felt his chest tighten. His calves twitched as they had the first day he'd ever set foot in a newspaper office.

Hearing Burns express his fears made it seem unreal, almost silly, the way another person describing personal religious beliefs always seemed to sound. There was a reason wars were fought over religious beliefs. When they were someone else's, they didn't make as much sense as the things you figured out in your own mind in the silence of the night.

Supernatural goings-on seemed ridiculous when Burns talked about them, even though they had crossed Trav's mind a dozen times on the way back from the Johnson house.

What if Burns was right? Neva had come from nowhere. She had come at a strange time.

Or were they persecuting her? People had hanged

women as witches because they happened to be in the wrong place at the right time. Were they doing the same thing to Neva, placing blame on her because her arrival had coincided with the animal frenzy and Alison's departure?

He looked at Chrisk, trying to find some indication of how she felt.

Seeing him looking, she lifted her hands. "My grandfather's always warned me to look out for haints," she said. "I'm prepared to consider anything. Besides, you remember that stuff that went on in Aimsley a couple of years back. All the people at the mental institution went into a frenzy, and there was supposed to be a girl who had contact with angels involved."

"I've talked to people about that. It happened the night of a big storm that probably got the patients upset," Travis said. He got up for the first time and paced around the room. "You know the spiel," he said. "I'm a journalist. I deal in facts. Just the facts, ma'am. If this is real, then we can find facts."

"We can go back through my library. I've got all kinds of books on myth and legend. The three of us could turn up material, enough that we can dig out information that parallels what's going on here. Then maybe we can discern the truth from the legend, and it will give us an idea of what we're up against."

"Like Dr. Van Helsing and Jonathan Harker."

"And Mina Murray," Chrisk added.

Travis paced a little more. His head was beginning to hurt. It was as if pieces of information bounced off the walls of his brain—the agony over Alison's departure, the attitude he had faced when he confronted her, Lory's suppositions, his own fears; all of it inundated him.

"When we find something in these books, what then?" he asked.

"We'll figure it out from there," Burns said.

"We should get my grandfather," Chrisk added. "He's been everywhere. What he knows may be helpful."

"Why do I feel like we should find Judge Hardy and ask for the use of his barn?" Travis asked. Then he nodded. "It sounds crazy, but I'm a desperate man. The good people of Bristol Springs may have to wait a day or two for their paper, but at least we'll find the answers."

A few minutes later they all left the office. The pages Chrisk had obtained in Aimsley remained rolled up on a chair where she had dropped them the night before.

Somehow, as he sat on his porch watching the sun go down the way he did every evening, Early Jackson knew they would be coming. He knew it as certainly as he knew he would go to heaven when he died and as certainly as he knew the sun would come up in the morning.

He knew it the way he knew all things. He had learned much in his day, had developed a sense of what went on around him, an awareness that allowed him to pick up on things. It was nothing out of the ordinary, just the wisdom of years and the grace of the good Lord.

Knowing they were coming was not what made Early uneasy. As the sun sank, he took comfort in the normalcy of the moment. Sunset was one of the constants of the universe which gave him a sense of solidarity.

He had watched the sun go down and come up since childhood; it was a perpetual event.

His belief in heaven had solidified in a revival tent around 1947. He'd been to church off and on all his life, but sitting amid a crowd of people shaking with religious fervor, he had begun to think more about eternity.

Early had traveled quite a bit by that time, had partaken of his share of worldly pleasures, and the talk of Jesus had made him reevaluate the direction of his life.

It was then that Early decided he would be going to

heaven one day, accepted it with certainty, while he had given it only a passing thought before.

He had come away with a new desire to help his fellow man and to do good where he could.

But as he watched the reverend's car pull up in front of his house, he felt a new certainty: something bad was going to happen.

Burns climbed out with Chrisk and Travis not far behind.

Early got up from his chair, shifting his palmetto fan to the hand that held his tea glass, and walked to the edge of the porch to greet his guests.

"It's getting dark," he said. "I was about to think about going inside. The mosquitoes are gonna get bad in a minute or two."

"We need you to come with us," Chrisk said.

He looked at them, at her face, at Travis. He nodded. "It's more wrong here than what we first thought," he said knowingly.

"We want to find out what is happening," Burns said.

Early followed them down his walk and got into the back seat of the car beside Travis. He didn't mention the rumors circulating. The boy looked like he was in enough pain.

As the car pulled into the street, Early sensed he would need all the faith he had ever learned for the coming days.

Chapter 29

They were called bobcats, North American cousins of the lynx. In appearance, they bore a resemblance to common house cats. Their heads were similarly shaped, but their ears were sharper, with little tufts of hair at the tips. On occasion, domestic cats inbred with them, however, making the resemblance even closer.

It was their hind legs which made the final distinction. Like the extra-large tires which lifted up the chassis on souped-up sports cars, the legs seemed to hoist the cats' backs up in a permanent arch. The hind legs were long and angled for jumping.

Adults stood about fifteen inches at the shoulder. In size, they were not particularly menacing. To dismiss them as harmless was unwise, however.

With their short tails and coats of brown, which blended with the forest, they looked wild, predatory.

Normally their evenings were devoted to hunting for food. They stalked through the trees, their wide eyes searching for prey.

Tonight, however, they felt a different urge. The summoning had found them. It had reached out to them each night, and they had stood prepared to obey, if necessary.

So far, nothing had come of the impulses which throbbed in their brains, but tonight the feeling was more intense. It seemed to indicate that they would soon be called upon.

They nestled together as the shadows took over the forest.

The message in the air was clear.

Tonight they would taste blood.

Briggs loaded his rifle carefully after cleaning it. He had not used it since a hunting trip the previous fall, so he had taken care to get it in perfect condition. He didn't want it to fail him at a critical moment. His life and the lives of his friends might hang in the balance.

Resting it across his knees, he wiped a cloth along the barrel and across the polished wood of the stock. It looked like the fine grain of a mahogany table.

Guns to Briggs were works of art. If his pocketbook had permitted it, he would have owned a whole collection of weapons. They would have been displayed in a cabinet in his den, offsetting the trophies he would have used to decorate the walls. He sometimes thought about big-game hunting. The notion of stalking dangerous prey was thrilling.

Tonight he would be doing something similar, yet far less appealing. Tracking a panther in the dark wasn't his idea of a good time.

Zipping his rifle back into its case, he walked through the house. Julie was still not back. She had left a note that she would be at a friend's house. She had not been acting right the last couple of days. She'd come in late the night before and had barely listened when Briggs lectured her about it.

He was troubled by the possibility that he and his daughter might be growing apart. He was also troubled by

326

the idea that she might be seeing some boy he wouldn't approve of, some little punk who'd drag her into the backseat of his car and put his fingers into her underwear.

If Briggs ever caught anyone up to that, he knew he wouldn't be able to control himself. He knew he would tear the kid apart.

Unfortunately, dealing with Julie would have to wait. He'd always promised himself that he would not neglect her while he did his work, but for the moment the hunt was more pressing.

If he found out she was seeing some scrounge, he'd handle that later. He'd keep her in line in spite of the teenaged tendency to rebel. He just wasn't going to tolerate any problems with her, and he wasn't going to have her quitting school because she was pregnant.

He stood still for a moment, letting his pulse return to normal. He discovered he wasn't worried about going into the woods at all. Hunting the cat was a job, something that could be handled without complexity. In a way, the thought of it seemed easier than the struggle of rearing a daughter.

Shouldering his weapon bag, he walked out the front door, his mind a jumble of concerns. He wasn't taking into account how things would function without him.

Doc hadn't hunted in years, not since the days when he was right out of medical school and getting his practice started in Bristol Springs. There had been more time in those days, more hours in the day. He'd always gone with his brother, a brother now long dead.

He could remember the hunts. He and his brother never killed much, but they enjoyed getting out together.

They had tromped through the woods with their jackets buttoned against the cold and their hats pulled over their ears.

They stalked squirrels. They rarely spotted them, scored kills even less often.

But they talked and laughed and drank coffee from their thermos.

Thinking of those trips put a warm feeling in the old physician's chest.

He missed his brother, more so when he did things that reminded him of activities they'd enjoyed together.

Doc had always been a witty man, a clown among the other students at medical school, and a charmer with his patients. Since losing his brother and his wife, his wit had sharpened and become more cynical. He used it as a form of survival. People interpreted it as the crankiness of age.

As he oiled his rifle, he shook his head sadly. Hunting with Briggs and Holyfield wouldn't be the same.

For his last hunting trip, it would offer little of the cherished pleasures he remembered.

Holyfield drove from his house near Penn's Ferry with the radio turned off. He didn't want to listen to the squawk of the dispatcher's calls. Since he was technically off duty, he didn't have to.

He would have preferred to spend the evening with his girlfriend, Elizabeth, a nurse who worked at Riverland General, but he felt an obligation to help Briggs.

The chief was a decent guy, and he was really on his own. Holyfield had seen enough of office politics to know the sheriff's department would be providing no assistance without real pressure.

Holyfield did not feel bound by the office protocol, however. He worked in Bristol Springs so frequently that he had come to like the people, and he felt a certain duty to carry out the role of a peace officer even if he wasn't under orders to do so.

He had become a cop because the pay and the retirement

328

enefits looked pretty good to a country boy in search of a ob, and because he liked the idea of helping people.

He hadn't anticipated the resentment people would how him because he wore a uniform of authority, but he ad learned to live with the down side.

That also included working above and beyond the call f duty, directing traffic at the parish fair or performing ther public service tasks. He accepted those as well and ried to make Liz understand. She worked odd hours, so vhen they were supposed to be off work, she wanted them o be together.

Tonight's hunting trip had upset her, because she had lanned to fix dinner for them at her apartment.

Navarra stood in the doorway of the resort. She had eturned from town an hour before sunset. Alison had een left at the Johnson house to rest. She was not yet ready o come to the forest. She would need a little more time to ccept the new reality to which she would be presented.

That would come, so Navarra was not concerned about er. Before leaving she had touched Alison's thoughts oftly, inducing a sleep that would continue until the ouch was removed.

There were more pressing things for the moment. She new the men would be coming. The owl had given its varning.

As it trailed the approach of their vehicle, she did not let ear seize her. The group was not as large as she had faced efore. She did not fear their approach.

"How many?" Blade asked, standing at her side. .angdon waited behind him, ready to respond to any ommands.

"Not many—not enough to worry about. My night rothers will protect us."

She did not offer more explanation, but she continued

to watch the darkness, and she did not rejoice with th
feeling it bestowed.

The energy of the night on which she thrived wa
present, but there was also a disturbance she could sens
She could feel the possibility of opposition. It did no
frighten her. She had lived too long to be frightened, bu
there was some concern.

He had bowed out as gracefully as possible. Althoug
he regretted that they would miss the dinner, at least it wa
just a hunting trip and not some nightmare like using
flashlight to direct the parking of cars at a high schoo
football game.

Hunting wasn't his favorite pastime, especially not on
hot night when they would be swatting mosquitoes a
every turn, but it was a lot quieter than dealing with ira
drivers. He wouldn't be listening to honking horns o
swearing motorists.

He pulled to a stop in front of the sheriff's office just as
was getting dark. The sky was fading from a dusty silver
full black.

He rolled up the sleeves on his old work shirt and the
got his Remington out of the backseat.

He stuffed spare cartridges into his breast pocket.
would be too warm to wear a hunting vest.

With his gun over his shoulder, he strolled into th
office, where the chief was sitting with Doc. They wer
drinking coffee.

"Let's go kill us a cat," Doc said.

The old man got up and lifted his own weapon.
seemed a little heavy for him, but he managed, an
together they walked out to the patrol car for the drive ou
to the springs area.

She was angered. Just as before, there would be morta

oppose her purpose. They would try to get in the way.

And they would fail. She had taken more precautions this time. She had a refuge here in the forest, a fortress, a castle with guards willing to do her bidding, and all round the night brothers were on hand.

Let them come with their wooden stakes and silver bullets. This time they would not reach her. They would not defeat her, and they would not turn her from her purpose. Her kind would continue. Her line would not die out. The ancient curse, the curse that had followed her sisters since the beginning of time, would not be completed.

The forces of darkness would serve her, and they would accept her bidding as they had served her kind since the beginning.

She was a part of the darkness, after all; she had been born of the darkness in the early days of creation.

She remembered the beginning now, how they had danced on the banks of the Red Sea, basking in the sunlight. There had been so many of her sisters then. They had gloried in the taste of the air and splashed in the sea.

It was a happiness short-lived and almost forgotten. She had watched so many of her sisters die, and she remembered the tears that had flowed.

Most of all, she recalled the determination among those who had not died. They had found a way to go on living, living for eternity.

She felt that determination again. She would continue. Those who opposed her would only serve as more sacrifices to appease the dark ones. She would not be topped. Not this time. Not at any cost.

They sat around a conference table at the church, sipping coffee made in the church kitchen, while they pored over a half dozen volumes of writings that ranged from the scholarly to the superstitious.

"What are we really looking for?" Travis asked, shoving aside a copy of *The Golden Bough*. "This is hopeless. What are two-thousand-year-old myths going to tell us?"

"Some aspect of legend may jump out at us," Burns said. "We're trying to find the reality behind the myths. Some references to control of animals might help."

"Didn't St. Patrick drive the snakes out of Ireland?" Travis asked.

"That's the wrong side of the street, isn't it? We need to know who would have been able to send the snakes after someone."

The look on Trav's face made it clear that he was not convinced. He did not want to continue to look for old stories that might offer answers. It was clear he wanted to take some kind of action instead.

From the way he stomped around the room, he seemed ready to throw something else.

"If this woman is a threat to Alison, I have to do something. I have to go over there and storm the place."

Burns got up from his seat. "If you do that, you'll be endangering yourself and Alison too."

"*If* there is a supernatural element. Listen to us. That's ridiculous. We're like scared old men around a campfire. I'm going to have to make Alison listen to me. That's the only thing that's going to do any good."

Chrisk got out of her chair and stood in front of him. "If you go over there and get yourself hurt, will you be doing Ali any good?"

"I don't know."

"And if we are all suffering from mass hysteria, then you'll look like a total asshole if you go busting in there like Dustin Hoffman."

He threw up his hands. "I've got to do something. You guys keep looking for the right answers. I'm going."

Chrisk stood her ground. "Then I'm going with you."

Early intervened. "You two being together is what started this mess," he said, getting to his feet.

332

"I can't let him go off like that alone," Chrisk said, running after Trav, who had stepped around her and already left the room. "He's a danger to himself and others."

She caught up with him in the parking lot just as he was climbing behind the wheel of his car.

She ran around to the passenger side before he had time to protest. When she was in the seat beside him, he didn't try to make her move. He just shoved the car into gear and went on.

They made the trip over to the Johnson house in silence, Travis staring at the road with intensifying anger.

His breath came in quick bursts through his clenched teeth, and the muscles in his forearms kept rippling with tension. Chrisk had never seen him so on edge.

By the time they reached their destination, she was afraid he was going to break the steering wheel with his grip.

He had been driving at a reckless speed. The tires screeched as he brought the car to a stop at the curb, and he was climbing from his seat before Chrisk could speak.

"Wait here," he ordered her.

She started to protest and reached out her hand to halt him, but he looked back at her with a gaze which made her stay put.

She watched him move in front of the car and up the walk at a jog. The house was dark and looked deserted, haunted.

He climbed up the steps and disappeared into the shadows.

Everything was quiet, and for a few seconds there was no sign of movement.

She saw the first dog just as the sound of his knock reached her ears. He was pounding on the door, rattling the screen in its frame.

The dog was a German shepherd. It apparently belonged in the neighborhood. It stood at the edge of the house, looking toward the porch.

Chrisk thought at first it was a neighbor's dog drawn to investigate a possible intruder, but as Travis stepped back from the door and tried to look through a window, she began to feel something was wrong.

Another dog appeared from the other direction, a mongrel of almost the same size as the shepherd. It too peered at the porch, toward Travis. It was almost as if the animal's course had been directed.

When the owl hooted, she almost climbed through the canvas roof. The low and sudden sound bit through the silence of the dark.

Ignoring it, Travis banged on the screen, determined to get someone to answer.

Chrisk watched the dogs draw closer to the edge of the porch. The fear crept up her chest and into her throat. She whimpered slightly, then twisted quickly in her seat.

Half leaping toward the driver's side of the car, she banged her elbow on the gearshift. It struck the bone, making her arm go numb.

With her other arm she shoved the horn bar down, sending a loud moan through the front of the car.

When she had scrambled back to her window, she could see Travis had heard the noise and looked around as she had hoped.

He stood at the edge of the porch now, looking down at the dogs. There were more of them now, mostly large ones. They had all bared their teeth. They snarled like wolves, saliva dripping from their jaws.

They were spread along the edge of the porch between Travis and the street. To get back to the car, he would have to traverse them, and they would rip him apart.

She saw him look around for a weapon, but there was nothing on the porch. He couldn't enter the house, and a couple of them stood at the end of the porch in case he tried to flee in that direction.

He backed slowly into the shadows, pressing his back against the wall. He tried to start peeling the window screen away to allow himself access to the house for refuge, but the dogs began to move forward then.

The Shepherd led the way up the steps, making a lunge for Trav's throat. Trav dodged it and ducked out of the way of another dog.

The animals slammed into each other and went bouncing across the planks of the porch.

A third grabbed at Trav's leg, its teeth hanging on the loose cuff of one leg of his jeans.

He kicked at it, shaking free as another dog grabbed for him. This one, which looked like a Labrador, sank its teeth into his forearm.

He tried to shake free and failed at first. The movement dug the teeth through his skin, and blood began to flow. Still another dog leapt at him, striking him with its weight and driving him backward.

He fell down the steps, rolling onto his back with his hands raised to shield his face and throat.

More of them moved in on him, trying to get him with their teeth. He curled into a ball in an effort to protect his throat and stomach.

Chrisk had been transfixed by the scene, but as she saw the blood spurt from his arm, she was drawn back into reality.

She looked over at the dash and saw that Trav had left the key in the ignition.

Taking care to miss the gearshift this time, she slid over behind the wheel and coaxed the engine to life.

Then, before shoving it into drive, she reached up and released the catches on the roof. The canvas popped out of its restraints, and the mechanical whir of the crank began to peel it backward.

The dogs were still after Trav, still tearing at his back and shoulders, but he had managed to keep them away from his vitals.

Chrisk's arm still throbbed from the job on her funny bone, but she forced the shift into place and backed the car away from the curb, spinning the wheel to the side so that she could angle the car toward the lawn.

She flipped the brights on, bathing the area with stark white light. Some of the dogs looked up into the glow, their eyes reflecting back bright green. There were almost a dozen of them now, all breeds, all sizes. They must be coming from everywhere.

Again she shoved the horn bar down, producing another loud moan. Then she stepped on the gas.

As the top slowly climbed backward, the car peeled rubber on the pavement and went bouncing over the curb and the sidewalk.

The wheels tore furrows in the grass as it shot toward the house.

Travis was thrashing about, trying to free himself. She aimed the car straight for him and gave it more gas, slamming the brakes down only a few inches from him. She stood up in the seat and screamed.

He grabbed one dog, what looked like a bull terrier, by the throat and forced it backward, then got to his feet, kicking at another, a pit bull of some kind. His foot caught it in the ribs, and from the force the dog went rolling with a loud whimper.

Trav's shirt was ripped apart, and claw marks streaked his skin. Blood was spilling through his hair and running out cuts on his face and arms.

The dogs continued to jump at him, and their barks rose into a loud chorus. They were not dogs anymore. They had become a pack of hideous beasts, hellhounds with only one purpose, to kill.

He thrust his fist into one of them, sending the creature sprawling. Summoning strength, he jumped onto the hood of the car, narrowly avoiding another set of gaping jaws.

All around the car the animals began to leap for him, scratching at the fenders and the tires. He clambered along the hood quickly, lifting himself over the windshield into the front seat.

"Get us out of here," he screamed, dropping into the bucket seat.

The dogs were scratching at the car now, trying to climb up on the grill.

One of the larger ones managed to place his front feet on the hood, but his claws could not grip the slick surface. When Chrisk put the car in reverse, the claws screeched along the metal until he was gone.

With hard thuds they began to crash into the sides of the car. The top climbed slowly back into place.

As blood dripped from his arms like perspiration, Travis got the catch back into place on one side.

A smaller dog came from somewhere and struck the plastic of the rear windshield, but the seams held, and the dog slid away with a yelp.

With the tires, Chrisk dug a deep rut in the front lawn, but she managed to get the car back onto the street.

It swerved from side to side, almost plowing up onto the sidewalk on the opposite side of the street before she got it under control.

Beside her Travis leaned against the passenger door, angling the air-conditioning vent so that it blew into his face.

"She was in there," he muttered. "I know she was."

"Those things were guarding her, Travis. Navarra left them to guard the house. They are under her control."

"Burns was right," he said. "I never would have believed it, but something very unnatural is going on. We've got to figure out what she is and then find a way to fight her. Before it's too late for Alison."

Chapter 30

Briggs halted in the darkness and swatted a mosquito which had settled on his face. He was covered with welts from the bug bites, so many of them that he had stopped trying to scratch.

The repellent that Doc had sprayed on him had worked for a while, but he had sweated a lot of it away. Besides, Louisiana mosquitoes were resilient: they didn't let a little thing like chemical warfare scare them off.

The three men had been at their hunt for more than two hours now with little success or sign of progress. They had done little more than wander in and out of the woods.

Leaning against a tree, Briggs sipped from his canteen and waited for the others to catch up with him.

After a while he saw Holyfield's light bob over toward him. Blinking his own flashlight, he got the deputy's attention and motioned him over.

"Any sign of anything?" Briggs asked.

"Besides the mosquitoes?"

"I found my share of them too," Briggs said. "I don't see how the damned kids keep finding this panther. We can't lay sight on him for hell."

"Maybe we're trying too hard."

"Maybe we ought to drag some fresh meat around."

"That's another thing that doesn't make sense to me," Holyfield said. "How come this bastard hasn't bothered anybody's cows? He just stalks people."

"I guess the cows haven't disturbed him," Briggs said. "Kids wander into his way." He knew that was not a legitimate answer.

He didn't admit that the notion made him quiver inside.

It was another fact in support of the thing he had been dreading: that there was something beyond his understanding going on in these woods and in the whole town.

If they did find the panther and killed it tonight, what good would it do? If something weird was going on, then other animal attacks would probably continue. How could they be stopped? As he'd said before, they couldn't kill every wild animal in this end of the parish.

Yet if the hunt tonight was unsuccessful in putting an end to things, Alden would probably take his band of merry men and try to do just that.

The fear of that group being out of control was as big a concern for Briggs as the fear he felt wandering through the trees out here.

He was frightened. He'd seen what had happened to the victims, including Jasper, who had been armed. The rifle he clutched in his hands was no great comfort.

"You want to keep moving?" Holyfield asked.

"Might as well. See if we can find Doc. He's been moving while we've been talking. He's probably way out in front of us now."

They adjusted their weapons, trying to find a comfortable position for carrying them as they began to move forward again, listening for the footfalls of panthers.

Doc was pausing to wipe perspiration from his face with his old blue bandanna. His feet were beginning to hurt, and every muscle in his body felt heavy and tired. He was discovering something he had forgotten about hunting with his brother—the experience was exhausting.

Part of it was the heat. The air was thick, and darkness had done little to cool things off. It was not as hot as it would have been at noon, but it was bad enough.

He wasn't sure how he'd managed to move out so far ahead of the other men. He hadn't been walking at a brisk pace. He had apparently had a path of least resistance, with fewer branches and shrubs in his way.

He thought about waiting for them, because he knew they would catch up with him shortly, and he was quite comfortable leaning against the tree. He took long breaths, letting the air replenish his lungs.

But then he heard something move a few feet ahead of him. It was a brief twitch of a movement. Something rattled a branch and then was still.

He was still tempted to wait for the others. If it was the panther, he wasn't inclined to attack it alone.

He was worried that it might get away, and that alone caused him to leave his leaning position.

He didn't want to lose what might be their only chance to get the creature. He'd seen what it had done to the young people, and although he hadn't said much about it except in quips, the carnage sickened him.

He felt no anger against the cat, but he didn't want it to go on killing. With his gun clutched in front of him, he began to move forward.

He hadn't crept up on anything in a long time. He tried to place his steps carefully. He made some sound anyway when he pushed around a bush which stood between him and the spot where he had seen the movement.

He paused, standing as if frozen, holding his breath, completely silent. Nothing moved ahead of him, so he walked on, stepping around the bush. His gun was raised, his index finger curled tightly around the trigger, ready.

There was nothing in the spot where he expected to find

340

the panther waiting. His shoulders sagged a little and he let go of the gun with one hand, reaching into his pocket for the bandanna again.

He was surprised by the amount of perspiration on his brow. It almost drenched the cloth. He was too old for these kinds of games. He'd heard a lot of men died on hunting trips because the excitement brought on by the sight of their prey caused an overload on their hearts that they couldn't handle.

And those were men hunting deer and other animals that didn't fight back. The trauma of spotting a great cat would probably send adrenalin flowing.

He pocketed the bandanna and brought his gun back into a ready position. The brush all around him formed a thicket. He glanced about on the ground to make sure he wasn't walking into any snake holes and then moved forward again.

The brush rattled, but he paid it less attention now. He wasn't creeping any longer, he was just covering ground, stalking perhaps.

The leaves were dry on the bushes. They clattered together with a swishing sound. Somewhere he heard an insect buzzing as well, and a mosquito lit on his forehead and stung before he could slap it.

He wiped it away and found a tiny smear of blood on his palm. He was learning this task could be unpleasant in many ways.

Waiting on patients in his air-conditioned office was better. Even examining dead people for Briggs was preferable. That was not an enjoyable task, but it could be done with more ease. No wonder he had given up hunting after his brother had passed on.

Using the barrel of his gun, he eased a branch out of his line of vision and looked ahead.

In the moonlight he saw only a stretch of trees. Except for the light breeze, there was no sign of movement.

341

He stepped out of the brush and began pacing along through the trees, which were spaced several feet apart.

With a little more room to maneuver, he felt better. It must have been claustrophobia he'd felt in the thick growth of brush.

When the first cat dropped, he thought a branch or a pinecone had struck him on the shoulder.

Only a second later, when the sting began to set in, did he realize something heavier had touched his back.

A heartbeat later the stinging turned to pain, and he realized he'd been gashed. Like razors, the claw had sliced through his shirt and into his back.

He let go of the stock of his gun again to touch his back. He felt the warm blood flowing over his fingers.

The panther came to mind, and he turned around with the gun ready to fire.

He didn't see anything, but he kept his finger on the trigger and took a step back in the direction he had come.

More of them dropped from above him. The second and larger one managed to stick onto his back, digging its front claws into his shoulders and bracing its weight against hind feet which found footholds in the small of his back.

Doc screamed as the cat bit into the soft flesh at the base of his neck.

As a reflex, his finger squeezed the trigger, sending a blast into a tree in front of him.

He dropped the gun then and tried to reach back and dislodge the cat. He began to spin about, screaming.

While his hands were busy, other cats moved up in front of him, leaping up at his torso, clinging to his clothes.

A few more dashed in at him from the shadows. As they began to rip at his legs he went down, landing on his knees. He was still struggling to get free of the one on his back.

Blood ran down his neck, seeping under his collar in a hot stream. He hit at a cat at his side and then tried to grab the head of the one on his neck. The teeth were piercing his flesh like needles.

He toppled forward and rolled over onto his back, crushing the bobcat under his weight. Lifting himself upward slightly, he bent at the waist and then let his upper body fall straight backward.

The cat let go when it slammed into the ground, and Doc, in spite of his years, wasted no time in rolling off it and getting onto his knees once again.

Picking up its carcass by the front legs, he began to swing it from side to side, striking its brothers and scattering them about.

The old man's heart was thundering now. He could hear the blood rush in his ears as he hammered at another of his attackers with the body.

The bones of the animal began to shatter until he had a bag of pulpy mess.

Dropping it, he attempted to stoop for his gun. That was a mistake. As he tried to pick it up in the darkness, a cat bit into his wrist and dragged him forward.

He fell hard, and another cat rushed in on him, trying to sink its stiletto teeth into his throat. He was trying to swat it away when the pain gripped his chest like a huge hand that had reached into his ribcage to squeeze his internal organs.

Clutching the area of the pain, he stopped battling the cats. He lay still, gasping for air, looking up at the branches above him in the moonlight.

The cats soon blotted his vision. A claw slashed across his left eye, slicing it open. He felt it part, and the socket quickly filled with the warm liquids of his pupils and with fresh blood as well.

Another claw raked across his throat, finding his

jugular. He began to choke on his own blood as the darkness closed around him.

Briggs and Holyfield heard the gunshot and jogged forward through the darkness, fighting their way through the thicket, where they could see signs of Doc's passage marked by broken branches and pressed-down brush.

Racing madly, they traversed the tangle of vines and limbs, ignoring the branches that ripped at their clothes.

They broke through together just in time to see Doc gurgling blood through his lips.

A circle of bobcats formed a perimeter for his body. The cats looked up with warning gazes as the lawmen flashed lights in their direction.

Holyfield raised his rifle and fired, killing the one that had ripped open Doc's throat. Its snout was covered in blood, and it went down with a roll which left it on its side in the dirt. Only a light whimper escaped its mouth as the death throes set its muscles to twitching.

The remaining cats didn't wait for quick death. Almost as a pack they charged forward, converging into a unit.

They struck Holyfield first, clambering up his body, using their claws and their teeth on him.

Briggs had no time to react before they were on him too, and more of them dropped from the trees to sink teeth into the men's faces and ears.

Holyfield felt half of his left ear separate into a cat's mouth.

He screamed, a scream that could not drown out the chief's own.

Both of them tumbled into the dirt at the same time, flailing their arms in a worthless effort to fight back.

Their blood picked up dust from the ground which stuck to their skin as they rolled about, trying to fight the monsters which clung to them with stubborn tenacity.

One managed to bite into Holyfield's arm, finding vital veins, which it ripped out.

Another bit onto Briggs's nose and caught the edge of his left nostril with its teeth. It yanked upward, and the skin peeled, tearing the flesh upward, away from his face.

Holyfield attempted to get up onto his knees. The claws of one cat dug into his back, and another one ran forward, leaping onto his chest.

Its weight struck him, forcing the wind out of his lungs. He fell over onto his side, and another cat went for his throat.

The deputy choked, tasting his own blood as it bubbled up into his mouth. As it spilled out over his lips he closed his eyes, trying to shut out the pain.

Briggs fumbled at his side to pull his pistol from its holster. Just as he was tugging the barrel free, one of the cats, a large one, bit down on his wrist. Its daggerlike teeth pierced one of his veins, uncorking a new flow of blood that seemed to spray out of his arm like a pressure hose with each beat of his heart.

The gun slipped onto the ground at his side. Clenching his teeth, he reached over with his other hand, struggling with his body, rolling to the side so he could reach the pistol.

It was difficult, reaching across his body as he was. When his fingers closed on the weapon, he had the barrel.

Cats were still ripping at his shoulders and back, but he forced himself to fall over onto his back with the gun resting on his chest so that he could turn it and get the handle into his hand.

Blood bubbled out of his nose and spattered across his face as he tried to get a grip on the gun. The flap of skin which had been ripped back from his nose left part of his sinus cavity exposed, and as he moved dust collected, burning as if it had been salt.

The cats were all over him, biting deeply. Once the gun

was in his hand properly, he slung his arm to one side hitting a cat with it first. Then he aimed it at another one.

The cat didn't pause from its assaults with its claws and mouth, so he pulled the trigger.

The explosion was loud and was followed by a burst of blood from the cat's chest and the smell of burned fur.

Then the cat continued forward, its eyes glazed but its jaws still dripping. The gaping hole in its chest pulsed blood forward into Briggs's face as it ripped into his jugular.

He died slowly, painfully, trying to scream.

He died thinking a silly thought, something that crept into his mind for no reason other than to distract him from the pain. *If a man screams in the forest and there is no one alive to hear him, is there a sound?*

As Navarra stood in the open doorway, the owl fluttered forward out of the darkness to alight on her arm.

She held it up as if she were a falconer, and it sat contentedly on her forearm.

The huge, almost human eyes peered at her without emotion, the rounded head turning slowly from side to side.

The eyes had witnessed all, and from them Navarra could perceive what had transpired.

The events made her feel even more powerful. All those who had sought to oppose her tonight had failed, had fallen.

She laughed deep and long, thinking about Travis Dixon's surprise when he tried to draw his wife from Navarra's clutches. He had not considered there might be obstacles involved.

The others had died as they deserved to. They reminded her of the men who had pursued her before, and she felt satisfaction in knowing of their pain.

She would not drink their blood. They had died the death of intruders, the death of necessity.

It was the death that would be tasted by anybody who opposed her. She was strong now. She controlled the forest, and in her makeshift castle she had gathered a circle of protectors.

She had learned from her mistake before and selected her circle, exploiting their needs quickly to fit her purposes.

Travis would come again for his wife, especially now that he had learned she was not turning against him, but was instead under some outside influence.

She would have to bring Alison here before dawn, because the house would not be as well protected in daylight. Her power would not extend into the dawn.

With the policemen dead, attention would be aroused tomorrow, so everything would have to be completed as soon as possible. As soon as night fell tomorrow, she would have to take Alison through the transformation.

As the chosen one, Alison would be the one of this generation to receive the changing and the strength.

The oracle would be ready, and even if the isolation of the resort did not prevent them from being found, whoever ventured into the forest to oppose her would be destroyed.

The oracle would be ready. She could feel the power growing even now. If the isolation of the resort did not prevent her group from being found, whoever ventured into the forest to oppose her would be destroyed.

She lifted her arm, dispatching the owl skyward, and her lips twisted into a smile. Then she began to laugh, and her laughter echoed through the night.

347

Chapter 31

After a shower, Travis was still not as good as new.

A scratch stretched across his left cheek made him look like an escapee from a chain gang, and various other spots where the dogs had gotten to him ached.

He sat on the lid of the toilet in Burns's bathroom with a towel around his waist while Chrisk attempted to apply first aid to the worst places.

He groaned through clenched teeth as she dabbed a cotton ball soaked in alcohol onto a cut along his ribs. It was bad, but not quite deep enough to require stitches.

After cleaning a bite on his arm, she wrapped it with gauze and adhesive tape and did what she could for a couple of other bites.

He got to his feet shakily and leaned against the sink.

"You missed your calling," he said. "Ben Case couldn't have done a better job of putting me back together."

"You probably need to see a doctor," she said, "and get a tetanus shot."

"I can't face a needle after being mauled by all those teeth," he said. He looked up into his reflection in the mirror, studying his eyes.

"Just making sure I'm sane," he said.

He put his jeans back on and slipped on a sports shirt
ory had provided. He left the tail of it out and with
hrisk's help half walked, half limped back into the
iest's den, where the others were still poring over
lumes of old books.

Plopping down into a chair, he brushed his wet hair
ck over his ears.

"Do you need medical attention?" Burns asked.

"None of the gashes are that deep. I probably need to
ave rabies shots, but I'll cross that bridge when I come to
"

"She knew you would be back," Burns said.

"So she left guardians," Chrisk said.

"Night guardians. Which means she must be some-
here else tonight."

"Killing somebody," Chrisk said.

"Or getting animals to kill them," Travis said. "I'd be
ead without Chrisk's help. Is there any logical explana-
on for this? Any kind of animal training she could have
mployed?"

Burns shook his head. "Not for so many different kinds
f animals. The dogs are one thing. That might be
ossible. I don't know if it's possible to train bats, but I'm
ure it would not be an easy task."

"The only thing remotely scientific might be that she
tilizes some kind of psychic energy to control the
nimals."

"That would mean it's not supernatural. It's just
omething natural we haven't recognized yet."

"Something that would have looked like magic to the
ncients," Chrisk said.

"I'm inclined to look even deeper," Burns said. "To the
rigins. Where did the power come from? Is it natural, or
as it been drawn from something beyond this realm of
nderstanding we call reality? It's a question I've asked all
ny life. Is this world all there is? If it's not, then the other

349

question is: are all the things outside our understandin
forces for good? Or is there outside evil? By the way she ha
acted, I'm inclined to believe her power is not a source fo
good. We have to find an explanation of what she is."

"Is it in the books?" Chrisk asked.

"Only the framework. The only real answers lie i
determining the truth among the legends. We have t
learn what she really is. Is she a witch? Is she a succubus? A
wood sprite?"

"The Bible talks about witches," Early said. "'You shal
not suffer a witch to live.'"

Burns nodded. "There is mention in the Bible of contac
with dark forces being forbidden. There's not a great dea
of elaboration on what that might be. The Bible is no
solely a history book. It doesn't recount all of what wa
seen by the people of ancient times."

"But I think it's the truth," said Jackson, his voice dr
and cracked. He was awake long past his bedtime, bu
determined to offer his experience.

"He's making a significant point," Burns said. "If th
Judeo-Christian teachings are correct, as my persona
beliefs have always held, then this woman must b
something out of that biblical history."

"And other people at other times would have inter
preted her based on their own superstitions," Chrisk said

"Just as we in our time would attribute her actions t
psychic phenomena and mental energy," Burns said.

"The big question for me is, how are we going to banish
her and get my wife back," Travis said.

"That's difficult to say," Burns said. "We still don'
know what she really is."

"We're not going to have a lot of opportunity for trial
and error," Travis said.

He swore under his breath. "I feel so helpless. I feel like
I'm in a dream. This can't even be real. It hasn't even hit
home yet. One minute I was arguing with my wife, and the
next minute I'm being eaten alive by hellhounds."

"Righteousness should be our shield," Early said.

"If she is evil, that is probably true," Burns said.

"Preacher, it has to be," the old man said. "We'd better k Jesus to protect us."

"That is so," Burns said.

He bowed his head and began to pray.

Denise Jowers, the part-time dispatcher/receptionist for e Bristol Springs police department, was surprised to nd the office empty when she arrived for work at 7 A.M. Vednesday.

Usually Chief Briggs was in his office by the time she rived and he already had coffee brewing. Seeing the pot npty, she guessed that he had stayed out late on his hunt d decided to sleep in.

She put her purse and her new Danielle Steel novel on er desk and set to work on the Mr. Coffee.

The coffee had just begun to brew when the phone rang. was Deputy Holyfield's girlfriend. He had not come ack from Bristol Springs and she was worried.

Denise hung up and tried the chief's home number.

No answer.

She tried Doug Langdon.

No answer.

Her concern grew. She drummed her fingers for a few 10ments and then went to the radio, where she got the ispatcher for the substation.

They hadn't heard anything from Holyfield since the revious day. Since they didn't have a unit available, she nally managed to raise a state police officer who had ɔme on duty an hour earlier.

Bored with watching the traffic pass and faced with leven more hours of his shift, he agreed to make a check of ie springs area.

His name was Donny Houston, a cop everybody ɔnsidered one of the good guys.

He was the one that found the bodies.

The sight made him begin to think seriously about different career. The coroner's office sent cars out in caravan, and the sheriff's office sent investigators.

Two cops were dead. Some reaction was required.

At the scene, the coroner determined quickly it was not criminal matter.

There was no clear set of rules for dealing with th problem that faced Bristol Springs because nothing lik this had ever happened before.

Now that local law enforcement was out of the picture, bureaucratic tangle developed with no one really sure wh had to do what.

After all, what could be done? Every animal couldn't b killed. A lot of people started to pray for rain, believin that would end the problem. They still thought th animals were thirsty.

But the thirst was not for water, though they had no wa of knowing that.

When news of the deaths reached Alden, he realized he' waited long enough to rally his support, and he saw it as prime opportunity to build his reputation.

He was confident that the drought would end and tha the agonizing demise of Bristol Springs would be turne around.

If he brought this crisis to an end, or at least appeared t do something about it, he'd be in high cotton, as th saying went. Once the town was back on its feet, he woul be in a position of power.

A seat on the town council followed by a shot at th mayor's office wouldn't be out of the question.

With his straw hat pushed back from his brow, h looked around the diner at the men Dex had gathere together. They had left their jobs or their farms because o their concern about the safety of the town. They didn'

ave much business or work to do anyway, with everybody
either broke, discouraged, scared to death, or just plain
dead.

"It's high time we did something," Alden said, facing
the group. "We left it up to the chief, and now he's dead.
He was a good man, but it was too much for him to handle
alone. It's gonna take each one of us. Now every man here
grew up huntin', so we've got the skill to remedy the
nightmare that's gripping this town." He liked the sound
of his last statement. It had an eloquence he had seldom
discovered in himself.

He started feeling like the guy in Julius Caesar, which
he vaguely remembered from high school English class,
who wooed the masses after somebody died.

"My friends," he said, summoning a memory of the
soliloquy, "It's time for us to take up the sword and do
something to protect our town and our families. This has
always been a good town, the kind of town where you can
walk the streets at night without worrying that somebody's going to knock you in the head. We owed a lot of
that to Chief Briggs. Something's come along now that
got the best of him, so now we'll have to go on in our own
way. We'll have to fight back the wild things the same way
the great men who built our town did."

"We'll get our guns, and we'll fight for our town. We're
going to find those cats out there wherever they're hiding.
Then we'll put a stop to what's gone on here. We'll make
sure nobody else has to die. We'll destroy the threat to our
own, and we'll all pull together."

"We'll ride out this drought, too, because nothing is
going to tear down Bristol Springs. This is Bristol
Springs, Louisiana, America, not Bristol Springs, Louisiana, Russia. It's *our* place, and the wild animals or
the drought or the drug pushers or whoever wants to take
it away from us will find they've made the wrong choice."

* * *

353

Dex had to admit that while Alden wasn't really saying much, he was saying it well, and people were responding. All of them were fed up with the weather and the fear and the threat of having to file Chapter Elevens, so they liked the idea of having something to fight against.

With Alden leading them, they'd be able to feel that they were doing something to regain control of their lives.

Not bad, Dex thought. It ought to be interesting to see what was going to happen.

Denise couldn't seem to find the chief's daughter. She kept calling places she might be, the homes of friends, without success.

She hadn't heard the chief mention her going away anywhere, and she felt she had to locate her. Somebody needed to try to break the news of Briggs's death to her gently. She was going to have a rough time of it with her daddy gone too.

As various law enforcement people passed through the office and used the phone lines, fielded questions from the media that called in, and did assorted police business, Denise tried to reach Langdon again. He would have to pick a time like this to get sick and drop out of sight. He was as weird as everybody had always said he was.

She hung up the phone. No one from the *Gazette* had called about the mess either.

Things were really screwed up in this town.

Travis sat in the back seat of Burns's car as they headed over to the Johnson house. Chrisk kept looking back over the seat at him as the priest eased the car along.

They had received word of the latest slaughter early, and it had hit Travis hard. He had spoken only a few words since hearing about it, and his growing anguish was

354

isible in his sullen face.

"Are you sure you're okay?" Chrisk asked.

"I'm fine," he growled. He sat with his shoulder against the door and his forehead resting against the glass. He peered out at nothing, not showing signs of fear, even though they had turned up nothing of value in their research, which had continued until just before dawn.

Eventually they had talked Early into getting some sleep, and while Chrisk and Travis drank coffee, Burns had gone out for breakfast.

He'd learned of the new deaths, and Travis had insisted that they go over with Burns as mediator to try and establish a dialogue with Alison.

They had no idea what kind of power Neva might possess, but Travis reasoned that she had not made any moves to reveal herself as anything other than a visitor. He didn't think she would start now, because she obviously wanted Alison for some purpose, something she didn't want to jeopardize.

The car pulled to a stop, and they climbed out together. There was no sign of movement in the house as they stood at the end of the walk. No curtains fluttered back, no doors opened.

Adjusting the cuffs of his shirt beneath his jacket, Burns led the way. Travis and Chrisk followed slowly. When they reached the porch, Burns went up the steps alone, leaving them waiting at the foot of the steps.

They had deemed it better for Travis not to be readily visible in the doorway.

Burns knocked, waited, knocked again.

Several seconds passed with no answer.

He turned back to Travis and held up his hands. "They're not coming out."

"Do you think they're still in there?" Chrisk asked.

"Most of the other deaths have taken place in the woods," Burns said, "as if she had to protect herself out

355

there. Maybe she's got a hiding place somewhere in th
forest."

"The dogs aren't around," Travis said. "All of th
deaths have taken place at night. Maybe she doesn't hav
any power in the daytime."

"The deception of posing as Mrs. Johnson's cousin
would lend itself to that," Burns said. "She took great car
to keep me away from Estelle. If she was all powerful sh
wouldn't have been afraid of anything. Her ability t
mesmerize seems consistent, however. Once it's estab
blished, it doesn't fade."

"You think Alison's still in there?" Travis asked. Hi
voice was grim, and his face looked like it was chiseled i
stone.

"I got in here once before," Burns said. "I guess I can d
it again. Watch for dogs."

Chrisk and Travis waited at the front door while Burn
disappeared around the house. A few moments later the
heard breaking glass.

When he opened the front door, the priest wa
perspiring. "I'm not as young as I used to be. I don't thin
I have a career as a second story man."

They stepped inside, into darkness and stifling heat
There was no air-conditioning turned on, and apparentl
all of the windows had been closed and locked.

Spreading out, they checked all the rooms, winding u
together again in the back bedroom.

The bed was rumpled, and a few towels were wadded u
on the floor.

"This is where Alison must have been," Travis said. "
can smell her hairspray."

"So she's been moved."

"You got too close," Burns said.

Travis sat down on the foot of the bed. "I guess we'r
going to have to go out into the woods and look for her. I
that's where she is."

356

"That's her element," Burns said. "We've got to know [wh]at we're doing, what we're up against."

"We've already spent the night trying to do that, Travis. [If] we're going to do much more research, we'd better do it [qu]ickly. We're wasting daylight."

In the same trucks they had driven the day before, Alden [an]d his followers headed out to the springs.

They were crowded into the cabs and loaded into the [be]ds of the vehicles. There were four trucks hauling [tw]enty men heavily armed with rifles and shotguns.

Their cheeks were stuffed with wads of tobacco, and [th]ey swore frequently in conversation. They were ready to [st]rike down the panther that had killed their townspeople, [an]d nothing was going to stand in their way.

The sheriff's detectives had left only one man at the edge [of] the forest. He was leaning against his car, wiping sweat [of]f his neck when he saw the trucks pull down the road [st]irring up a huge cloud of dust. It looked like a tornado [ap]proaching.

"Y'all cain't go in there," he said in a deep drawl.

"We got to," Alden said, climbing out of the first truck. [Y]ou boys have had your chance to do something, and it [h]asn't done anything but leave more people dead. We [g]onna do somethin' now."

More people piled out of the trucks behind him, spitting [to]bacco juice into the dirt, cocking their guns at the same [ti]me.

The deputy got out of their way. By the time he was on [h]is radio to report what was happening, the crowd had [d]isappeared into the woods.

Alden and Dexter led them, tromping back through the [fo]rest, kicking branches aside and fanning out in a line, [re]ady to blast anything in their path.

Chapter 32

The bier which had served as Navarra's resting place ha[d] been transferred into the center of the swimming pool, an[d] Alison slept there now, her face peaceful, her hands folde[d] gracefully across her chest. She might have been dead, an[d] only the gentle movement of her eyes beneath their li[ds] indicated she was alive. Navarra stood looking down [at] her but not touching her.

Alison reminded her so much of the ancestor, in h[er] features, in her speech, and most of all in the vibration[s] which trembled out from her like ripples across the surfa[ce] of a pond.

The touch that Navarra had given to Sarah Wilson s[o] long before had managed to carry forward to her grea[t-] great-great-granddaughter.

Just as the fair hair and pale eyes had lingered, so ha[d] the beginnings of the transformation, beginnings n[ot] pursued for more than a hundred years. Beginnings whic[h] waited now for consummation.

Gently she touched Alison's hair, then bent forward an[d] and kissed her forehead.

Time was close. Darkfall would bring the hour of th[e] ceremony. Already she could sense the stirrings in th[e] fabric of the universe. Tonight the curtain would dra[w] en, perhaps for the first time in an age.

Nothing would be allowed to prevent the creation of a
w sister, one to carry on the line. Navarra's army of
ght brothers would be on hand, her protectors would be
place.

When she summoned the demon goddess she and her
sters had come to know as Hecate so many ages past as
ey lay dying on the shores of the Red Sea, the gift of life
ould once again be renewed, and the cursed line would
nce again be prevented from dying out.

This time she would not be turned from her task.

She walked to the end of the pool where the altar was
onstructed and the idol of Hecate had been placed. The
nergy was stronger than ever.

Blade had gathered the herbs from the forest to create the
ncense to summon the dark spirit in the time-prescribed
tual.

He stood there now, looking at the features he had
arved.

"Is it time?"

"It will not be long. There will be those who try to
revent us from reaching our goal."

"I won't let them stop us," Blade said. "Not for
nything. I'm the black knight."

Navarra smiled. "Guard me well, my knight. I must
est. When the hour of darkness comes, we will begin."

Travis, Burns and Chrisk walked into the front room of
he police station and drew the attention of all present.

Several uniformed cops were sitting around smoking
nd drinking coffee while a sour-faced deputy with sweat
tains under the arms of his uniform tried to deal with a
ouple of reporters from Aimsley.

He didn't look happy about seeing more people in the
oom.

"If you folks will give us a few minutes . . ."

"We need to see files on the cause of death," Travis said

The cop's mouth dropped open. "What's that?"

Travis spoke slowly, clipping each word. "W . . . want . . . the . . . fucking . . . cause . . . of . . . deat . . . files . . . that . . . you . . . cocksuckers . . . are . . . si ting . . . on."

Burns took his arm and steered him away from the cop speaking softly into his ear.

As Chrisk moved to stay with Travis, Burns turned bac to the policeman and introduced himself.

"We believe there's something out of the ordinary goin on here. There may be something in the autopsies on th previous deaths which could shed some light on thi matter . . . something *we* might be able to recognize tha you overlooked."

"This case is still under investigation," the cop said.

"I believe your initial reports on such matters are publi record," Burns countered.

"If it is, I'm not authorized to release it."

Burns eyed him steadily. "Your authorization is nc pertinent. The custodian of public records is civilly an criminally liable for failure to release them, and an ordinance set up by your department to subvert that is i violation of state law."

"You can have me put in jail later, Father. You're nc seeing them, and you're interfering with importar business."

"Typical police bullshit," Travis said, pulling awa from Chrisk. "We're wasting time." He left the office wit Chrisk behind him. Burns followed.

They were about to pile back into the car when Denis stepped out of the office.

She had obviously been crying. "Reverend Burns," sh said.

Burns turned to her. "Yes."

"There is something strange going on. The chie

ieved that before he was killed, I could tell it. Now his
ughter is missing, and I don't know what's happened to
ngdon. These deputies don't know what to do. Nobody
es."

"We're not dealing with a typical problem," Burns said.
"You think you can do something about it, don't you?"
"I'm trying to. Before others are hurt."
"Doc was killed too, but he examined one of those
dies. He and the chief talked about it quite a bit in the
ief's office. I don't know what it was all about, but the
ief seemed bothered by it. I overheard very little of it."
"Did he make a report?"
"I can't get you anything out of the office here, but I'm
re Doc would have records of his own in his office. You
dn't hear this from me either, but there's a key in the
rch lamp by his office door. He always kept it there
cause he got forgetful after his wife died."
"Thank you very much," Burns said. "May you be
essed."

By 4 P.M. Alden's band had been about their task for
out two hours. They were ready to stop for a rest and to
t the sandwiches they'd had prepared at the diner before
parting, and they had not seen any sign of a panther.
The only things they had killed were a squirrel
nfortunate enough to have rattled a branch and a bluejay
hich fluttered out of a bush while Lester Ingram was
alking toward it.
All the men were sweating, and they'd grown more
ritable. Their swearing had increased considerably, but
s they discarded their tobacco wads and began to shove
od into their mouths, they started to talk about old
unting trips—the animals they had killed, the trophies
ey had collected, and the quantities of beer they had
nsumed.
They were veteran woodsmen with memories of many

361

animal slaughters. Deer and squirrels and chipmunks h
all fallen to their guns. They were doing the animal
favor, they all said. They had to kill some of the anim
off. Without hunters, animals would deplete their fo
supply and they would starve to death.

It was a never-ending justification for their own love
killing.

"We sure are getting deep into these woods," Dex
said.

"We're not even to the place where Jasper got kill
yet," Alden said, flicking a piece of ham off the corner
his mouth.

Dex took off his cap and wiped his hair back off h
forehead. "How long are we going to stay at this?"

"Long as it takes," Alden said. "We've got to let t
people know we did what we set out to do."

"Sheriff's office didn't say much."

"They probably hope we get the job done for them
Alden said. "They'll haul most of their people back out
here by tonight. Leave a couple of deputies to operate t
police office until the council can appoint someboc
Otherwise, this is just a pain they don't want. It's like
burden we're relieving them of."

"Where do you suppose that old panther sleeps?" D
asked.

"Beats the hell out of me, but if all of us can't flush h
out, maybe we'll run him back to Texas."

"What if it gets dark on us?" Dex asked.

"We'll have to keep at it."

"That cat'll have an advantage on us in the dark."

"We'll send somebody back for some lanterns and stu
We've got to get him. We wait until tomorrow, a man
two will drop off. Then a couple more the next day. The
the cat will get away and we won't have proved anythin
and the next thing you know, somebody else'll get kill
and we ain't done any better than Briggs did."

"Guess you're right," Dex said and poured a sip

oca-Cola down his throat.

In another twenty minutes they were on their feet again, sted and ready to wreak more havoc.

The entry into the doctor's office worked just as the olice dispatcher had promised. They piled into the small ffice together and again found a place filled with stifling eat.

Chrisk located a fan and switched it on, while Travis fled the desk and then the file cabinet.

Burns made no effort to stop him. He knew it wouldn't o any good. He just watched until Travis came up with e file he needed.

Plopping down into the swivel chair behind the octor's desk, he flipped open the manila envelope and pread the handwritten notes out across the green blotter.

The doctor's handwriting was a shaky scrawl, and it pread out across the unlined paper like the trail of some lithering reptile dragging a jagged tail.

Travis pored over it and passed it to Burns. "I think it's vritten in Greek," he said. "We may need you to interpret . It's worse than my handwriting."

The priest took the pages, his eyes scanning them uickly. As he read, the color drained from his face.

He slumped back onto the desk.

"What is it?" Travis asked.

The pages slipped from his hands. Chrisk picked them up and tried to decipher them herself.

Burns swallowed. "It's something I never thought bout."

"What?"

"Does it say what I think it says?" Chrisk asked.

"It says he was completely drained of blood," Burns aid.

Chrisk's face took on a haunted look. "My God."

"I don't know what I was expecting," Burns said.

"Anything but a vampire?" Travis said.

"Or the being that started the legend."

"If I hadn't seen what I have in the last few days, I'd never believe it," Chrisk said.

"She controls animals. Just like it said they could in *Dracula*," Travis said.

"She's been using them to try to cover the cause of death," Chrisk said. "You said there should have been more blood at that first killing."

Travis nodded. "She must drink the blood and then have the animals rip her victims apart."

"It worked," Burns said. "All of us were thinking what we were supposed to think—that it was just animals, and Briggs was apparently too frightened to believe what he was reading in the medical reports."

"Does this shed any new light on your research?" Travis asked.

"It probably makes it more complicated. How do you know what part of the stories are real?" Chrisk asked.

"Obviously there's some truth to the legend," said Burns. "I doubt she got bitten by a vampire bat and developed this desire and power. There must be some other explanation."

"The blood must serve as some sort of transfer of the life energy, something that sustains and feeds her psychic ability."

"So do we drive a stake through her heart?" Travis asked.

"It might not hurt to prepare for every contingency," Chrisk said.

"Where did she come from?" Burns wondered. "Why is she suddenly here? Did the drought have something to do with it? There are so many questions to answer."

Chrisk nodded slowly. "The woman who lives beneath the waves. The first death took place at the springs, where we've always been told the woman lived. The water was ied up out there."

"So whatever happened out there after the Civil War ust be true," Travis said.

"We never read the newspaper accounts I found," hrisk said. "They're still back at the office. They might ed some light."

"Let's haul it," Travis said. "We can make some ooden stakes out of the furniture."

The sheriff's detectives and deputies who had come into ristol Springs began to filter out again as the afternoon ragged on. There was not a great deal to investigate. The ause of the deaths was not in question, and there was no ispicion of foul play.

The hunt was a cause of limited concern mainly because f the fear it might result in someone getting shot ccidentally.

Although it was not sanctioned by the sheriff's office, it id have the potential to bring in the panther.

If it failed, the sheriff was not truly associated with it, so t was politically safe.

Only two deputies were left posted at the edge of the oods in case something bad happened.

Otherwise the men of Bristol Springs were left to ontinue their hunt without disturbance or interference.

Kirby Smith followed an overgrown trail through the oods, stalking along it because it made for a little easier raveling in the heat. He didn't really expect it to lead him o the panther. He was just tired of getting branches in his ace every few feet.

A rabbit stirred some weeds a few feet in front of him, nd he almost shot at it before he saw the white tuft of its ail disappearing into some brush.

Kirby was as concerned about the town as anybody, but he wasn't quite as itchy on the trigger as some of the others.

He was a quiet man, and many folks said he resembled Henry Fonda, both in his looks and in his mannerisms and speech patterns. He reminded people of many of the strong figures Fonda had played in his career.

He'd been away from the town, working as a truck driver in Denver and the northwest before coming back home to tend the family farm.

Nothing he'd ever tried had been terribly successful. He'd managed to keep food on the table, which he considered enough.

Hunting had always been a pastime for him. He was a decent hunter when it came to squirrels. He'd never had much experience with panthers.

The path he followed finally wound around a stand of pine trees, and he spotted the overgrown structure which had once been a resort.

The path had been the secondary access. The remains of the old highway which had been closed for ages led up from the other side. There was very little of it left which had not been claimed by the forest.

Like most, he had forgotten the resort was there.

Looking at it now with its cracked glass and the brush which half shrouded it, it looked like it might be a good hiding place for a panther which had some mountain lion blood in its veins. The old resort might remind the cat of a cave.

Easing the safety off his rifle, he pushed forward. His legs began to tremble a little as he moved. He didn't know what to expect in confronting a panther. He'd hunted raccoons at night, but he'd never actually seen one. He'd had his doubts there were any around up until now. People claimed to hear them scream, but he knew people often exaggerated.

Reaching the edge of the building, he tried to look in ne of the windows, but it was covered in dust from the .side.

Flexing his fingers on the weapon, he eased around the .de of the building, following the wall in hopes of cating a door.

Rounding a corner along the back of the building, he ootted the kid, a muscular teenager wearing black pants nd a sleeveless black t-shirt.

He was working on a motorcycle with a ratchet. When e heard footfalls, he turned around and straightened up.

"How's it going?" he asked. His hair fell across his face ntil he brushed it away. He was rough looking, but his ice spread with a smile.

"Okay," Kirby said, lifting his rifle so that it wasn't ointing at the boy.

"Name's David," the kid said.

Kirby released the barrel of his gun and shook hands autiously, watching closely to make sure the kid didn't ull a tire iron or anything. You couldn't be too careful.

"It's kind of hot weather for hunting," Blade said. "It's ot the season, is it?"

"Special case," Kirby said. "There's a killer panther in aese parts. We're trying to hunt it down. All the animals ave been acting kind of crazy."

"It's weird. I've heard about that. I'm kind of camping round here. I've been in this old steambath here a couple f days."

"That's what I was checking," Kirby said. "I thought it aight be holed up in there. Kind of like a lair for it, you now."

"Well, I haven't seen any big cats in there since I've oread my sleeping bag out. It's kind of nice to be out of ae weather. This is so old I didn't think anybody would aind."

Kirby felt a little relief. Now he wouldn't have to go in

367

there, which suited him just fine. He hadn't really wanted to wander around in the shadowy interior of the place.

Deserted buildings were spooky enough without having to watch for a panther to jump out at you.

"I guess I'll move on," Kirby said. "I'll tell the rest of my group there's nothing back here so they don't bother you. I guess it's O.K. for you to be here."

"Thanks," the kid said. "I'm going to be heading out of here as soon as I get my bike fixed. I'll try to watch out for wild animals."

"Good," Kirby said and headed back around the building. Back on the trail he met another of the party, Berton Sanders, and turned him back with the message that the direction was futile.

"There's only one of those weird hippie kids over there," he said.

"Probably a satanist," Berton said, and together they headed in another direction.

Blade slipped the iron rod from beneath his shirt, where it had been ready if he'd needed it.

Navarra had told him to turn people back by fraud rather than violence, if possible. Attention was unavoidable, but she felt the less the better.

She was sleeping now, deep in the trancelike state which would give her the strength she needed for tonight.

Blade could feel his own excitement building.

With any luck, the old-timer would do as he had promised and keep the others away.

If they did come here, Blade was prepared to do whatever was necessary to keep Navarra safe. Inside, Langdon was waiting to do the same.

Nothing would deter the transformation she had called for. She had said the girl's husband would come. Blade would be ready for that. He wasn't squeamish any longer.

368

He was loyal to the cause. He knew he could not receive Navarra's ultimate gift as the woman would, but her other rewards and the enlightenment she could provide made it worthwhile enough.

Worthwhile enough for him to do anything.

Travis slammed the front office door open and plowed across the room to snatch up the rolled photocopies.

Nightfall was still a few hours away, but he knew time was important. Once they knew what they were doing, they would still have to find where Navarra was keeping his wife in the forest.

He spread the paper on the drawing table and began to scan the columns of print. It was small and difficult to read. The copy was grainy and dark.

Chrisk and Burns moved up behind him to look over his shoulders at the article: *Mystery Woman Disappears After Sheriff's Death.*

Sheriff Vince McKinley died late last night as he led a posse after a woman suspected of murder.

Witnesses said the sheriff was trampled to death by his horse. Some speculated the woman may have managed to spook the horse in some way.

Others still allege that magic was involved. Rumors that Navarra Dorsey was a witch have circulated through Bristol Springs for several weeks.

Acting on the rumors and the discovery of several bodies that were apparently mutilated, McKinley was pursuing Dorsey for questioning.

Reportedly she was warned of the matter by a friend, Sarah Wilson. She fled her home and dress shop before McKinley could arrive.

Some say she fell into the springs, although there was no witness to the event.

369

Acting on behalf of Sheriff McKinley, Amos Williams, recently deputized, questioned Miss Wilson.

Because she was close to Miss Dorsey, she was suspected of complicity. Rumors of black magic have also surrounded Miss Wilson.

Miss Wilson was to have married recently, but later declined the proposal of Steven McCullers.

She was seen frequently about town with Miss Dorsey. She visited often in the dress shop Miss Dorsey ran, and the two often took meals together.

Mary Gaines, a friend of Miss Wilson's, said there seemed to be a change in Miss Wilson's behavior. "She began to act strangely after she broke off the engagement," Miss Gaines said. "She was like a different person. She acted very distant."

A search for Miss Dorsey has so far been unsuccessful. Some have speculated she might try to return to her shop if she did not drown. It was rainy the night she disappeared. A search of the water has not revealed a body.

With the hint of magic and superstition, people in town have been talking a good deal about the incident.

It appears all of the answers may never be found. Bristol Springs has its very own mystery.

"A legend is born," Travis said when he had finished reading. "Otherwise, it's useless."

He tossed the paper aside and walked over to a ladder-back chair. Picking it up, he slammed it across a table. It splintered, and he took one leg of it to fashion into a weapon.

"It doesn't give us much new information," Burns sighed, glancing back at the paper.

"Maybe it does," Chrisk said. "I think we're missing

mething. The woman they questioned was named Wilson."

"The same name used by our vampire woman," Burns said. "Neva is a variation on Navarra. She built an alias. It seems to confirm she was around in those days. We already suspected she was supernatural."

"She took the name of her friend from the old days," Chrisk said. "Travis, think for a minute. Alison is from here. You know how she'd been researching her ancestry. Look at the pictures of the gravestones. Some of her family was in town back then. She showed me some gravestones when we did that piece on the old cemetery last month."

Trav paused in his work. "Delta Marie Wilson," he whispered. "She always liked the sound of that name. That was one of her great-great-grandmothers." He looked over at the wall where the framed photographs hung. Among them was a shot of a weathered tombstone decorated with a white stone Bible which bore that name.

"Sarah must have been one of the ancestors also," Chrisk said. "Although Wilson was a maiden name, it seems. Maybe Delta was Sarah's mother."

"Who knows how names are handed down? She must be related," Travis speculated. "It's probably in that book Ali was keeping."

"So Navarra was drawn to Alison because she knew her ancestor?" Burns said.

Travis nodded slowly. Connections were being made in his brain.

"Maybe some of Sarah Wilson's things would still be around in the family home where Ali's cousin lives."

"You think there might be something there?"

"I don't know. We don't have the time to keep checking out these things."

"Any information could be valuable," Burns said. "We're facing great danger here. We need to split up. Mr. Jackson must be rested by now. He and Chrisk could go

371

over to the house and check for whatever might be there You and I can go ahead to the forest and start looking We've still got some daylight. It should be safe for while."

"I hope several hours is enough," Travis said, tossin another chair leg to Burns.

"That won't work," Chrisk said. "Reverend Burns, yo can spot something pertinent quicker than I can if ther are any of Sarah Wilson's things left. I can go wit Travis."

"It's too dangerous," Travis said.

"Damn it, I want to help," she protested. "Besides, it' unlikely they'll find anything at the house. They probabl won't be far behind us."

"We're wasting time," Travis said. "Lory, you searc the house. She's right, you'll know if you're findin anything worthwhile before any of the rest of us will. M Jackson might be able to help you."

"You're talking about more than a hundred years ago,' Burns said. "There's probably nothing like Chrisk said.'

"You haven't seen the attic over there," Travis said "Besides, Sarah Wilson knew Navarra personally. Sh might have kept something that could be worthwhile. If go out there now while it's still daylight and I screw up it's going to take more than good intentions to best tha woman. We know what she can do at night, and the wood are full of friends for her. You'll have to have some kind o trump."

Dexter picked out a spot in the shade and sat down to le his feet rest. He was used to working in the heat, for he' lived without air-conditioning as a kid, but his feet wer aching. This was shaping up to be one of Alden's mor grueling efforts to rise to power in Bristol Springs Extended time in the woods would take its toll or ybody, and he was getting bored above all else.

He would stick around only because of the loyalty he'd
lt toward Alden since they were kids. They'd been
addies for years. Good friends were hard to come by, and
sides, if Alden got to be mayor, he would get Dexter a
od job as supervisor of town workers or something.

Alden caught up with him and sat down. "You think
e're going to get anywhere before dark?" he asked.

"It's a while yet. I don't know. Panthers must hole up
mewhere in the daylight. Nobody ever sees 'em, I can
ant you that."

"He'll be on the hunt again tonight."

"It'll be dangerous as hell out here," Dex said. "It ain't
en just the panthers that have been a problem."

"We can make some torches. As long as we're careful
ith them, we won't have a problem. If that fire from
bley's truck didn't set off a forest fire, nothing will. And
u know ain't no animal gonna make a run at a torch."

"Guess you're right," Dex said. "We'll have a good hunt
me dark."

Early had been awake for a couple of hours and was
rowing tired of the waiting when he saw the priest's car
ull up again. Travis drove up behind him a few seconds
ater with Chrisk on the passenger side. It made the old
an feel a little more at ease. At least it let him know
othing bad had happened so far, but he didn't feel any
reat relief. He knew things were far from being over. He
lso felt a twinge of regret seeing Chrisk still riding with
Travis.

He walked out the front door and greeted them at the
loor. It was Chrisk who bounded up the steps first. Her
air was falling across her face, and her hands were
rembling when she touched his arm.

Her words flooded from her mouth, rattling out a story

373

that sounded half mad. He nodded a few times, unsure
what he should believe. Looking past her, he could s
Travis and Burns were taking her seriously.

"We've got to get out there to the springs and look f
Alison while it's still daylight," Chrisk concluded. "A
you feeling up to helping Reverend Burns search the o
house?"

"I don't mind helping the reverend," he said, "but
don't like the idea of you going out in those woods."

"We have to, Grandpa. There's not much time left. Th
is Alison's life. She might not be out there if it weren't f
me."

Travis started to speak, but Early raised his hand. "
won't hold you back," he said. "You think they're in tho
woods?"

"That's where everything has happened," Chrisk sai
"She has to be out there somewhere."

"I suppose you're right." He rubbed his hand across h
face. "I've been thinking. There used to be a resort ou
there a long time ago. That'd be the likeliest place whe
she'd be holed up."

"I have heard of it," Chrisk said. "It closed down when
was little."

"It's been mostly forgotten," Early said, "but the ruin
are still there."

"How can we find it?" Travis asked.

"There's no road anymore. Still, you just might be ab
to cut your car partway through the woods and make
little time. You go out past the end of the springs and hea
due west. You might be able to go a good distance 'fore th
trees stop you. It's going to be rough going," he warned

"We'll have to manage," Travis said.

"As soon as we find something, or as soon as we kno
there's no hope of finding anything, I'll be right behin
you," Burns said.

"Say a prayer for us in the interim," Travis said.

"I will," Early said. "Take good care of my grand-daughter. Don't let that witch drink her blood."

"I'll do my best," he said.

Once they were on the highway, Travis pushed his convertible to a record speed, ignoring the groans of protest from the engine and the ensuing shudders and vibration. The stakes he had fashioned out of the old chair rattled together on the backseat, and Chrisk held onto the dash for support.

"I can't believe this is happening," she said.

"It's a bad dream," Travis said. "I just want to make sure that when we wake up from it, things will be all right again."

"I'm sorry for what I caused."

"Don't blame yourself. Navarra already had her plan in motion. She would have found some way to get Alison no matter what."

"What could her purpose be?"

"I don't know. It has to be more than she wanted from the others. Ali would already be dead if that were the case. Navarra probably wouldn't have lingered here this long without some special reason. She's made a lot of effort to conceal herself."

"Do you think there are others like her?"

"If there's one, who knows? People are unwilling to believe in things they don't understand, so there's a bonus for her right there. With all the homeless and the missing children they probably have plenty of prey that don't get recognized for what they are."

"Trav, do you think she turns the others into vampires?"

"I don't think she's a Bela Lugosi type. We haven't seen the dead walking. It looks like when she kills, they stay dead."

375

The car fishtailed as he jerked it off the roadway onto t[?]
path to the springs. Chrisk felt herself tossed about a[?]
had to grab onto the door to steady herself.

She realized how afraid she was now. It was possib[?]
she'd never make it to college. She'd never thought mu[?]
about dying, but the concept was becoming very real
her.

The car reached the end of the road and fishtailed aga[?]
in the loose sand as Travis piled it down the embankme[?]
and sped along beside the dry spring bed.

The bed reached about a hundred yards parallel to t[?]
woods, and at the end of it the land sloped downward,
dry expanse of more dust which stretched back to meet t[?]
woods where it curved around.

With his foot heavy on the gas pedal, Trav headed dow[?]
the slope. The shocks were bad on the old vehicle, so
bounced up and down as it moved.

At the edge of the forest, he aimed it between a couple [?]
thick pine trees. Once between them, he had to jerk th[?]
wheel hard to the right to miss a big oak which sproute[?]
near the pines.

The ground was uneven. The tires crunched over it a[?]
the bouncing grew worse. Chrisk attempted to ancho[?]
herself.

Travis gripped the wheel and pressed his back again[?]
the seat, wedging himself to keep steady.

Branches scraped along the side of the car and swatted [?]
the windshield as he zigzagged between trees and bul[?]
dozed over smaller bushes.

Fallen branches raked along the undercarriage of th[?]
car, thumping against the floorboard beneath their fee[?]

The sun was still high, but its rays angled dow[?]
through the branches. They were going west . . . towar[?]
sunset. An unsettling thought.

Just ahead, a gully furrowed through the forest floo[?]
Travis braked to keep from plunging the car into i[?]

376

utting the vehicle hard to the right, he guided it ongside the rut until he found a place flat enough to oss.

More branches whipped at the windshield. Things emed to be growing closer together, and more stumps nd obstacles dotted the landscape.

Travis steered around the remains of a fallen oak and lowed the car through a thick growth of briars and nderbrush.

Chrisk felt her heart thundering in her chest. Trav was xercising some caution, but he was not giving any uarter to the opposing vegetation.

She didn't try to speak to him now, Uttering a "be areful" would be meaningless.

Her eyes locked on the scene in front of her, the rushing rees, the branches, the brush.

The land made another slope downward. It was steep, ut Travis didn't avoid it. He tried to keep the car straight s he plowed over the slope, but the wheels didn't hold.

The vehicle skidded sideways and slid downward. Chrisk braced herself for a crash, but the car came to rest vith a gentle thud in another gully along the base of the ise.

The car was at an angle, a bad angle for exits. Her door vas on the uphill side, and it was too heavy to push upward.

"Roll the window down," Travis said when her attempts failed.

She complied, and he pushed her upward. She climbed hrough the escape hatch and accepted the stakes when Travis passed them up to her.

He scrambled out on his own and took her arm to usher her around the car. They started the trek on foot at a jog.

Daylight wouldn't last forever.

Chapter 33

The house was old but not ancient. It was a white fram home of the variety popular in southern towns just aft World War II. It sat back off the street in the shade of willow tree that dangled weeping boughs over the edge the front porch, where a swing creaked back and forth o rusty chains.

The white paint had cracked in a few places, but it wa not peeling too badly.

Burns and Early were greeted at the front door by woman of about thirty-five. She bore only a sligh resemblance to Alison. Her skin was a little more pale, an she was a good deal heavier. Her name was Skitsie, an people were wont to talk about her. She was considere strange. Her father had left her a little money and a goo insurance payment, and with the house in the family, sh had a free place to live. Living in the house was about al she did as far as anyone could tell. She had no boyfriends and even the rumors about girlfriends didn't seem to b true.

Her bleached hair was limp and slightly oily, with darker roots showing where it was growing out.

She wore faded overalls over a t-shirt. There was no much mystery about why she spent most of her time alone

She had apparently been watching television, because the voices from a soap opera were blaring somewhere behind her.

"You're the preacher, aren't you?"

Burns nodded. "I'm a friend of Alison and Travis," he said.

"Yeah, I've seen what you write in their paper."

Early nodded and tipped the cap he was wearing. "I'm Early Jackson," he said. "I knew your daddy."

She nodded. "What can I do for you gentlemen?"

Burns studied her features, unsure of how much she had heard about what was going on in town. From the times he'd heard Travis speak of her, he'd gathered she was not well informed.

"We're here for Travis," he said, careful to make sure he was phrasing his words so that they were not lies. "We need to look in your attic for some old family items. They might be of help to Alison."

"For the paper?"

"I believe she'd spoken to you about going through the old things?" Burns said. "She was trying to trace the family tree."

"If we could just have a look, it would let you get back to your program, Miss," Early suggested.

"Okay. I'll show you to the hatch."

The hatch was a hole in the ceiling between the closet that housed the hot water heater and a narrow pantry.

They had to dig a step ladder out of another closet, knocking over several boxes filled with Harlequin Romances in the process.

Early tried to pick them up, but Skitsie shooed them away. "Y'all don't bother with that. I'll clean it up later."

She apparently saved everything until later. The house was a mass of clutter. Old newspapers and magazines were strewn everywhere, as were discarded items of clothing.

Passing the kitchen, Burns noticed food items on the

stove and on the countertop which were starting to look frightening.

He set the ladder up quickly and climbed up it to push the board which covered the hatch out of the way.

Climbing back down, he helped Early scale the rungs. The old man moved slowly, placing his feet carefully until he reached the top. With difficulty he disappeared through the hole.

The attic was dark and the heat oppressive. The air conditioners in the house did little to cool it, and the atmosphere was thick and musty.

Burns said a quick prayer of thanks that at least the light worked when he pulled the chain to switch it on.

Its white light brought them into a world of boxes. They were stacked everywhere, one on top of the other, spilling out old letters and brown fragments of newspapers used for packing insulation.

The room was larger than Burns had expected and floored with plywood which allowed almost all of it to be utilized for storage.

Trunks from several generations were on hand, and unused items of furniture were stuffed into corners.

He took a step and kicked a small cardboard tray spraying powdery rat poison across his shoes.

"How did they get those things through that hole?" he asked, nodding at some chests of drawers which were clearly larger than the hole through which they had been squeezed.

"Maybe they put them up here first, then built the hole," Early suggested. He was already wiping away sweat.

Burns unbuttoned his collar and rolled up his sleeves.

"You go that way, I'll look in this direction," he said.

"Needle-in-a-haystack time," Early said.

"We just won't spend a lot of time with it," Burns said. "If we don't think we're into the right era in about an hour, we'll go find Travis and Chrisk."

"Sounds good to me," Early said. He picked up an old white shoebox that was tied with string and peeled it open. "Steerage papers for old-world ancestors," he said.

"Wrong side of the family," Burns said.

"I vote we dig into those trunks," Early said.

Burns agreed.

Naturally, they were locked.

The branch of a myrtle tree rattled, and Hoyt Atwood aimed his shotgun and yanked the trigger back in an unprofessional manner, causing both barrels to explode.

Feathers began to float in the air. They were brown, and they sort of drifted the way feathers from pillows did if the pillows happened to get ripped open.

"I think they were thrushes," said Doyle Menger, tilting his hat back on his head.

"Well, dat blast it," Hoyt swore. "Ain't no panther within a hundred miles of here."

The men around him began to chuckle, but they shared his frustration. It was hot even though the sun was slowly beginning to creep down. Several people had given up on the effort, and everybody else was beginning to consider the same move.

"Good thing you got those, Hoyt," someone said.

"Yeah, we ain't gonna be menaced by no birds now."

"Well, shit on it," Hoyt said, spitting out his tobacco. "I'm going home. This ain't gettin' us nowhere." He took a few steps and then stopped, looking back at a few of the others. "Is anybody coming with me?"

A few of the men had ridden with him. They didn't have to think long before they agreed to tag along with him for his departure.

Dex and Alden watched them go. They had about six men left in their party now, mostly the ones who'd ridden in Dex's truck.

"We've still got a job to do," Alden said. "I know

381

everybody's tired, but that don't mean we can just up an[d] quit. If we do that, somebody else is gonna wind up dea[d] from that monster.''

The men all nodded, but they were grudging nods. Morale was getting low.

''We'll take a little rest break,'' Alden said. ''Then we'[ll] move on.''

As several of the men moved over to some trees to reliev[e] themselves, Alden turned to Dex.

''We've got to do something. We've got to find tha[t] thing.''

''If he ain't here, he ain't here,'' Dex said.

''If we don't find him before it gets dark, we're gonn[a] have to take those precautions.''

''We'll stay in a group.''

''That might not be enough. It's gonna be dangerous.''

''So? Should we go back when it gets dark?''

''I ain't goin' back empty-handed,'' Alden said. ''We'r[e] out here to prove something as much as we are for the goo[d] of the town.''

Dex didn't argue.

''The thing is, we need some way to take care o[f] ourselves out here,'' Alden said. ''I don't want any of thes[e] monsters stalking us.''

''What do you suggest?''

''No animal in the world will run at fire, even if they'v[e] lost their fear of men.''

''Torches? Like you talked about?''

''We got to.''

''It's a powder keg out here.''

''We'll be careful.''

''If you say so,'' Dex said.

Alden called the men together and told them what h[e] wanted them to do. Then they turned and began to gathe[r] sticks that would be usable.

* * *

hrisk felt as if the briars were reaching out to grab her
she fought her way past them, following Travis
ugh the tangles of vines and branches which ob-
cted their path.

He was using the sticks he carried to knock things aside,
mpting to clear a trail. He was not a hundred percent
ctive.

Both of them were covered in sweat, their clothes like
rags on their backs. Chrisk could feel drops of
spiration spilling down her back.

Trav kept trying to pick up speed, but as soon as they
an to gain ground, more obstructions appeared. They
re in territory which had not been traveled in a long
e.

"I perceive that we haven't found the easiest route
ilable," Chrisk said. "Do you think we're getting close
he resort?"

"Hard to say. I think we're still headed in the right
ection."

He ducked under some intertwining branches and
most slammed into a man in a rumpled fedora who
ked a little like Jed Clampett.

"Stanley," Chrisk called. "We've found Dr. Living-
n."

The man looked at them with a puzzled expression. For
me reason he seemed to find it odd to discover a pair of
ung people in jeans and tennis shoes taking a safari
ough a briar thicket.

"You two lost?"

"More along the lines of confused," Travis said.
We're from the *Gazette*," he added, to quell further ques-
ns.

"I'm Kirby Smith," the man said.

Travis shook his hand. "Do you know these woods?"

"Nobody knows parts of these woods, but I've learned
me of them this afternoon. I was out with Alden's crowd,
t I got tired of being around those old boys."

383

"You happen to know about an old resort arour here?"

The man nodded, still puzzled by the encounter. "R across it this afternoon, as a matter of fact. You head ba another three hundred yards, you'll find an old road th leads up to it. It's overgrown, but you can walk it. It'll easier traveling."

"You were there?" Travis asked.

"Yep."

"Did you see anything out of the ordinary?"

"Some biker was hanging out there. Otherwise no. didn't go inside. He said it was empty. You better careful out here, you two. You know what's been going (in these woods."

"We will," Trav said.

Kirby studied them a moment longer, suspicious their presence. He eyed the sticks through narrowed lie but finally he turned his gaze away.

Travis and Chrisk looked at each other. She shrugge

A new worry had crept into Trav's eyes. If the resort w the wrong place, the uncharted woods left a broad area search.

"What are you looking for?" Kirby asked.

"Vampires," Travis said, setting off again withou offering explanation.

"Journalists have to check out all rumors," Chrisk sa and followed.

Kirby didn't follow.

She had to jog to keep pace with Trav's brisk movemen

"Who do you think the biker is?"

"Renfield." He handed her one of the stakes. "You ma need this."

The man in question sat near the doorway of the reso with his club resting on his lap. Across from him, Dou

384

gdon, with his uniform shirt unbuttoned almost to his
t, sat spinning the cylinder of his revolver.

t won't be long until dark," the policeman said.

t's still too long," Blade said. "Too long for my taste. I
t want interference. I want to see what's going to
pen."

f anybody tries to mess with us, we'll get 'em," Doug
, pointing his gun and peering down the barrel.

Whatever it takes," Blade agreed. "We've come this far.
e can't keep them away with a bluff, we'll kill them. It
sn't matter who shows."

Do not be too hasty in your judgment," a voice
spered from the shadows of the room.

oth men looked around to see Navarra. She emerged
vly, her eyes bright and rested.

What do you mean? I thought you didn't want
body here," Blade said.

Perhaps some of our visitors can be of value to us."

Who?"

Alison's husband, and the ebon girl might come. Bring
m to me when they arrive. When night falls I will have
of them. Perhaps. If not, they will die no less easily
ide as they would outside."

True," Blade said, and his smile was as grim as
varra's.

A search of the kitchen provided Burns with an old ice
k with a wooden handle which bore an endorsement for
ne forgotten feed product from the forties. The whole
use was like a museum of uncatalogued artifacts. If they
uldn't find anything here, there would be no hope.

He scaled the ladder and found Early sitting on the lid of
old gray cracker barrel, going through a stack of letters.

"Alison's father wrote poetry while he was courting her
ther," Early said. "No wonder she made a journalist."

He dropped the letters back into the box where he found them and sighed, the momentary brightness fad

"I hope we can help her," he said.

"We might," Burns said, kneeling before the first tru which also looked like the oldest.

He had rolled up his sleeves, but sweat was pour down his forehead. He began to jiggle the latch on chest.

He had to remove his glasses. Rubbing his arm ac his head and face, he stopped some of the stinging.

Putting his glasses back on, he slipped the slender p of the pick into the lock once again. He had no experie with breaking into things, so he had to feel his way alc jabbing at the tumblers.

The lock was old and did not give easily. Inside keyhole, things scraped and clicked without submitti

With the stuffy atmosphere in the room, Burns quic felt a flood of perspiration washing down his forehe

Pulling back, he wiped his brow, checked the tip of pick, and then plunged it back into the latch.

Things began to click again. He tried to push tumb about, hoping to spring the mechanism.

The sweat began to sting his eyes.

He wiggled the pick in another direction, and so thing popped inside the latch. Withdrawing the inst ment, he found he was able to slip the latch open.

Lifting the trunk lid, he found it filled with old dres

"'Least now you got the hang of how to do it," E: said.

"Right."

Burns pulled out his shirttail and bent to wipe his f on it. The sweat soaked the fabric.

Almost reluctantly he set to work on the second ch Since he was not quite sure what he had done right the f time, it was almost like starting the process from scrat

It didn't take quite so long this time around.

386

he open trunk offered no surprises.

was the third trunk which opened to reveal a stack of
ks, more envelopes, and particles of crumbling paper.
here were old novels with dusty black covers and a few
kled books of poetry, and at the very bottom was a
riorating old diary.

pening the first page, he found Sarah Wilson's
ature on the yellowed endpaper.

e held it up to Early with a smile before he began to
mb through it.

Will it do us any good?" the old man asked.

Hard to say."

did not go back to the Civil War days. Sarah Wilson
lived until 1915 and had written the book during the
years of her life.

Vater had touched it at some point, although Burns was
eved to find it was only a few drops that did little more
n create some brown stains across the first few pages.

Ie discovered it was not really a diary as he read the first
lines.

What is it?" Early asked.

A confession," Burns said. "And maybe a warning."

rom the volume by Sarah Wilson Davis:

*Most have forgotten the days after the war.
Although I was an outcast for many years, that has
passed. The loneliness is gone, and I have found
some measure of happiness in life. I have married
and have had beautiful children who have grown to
become beautiful adults.*

*I am fortunate and blessed by God, whom I once
turned my back on. It is good that He is forgiving, for
He has not held against me the mad moments of my
youth, when the promises of the witch woman*

seemed so sweet.

I know now that it was more than just he
promises. Her devil's magic touched my thoughts.
was but a girl. I was twenty-five, and that was not a'
age of wisdom. I had lived all my days in Brista
Springs, never seeing anything outside the bound
aries of the community.

So much is different now. The automobile came te
town last year, and they say it will all but replace th
horse-and-buggy in its time.

The old days are no more than a faded memor
now. I almost believe it was just a dream.

I am not so deluded that I accept that. It was real
and I write this now because it may someday benefi
someone who happens to encounter something
similar.

She came to Bristol Springs . . .

Burns skipped over a few pages which told of Navar
arrival in Bristol Springs and the establishment of
dress shop. He continued reading a few pages later w
Early looking over his shoulder.

I found myself fascinated by the things of which
she spoke. She filled my thoughts with stories of
faraway places where she had traveled. She had lived
for so long. (I did not believe how long when she first
told me.) She had been to the fabulous cities of
Europe and along the River Nile, and she had lived
in New York City and later New Orleans.

Burns flipped over a few more brittle pages, skimmi
until he found something else that seemed pertinent.

She told me she had lived since almost the
beginning of time. She spoke of her birth on the

388

hores of the Red Sea in a time very different from urs. It was then that I began to understand she had old me the truth about her life. She had lived forever ecause she was not human. She was the child of a monster from the depths of hell, one of a sisterhood f demon offspring who were cursed by God.

To survive they began to feed on the lifeblood of thers, and it has carried them through the centuries.

Navarra did not speak in detail about her past, only to give me brief hints of what had come before. Some I pieced together. I came to understand later he was an enemy of humanity. She hated us, and she aw me only as a means of carrying on her line.

Only one in a generation could be transformed, and that had to be a willing transformation. She elected me. I was a quiet girl, easily wooed by the promises she made. I would have made the change if it had happened as she intended.

She explained that I would become like her. I would have to draw the dark blood from the souls of men to survive. It would be necessary to drink the life essence of others, for there was an energy contained in it which held back the curse.

It was something she and her kind had learned when they began to die. They were not really of this world. They were from an unholy union that cursed God's will, and so they could not survive without the feeding.

From their patron in the darkness—I realize this will sound like the madness of some aged woman when it is read, but this is what I was told. They spoke to the figure of the night, who lived in the nether region on the coasts of hell. Some called her Hecate and later worshiped her in other ways. I do not know her real name, but it was she who helped those of Navarra's kind.

389

Through some oracle in her likeness they called t[...]
her, and she taught them to sustain themselves o[...]
blood and convert others to their ways so that the[...]
line would not be destroyed.

The she-demon known as Hecate was a servant o[...]
the great Fallen Angel, the Dark One whom we ca[...]
Satan. I know that now, but in those days it seeme[...]
like the light of the universe was shining in her eyes[...]
She convinced me how perfect it would be.

From one of her dressmaker's dummies, sh[...]
fashioned a likeness of Hecate which was to have[...]
served to summon her, just as the witch cults in th[...]
ancient days called on her.

She spoke to them through the oracle and[...]
bestowed the touch of darkness to replenish the rank[...]
of the damned.

All those members of those ancient cults could no[...]
expect eternal life . . . only the selected soul. Yet the[...]
others served their half-demon queen with willing-
ness because of the rewards she was able to bestow on[...]
them.

I wanted those dark blessings once, was ready to[...]
sell my soul for them. I thank God now that she was[...]
driven away by the men of the town. It cost our
sheriff his life, but it stopped my destruction.

The witch queen was plunged into the depths of
the water, and she could not free herself from that
prison. I do not know why she feared water. Perhaps
it was its purity. I pray now that if she is ever
resurrected, this will reach the hands of someone
who can somehow use this knowledge to prevent
the corruption of other souls.

Burns closed the book and let it rest in his lap.

"She was an old woman," Early said.

"You've got all your faculties," Burns said. "I c[...]

ve what you tell me. Why should we dismiss her
s just because of her age? It's farfetched, but there's
ence that it's real."

e got up from his seat and helped the old man move
rd the ladder.

rly struggled through the hole, his legs quivering as
oved.

Age affects different people differently," the old man

rns followed him to the floor, and together they
ed through the house. The cousin was in front of the
vision, so they didn't disturb her as they headed out the
t door.

hey'd spent enough time here. Both of them wanted to
o the forest to help Travis and Chrisk. They agreed the
thing they could do was stop by the church and then
out to the forest as soon as possible.

You're trained in theology," Early said as they climbed
the car. "Does any of what she wrote fit with what
've learned?"

All of it does," Burns said when he climbed behind the
el. "We just called it mythology."

e coaxed the engine to life and peeled rubber for the
t time in his life. In his rearview mirror he could see
k streaks stretching from behind the vehicle.

e didn't look back at the dash where the red oil light
come on again. He'd grown too accustomed to
oring it.

Some of it I've even reread in the last few days," he said,
hile we were researching. It just never fit together until
v. All of it makes sense. Hecate's followers summoned
atures of the night. They were supposed to be spirits.
e Greek word was *epopides*. Now I see they weren't
rits at all. They were animals like we've seen here,
mals under the influence of the mental powers
sessed by half-demon minds.

391

"Half-demons? That's hinted at in the Bible, but I ne
thought I'd see one."

"The myth was that Lilith, the first wife of Adam,
banished from the Garden of Eden."

"You think that's so?"

"I doubt that, I mean that she existed as a wife of Ad
I suspect she was some kind of witch who emerged fr
the ancient Hebrew tribes, rebelling against their mo
order. As the story of her was repeated, it was proba
incorporated into the oral traditions from Genesis. Peo
like for things to fit together."

"What happened to this Lilith?"

"She went to the shores of the Red Sea and conju
demons, and she lay with them and bore childr
Hundreds and hundreds of demon children.

"They were cursed by God, and they began to die. W
the help of some demon spirit they found a way to surv
by feeding on the blood of humans. There must be so
kind of energy or something in the transfer of the blo
which allows them to live.

"The legend says Lilith would molest the children
others. That must have developed from the feeding. Th
used charms with the names of angels in an effort to w
her off.

"Apparently, fighting destruction, they found so
way to convert humans. It was a way for their essence
live on. That's why she wanted Alison, and I guess si
she had touched Alison's ancestor, there was some allu
Maybe she viewed it as a task left incomplete."

"Is there a way to stop her?" Early asked.

"There was before. This time I don't know. I guess w
find out."

Chapter 34

Travis pushed back some branches and found himself looking at the ruins of the resort.

As the shadows of the late afternoon crept over it, he found it did resemble an old castle, like the kind always found in the Hammer horror films where Christopher Lee lurked and Peter Cushing hunted.

Mold grew along part of the wall, spreading a broad green stain across the stucco-like surface, which was cracked in several places.

"Do you think they're in there?" Chrisk asked.

"Somebody must be." He was holding the stake in front of him in both hands.

He slipped through the brush, crouching low as he moved toward the building. Chrisk followed him, her own stake clutched in her hands.

When they reached the wall, they pressed their backs flat against it, waiting, panting.

Seconds passed without any movement or sound. Travis moved cautiously around the corner and crept along until he reached a dingy window.

Cautiously he lifted his head over the edge of it.

Looking through it, he could see only some dusty tables and chairs. The sight was spooky, the way vacant places

often seem when the ghosts of their former residents see
to lurk somewhere nearby.

Slumping back against the wall, he adjusted his grip o
the stake.

"What's next?" Chrisk asked.

"We have to keep checking."

He was breathing heavily now. He could feel th
pounding of his heart in his throat. It felt as if his bloo
vessels were ready to burst.

He ducked beneath the window now and moved o
along beside the jagged wall until he reached the ne
opening.

The scene inside was similar. This had apparently bee
the restaurant where the guests had replenished them
selves after grueling workouts and dehydrating stean
baths.

He dropped back from the glass just as Chrisk reache
him. She knelt beside him, trembling.

"No sign in there either." He wiped sweat from his bro
and gave a quick look around to make sure they were sti
unobserved.

They rose and crept along the ground until they reache
a sidewalk which curved around the building an
stretched toward a second building.

"The baths," Chrisk said. "There's supposed to b
magic water here or something."

They were halfway to the second building whe
something moved to one side.

It was Blade.

"Greetings," the biker said. He was resting his club o
his shoulder. A broad grin had spread across his face.

"I'm looking for my wife," Travis said.

"She's waiting inside."

Travis held his stake in front of him, the point tilte
slightly toward Blade. Chrisk, at his side, did the same.

"You two look like you're out hunting a tiger," Blad
said, moving toward them.

"I want Alison," Travis said.

"I know what you mean," Blade said, cupping the [cr]otch of his jeans with one hand and making a thrusting [m]otion with his hips. "She's a piece."

"You son of a bitch," Travis said. "If you've hurt her, I . . ."

"Relax, dude. She's fine."

"Then take me to her."

Chrisk touched his arm, "Trav, what if it's a trap?"

He hesitated, then shook his head. "I've got to take the [ri]sk."

"Come on," Blade said. He took a couple of steps as if to [le]ad Travis into the building.

Trav was on the verge of following when the biker [ab]ruptly swung his club. He was aiming for Trav's head, [b]ut Trav still had the stake in front of him. He managed to [u]se it to block the blow.

Off balance, he staggered and got the stake in front of [h]im again at about the same time Blade resumed his [fi]ghting stance with the club drawn back over his [sh]oulder.

Travis jabbed at him with the stake, forcing him to back [u]p a few steps.

The biker was watching for an opening so that he could [s]wing the club.

Chrisk took a position to Trav's left in an effort to keep [t]he biker at bay.

His eyes moved from one to the other for a second, [c]ontemplating. Then he turned around and jogged [t]oward the doorway to the baths.

Travis and Chrisk followed, rushing down the sidewalk [a]nd reaching the door just as it closed behind the biker.

Grabbing the latch, Travis yanked backward. He [e]xpected it to be locked, but it gave easily.

Keeping the stake raised, he moved into the shadowy [i]nterior.

There was not a sign of Blade now. He paused, taking

Chrisk's arm as their eyes adjusted to the light.

"Where did he go?" Chrisk asked.

"Over here," Blade said.

When they turned they found themselves looking dow
the barrel of Doug Langdon's service revolver. He alread
had it cocked.

The stop at the church on the way out of town was
brief interruption of the journey. In the sanctuary the
picked up a heavy metal candle stand which had potentia
as a weapon.

After he had unscrewed it from its base, Burns hefted
into his hands, checking the weight of it. It was heavy.
would make a good weapon.

The priest also took a crucifix and slipped it into hi
belt.

Early was showing signs of tiredness again. "Maybe yo
should wait here," Burns said. "This could get rough."

"My granddaughter's out there," the old man said. "I'v
got to make the trip. If anything happened to her, I don'
know what I'd do."

"Are you sure you're up to it?"

"I'm gonna have to go to show you how to get there
Time's running out."

Reluctantly Burns nodded. "Let's go, then."

They left the building and piled back into the car. The
sun was beginning to dip, but nightfall was not close.

There was plenty of time even with the distance they had
to cover. Burns was worried, but he wasn't terrified. If she
didn't have her full strength, they would be all right. They
would stand a chance.

Burns attempted to pick up speed, but the vehicle begar
to sputter for the first time. He looked down at the pane
and noticed the red light was glowing.

A sound like a threshing machine was issuing from

der the hood, and white smoke was seeping out.

"Checked your oil lately?" Early asked.

"I'd been meaning to," Burns said as the car creaked to a
op.

When they raised the hood, more smoke billowed out,
d the smell of burned oil fouled the air.

Early leaned over the engine for a moment and then
raightened up again, shaking his head. He took his hat
ff and wiped his face.

"We ain't goin' anywhere else in this car," he said. "The
ngine's burned up. I did that to a car myself once. Some
nd of clog kept the oil from getting to the pistons."

"What did you do?"

"Walked."

They were about a quarter mile from the turnoff to the
prings.

"Our advantage is gone," Early said. "We'll have to
alk it. We can go at an angle, cross country, and save
ome time."

"Are you up to the trip?"

"I'll stay with you. We're all gonna be in trouble."

Burns took the candle stand from the back seat and
lung it over his shoulder.

He hoped for someone to happen along to give them a
ide.

No one did.

The sun dragged a slow path across the downward curve
f the sky.

Travis watched the shadows crawling across the bottom
of the empty swimming pool like flat black figures
lawing across a barren desert.

They had tied him up with his own belt, yanking his
hands over his head and binding them around the metal
ladder set in the concrete at the deep end of the pool. He

dangled there.

He began to lose feeling first in his fingertips. A coldness set in and crept along into his palms while the underside of his arms began to ache from being held in an awkward position.

His feet touched the floor, but not firmly enough to allow him to take any of the tension off his forearms.

In this position, there was also a strain on his rib cage which made breathing difficult. Without enough air, his brain began to fog.

His eyes kept wanting to close. He refused to let them concentrating on the pain to keep himself alert as he scanned the scene in front of him.

The altar was complete with a statue in the likeness of a woman standing at its center.

Candles burned around it, and Chrisk had been tied to one side of it in a kneeling position.

Langdon sat on the pool steps at the edge of the altar watching her, while Danya knelt beside him, massaging his shoulders.

Estelle Johnson sat back against the wall, curled into a fetal position. She was withdrawn and silent.

He could see no sign of Alison, Blade, or Navarra.

Struggling against his bonds, he tried to wriggle his wrists free, but he succeeded only in irritating the flesh where the leather touched.

With his arms, he tried to lift himself. It didn't work, so he tried pushing his weight away from the ladder in an effort to break the strap.

That effort was also futile. He was wearing faded jeans and a t-shirt. The soles of his tennis shoes were worn almost smooth, but he had a belt that could have been used to bridle a bull.

Sweat was pouring down from his armpits and soaking through his shirt at the chest. The air was heavy in the building.

As he watched, the shadows continued their journey. How long had they been here now?

Did it matter? Darkness was coming. He would still be here when it arrived, and Chrisk and Alison might be sacrificed before his eyes while he was helpless to take action.

Navarra was powerful. In the darkness she might be able to summon something to rip him apart.

His eyes moved over to the altar again, and he saw Chrisk look back at him. She was frightened, but there was a question in her eyes, too. She expected to escape and was checking to see if he had a plan yet.

He shook his head slowly to let Chrisk know he had no ideas. She nodded back.

The feeling was now gone from his palms. He believed his heart was hurting also, perhaps working too hard in his present position. He couldn't be sure if the ache was imaginary or not.

A coronary would seal his fate and everyone else's as well.

Drops of sweat stung his eyes. He tilted his head back and stifled a cry as another bead of sweat streaked down the side of his face.

He gritted his teeth against his growing anger.

The shadows were still creeping across the pool. The shadows were dragging the darkness with them.

The shadows were enveloping everything, devouring all hope.

Greer Pennington, known as Deke, was one of the hunters who had decided to stick with the game. He was a big guy who wore a plaid shirt with the sleeves cut off and an old camouflage cap.

His arms were brown and weathered, stained with blue ink tattoos he had carved himself with a pocket knife and a

Bic ballpoint. They consisted of his initials and those of a girl he hadn't seen in years, a jagged marijuana leaf, and a peace symbol that had been popular in his high school days.

Hunting was one of his joys, so he didn't mind sticking with the effort. Hours in the woods were no problem for Deke. He did it all the time.

He didn't have much respect for the men accompanying him, but it didn't matter. They weren't a hindrance, just an annoyance. If he came upon the panther, they wouldn't stop him from taking the bastard out.

He was balancing his gun in one hand, keeping the torch raised with the other. The woods were getting dark, the sky faded now to a dull charcoal gray that left little light.

The flickering flame blazed an orange path out in front of him, toying with the shadows cast by branches in his path.

The sound of movement came through the stillness, heading toward him. He was able to look forward and see the rustle of branches.

Raising his rifle at his side, he tried holding the torch higher to get some sign of what was out there.

He didn't want to fire at random. He knew better than that. He didn't want to take down Alden or Dex accidentally. Even though the movement did not appear to be a man, Pennington was not the type to blast aimlessly.

He might have saved his own life if he'd been a little less cautious.

Instead, he decided he couldn't shoot without seeing what he was firing at. Cursing the torch because it was not his Coleman lantern, which he hadn't had the foresight to bring, he began to move slowly through the bushes in front of him, careful to keep the flame away from the dry brush.

was insane to be doing this, but he had to try and kill
cat before it harmed someone else. He had the same
vation as everybody else in Bristol Springs.
sides, it would make a great trophy.

ith the barrel of his gun, he pushed aside some
ches which dangled in front of him. He stepped
tly the way he had been taught, weaving through the
h cautiously.

is finger was curled on the trigger, even though it was
cult to keep the weapon ready, carrying it as he was in
hand. He wished he had a pistol. He wished
umstances were ideal.

e bent his shoulders slightly in an effort to make his
ement less noticeable. He squinted to try and see better
ugh the brush.

bove him, the night wind rustled the leaves of the trees.
as a noisy rattle, a whisper from a scratchy throat of the
kness.

he cat was staring into his face before he realized it, its
n eyes gleaming like blazing emeralds from its black
.

t was not afraid.

e tried to squeeze off a shot, but the panther was
ady crouched and ready. As his finger began to tense, it
ang, claws striking his chest and digging into him,
cking him backward.

he shot flew wild, and then the jaws were at his throat.
screamed just before the teeth pierced his flesh, taking a
nk out of him. Blood vessels peeled free, and the
ular opened.

His fingers let go of the torch, and the flames rolled from
tip onto the dry branches. The blaze climbed along
bs quickly, spreading to another bush, then another.
As Pennington died, he watched the forest around him
ite. He felt his blood covering his neck and chest, felt
cat's claws ripping into him, while all around the

night was turning orange. Bright orange. Bright, bri
orange.

The shot alerted Alden and Dex that something
wrong. They were not that far from most of th
remaining in the party, so Alden called out for then
join him.

In a few moments they had all gathered. Together t
began to move in the direction of the shot. All of them
their guns ready.

They rushed, kicking through the underbrush w
fingers twitching on their triggers.

The sound of the fire reached them first, a lo
crackling of branches and leaves being consumed.

The smoke touched their nostrils, burned their thro
and eyes.

Stopping, Alden and Dex looked at each other, e
wide with fear. The blaze was already out of control.

"It had to be Pennington, that shot," Dex said.

"If it was, he must have been trying to warn us about
fire?"

"Or maybe something got him."

Alden peered into the blaze. "If he's in there, ther
nothing we can do for him."

A bundle of fur suddenly darted out of the thicket, a
two people shot at it.

One blast ended the life of the raccoon that had be
fleeing the flame.

The other one put a fist-sized hole into Alden's thig

He thudded to the ground, clutching the wound as h
face twisted into a network of wrinkles displaying h
pain.

Dex knelt beside him and yanked his belt off, quick
using it as a tourniquet.

He barked orders to the others.

t was an accident," someone protested.

ine, we don't have much time. We've got to get out of
 before this whole place goes up, so find some sticks
 stretcher."

o cars had come along to help Early and Burns in their
ney, so night had fully settled by the time they reached
 edge of the springs. They began their trip back
ugh the trees at about the same time a stretcher was
g constructed for Alden.

ithout flashlights, it was difficult to see, but there was
int trail in the dust and some broken branches which
ained from Trav's passage through here in his car.

arly leaned against the priest for support. Aches had
ead up and down his back, hampering his movement,
 his lungs labored for each breath.

urns's youth allowed him a little more strength, but it
 also been some time since he had traveled a great
ance on foot.

The calves of his legs were growing sore, and pain shot
 through the balls of his feet.

He was wearing leather shoes with hard soles, not made
 travel across rough terrain. He'd almost twisted his
kle with several steps on the uneven ground.

By the time they located Trav and Chrisk, they probably
ren't going to be in much shape to offer help, Burns
ught. The candle stand was growing heavier by the
ment in his hand.

"It's full dark," Early said. "We're in trouble."

"God will be on our side," Burns said. He had never
ven much consideration to divine intervention in a
uation of pure and tangible evil, but he reasoned that if
avarra was real, she validated what he had believed most
 his life about eternity.

"He knew the old man's faith was real also, and that

comforted him. He was afraid, but he was not defeate‹

He helped Early steady himself as they found t‹
downward slope and moved down it to the abandoned c‹

"He got stuck," Early said.

"Doesn't look like they were hurt."

"Not by the wreck. But it ain't over till it's over."

"Are we still headed toward the resort?"

"As much as I can remember, we are. We might as w‹
keep going."

They moved past the car, heading on through the fore‹

They didn't see the beginning glow of orange agair‹
the sky in the distance, and the smoke was not yet reachi‹
them to alert their sense of smell.

They didn't know it, but they were walking into he‹

Navarra awoke.

Her eyes opened slowly, and she inhaled deeply, feelin‹
the energy of the night all around her. She felt strong‹
than ever.

Her brothers were at hand to do her bidding, and h‹
protectors had served her well. She could sense it as s‹
slowly got to her feet.

Alison was waiting, the night was alive. She did not fe‹
her opposition. All was well. She walked slowly into t‹
pool area, her soul tingling with anticipation.

She saw what her thoughts had already told her: Tra‹
dangled from his bonds at the ladder and Chrisk sat at t‹
end of the altar.

Blade and Langdon walked over to her, waiting f‹
praise as much as instruction.

"Well done," she said. "Let us prepare. Bring Alison‹

They moved away at a brisk pace, in a hurry to do h‹
bidding, anticipating the night.

When he saw her, Travis began to struggle anew a‹
curse at her. She only smiled as she walked over to the ed‹

he pool, where she peered down at him.

was like looking down into a cavern. He had to twist
nd and tilt his head back to stare up at her.

What do you want from us?" he demanded.

Survival. That's all, Mr. Dixon."

Why my wife? Let her go. Let Chrisk go."

he shook her head, feigning sadness. "I can do
ther," she said. "Your wife is the descendant of one I
ıld have called before. The lineage already bears my
ch. If she chooses, willingly, she can become immortal.

you think she will turn that down to continue
ıggling with you at your little newspaper?"

'As for the negress, I must have her blood. Hecate
nands more than obedience and fealty when she is
nmoned to bestow her blessings."

n a sudden burst of struggle, Travis strained against the
t. His weight jerked from side to side and the muscles of
forearms tensed as he pulled against the leather. His
ists strained, and he gritted his teeth.

The strap was too stout for his efforts. After a moment
: thrashing stopped.

Navarra walked from the edge of the pool without
eaking. She was looking toward the other end of the
ɔm.

A groggy, staggering Alison was being led into the area
tween Langdon and Blade.

Navarra met them at the head of the pool and took
ison's face into her hands, moving it so that their eyes
et. She spoke softly to her, soothing her confusion with
ɔmises of eternal life.

"Do you trust me?" Navarra asked. "No harm will come
you."

"I understand," Alison said.

Navarra nodded to Blade and Langdon, who complied
guiding Alison carefully around the edge of the pool
d down the steps so that she was standing in front of

the altar.

The men carrying Alden staggered with his wei
balanced awkwardly between them. The stretcher they
fashioned from a couple of shirts and some sticks was lo
and fragile, and Alden didn't help matters. He rolled fr
side to side, moaning and pressing his hands against
wound in his leg.

As they struggled along, the flames seemed to ch
them. They were staying just ahead of the blaze a
reached up to ignite branches and spread along the fo
floor.

"I've never seen anything like this," Dexter called ou
he trotted along at Alden's side. "It's going to eat
whole forest in a few hours."

"We had to have it," Alden said. "It'll clean out th
crazy damned animals. That it'll do for sure."

Dexter didn't argue with him about the price of
victory. He was too busy trying to elude the flames.

He knew there were some people who would cla
getting rid of Alden was a blessing, but he wasn't one
them.

If they got out of these woods, he wouldn't look ba
until he got Alden to the hospital in Penn's Ferry. It w
old, but it was close. They could answer questions abo
the mess later. He prayed they wouldn't face arson charg

The owl swept over the flames, flapping its wings rath
than gliding so that it remained high above the heat.

Its night eyes continued to scan the ground below wh
it had swept past the reach of the fire. The panther w
visible to it, moving toward the resort where t
summoner was at work.

Many creatures, the brothers of the night, were fighti

own battle to escape the flames, but the cat was
dy prepared to guard the perimeter of the building.
ould not disobey the commands that thundered in his
. He was needed by the woman, and he was ready to
ply, to protect her.
he owl spotted the two men moving toward her
ling as it made a loop over the edge of the forest. It did
ing to alter its course. It knew, as it saw them, that she
them too.

rom the edge of the forest, Burns could see the resort. It
  dark and empty looking, yet through one of the
dows he detected a faint glimmer of light somewhere
de. They were in the right place.
e was about to lift the candle stand and move toward
  building when he saw the cat padding around the
her of the structure.
ts stride was graceful as it plodded along the edge of the
rt building.
He's guarding it," Early whispered.
What do we do? We can't fight that thing with this
thpick."
"We'll have to distract it," Early said.
"I'll do it," Burns suggested.
"No. You need to try to get inside and see what's going
  I'll get his attention and then get out of his way."
"He'll kill you," Burns said.
arly's wrinkled face did not change expression. "It's a
nce I'll have to take," Early said. "I've had a good life.
risk hasn't lived yet. Those kids in there haven't lived.
rifice is what our faith is all about, isn't it, Reverend?"
Burns could not argue. Picking up his weapon, he
gan to move along the edge of the forest. His legs were
rting worse now, and his back was growing tired.
Selecting a spot which kept him concealed, he watched

407

the play of shadows created in the pale light beyon[d] resort windows.

The cat continued its silent patrol.

The priest waited for the old man to make a mov[e] soon as the cat turned, Burns would head towar[d] building.

Early moved a few paces to his left and reached u[p] break some branches off a tree.

Their leaves made a protesting rustle as he clashed t[hem] together. Keeping silent otherwise, he continued to n[...] away from Burns.

The cat's ears perked and it turned, raising its head [...] eyes probed the shadows.

It took a few slow steps toward Early in an effo[rt] determine the source of the sound.

Early thrashed the branches together in front of even harder, hoping he sounded like a small ani[mal] trapped in some brush.

The panther stood still, eyeing the movement.

Licking his lips, Early whistled, doing his bes[t] imitate a bird of the night.

Burns raised himself onto the aching balls of his f[eet] The leather of his shoes squeaked in protest of movement, and his ankles sent messages of discomfo[rt]

He used the stand to balance himself, bracing one en[d] it in the dirt so that he could use it to push off. He waiting for the cat to make a move toward the forest, bu[t] far it was like a statue.

It wouldn't move. It just stood there, and if he hea[ded] toward the building, it would see him.

Why didn't it move? Wasn't it curious about the sou[nd]? Or did it somehow know what was going on?

408

If something didn't happen soon, he was going to have to chance a run for the building.

Early threw down his branches. He wasn't going to lure the cat like that. The only thing left was to confront it.

He closed his eyes for a moment, his lips moving in one final silent prayer.

Then he stepped forward, out of the concealment of the forest and into full view.

The cat saw him and uttered a low warning growl.

Early took another step, letting the cat see he intended to move past it to head into the building.

The cat lowered its head and let its mouth drop slowly open to reveal the rows of its teeth. Strings of saliva stretched from the ends of those jagged daggers, and another growl came forth.

"Go, preacher," Early said, stretching his arms out in front of him as the cat lunged.

His arms did little to ward it off as it plowed into him, knocking him onto his back and pinning him in the dirt.

He felt its claws splitting his skin, and the weight of it had knocked the air out of his chest.

He clutched at its neck but was unable to get an effective grip.

The razors in its claws sliced along his chest, ripping narrow lines through his skin.

He had not expected to survive, but the pain was more than he had dreamed. He could not suppress the scream that welled up in his throat.

The cat went for that throat, silencing the cry.

Early's mind began to spiral toward unconsciousness. Remnants of his faith spilled up from his brain. He remembered the promises of Jesus, telling him about eternal life.

He waited for the angels, and he prayed that his sacrifice

would be enough.

"You died for my sins, Jesus. Let my death save Chrisk's life. Please."

His head rolled back then, and he prayed no more.

The old man's screams were torture for Burns. They began when he was halfway to the building, and it took all of his willpower to keep moving.

He wanted to turn back, to run to the old man and hammer at the cat with the bar he carried in his hands.

Only the knowledge that Early would not want that kept him moving toward the resort.

Both of them had known the risks, and Early had stated it correctly. Sometimes sacrifice was necessary.

As the screams began to die, he reached the edge of the building and crept along until he could stare through a window.

It did not offer a vantage of anything except more shadows on the wall, reflected from somewhere inside the building.

There was movement, but little more could be detected.

He pulled back from the window to head around the end of the building in search of some way to get inside without being noticed.

He had just stumbled on a narrow hole in the ground covered over with a heavy metal grate when the bats began to pour from the sky.

The fire raged onward, an unstoppable force. While the lack of moisture had strangled everything else in the forest, the blaze fed on the dryness, consuming the lifeless branches and crawling through thickets and up into the trees.

There was no darkness now. Everything was brilliant,

indingly so.

The hunters had departed, and the forest creatures
hich remained, the squirrels and rabbits and chip-
unks, didn't look back. They were trying to find refuge
s well.

For Matt Fennaday, it was no more than a spot of light
n his binoculars.

He turned off the Walkman which he wore to pass the
ong hours in the Penn's Ferry Fire Tower, and took a
eading on the location.

The night shift had a way of being boring, and Matt
ndured it only because he needed the money.

Moments like this got his blood going, however. He put
n the shortwave headset and called his counterpart near
he parish line.

"You need to take a gander toward Bristol Springs," he
aid. "There's a burner over there that's about to make that
ne at Kisatchie last year look like a high school bonfire."

"At least that ain't no wilderness area by Bristol
springs," Beth Andrews radioed back. "Maybe we can get
ome bulldozers out there to put this one out."

"I hope so," Matt said, flicking his alarm button. "If
omebody doesn't get a fire line cut along there soon, we'll
e missing one municipality in this parish."

"Nobody'd miss it," Ruth chuckled. "Still, there's a lot
of nice forest to be saved. I feel sorry for anything that gets
n the way of that blaze."

Matt lifted his binoculars to his eyes again. It was like
looking into film footage of a bomb blast. It would take a
while to get anybody out there.

He was thankful he wasn't in its path.

Travis watched as Navarra stood beside Alison in front
of the altar. She stroked Ali's hair gently and urged her to
stare forward into the eyes of the statue.

411

Slowly Navarra raised her hands and bent downward in a bow that placed her at the rough figure's feet.

Kissing the base of the statue, Navarra whispered something in a forgotten language.

When she rose again, her eyes had begun to glow. With her slender fingers, she reached out to Julie, who stepped forward and knelt beside her.

Navarra looked into her eyes, silently asking some question to which Julie responded with an affirmative.

The dark woman placed a hand behind the girl's head and stroked her hair softly, sliding her palm around to gently touch the girl's cheek.

Very gently she bent forward, touching her lips softly to Julie's forehead as the teenager closed her eyes.

Navarra's hand continued to slide downward under the girl's chin until the fingertips rested against her throat.

In a quick, sharp movement, Navarra plunged her thumb into the girl's flesh.

Her nail was sharp, and it seemed to split the skin easily. The throat opened like a fountain, and Navarra grasped the girl's hair, pulling the head back and angling the spray of blood onto the base of the likeness.

Hecate could not be summoned without a price.

When Julie had stopped moving, Navarra let her slide from her grasp and then turned toward Chrisk.

Blood dripped from the fingers which caressed Chrisk's cheek. The black girl tried to scream, but Navarra clamped a hand across her throat.

Travis made another lunge against his belt, without success.

Navarra smiled, grabbing a handful of Chrisk's hair in the back and yanking.

Chrisk's face was forced upward, her throat exposed.

Navarra bent and kissed her hard on the mouth.

Chrisk spat at her when she pulled back.

Navarra only smiled and ran her tongue across her

ower lip where there was a drop of blood. She had bitten Chrisk's mouth.

Releasing Chrisk's throat, she raised the hand she had used on Julie and licked the blood from her fingers.

A bloody handprint remained on Chrisk's neck.

Navarra put a fingertip against Chrisk's lips and let it trail slowly downward across her chin toward her jugular.

"Unlike Alison, your choice does not have to be a willing one," Navarra said. "Hecate accepts all gifts without question."

The first bats struck Burns in the back, darting into him and bouncing off. He swatted at them and then tried to lift the grate. It was heavy and rusted and wouldn't give.

The next flurry of the animals assailed him, their leathery wings swatting at his face and shoulders as he flailed his arms.

Something bit his face, and instinctively he clawed at it, yanking the bat away. Its teeth were clenched against his cheek, and a strip of skin peeled away.

He swung the candle stand wildly, striking several of the creatures and knocking them about.

Jabbing upward, he impaled another with the threaded end of the stand.

They continued to flap in at him, their cries shrill as they sought exposed flesh.

He forced himself to ignore the assault even as they ripped pieces of his skin open. He bent over the grate with the candle stand.

Slipping the tip of it through the edge of the grate, he used it for leverage and began to pry upward.

Reluctantly, with a metallic groan, the cover budged only slightly.

Burns strained his arms, feeling the tension in his shoulders as he struggled to move the grate.

It moaned some more, scratching against its frame, the rust around it slowly crumbling.

Slowly it began to slip upward.

The grate was moving now, giving way.

The pain in the back of his neck was so severe, his hands slipped off the stand.

One of the bats had somehow slipped beneath his collar and found a sensitive spot.

He struggled to reach it, stretching a hand over his shoulders at first, then trying to bend his arms behind him. It was like a scene from a film in which a stabbing victim tried to pull a knife from his back.

Finally his hands clutched around its small furry body, and he pulled it free. More flesh ripped, but the teeth were no longer in his flesh.

He crushed the bat in his hands and threw it aside. Thoughts of rabies had already flooded his mind, but he did not let them slow his progress. Later he would take shots . . . if he survived this night.

He swatted at a few more of the bats before picking up the bar again and inserting it into the grate once more.

His previous effort had loosened the metal, and it budged a little easier this time.

The bats continued to strike at him, thudding against his back and sides. He hunched his shoulders, trying to make himself a smaller target.

The metal rose further now, slipping free. Keeping one hand on the bar, he reached down with his other and lifted upward on the grate, sliding to one side so that an opening was available.

He made one final swipe through the air to drive some part of the hoard back before dropping into the opening.

A few bats followed, but quickly he reached up and slid the grate into place, shutting most of them out.

They fluttered and screeched, trying to slide through the metal bars, which were too narrowly spaced to allow em passage.

Those that had entered the hole with him flapped ound him, but he killed them quickly with the stand.

Then he sat down on the stone floor to let his lungs draw ep breaths and slowly regain strength.

He was inside a culvert which had been used to channel ater into or out of the resort at one time. Now it was usty and dry. No water had passed through here in a ng time.

It was a narrow passage with a line of grit and other eposits streaked along the center of the floor.

He dropped to his knees and began to make his way long. The dust scraped onto his pants and covered his alms. He had to draw his shoulders in to allow free novement.

He had no idea where he was going to come out, but he rayed it would lead him inside. He was on his way to the scue.

Chapter 35

The blood glistened in a black-red pool around the base of the statue. It washed around Navarra's ankles, but she ignored it, enjoying the agonies of Chrisk's struggles.

She moved her thumb back and forth across the jugular, a smile on her lips.

Chrisk's lips trembled; her shoulders shuddered, and tears dropped out the corners of her eyes.

"You might have made a good sister," Navarra said. "A pity you came at the wrong time."

She began to apply pressure, preparing to drive her thumb into the throat.

"If you need a sacrifice, why don't you take me?" Trav called out.

Navarra withdrew her hand from Chrisk's throat and turned toward the end of the pool.

Tugging against the belt, Trav managed to rattle the ladder in a protest of clanking metal.

"Is that what you would like?"

"If you let Chrisk go."

"What of your wife? You have nothing to bargain with for her release?"

"Does she have a choice?"

"She has to choose. I cannot order her. I believe your

416

nds say a vampire cannot enter a house uninvited. l, that is not quite true, but Hecate will not bestow her sings on one who does not choose to receive them. Yet o would not choose eternal life?"

rav's face remained stern. "If she chooses, then I have choice but to accept that. There's no reason for Chrisk ie too, though."

Chrisk looked at him, shaking her head. "Trav, you 't."

You wouldn't be here if it weren't for me."

Navarra pulled free the rope which bound Chrisk to the r and nodded toward the ladder.

Release him," she said to Chrisk. "He replaces you, so d him here."

lipping her hands from the rope, Chrisk walked down pool floor to stand in front of Travis.

"You can't do this."

"I have to."

She reached up to his wrists, pressing against him so t her lips were near his ear.

"Do you have a plan?"

"Part of one. Once you untie me, it gets a little foggy."

She pulled the belt loose and his hands slipped away m the rung. He lowered his arms gratefully, massaging wrists first and then rubbing the muscles of his upper ns until feeling began to ebb back into them.

Blade was beside him in a few seconds, the club folded in arms. He escorted Travis along the length of the pool til they were standing before the altar.

Alison did not look at him. Her head was bowed, her ns folded in front of her. She wore an elegant white wn, and her hair was brushed down her back in a golden ass of curls.

"You don't need to guard him so closely," Navarra said Blade, but her gaze was on Travis. "He will not flee."

"What are you?" Travis asked. "What is your purpose?"

"To continue my heritage. To defeat death."

"You've killed. That's a high price for immortality.

"I kill to combat the curse. The curse from the creat who damned us."

"Who are you?"

"We were called the *lilim*, daughters of Lilith, the spi of the wind. She sought to be a priestess and fled the trib of God's chosen. She found pleasures and communic amid the demons on the shores of the Red Sea. She reach for something akin to godhood.

"From the coupling we were born, more than o thousand. More than two thousand. We played togethe learning to make ourselves one with nature and to dan in the sunshine.

"He frowned on that. The demons were the followe of His rebellious servant, and we were some unho offspring.

"Lilith was ordered to return to her people and forsa her casting of spells and coupling with the forces of t beyond.

"When our mother refused, He leveled his curse. V began to die. Our bodies withered and our tongues gre swollen. Hour upon hour we perished, until there we only a few of us left.

"Darkness had fallen, and somewhere in the night v heard the call of the dark angel known as Hecate Prosperina. The howling of the hellhounds foretold h presence as she journeyed from the depths of the abyss a offered us her aid, for she hated Jehovah just as the Son the Morning did.

"She could not undo the curse, but she could offer us alternative. No more could we enjoy the power of t sunlight and the dance beside the sea. No, now we mu dance in darkness, and shun the ripples of the water order to survive. We had no choice but to drink the da blood from the hearts of mortal men.

From the forces she was able to channel through [n]ure, she bestowed power on us, and like the creatures [ ] commanded, she gave us the knowledge to control [ani]mals on this plane. We beguile the Creator's little ones [jus]t as we beguile men.

The world has changed much since those days. The [dem]ons no longer live in this realm, the giants were [des]troyed in the flood, the Nazarene walked the earth and [defe]ated death, but we remain. Hecate has given us the [stre]ngth to withstand the onslaughts. And she promised [she] could bestow her grace upon one in each generation in [ord]er to carry on our power and to defy Him.''

"If it is accepted willingly?'' Travis placed his feet a few [inc]hes apart, balancing his weight carefully.

"He gave all free will. Freedom to choose light or [dar]kness.''

"Old stories have a lot of truth in them,'' Travis said. [Fro]m the corner of his eye, he looked over at Blade, who [sto]od listening to Navarra. He was hearing it all for the [fir]st time as well, and it seemed to hold him enthralled. [Th]e club was still cradled in the crook of his arm.

"Many have heard the stories and tried to form cults that [fol]lowed them, seeking to gain the power and energy [thr]ough nature that we have enjoyed. There is too much [ign]orance mixed in when mortals try to make themselves [lik]e us.''

"Demon children?''

"I am what I have become. I have become what I am.''

Travis gave a slow nod. As he did, he stiffened his hand [at] his side, tensing the muscles in his arm while keeping it [pr]essed against his side to remain inconspicuous.

Navarra was looking into his eyes. She smiled. He [sm]iled back, blocking his thoughts with anger. No one [ex]pected the chop he placed across Blade's throat. He [ai]med for a pressure point that would do the most damage. He connected somewhere near the Adam's apple and

419

stunned the biker. Blade reached for his throat, gagg
and choking.

Before Langdon could make a move from his corr
Travis gripped the kid's shoulders and drove a knee i:
his abdomen.

That caused him to double over, and Trav kicked him
the face without hesitation.

Navarra screamed. She had not sensed the intent,
caught up was she in her own mythology.

She tried to claw at Trav, but he ducked past her han
and picked up the club.

Langdon leveled his gun toward Travis, but Chr
slammed into the policeman, causing his shot to go w:

"No!" Navarra screamed as Travis hurled the cl
toward Langdon.

The weapon struck the cop on the forehead, twisti
him sideways. As he fell, his face struck the side of t
pool. Teeth shattered, and blood began to pour from l
nostrils.

Navarra did reach Travis now, and her grip was ha
Her hands dug into his shoulders, and she lifted him a
shoved, sending him crashing onto the rough floor of t
pool.

He rolled onto his side, across his arm, and somethi:
cracked under his weight.

When he flopped onto his back, he realized it was his l
arm. It lay at his side, limp and filled with pain.

He felt strength ebbing from him, and his lungs let ou
long sigh of air.

Chrisk rushed at Navarra, who only laughed a:
grasped the girl's hair. With a tug, she slammed her in
the side of the pool and pushed her onto the ground.

When she laughed again, it was a high and sinist
sound.

She was still laughing when the smoke began to see

420

the room.

The men from the forest service hauled a heavy old bulldozer out of its storage warehouse near Penn's Ferry and put it on the back of a flatbed truck.

With volunteers from local departments, they quickly assembled a team to head out to Bristol Springs to try and cut a fire line that would at least isolate the blaze and keep from consuming the entire forest.

"It's burning pretty good," Fennady told them on the radio. "You're going to have a real mess to contain."

"We've done it before," Charlie Perkins told him. "We'll do it again. I knew this was bound to happen when everything got so dry."

They yanked out the portable fire tents and issued them to the crewmen. The small silver packs were worn on the belt. When opened, the tents could be pulled over a person to shield from the flames. On occasion, they had saved the lives of people who huddled beneath them while fire burned all around.

Perkins liked to have everybody who worked under him equipped with one. It was a good safety precaution.

Burns was tasting smoke when he used the stand to knock loose the grate in the steambath where his tunnel had finally led. It had not been an easy journey. He had scraped his hands and elbows, and the knee of one pant leg had ripped as he crawled along. The flesh on his kneecap had scraped away as well.

At the end of the culvert, he had discovered a network of pipes and shutoff valves. With difficulty he climbed up through the maze, finally making it to the steambath. The tunnel was apparently a long-forgotten channel

421

which had been used to divert the natural water into bath area years before. It had been converted to a dr: when different methods had been developed. The pip that curled up through the end of it had later become method of getting water into the bath.

When the grate gave way, he found himself insid small, enclosed area where the water had been held.

Climbing out, he crept across the room and into hallway. He could hear some movement along the end the corridor, and faint voices echoed off the vacant corn of the building.

With the hard soles of his shoes, he found it difficult walk silently. He stayed close to one wall and slid his f along. He held the heavy metal bar at a diagonal, as i were a rifle.

He inched along, wondering if he would be able to of any help to Travis and Alison.

Early had died to give him this chance. He had to ma good on it.

He inched along the corridor, following its windi path around the individual massage rooms until he w near the doorway that opened into the pool area.

The door was gray, with a sheet of grime which h formed on the glass, but he was able to brush a view h with his sleeve.

The chaos inside the pool met his gaze. He recogniz the style of the altar from his studies of Greek and mediev myth, a mélange of symbols.

The truth behind the legends hammered into him. was almost impossible to believe everything he was seei was real, yet it was indisputable. He was not hallucina ing. He was seeing a convergence of myth, of the Gre and the Hebrew.

He also realized there was more smoke filling the roor There was fire outside, and it was getting closer. If the weren't out of this place soon, they were going to be l trouble.

At the edge of the springs, the firefighters pulled their
icks to a stop. The glow of the flames was visible above
e treetops in the distance, an orange shade against the
ick sky.

"It's a burner, all right," Charlie said. "If we don't get to
quick, we're going to lose this whole stretch of woods."

"That's way back in there," one of his men said.

"Rough country," he agreed.

The forest behind the resort had become a wall of flame.
if it were alive, the blaze jumped from tree to tree,
vouring the brittle leaves and crawling along the tree
inks.

It quickly ignited the brush and weeds that lined the
ill of the resort, and shoots of flame curled up the trees
iich grew near the building.

The dry branches caught like exploding canisters,
rning away from the tree and plummeting down onto
e rooftop, where they formed pools of flame.

Within minutes those pools were burning through the
of, while other arms of the fire continued to spread out
hind the resort. Before long, the flames would be
iching around it.

"What do you want us to do?" one of the firefighters
ked.

"We're going to have to get a crew back there quick,"
iarlie said. "Everybody suit up and get your equipment.
e're going to hike it."

He nodded toward Kyle Perkins. "Unload the dozer."

"These trees are pretty thick here," Kyle noted. "Too
ose together. Rough traveling. It might not fit."

"The ground's going to be rough, too. In the dark he

might drive it into a gully," Terry Hatch added.

Charlie rubbed his eyes. "A couple of you—Bench Carson—run interference."

He pointed toward the opening at the edge of springs. "It' a little thinner over there. It's going to t longer, but you guys go that way, get some chain saws cut him a path if there's stuff in the way. We've got t back in there as soon as we can, and we're going to need tractor."

Nodding, the men pulled on their bright yellow jac and their helmets before they moved to the back of truck to help Kyle unhitch the tractor.

"We're in for a long night," Bench said. He was a t lanky man in his twenties, with a pointed nose and da oily hair.

Carson, who was heavier and several years ol scowled, adding even more wrinkles to his weathered fa

"We'll do what we have to," he said. "If we don't, thi going to be a charred mess by morning."

The group left following Charlie, and Carson picked his flashlight. While Kyle backed the dozer off the trai they walked to the edge of the woods and began to lo around.

"Looks like somebody's been driving through her Bench said.

"Maybe they cut us a path," Carson said. "Let's hope s

"Maybe somebody drove a car back in there and star this mess."

"Could be."

They began to walk.

Toward their deaths.

Burns studied the scene before him. Navarra w kneeling at the altar, while Alison stood at her side.

Travis was on the floor against one wall of the po

...isk against the opposite side. Both of them looked
...ered and dazed.

...oug Langdon was in a huddle near the steps of the
...llow end, and a kid in black leather was hovering over
...

...bove him, Burns heard the shift of timber. He realized
...d better move soon if he was going to do anything.

...aking a step backward, he slammed his foot into the
...or and sent it crashing inward.

...hen he ran forward, the bar in his hands at the ready.
...didn't try to cover the sounds of his feet now as he ran
...ng the edge of the pool and jumped from the side.

...He landed on his feet near the upward slope from the
...p to the shallow end. The impact sent pain up through
...ankles, pain he forced himself to ignore.

...Navarra spun around suddenly as he charged toward
..., holding the candle stand like a lance. If he could
...pale her with it, perhaps she would be subdued, as the
...ends had promised.

...f he had been a little faster, he might have found out,
...t Blade moved quickly. Pushing away from the steps, he
...oved toward the priest in a diagonal path, meeting him
...out five feet from Navarra.

...With all the force he could muster, the biker slammed
...o Burns, sending both of them to the ground.

...The rough concrete ripped through Burns's coat sleeve
...d scraped off the flesh on his left arm from elbow to
...ist. The bar rolled out of his hands, clattering across the
...or, out of his reach.

...A loud moan escaped his lips as his body hit the floor,
...iving the edge of the cross into his side. He felt the corner
...it tear open skin and muscle.

...He didn't have time to pull it free because Blade was
...ready scrambling on top of him, grabbing for his throat
...d trying to connect a blow to his face.

...Almost instinctively, Burns blocked the strike with his

425

right arm.

Blade drew his fist back again, straddling the priest a
preparing to slam a blow hard against his forehead.

Although there was pain shooting through his left an
Burns forced himself to use it to reach to his belt and
out the cross. He had to bite his lip to hold the roar
agony in his throat as the crucifix pulled away from
wound.

As he brought his right arm up again and blocked
new strike from the biker, he lifted the cross as well.

Holding it by its base, he raised it in a backhand
swing that connected with Blade's face.

The hard crosspiece cracked the biker's jaw and se
him crashing against the floor. When his head struck
concrete, it split open, spraying blood across the pale bl
finish.

He didn't move, and Burns wasted no time
scrambling away from the body.

Navarra was now standing near him. She had picked
the candle stand.

"You amuse me, priest," she said, and bent the bar into
twisted knot. "And you have brought a crucifix."

He held it out in front of him.

"The priests in the past used those," she said. Her fa
was twitching slightly.

Burns kept it high. It was evident that it made h
uncomfortable.

"Before the Nazarene walked the earth, they called
their angels to protect them. That never worked w
either. Your intellect is far too inferior."

Burns took another step toward her, and she had to tu
her face away.

"You cannot tolerate the symbols of the heavens
Burns warned. "You are impure."

She raised one arm, and he touched the cross against
The metal seared her flesh, and she cried out.

426

He kept pressing it against her, applying more pressure
she began to waver on her feet. The skin blackened and
bbled around the burn.

Burns failed to notice Danya moving along the side of
e pool. She was carrying one of the stakes which had
en taken away from Travis.

Chrisk, who had been trying to pull herself to her feet,
oked up and screamed. Or tried to scream. Her voice
me from her throat as a dry croak.

The warning came too late for Burns, who had time
ly to turn partially before the weapon was hurled like a
ear.

It pierced his upper arm near the shoulder, sinking in
ly a fraction of an inch, since it was not a well-crafted
apon. That was enough to make his hand relax so that
e crucifix could clatter to the floor.

Navarra retaliated immediately, grabbing his throat
th a grip that choked his voice away before he could
eak.

Smiling, she tightened her hold, squeezing until the
iest sank to his knees, gasping for breath, choking.

"You might have stopped me with your knowledge,
iest."

She touched his forehead and smiled. "You have learned
uch. You speculate much. You might indeed have
lped your friends as you had hoped to." Her eyebrows
se as she read his thoughts. "And fulfilled the worth of
e old man's death."

"Grandpa?" Chrisk whispered.

Burns wanted to tell her that he had died bravely, but he
uld not speak. He looked over at Travis, who was trying
get up to move and help him, then at Alison. She stood
zed and confused near the oracle.

He closed his eyes, coughing from the smoke and the
oke hold. The last sound he heard was Navarra's laugh.
It came just before she forced her hand through his

chest. The skin gave way, the ribs cracked and parted, ashe grasped his heart and tugged.

As it pulled free, the muscles and flesh around it toopen. When it exited his chest through the gaping hoveins dangled around it like small worms from
uprooted clod of earth.

Lifting it high over her head, Navarra let out a primcry of triumph. When Burns slumped to the floor at hfeet, she did not look down.

She looked upward at the mass of tissue in her han
Blood streaked down her arm and spattered from tremains of the aorta and other veins.

Sticking out her tongue, she caught some of tdroplets, then closed her mouth as if she were tastinambrosia.

Then she lowered her arm and clutched the heaagainst her breast. It stained her white dress with a dark rsmudge as she moved to the statue.

Gingerly she laid it at the base of the likeness and bowagain, dropping to one knee.

"The heart of a holy man, dear Hecate. The secorsacrifice. Now I call on you to bestow the gift on nsister."

She reached up and took Alison's hand, urging her
kneel as well.

Travis was on his feet now. He staggered, the pamaking him dizzy as he moved.

Smoke hung thick in the air. He walked through
slowly until he was only a couple of feet away fro
Navarra and Alison.

Swaying slightly, he stared at Alison and parted his li
"She has not made her choice yet," he rasped.

Navarra rose and faced him, her eyes aglow and readycut through him.

"Her choice is clear," she said. "I offer her eternity. Twonders of the universe. You think she would choose y

...d your petty existence in exchange? You have nothing ...give her. Nothing."

"Let her make the choice," Travis said.

Beyond them, he could see Chrisk moving. She was ...w. The side of her head was matted with blood, and it ...eamed down her cheek like a scar.

Navarra did not seem to notice her. Her attention was on ...s challenge.

Alison looked at him, her eyes revealing her pain and ...nfusion. Tears spilled out over the rims of her eyes, and ...r lips trembled. She bowed her head and folded her arms ...ound herself, her shoulders bouncing with her sobs.

"You said she had to make the choice," Travis said. "Let ...r make it."

"It is made. You have nothing to offer. Nothing," ...avarra repeated. "You worship a God that offers nothing ...til your death. You slave in an endless cycle at your ...wspaper. You live where there is nothing. You are ...thing. I can give her everything."

He stepped forward and reached beneath Ali's chin with ...s uninjured hand to tilt her face up to him.

"I can't offer anything like she promises. I know there's ...price for what she's giving you, but I won't argue with ...u about it. I'm sure you've realized that by now."

Chrisk had reached Burns's body now. The hideousness ... his remains made her shudder as she touched his ...oulder. He had fallen on top of the crucifix. She reached ...der him, trying to pull it free.

It would not budge at first. She had to touch him, lift ...m off it, and reach under the gaping cavity to grasp the ...oss.

Trav swallowed, fighting a cough from the smoke. His ...es were tearing also, as much from emotion as from ...oke.

"I can only tell you that I love you," he whispered. "Not ...r anything but love's sake, and that's all you ever asked

429

of me before. And now that's all I ask of you. That
think of that, and that if you still love me, 'let it be
naught except for love's sake only.' Don't worry about
paper or the future or anything else that fades."
paused, pursing his lips and fighting more tears. "
'love me for love's sake, that evermore thou mayst love
through love's eternity.'"

Alison looked into his eyes. She began to weep.

Navarra opened her mouth wide, her lips peeling b
to reveal her teeth. She lifted her hands, holding them
claws to reach for Travis.

He lifted his good arm, hand opened, and Chrisk th
the crucifix. It arched through the air and slapped into
palm.

Navarra took a step toward him, and he brought
cross down on her face. She cried out with the pain a
burned into her, turning flesh black and sizzling as wi
of smoke curled back from it.

She slapped his hand, sending the crucifix flying,
he'd bought the time he'd wanted. The spell had ebb
Alison moved away from her, stepping back from
oracle and whatever psychic energy might be emanati
from it.

The smoke was thicker in the room now, and near c
wall a beam collapsed, raining flaming debris down or
the floor.

Splinters scattered out across the floor, some of the
dropping into the pool area. They continued to blaze, a
the ceiling was quickly becoming consumed. Oblivious
the fire, Navarra clutched at Travis, forcing him backwa
onto the floor. His shoulders slammed into the concre
and he was unable to protect his broken arm. It flopp
out at his side, sending reverberations of pain throug
him.

He could not contain a scream.

Navarra screamed also and started to move on top

430

a, teeth bared to plunge into his throat. Since Alison had turned away from her, she had grown pale, her flesh wrinkled. She had been feeding on Alison in some different way, Travis realized. She had been drawing some sort of energy from her. Now the connection was gone. She intended to make up for the loss now with Trav's blood.

Chrisk pulled the stake from Burns's shoulder and handed it to Alison, who rushed forward with it, shoving it into Navarra's back.

It was placed near the center left. Ali had tried for the heart. Navarra jerked backward immediately, her hands clawing behind her in an effort to pull the obstruction free.

She screamed even louder now, arching her back and tilting her head toward the ceiling.

As Alison tried to help Travis to his feet, Navarra managed to tug the weapon free from her wound, which was spilling blood in a steady flow.

The wrinkles were continuing to show in her skin, and muscles were pulsing, causing bulges in her cheeks and along her arms.

Clutching the stake in her hand, blood dripping from one end, she stood slightly stooped. Her eyes were glowing even brighter, and her jaw sagged open. Saliva dripped from her lips, and with her hair wet and plastered about her face, she looked like an animal, more a beast of the night than a human. The part of herself which was kept hidden had been revealed.

Travis held his uninjured arm in front of him, preparing to strike her if she rushed at him, but Chrisk moved behind her, grasping the statue and shoving it off its pedestal.

It splattered into the blood on the floor, and she quickly grabbed one of the flaming fragments of wood and dropped it on the likeness.

431

"*Noooooooooo*," Navarra screamed, spinning and sta[?]ing as the fire consumed the wooden object.

Chrisk ran past her to Travis and Alison.

"We've got to get out of here," she said.

They moved together up the steps and started o[?] toward the doorway where they had entered, but befo[re] they could reach the exit from the pool area, another bea[m] crashed, blocking their path with flame.

"The other way," Travis said.

They turned and started along the end of the pool.

The destruction of the oracle further served to al[ter] Navarra's state. More emaciated now, she pulled herse[lf] over the edge of the pool where Mrs. Johnson was lyi[ng] against the wall on the opposite side.

"Oh my God," Alison called, but before they cou[ld] move to help, it was too late.

Kneeling beside the woman, Navarra ripped open h[er] throat and pressed her lips against the wound, drinking [in] the blood.

It replenished her quickly, and she turned again in the[ir] direction, snarling. Her hands were still extended in fro[nt] of her.

"They locked that door we came in when they grabb[ed] us," Chrisk said. "It was blocked from the insid[e.] Reverend Burns must have found another way in."

"He came from that way," Travis said, pointing towar[d] the end of the pool.

Chrisk took Alison's hand and pulled her along wi[th] Travis following.

They entered the corridor at a dead run.

Another portion of the ceiling crashed just as the[y] passed under it.

"Maybe that'll slow her down," Chrisk said.

"I doubt it," Trav muttered.

They rounded a corner and found the entrance to t[he] steam room. Smoke clouded the air, but they ducke[d]

432

ugh it.

ehind them, Navarra traversed the flaming rubble and owed.

This whole place is engulfed," Travis shouted.

hrisk and Ali moved on through the smoke. They were king for a window, and they almost stumbled into the ning Burns had left.

There's a hole over here," Chrisk said. "A pipe of some d. A drain."

How big?"

It'll hold us. But it may lead nowhere. There are a nch of pipes here."

It must be how Burns made it in."

It has been chipped open."

You and Ali go, then."

We can't leave you," Alison protested. "You're hurt. u can't fight her."

Chrisk took Ali's hand and guided her through the rrow opening and then started to follow.

It's dark," Chrisk said. "We won't be able to see."

It's got to come out outside," Travis said. "It's the only ance we've got. Go on. I'll be right behind you."

You can't fight her," Alison protested again.

I've got to try," Travis said. "It'll buy you time."

The ceiling near the corner of the room split open. The me showered through it and began to crawl along the ll. The crockery shattered, giving the fire access to the ams beneath it.

Travis moved over to the wreckage and picked up a ece of burning wood, a fragment of a small support am.

Keeping his injured arm as close to his body as he could, moved back to the entranceway and waited.

The pain was still throbbing, hammering at his brain. e swallowed back bile that wanted to spill into his roat and fought the waves that were flowing through his consciousness.

Navarra burst through a moment later. He held beam in front of him, trying to touch it to her gown.

She screeched at him and stretched her arms outward an effort to rip at his face and his eyes.

The flame kept her back.

"I guess we've found another portion of the lege that's true," Travis said. "Fire frightens you."

She did not speak, but no fear showed on her featur She remained in front of him, her teeth bared.

Travis threw the beam. It brushed past her sleeve, a the flame touched the fabric.

But it didn't burn.

She dove then, her fingers reaching Trav's throat. As toppled backward, she clutched at his windpipe, the sha nails on her fingers cutting his skin.

He fell onto the floor again, almost repeating t previous experience. His broken arm fell at his si almost causing him to faint.

He wanted to lie still and let unconsciousness take hi He was almost ready to let her finish him. His strength w ebbing; his sanity was dangling by a thread. If he had n known that she would go after Alison, he would ha stopped struggling.

As she tried to bring her teeth to his throat, he kick upward, driving a knee into her side.

She ignored the pain, but the blow threw her slightly balance. He followed through, rolling with her, forcin his weight on top of her.

She clutched at him, thinking he was trying to get aw from her. He rolled over again, his injured arm flailin wildly, bringing new pain with each movement. It stru the floor again, swinging at a bizarre angle.

Navarra scratched his throat and ripped at his shi trying to break through his flesh.

She didn't realize until they were upon it that he wa

ing toward the debris in the corner.

Vhen they reached the edge of the flaming timber, she
d out. The heat it emitted touched their flesh.

he tried to pull away, but Travis held her now with his
d arm, rolling on over into the rubble.

t the same time he forced his knee up between them
used it to push himself away from her.

Iis arm touched some of the flame, and the hair burned
ay from his forearm. A streak of the wood brushed his
h, searing a six-inch scar across his upper arm before he
out of the flame.

Vavarra was not so lucky. Her hair fell into the blaze
ignited.

The orange fingers climbed along to her scalp in an
tant, turning her black hair into a mass of gray powder
ich spilled back away from her skull.

Screaming, she began to scramble out of the rubble. The
of her head was raw and pink with slugs of melted
sh spilling down across her forehead.

Before she was clear, her gown caught fire and burned
well, scorching her flesh and searing the upper layer of
n away in several places.

She never stopped moving. The flame encircled her,
arring her, scorching her arms and shoulders, turning
r face into a pulpy mass.

She rushed toward Travis, screeching at the top of her
ngs.

He dodged her and dropped down into the hole. It was
mpletely dark inside, and smoke had filtered into the
nnel. Alison and Chrisk had already covered a good bit
ground, apparently, because they were no longer
ound.

He forced himself to move along, climbing down
rough the pipes while cradling his broken arm in front
him. He knew the pain would be worse if he continued
let the arm dangle.

435

The burned spot ached as well, brushing against thi[gh?]
as he moved.

The valve wheel caught his attention as he neared [the]
bottom of the pipes.

On an impulse, he pulled it. It budged only slight[ly.]

Above him he could hear Navarra's screeches. S[he]
would be after him in an instant.

Wrapping the fingers of his good hand tightly arou[nd]
the handle, he leaned into it, using his weight to force [the]
ancient crank.

If he could flood the tunnel, it should keep Nava[rra]
away. She might not be able to travel through the wat[er.]

When the wheel had made its full rotation, disappoi[nt]-
ment followed. Only a moaning gasp of air pushed its w[ay]
through the pipes.

Still pressing his arm against his body, he climbed
down through the pipes and started to move along t[he]
culvert.

Behind him Navarra crashed through the opening, t[he]
flame around her flashing into the narrow passage befo[re]
it was extinguished by the lack of air and her moveme[nt.]

She did not land on her feet, and she did not try to ri[se.]
Instead, she pulled herself along. Travis listened to t[he]
sickening sound of her ruined body scraping along t[he]
culvert.

She was able to move better than he had hoped.

He felt a new fear leap into his heart. He did not want [to]
fight her again, did not want to face the hideousness of h[er]
burned countenance.

Behind him, he heard the crash of more debris. [It]
dumped a pile of rubble into the hole. He felt the tunn[el]
tremble with the impact, and he realized the room they h[ad]
been inside must have collapsed, sealing that end of t[he]
drain.

If they were going to get out, they'd have to find the w[ay]

436

Bench and Carson made better time than they expected
the woods. With the dozer grinding along behind them,
·y made their way through the trees at a brisk walk.
Although the terrain was rugged and uneven, the tread
the machine allowed it to cover most of the ground.
Kyle trusted them as they led him along. From his seat
 watched the outlines of their yellow coats in the
·rkness, and only when they came upon the abandoned
·r did they have to direct him around anything.
Bench took a flashlight and waved it to give Kyle
·ection.
Cautiously they guided him around the gully and
·ntinued in the direction of the blaze.
They could see the blaze more clearly now. It was
·ching high into the sky, peaking above the trees which
·d grown for an eternity.
The signs of its severity urged them onward. Both of
·em knew that the cost of destruction would be great. The
·rest could not be replaced except by time.
They also realized the danger of letting it burn out of
·ntrol, so they rushed.
A couple of times they had to use their chainsaws to get
·all trees out of the way. There was usually enough space
·tween the larger trees to accommodate the machine.
When they reached the clearing near the resort, they
·und the building engulfed in flame, with fire spreading
·t behind it.
"We've found the place to start," Carson said, raising
·s voice to make it heard over the racket.
Kyle, who was still a number of yards behind them,
·gan to grind the gears of his machine, moving it forward
·d preparing the blade to begin pushing a furrow. A

backhoe would have been better for digging a fire tren
but he would have to make do with what he had.

"How many acres you think it's got?" Bench asked

"Plenty," Carson said. "Plenty."

He was about to speak again when the panther hit h
from behind. Its paws struck the center of his back, and
went down, hitting the ground on his stomach. He h
rolled over. He didn't have time to cry out before the
was upon him, its claws digging into his shoulders and
jaws ripping into his neck.

Bench pulled the small chainsaw from his belt a
began to fumble with the crank cord. His fingers k
slipping, and he didn't get an effective grip for seve
seconds.

The other firefighter's screams filled Bench's ears, a
his stomach felt like it was turning inside out.

When he finally got a firm hold on the cord handle,
yanked it backward. The motor sputtered but refused
awaken.

Carson's screams turned to a gurgle of blood.

Bench found it almost impossible to breathe. His lun
were tight.

He gave another tug on the cord. This time it worke

The motor came to life. Bench started to move forwar
holding the saw so that the whirring blade was in front
him.

The panther looked up from Carson's body, blo
dripping from its jaws and whiskers.

It growled a warning at Bench, who stopped in l
tracks. When the panther sprang, he stumbled, twistin
his ankles together and falling onto his back.

His final moments were filled with pain. The bla
came down onto his throat, the chain spinning throug
flesh, then through his collarbone. It spat flecks of his sk
and sprayed blood into the air. He was dead before the c
reached him.

yle halted the dozer and jumped from the seat when he
ized what was happening. It was a panicked effort, an
onceived attempt at a rescue. He had grabbed a fire ax
a behind his seat, but the cat had him as soon as he
hed the ground.

e swung the ax at the cat's head.

Missed.

he cat knocked his legs from under him and was on top
im in an instant, the massive jaws once again doing
r work.

he fire continued to spread.

lison and Chrisk crawled over the dead bats at the end
he tunnel and saw the glow of light through the grate
ve them.

"It's too high," Alison said.

"We have to go out this way," Chrisk said. "The rest of
leads nowhere. It probably comes out in the river, and
not up to treading water."

"You'll have to get on my shoulders, then," Alison
l. "That's the only way."

"Can you hold me?"

"I'll have to."

Dropping to one knee, Ali braced her hands against the
e of the culvert and clenched her teeth.

Slipping her shoes off, Chrisk took a quick breath
ore she climbed onto Ali's back. Ali's frame was thin,
l she shuddered under Chrisk's weight.

Sliding her hands up the walls of the access passage,
risk tried to find a handhold as she placed her feet on
's shoulders.

Alison struggled to keep her balance as she straightened
her full height to give Chrisk a maximum reach.

Chrisk hit the grate with her hands. It didn't budge. It
s heavy.

"Brace yourself," she warned Alison.

Curling her hands through the bars of the grate, lifted upward. When she applied pressure, the muscle her back and shoulders strained, and the ache bega ripple down her spine. She gritted her teeth and contin to force the grate upward.

Alison staggered beneath her, trying to anchor herse provide the needed support. It was not an easy task.

Through the tunnel there were echoes of movement, she had no way of knowing who was making them.

Chrisk grunted, summoning all the strength she co muster to battle the weight.

The grate held fast.

Alison wavered, and Chrisk had to press her ha against the sides of the passage to steady herself.

Only when Alison had regained her stance did Ch return her hands to the grate. With a loud moan pushed upward. The muscles of her arms and b strained, and a new burst of sweat covered her.

And finally the grate eased out of place. With an eff she pushed it to the side to make an opening.

Her lungs were heaving now, and Chrisk had to g several seconds before she could struggle upward throu the space.

Lifting her legs was tough, but she managed it. O she was on the ground, she rolled back around on stomach and offered a hand down to Ali.

Stretching upward, Ali caught her palm. They co hear footsteps in the tunnel now.

With both hands Chrisk clasped Alison's arm and lif upward.

With her feet against the sides of the passage, Ali pushed as much as possible until she was able to p herself up.

Finally she was on the ground.

The flames were spreading all around them, mov

m the building and the area behind it to the woods
ide the building. It would not be long until it had
ead well past it, trapping them.

They saw the firefighters lying on the ground a few feet
ay and were about to move toward them when Travis
led from the hole.

Together they leaned over it, looking down at him.

'Thank God," Alison said.

'We're not out of here yet," he warned.

Alison and Chrisk leaned down together, clutching at
good arm, gripping his shirt. They were both nearing
naustion, and with his broken arm, he wasn't able to
er as much assistance.

Struggling, they tugged upward, eventually getting
eir hands under his arms to pull him out.

For a moment he sat panting on the ground.

"She's coming," he warned. "She's coming, and she'll
l us all."

He spotted the firefighters for the first time and shook
s head. "The cat again. It's still out here." He peered
ound through the darkness.

He and Chrisk spotted Early's body at the same time.
She started to get up and move toward it, but Travis
abbed her arm. The panther was standing at the edge of
e forest in front of the resort, watching. Its emerald eyes
ere filled with the evil glow of its possession by Navarra's
ower.

Chrisk pressed against Alison, fighting tears.

"This whole area is about to be ablaze," Travis said.
"The cat'll get us if we move."

He nodded toward Carson. "Get the chainsaw. And be
reful with it."

Chrisk and Alison scrambled together toward the body.
hen they reached him, they began to pry the handle from
s dead fingers.

Alison almost vomited as they tugged the blade from the

tissue of his throat, where the sticky blood had begun
congeal around it. Bits of flesh peeled back as t
removed the blade from his neck.

The cat eased from its perch in the low branch
placing its steps cautiously, head bowed.

"Crank it," Travis said. He was running toward
bulldozer. "Let it hear the motor."

Chrisk tugged on the pull cord, but it didn't start.

The mechanism sputtered and coughed and was sti

Still cradling his injured arm against his body, Tra
pulled himself up onto the bulldozer with his good ar
sliding into the seat.

"Choke the damned thing," he shouted, coughing at
smell of diesel that filled his nostrils.

Fumbling with the saw between them, Alison a
Chrisk pulled and twisted things on the chainsaw, th
pulled the cord again.

Nothing.

The cat neared them, crouching.

"Hurry up," Travis called. He hit the start button on t
dozer and cranked it to life.

The cat uttered a low growl which was drowned out
the dozer.

"It's going to jump," Alison screamed.

The cat did spring, and in the same instant Chri
pulled the cord again and coaxed the blade to life.

Grasping the instrument in front of her, she turned h
face aside. The cat's body landed on the blade, impali
itself. She fell under its weight, but kept the saw upraise

The chain chewed through the cat's sternum, sprayi
blood everywhere. Chrisk was drenched, but she held on
the handle, pressing it upward to keep the cat off her bod

The cat shuddered. The blade began to choke dow
sending exhaust into the already smog-filled air.

She coughed but held on until the motor stopp
entirely. Finally she let go, pushing it aside and rollin

from under it. The cat dropped into a heap on the
und, the muscles in its legs twitching and blood
ning through its mouth.

lison moved to Chrisk, pulling her away from the saw,
ging her, trying to control her own sobs. The blood
ared onto both of them.

ravis had managed to partially turn the dozer toward
mouth of the tunnel, but he wasn't having much
cess with only one arm to operate the levers.

I could use one of you up here," he called out.

he flames were billowing around the building now.
es continued to ignite, and the pine straw on the forest
or was blazing. In moments they would all be
sumed.

lison detached herself from Chrisk and ran toward the
er, hauling herself to his side.

'Won't the fire get her?"

'She walked through flame a minute ago," he said.

Together they orchestrated the controls of the machine,
king and pushing until they had it aimed at the mouth
the tunnel.

The flame crawled from the roof of the building and
lled down onto the dry grass beside it. The blaze began
creep onto the brush all around.

t the same instant, Navarra's head appeared through
opening of the tunnel.

lison pulled the control back, lifting the blade in front
them as Travis grabbed the knob on the gearshift.

He shoved it into forward just as Navarra began to pull
self out of the opening.

When the blade struck her, it cut her in two, jamming
ough her ribs and internal organs. There was a spray of
mson as torso separated and the upper portion toppled

Flagging gray ropes of entrails snaked out of her
domen.

As the upper body thudded into the dirt, her hand began to claw the earth, attempting to right the torso.

Travis yanked the gear into reverse.

Navarra reached upward with one hand while still dragging herself along with the other.

"Take the blade down," Travis shouted.

Alison complied, and he shoved the machine forward again. The scoop dug into the ground, missing the torso.

The fire roared as it consumed more brush.

As Travis jerked the dozer about with his good arm, Alison manipulated the scoop once more.

When Trav forced the dozer forward, the scoop did catch Navarra, shoveling up the upper body as a new scream croaked through her lips.

Yanking at the controls, Trav dumped it back into the hole with the mass of earth that had been scooped up around it.

With a nod he urged Ali to lift the scoop again. When she brought the lever down, it hammered at the mouth of the tunnel, caving it in.

The flames were around the hole now, but he shut the engine down, urging Alison off the machine.

Chrisk was watching, panting. Blood covered her face like a mask.

"We'll never get out of here," she cried.

Travis nodded toward the dead firefighters. "Get those packs off the belts," he shouted, dropping to a sitting position, holding his arm tightly.

He was near collapse.

"What are they?" Alison asked.

"Compact tents. They're made to withstand intense heat."

Together Chrisk and Alison bent over the dead men and detached the silver packets.

Then they moved back to Trav and helped him up. Together they staggered a few feet.

444

he flames crawled over the bulldozer.

ravis urged the women onward a few more feet,
ping when they had moved as far as possible from the
r.

Pop the tents and catch some air in them," he ordered.

hey ripped the packets open and pulled them through
air as if they were straightening towels.

he foil-like tents unfurled, billowing outward.
ckly the three crawled under them, pulling the pockets
n over their heads.

n instant later the bulldozer's tank exploded, sending a
d of flame into the sky.

he sound of it rattled the night. The force of the blast
ok the tents, but they held.

s the flames swept around them, they prayed. The air
de was thick, and the heat bathed them. It was like
g baked alive.

t was as if they were inside the mouth of hell, but they
ed huddled under the protective coverings, breathing
wly to preserve what oxygen they had.

he fire burned around them, exhausting its fuel as it
ved on to consume more brush and trees.

t seemed to take an eternity. Isolated as they were
eath the coverings, they had no idea who had survived.
en they finally felt safe to push the heavy bags off them,
y found themselves in a desert of black soot and
ldering debris. But each was still breathing.

he building and the dozer were still ablaze, but those
nes were beginning to die down.

he trees were no more than splinters of black wood,
smoke curled up from the ground.

tepping together, they hugged each other, laughing
weeping at the same time.

"It was a nightmare," Alison said. "I can't believe this."

"It's over," Travis said. "Over."

hrisk looked beyond them, where the fire still raged.

"We can't go out through there," she said.

"We'll just have to wait awhile," Travis said.

They sat down on the ground and watched.

At dawn the rain began, pelting down at first, th falling in a steady sheet.

They ignored the rain. It was nothing compared to t night.

"Do you think she's finished?" Chrisk asked.

"The water held her for so long," Travis said. "Som how or other she was susceptible to the elements. T fire didn't stop her, but it slowed her down. Maybe t earth on top of it has some power as well. Lory might ha known more, but we may never know."

"We would have died without him and Chrisk grandfather," Alison said.

Chrisk shook her head sadly.

"She was evil," Alison said. "She hurt so many peop And the animals too, she just used them." She rested h head against Trav's shoulder. "You saved my life. I was terrible to you, and you came after me."

"It was in the vows," Trav said. "Better or worse."

His lips met hers in a soft and gentle kiss.

Rising, Chrisk walked into the rubble of the buildin After a while she found the sunken spot of the swimmi pool and picked around until she found the cross. It w hot to the touch and melted almost beyond recognitio Finally she found a charred cloth with which to grasp

Carrying it back to the spot where the dozer's hu remained, she stuck the cross into the ground.

"Just for safety's sake," she said.

Travis laughed. "For safety."

He struggled to his feet with Ali's help, and togeth they began to walk in the direction of the road.

From somewhere, a little gray rabbit darted. It w looking for shelter from the rain, and its ears twitch against the droplets.

ison's lips parted in amazement. "How do you think
rvived the fire?"

"he same way we did," Trav said. "Providence." He
n to laugh again.

ison laughed too. For the first time in days, her
ghts were clear. She put her arms around Travis,
ng her head on his shoulder.

felt good to have him close. She closed her eyes for a
nent, thinking about the town, the paper, everything
nce.

here would be much to do. Maybe things weren't
ect here, but it was something.

was the place they had chosen for their work, their

"Come on, Dixon," she said, smiling up at Trav.
"'ve got a newspaper to put out, and it's past deadline
ady."

accoming
sable

Epilogue

From international wire dispatches:

Jan. 26, 1989
NEW DELHI, India—A herd of elephants stormed a small village and destroyed homes and property in the forest on Thursday, according to United News of India.

The elephants were believed to be looking for a lost elephant calf which had fallen down a well.

Officials have been able to come up with no other explanation for the stampede.

Jan. 29, 1989
NICOSIA, Cypress—Wolves have mauled fourteen people in the past two nights in the city of Bakhtaran, according to reports from the Islamic Republic News Agency.

Authorities believe the wolves are reacting to the lack of food created by the severe winter weather Iran has been experiencing. Heavy snowfall and freezing temperatures have been reported and have caused wild animals to move about over a two-week period.

Police are making efforts to prevent further attacks.